"Only lightning can str... thrilling romantic suspense..."

—DiAnn Mills, author of *Firewall*

"In *Under a Turquoise Sky*, Lisa Carter has created some great characters, especially Aaron, and a compelling storyline. This book is a page-turner you don't want to put down."

—Margaret Daley, author of *Severed Trust* and *Bodyguard Reunion*

"Don't miss another trip to the Navajo Nation in Lisa Carter's *Under a Turquoise Sky*, where a southern belle with a core of steel and an undercover agent who's lost his way face off against a drug lord with everything to lose. Besides a heart-warming romance, plenty of spiritual truths, and a hefty dose of suspense, Carter gently pulls back the curtain on the Navajo Nation and lets us glimpse a culture many of us will never experience. I thoroughly enjoyed it!"

—Connie Mann, blogger at Busy Women/Big Dreams, boat captain, and author of *Angel Falls*

Other books by Lisa Carter

Aloha Rose (Quilts of Love series)

Carolina Reckoning
Beneath a Navajo Moon

UNDER A TURQUOISE SKY

Lisa Carter

a novel approach to faith

Nashville

Macro Editor: Teri Wilhelms
Published in association with the Steve Laube Literary Agency

Library of Congress Cataloging-in-Publication Data

Carter, Lisa, 1964-
    Under a turquoise sky / Lisa Carter.
        pages cm
    ISBN 978-1-4267-5802-7 (binding: soft back, trade pbk. : alk.
paper) 1. United States. Federal Bureau of Investigation—
Officials and employees—Fiction. 2. Navajo Indians—Fiction.
3. Witnesses—Protection—Fiction.   I. Title.
    PS3603.A77757U53 2014
    813'.6—dc23

                                            2014006605

To Kathryn—You always make us laugh and remind us not to take ourselves too seriously. I pray you will love, honor, and serve the Lord all the days of your life. I can't wait to see where the journey with Him takes you. Let the adventure begin…

For the broken, wounded, and scarred—*You who've struggled to just survive. Despite the lies you've been told and maybe still believe, may you discover no one is too broken that God cannot mend. Remember the turquoise—You were worth the price He paid. Whatever your past, whatever you've done or has been done to you, I pray you will find in Jesus the bridge from broken-ness to wholeness and go forward in God's strength.*

Acknowledgments

David—Thanks for cooking dinner when deadlines loomed. Thanks for being there for me at speaking and book signing events this year.

Corinne—Gracias por compartir tus conocimientos de la lengua española.

Nancy Adams—Thanks for allowing me to use your name. Like you, my fictional Nancy Matthews is a great mother. I'm so glad we're family.

Bekki Brantley and Cathrine Bass—Hairdressers Extraordinaire, thanks for professional insight. You, like Kailyn, are both so gifted at bringing out the beauty in people.

Hope Dougherty—My thanks for your willingness to critique each manuscript and be my friend.

The Precepts Class & Marcia Miles—Thanks for the year we explored Isaiah. God used all of you to weave strands of Isaiah into Aaron and Kailyn's journey. And mine.

In memory of the late Les Kunes—I think with such fondness of our family trip to Santa Fe. And of your patience at the Palace of the Governors while I—like Kailyn—took forever to find the perfect turquoise ring.

Ramona Richards—Thanks for your wisdom and insight, for giving my book dreams wings to fly. You are the best.

Teri—This book was such a fun one to work on together. Thanks for making it better.

Cat Hoort, Susan Cornell, and the sales, marketing, and production teams—Thanks for your hard work and all you do to bring Christian fiction to readers.

Tamela Hancock Murray—Thanks for your wisdom, guidance, and optimism. You make this journey fun.

Readers—May you walk in beautiful obedience to the Shepherd of your soul. I pray you will discover the name by which He calls you—beloved—and fully embrace its significance. And, I hope you have as much fun reading this as I had writing it.

Jesus—Out of the tangled skeins of my life, You have woven mercy and grace. In spite of my weakness, You are strong. Thank You for loving broken vessels. For calling me Yours—and never letting me go.

*O afflicted city, lashed by storms and not comforted, I
will build you with stones of turquoise,
your foundations with lapis lazuli.*
— Isaiah 54:11

1

As soon as the elevator doors closed behind her, Kailyn knew she'd made a mistake.

Music blared in a mind-numbing, ear-deafening pulse from the penthouse suite stereo. Clutching her beaded purse, she placed her hands over both of her ears. A Latin beat, coupled with a heavy, chest-pounding, thumping bass, jangled her nerve endings.

Where was Dex?

Scanning the crowded party, she wrinkled her nose at the pungent odor permeating the room. An aroma once smelled—as any college student could testify—never forgotten. Bodies writhed and gyrated.

Kailyn's lip curled, the lyrics penetrating her consciousness. Gangsta rap.

Spanish gangsta rap.

Couples lounged on the couches, twined into each other. She pursed her lips at the faint lines of a chalk-white powder on a coffee table.

Dex had warned her to wait in the car. But she'd refused. No way she wanted to hang out in a deserted parking garage once night fell.

He said he'd be gone only a few minutes. Told her his biggest client wanted him to do a meet-and-greet with an out-of-town business associate. Promised they'd be on their way to the charity ball soon.

She crossed her arms, hugging herself. This was so *not* the charity ball. She tapped her foot on the hardwood floor. Dex better get a move on or her grandmother would have a cow.

Let Golden Boy explain their way out of this one.

It came to her attention that, of all the occupants in the room, she was the only blonde. Probably the only native English speaker, too.

The only woman whose décolletage wasn't cut to her navel and whose hemline wasn't hiked to her thighs. Self-conscious, she smoothed a hand across the ice-blue floor-length Vera Wang she wore. She didn't belong here.

Her skin prickled the way it does when you feel someone staring. Someone across the sunken living area. Against the glass-enclosed walls overlooking the twinkling lights of downtown Charlotte, she locked onto the penetrating glare of a thirty-something Latino man. His black hair scraped back from his sharply cut features, and a pencil-thin mustache and goatee framed full, sensual lips.

Gold studs glittered in both his ears. He'd been dancing—her brow arched—a euphemistic word for what she'd never describe as dancing. The voluptuous Latina continued to bump and grind. He'd gone stock-still. His dark chocolate eyes narrowed.

She lifted her chin, noting his skintight black pants, the gleam of gold chains against his well-muscled chest. And the smaller silver turquoise cross in the hollow of his throat. His white silk shirt hung open all the way to his—

Her feelings must have shown on her face for he moved around the woman, dodging the other revelers with the grace of a jaguar. Her mouth went dry. Out of her peripheral vision, she noted three other men from the corners of the room advancing.

With a flick of his hand, he motioned the other men away. But he kept coming, his face unreadable. Her chest hammered. She reminded herself this was America, not Colombia. She was an American citizen. She had every right to—

⁂

"You don't belong here."

The blonde stiffened. She stared for a moment at the cross he wore about his neck. He fought the urge to touch it for reassurance. She cut her eyes at him, the look she gave him derisive.

He folded his arms across his chest. "Go back to where you belong, chica."

She squared her shoulders. "I belong where I say I belong."

Defiance sparked from her iris-blue eyes. He scowled. "Not here, you don't."

Her nostrils flared. "I'm waiting for my date, Dex Pritchard."

The tension between his shoulder blades eased. He'd spotted her as soon as the elevator doors parted. One look at her designer dress and smooth, flaxen chignon, and he'd strode over thinking to provide a lifeline to an innocent who'd wandered into the wrong place at the wrong time.

His bad.

Not an innocent. Not if she kept company with a weasel like Pritchard. Still, the situation was sensitive. Time she got a move on. Perhaps a new tactic was called for.

He broadened his chest and bared his teeth. "Ah." He allowed his shoulders to rise and fall. "Perhaps if I upped your hourly rate."

The woman's eyes widened. Her lips parted, her mouth opening into a round O.

In a reflex move he admired for its swiftness, she raised her hand. He caught it in a hard vise inches before she could make contact with his face. She twisted, yanking her hand free.

He loomed over her. "Such passion, señorita. Bueno. I think you and I, we could work out some arrangement."

She took a step backward against the closed elevator doors. With deliberation, he positioned one hand on the space to the right of her head. Trapped—for the first time, fear shone from her eyes.

"Get away from me," she hissed. She pushed at him, her palm cool against his bare chest. Strained with all the consequence of a gnat attempting to shift a burro.

Silently, he applauded her courage, her spunk. While he bewailed her stupidity.

He allowed his lips to curve. He leaned into her, her short gasps of breath fluttering against his cheek. "Let me introduce you to Latino-style love. I promise, once you've—"

"Can I never leave you unchained for a moment around the women, mi amigo?"

He closed his eyes at the sound of Esteban's smooth tones. He'd hoped to get the woman out of here before his boss emerged from the conference room at the rear of the suite.

"Get your hands off her." The Anglo lawyer, Pritchard, fair and blond like her, shoved his shoulder. To as much avail as the woman.

He planted his left hand on the other side of her head. "Maybe now she's had time to consider the advantages of—"

"Call him off, Esteban," growled Pritchard.

"You should have never brought the *cordera* here." Esteban's voice if anything grew colder.

Pritchard, not as dumb as he looked, managed to catch its glacial chilliness, too. "I—I told her to wait in the car. When I received your urgent text, I came right over."

At Pritchard's words, the woman bristled. Leave it to Pritchard to hang himself by throwing his date under the proverbial bus.

He gave her a slow, menacing smile.

If this woman was half as intelligent as he read in her eyes, she'd realize Pritchard was no friend. In fact, though she didn't know it, he was her only friend in this room. Her only chance.

Esteban snorted. "What? You couldn't have dropped her off at home first? You brought her into our business? Estúpido."

With more credit than he'd initially awarded her, the bimbo kept her mouth shut. A shapely, elegant bimbo. High-class. Nothing but the best for the Pritchards of the world.

"She won't be a problem, I promise."

He broke eye contact with the woman, throwing a glance over his shoulder at the near-groveling Anglo. He despised those overprivi-leged, former frat boy, trust-fund types.

Esteban lifted one eyebrow, stretching the muscles of his face into the semblance of a grin. A caricature of the blending of his Aztec and conquistador heritage. "I will hold you to that." He clapped a manicured hand on Pritchard's shoulder.

The Anglo jumped.

Esteban focused his laserlike attention his way. "Let her go, Rafael."

He made an exaggerated sigh, the air trickling out from his lips. The woman turned her face away. "If you say so, *mi patrón*. I thought she might be part of the entertainment..." he licked his lips, "...package you provide for your associates." His body pressed hers against the elevator. She trembled.

Esteban laughed, the sound guttural. "Later, my friend, I promise. After our business is concluded. One day, I will introduce you to the keeper of my flocks."

The sound of Esteban's laughter frissoned across Rafe's spine, recalling to his mind his grandmother's tales of the evil *chindi*.

"Rafe..." The Latina he'd left on the dance floor called his name.

One of his names.

Esteban chuckled. "I think, *hermano*, you need my help not at all with the chicas."

Time to save this particular chica.

He tilted his head, his lips touching the strands of silken hair at her diamond-studded ear. "Run, don't walk, *querida*." She flinched. "And don't ever show your face here again."

To make his point, he raked his hand down the side of the woman's sequined dress. She shrank further against the elevator. His hand trailing down, she tensed, expecting him to touch her in a more invasive location, but instead he pressed the elevator button. The doors opened.

Knees buckling, she fell in backward. Sidestepping him, Pritchard caught her arm. Pritchard glared at him, placing a protective arm around the blonde's shoulders.

He blew them both a kiss. The doors closed, shuttering them from his view. And he let out an inaudible sigh of relief before turning to face Esteban.

But Esteban lounged halfway across the room in intimate conversation with one of the organization's female groupies. Esteban assumed—rightly—his orders would be obeyed and hadn't bothered to stick around to see them carried out.

Esteban's arrogance and overweening pride would make his job a lot easier in the long run. Be the drug lord's downfall.

Dismissing the Anglos from his mind, he wrapped his persona once more around himself, a second skin. Like her, he didn't belong here, either.

Or he hadn't when he'd first begun this operation. The longer he remained in this slime hole, the more he worried how much like them he'd become. But this kind of thinking would get him killed. Banishing his doubts, he hardened his heart from the unpleasant-ness of what he'd have to do to accomplish his mission.

Striding toward the woman he'd temporarily abandoned, he fingered the silver turquoise cross resting among the clanking gold chains. He had his duty to perform. And whatever it took…He gri-maced before painting the expected leer on his face.

Whatever it took to get the job done, he'd do.

2

Three months later

I'VE GOT A SURPRISE FOR YOU, MI AMIGA."

Amused, Kailyn glanced at her enthusiastic friend. She lounged against the deck chair, sipping her iced tea. "What now?"

She arched her eyebrows at Gaby. "Don't tell me you've ditched my color swatches and gone your own way?"

Gabriela Carmelita Flores Mendoza tossed her sun-streaked mane over a bare shoulder. She spread her coral-painted nails across the surface of the iron-scrolled table at the poolside cabana. "You've found me out."

Her dark brown eyes twinkled. "I've rejected your advice and chosen to paint the master suite—"

"Let me guess…" Kailyn adjusted the brim of her white hat to keep the afternoon sun out of her eyes.

Stalling while she formulated an answer sure to entertain her friend, Kailyn's eyes darted around the perimeter of the Flores's ten-thousand-square-foot mansion. Several months into their budding friendship, Gaby asked Kailyn to redecorate the Flores home. One exquisite room at a time, though the house needed no makeover.

But fledgling interior designers couldn't afford to be choosy. Not in this economy. And what were friends for, Gaby reminded, if they couldn't throw business a friend's way every now and again?

"Black."

Gaby choked on a swallow of water.

15

"You've chosen, against my advice, to paint the master cavern you call a bedroom black."

Gaby's lips twitched. "You've uncovered my secret."

Kailyn's eyes widened.

Gaby fell over the side of her chair at the expression on Kailyn's face. "Got you. So gullible. So naive. So…"

Kailyn made a move as if to scoot back her chair. "If I'd known I was only coming over here to be insulted…"

Gaby patted her arm. Her coral lips widened, revealing perfect white teeth glowing against the brown of her natural skin tone. "I love you just the way you are, Kailyn."

She squirmed, unsettled by Gaby's praise. "No, I think you were right the first time. All my life I've rushed headlong into situations where—"

"Where ángeles fear to tread?" Gaby crossed her legs at the ankle, brushing out a crinkle in her apricot-colored swimsuit.

Kailyn's lips quirked at the way her friend mixed her English with Español. Not that she understood much Spanish. Her grandmother had insisted she study French.

Which had proven to be so useful. Like a lot of things her grandmother had insisted she learn.

Not.

"Actually, I was kidding. You have impeccable taste as always. But I do have a gift for you—wait," Gaby countered at Kailyn's motion of protest.

"You don't have to keep buying me gifts. Your friendship means the world to me."

Gaby's face softened. "Right back at you, my friend. I don't know how I would've survived these months…" Her gaze flickered.

They'd been riding bikes next to each other at the gym for a week, same time every morning, before they'd acknowledged the other's presence. But their friendship hadn't blossomed until Kailyn inadvertently followed Gaby into the women's restroom and discovered the Latina leaning against a stall door, sobbing over a soiled tampon in her hand.

"My hopes and dreams died then." Gaby's lips trembled. "I realized the doctors were correct. I'd never conceive without medical intervention."

Gaby's hands fisted in her lap. "And I knew my husband would never agree to invasive procedures calling into question his very manhood."

Kailyn dropped her eyes and traced the condensation down the stem of her glass. She'd never met Gaby's husband. But she long ago realized all was not well in the Flores marriage.

She'd also come to the belated realization that Gaby only invited her over when Señor Flores was out of town on another business trip. Her childless friend had been lonely, hence their unlikely friendship when Kailyn offered a tissue and a shoulder to cry upon in the restroom. An unlikely, but mutually satisfying friendship between a pampered, sheltered Southern belle—Kailyn was self-aware if nothing else—and a vivacious, sheltered, convent-educated Latina.

Gaby cleared her throat. "You've given me so much more than sympathy. Your kindness…Hope of heaven…"

Kailyn shuffled her flip-flops on the concrete, truly uncomfortable now. "I didn't—"

Gaby seized her arm. "Oh yes, you did. More than you know."

"You don't have to shower me with extravagant gifts from Prada and Gucci just because my grandmother cut me off after I ditched Dex."

Gaby's mouth twisted. "You were right to dump that sleaze bucket."

Kailyn nodded. "You and I are in complete agreement there, but Grandmother didn't agree." She bit her lip at the memory of society maven Carole Eudailey's exact words about Kailyn's choice of friends.

In her grandmother's tunneled worldview, Latinas answered doors and scrubbed kitchen floors.

Gaby scraped her chair back. "You did far more for me. You brought me back to my faith. Come."

She followed Gaby around the pool toward the house. Gaby threw open the glass door on the tiled veranda. "Come see."

"What now? I really don't need any more Bobbi Brown makeup."

"Better, *mi hermana en Cristo.*"

Sister in Christ.

Kailyn sighed, resigned to her fate. It was a tough job to be the constant recipient of Gaby's thousand-dollar shopping sprees. But, hey, someone had to do it.

Gaby strolled into the Mexican-tiled kitchen. A kitchen she never used. A furious barking greeted their entrance.

Kailyn's eyes rounded. "What the—?" She swung her gaze to her grinning, *loca* friend. "What have you done?"

"Voilà!" Gaby swept her arm across the length of the makeshift pen corralling the ugl—One look at Gaby's adoring pet-lover face and Kailyn amended—most unusual-looking dog she'd ever laid eyes on.

Kailyn narrowed her eyes. "You said your husband hated dogs."

Gaby cocked her head. "He does. But this is for you. To greet you when you return to your condo after a long day placating impossible clients like myself." She bowed her chin to her chest. "This, I do for you, my friend. To warm your heart. A small token of all you've done for me."

Kailyn planted her hands on her hips. "My heart's less than warmed. I work long hours, Gab. What would I do with a pet?"

Gaby's eyes found hers. "You don't like dogs?"

"I—I didn't say that."

Gaby's chin jabbed at the air between them. "You tell me your grandmother did not allow pets after you came to live with her. How your parents had promised you a dog but after your mother's death..." She raised her shoulders and let them drop in the classic Latino gesture of she'd-done-what-she-could.

"Besides," she stabbed her index finger in Kailyn's direction. "You tell me to find something to expend my energy upon and so I volunteer at the animal shelter like you say."

Kailyn winced. Somehow she already knew how this would end.

"You tell me to lavish the love I have inside on those who need it most."

Kailyn had been thinking the senior center, not the SPCA.

"You say I should find the least of these and make their lives better."

Kailyn lifted her eyes to the ceiling.

"Nobody wanted this dog, Kailyn."

"For obvious reasons," Kailyn smirked, taking a long look at the powder-puff-sized mongrel. His hairless body suggested a strong resemblance to an oversized rat.

"This dog was going to be executed, if no one took him home."

Her lips jerked at Gaby's dramatic turn of phrase.

Gaby laid her hand over her heart as if preparing to recite the Pledge of Allegiance. "I rescue this dog from the path of destruction. I see beneath the..." She stumbled, searching for the right words.

"Splotchy gray skin?"

Gaby sniffed.

"Thinning patches of white fur on his head and paws?" Kailyn frowned. "He's not mangy, is he?"

"I see beyond the abuse he's suffered. I see the loyal friend he'll become. I see the special brand of courage he's utilized to survive to this point. I see this dog and I give hope. Just like you give to me."

At the word *abuse*, Kailyn studied the dog more closely. "He's been abused?"

Her heart constricted. As no doubt Gaby planned.

She hated being so predictable. A sucker for a lost cause.

Triumph glittered in Gaby's eyes. "And so I gift him to you."

Kailyn leaned over the pen. "Yeah, you gift him to *me*."

The dog, all five pounds of him, snarled in her direction.

"A real friendly gift, I see." Kailyn let loose an explosive breath.

The dog jumped half his height into the air.

"No loud noises. You scare our new friend, Kailyn." Gaby sank to her knees on the terra-cotta floor, allowing the dog to see her hand. The growling stopped. The mutt allowed Gaby to place one finger on his head.

"What in the world would I do with a dog?" She hunkered beside Gaby. "Especially a dog who needs so much attention and retraining."

"Love," Gaby corrected, making cooing noises.

"It's not a baby," and Kailyn regretted the words as soon as they left her mouth.

Pain slashed Gaby's face.

"I'm sorry. Forgive my thoughtless words."

Gaby gave her a sad smile. "No, you are correct. And upon reflection, I believe as always mi Dios knew best in preventing me from bringing an innocent bebé into my situation. I bring the dog home only because Esteban's out of town. It must go home with you or back to the death chamber." She sighed. "At least for now."

Esteban? An uneasy feeling niggled at the edges of her consciousness. Where had she . . . ?

Gaby placed her hands upon her thighs. "I will teach you everything I know about how to approach wounded creatures."

"Wait. You said the word *abused* before. Like you, Gaby?"

Gaby's mouth hardened. "Not what you think, *mi hermana*. But abuse comes in all shapes and degrees." She glanced out the window overlooking the side lawn. "I'm finally doing what I should've done the first time I suspected. After seeing you display such courage in throwing off everything you've ever known to do what is right, you've given me the courage—el Cristo has given me the courage—to face what must be faced."

"I don't under—"

"There are more gifts." With the grace of a ballerina, Gaby rose in one fluid motion. She snagged a turquoise leather tote off the kitchen island.

A doggy carrier? A five-hundred-dollar, fashion, doggy-accessorized carrier?

Kailyn settled onto her haunches. "More?"

Gaby plucked items from the bag. "Deluxe grooming tools." She laid the brush and comb on the granite countertop. "Gourmet dog treats." Those ended up beside the first items. "A collar worthy of a prince." Gaby laughed. "Even a dog deserves bling."

Kailyn groaned at the sight of the ruby-encrusted dog collar. No way she'd ever appear in public with a canine bedecked in such a thing.

Gaby continued with the canine essentials tour, ignoring Kailyn's weakening protests.

"Exactly what kind of dog is this, Gab?" She tilted her head. "Strains of Chihuahua mixed with a touch of pit bull mixed with Chinese crested?"

"A dog," Gaby set her jaw. "Who needs love and attention."

"So love me, love my dog, is that it, Gab?" She leveled her gaze at Gaby's oh-so-innocent features. "Just be aware, you're pushing the limits of my tolerance, *friend*."

"A temporary arrangement, I promise." Gaby nodded. "Until I can," she tensed, "make more permanent arrangements."

Kailyn sighed. "Temporary? You promise?"

Gaby clapped her hands together.

As if the outcome had ever been in doubt.

"What's the dog's name?"

Gaby smiled, a sweet smile. "I sense someone else will name my little darling."

"Darling?" Kailyn took another long gander at the wiggling mass of canine mush. "Huh. Some darling." She snorted.

Gaby fastened the collar around the dog's scrawny neck. "I'll teach you everything you need to know."

And for the next hour, Gaby was true to her word. Everything she'd learned from her work at the shelter about dealing with abused animals. At the sound of an engine, Gaby frowned. Glancing out the window, she stuffed the dog's accessories into the oversized purse.

"He still likes you better than me," Kailyn complained. Car doors slammed outside. "I don't see how in the world—"

"*Mi esposo's* supposed to be in Miami this week." Gaby craned her neck as a trio of men exited the black SUV parked in the driveway.

"Here," Gaby scooped the dog from the pen and deposited him inside the super-sized tote. "Why don't you take him upstairs, retrieve those color swatches in the bedroom, and apply more sunscreen to your lily-white Anglo skin? You're blinding the neighbors."

She thrust the purse—and the dog—at Kailyn.

"Is this your—?"

"He probably forgot something." Gaby swallowed. "He never stays at home for long during a workday. I'll see what he needs and—"

"I'd like to meet—"

"No." Gaby prodded her toward the hallway. "Best you stay upstairs. He doesn't like strangers in the house. He doesn't know about our friendship, and I think it's best to keep it this way."

"What's going on, Gaby?"

Kailyn strained around her friend, watching the three men. Clad in black business suits with dark polarized sunglasses concealing their features, they entered through the side gate and emerged into the privacy fenced–enclosed backyard.

"Go," Gaby hissed, hustling her to the stairs. "Please, my friend. Do this for me. They can't find you. Whatever happens, whatever you overhear, do not, I beg you, leave the house. I'd hoped to be away before…"

Gaby's voice caught and smothered a sob. "But everything now depends on…" She squeezed Kailyn's arm. "Promise me you'll always take care of my dog."

"What's going on? You're scaring me."

"Promise me, for the love of Dios."

"I promise, but I don't—"

Gaby pushed her backward.

Kailyn stumbled up the staircase. The dog poked out his head, snarling and revealing yellowed fang teeth.

"Gaby…"

But Gaby turned her back, squaring her shoulders and lifting her chin when someone bellowed her name.

Kailyn paused at the top of the landing overlooking the cathedral ceiling entryway. Goosebumps scurried up her bare arms. She'd left her wallet and keys in her bag at the cabana. She wished she'd brought her wrap inside. She promised herself as soon as Gaby's husband left, she'd gather her things and leave.

Hurrying into the master suite, she spotted the fabric swatch board where she'd left it on a bedside table. At the sound of angry voices, she sidled over to the Palladian window overlooking the pool. She stuck the swatches inside the bag.

The dog's jaws snapped.

"Hey," she yelped, barely removing her fingers in time from the proximity of the dog's teeth. "Watch it."

"What have you done, Gabriela?" the man raged. From this bird's-eye angle, her depth perception was skewed, but she judged him to be a few inches above her own height of 5'6" from how he towered over his more petite wife.

"I've done nothing, Esteban, *mi esposo*." Gaby's voice had taken on a soothing tone, like one attempting to placate a fractious child. Her hand reached to cup her husband's chin.

He slapped her hand away.

Kailyn jolted.

She'd had about enough of this. She'd not stand by and allow anyone to be abused. Not a dog, much less her friend.

Kailyn considered rushing to Gaby's rescue until…Gaby's husband pushed his glasses onto his head, and she recognized him as the same frightening Esteban from the hotel several months ago.

"Where is it, Gabriela? I'll have none of your games."

"Games? I don't know—"

He smacked Gaby so hard her head whipped around. The dog, his eyes bugged to the glass, growled. The two men grabbed Gaby by her forearms to keep her from hitting the ground.

Kailyn's eyes darted around the room, spotting a cell phone. She dialed 911.

A woman's voice answered. "State your emergency."

"I'd like to report a case of domestic violence in progress right now. Hurry. I'm afraid for my friend's life."

A woman's voice on the other end sharpened. "Please tell me your name and your location."

"I don't know the physical address from memory. I've only been here a few times and after typing it into my GPS, I forgot it. Somewhere on Marietta Lane. But I know you can trace this call and the location from the phone. I'm looking out the second-story window, watching this play out in front of my eyes. The other two men have grabbed hold of her—"

"You said this was a case of domestic violence. There are three men? Do you see any weapons? Are they armed?"

"No. Yes. No. Maybe."

Her hand shook. "They're wearing suits in this heat. I can't tell underneath the bulk. Please," she whispered. "Hurry, they're hurting her."

"Miss? Miss?"

"Kailyn," she murmured. "Kailyn Eudailey."

"Ms. Eudailey, I've dispatched two units to your location. Please stay on the line. Don't hang up."

"Oh, God, help us." Kailyn clutched the phone to her ear. "Hurry, hurry," she begged.

Going berserk, the dog launched himself against the glass pane.

"Hush." She stuffed the dog farther into the recesses of the purse, terrified the men would hear.

"You will tell me, Gabriela," Esteban Flores shouted. "One way or the other, you will tell me."

Kailyn tuned out the dispatcher and directed her attention once more to the scene below.

Gaby struggled against the men's hands, holding her like fetters. "I don't know—"

"Two things, *mi esposa*," Flores growled.

He held up two fingers. "Two things I've required from you from the beginning. To beget me a son and to give me your undying loyalty. Both of which you've failed miserably to do thus far."

Lunging against the men restraining her, Gaby spat in his face.

But instead of the explosive reaction she'd expected from Flores, an icy calm settled over his features. Which somehow managed to terrify Kailyn more than his temper.

He flicked his fingers at his men. They released Gaby. She staggered.

"I think a reminder of the punishment for disloyalty is due your way." He unbuttoned the top of his white dress shirt and loosened his silk tie. He shrugged out of his jacket, tossing it to one of his goons.

Unhurried, methodical, he rolled first one sleeve to his elbow and then the other. The expression on his face reminded Kailyn of a snake she'd once seen in the woodpile as it cornered a mouse.

Kailyn shivered.

"I will tell you nothing."

"Oh, yes, you will, Gabriela. Or see me in hell first."

Gaby's laugh rang out over the sultry southern summer air.

His face darkened.

Gaby lifted her eyes to the Carolina blue sky. "One place I can assure you, gracias a Dios, I will never be."

Something so evil, so sudden, leaped across the man's countenance, twisting and misshaping his face. Even from a distance Kailyn recoiled, dropping the phone.

Kailyn scrambled, fumbling to retrieve the phone from where it had scudded across the Persian carpet. She accidentally punched the power button OFF, severing her connection with Dispatch. She moaned.

"Oh, God. Oh, God." Stupid, so stupid. Why had God made her so clumsy and stupid?

By the time she resumed her watchful position by the window, Flores had grabbed Gaby around the neck. His face convulsed with fury, he dragged her kicking and screaming toward the pool. He shrieked words Kailyn surmised as obscenities in his native Spanish tongue.

Before she had time to think, to react, Flores hurled her friend into the shallow end and plunged after her, the water to his chest. He shoved Gaby face first into the turquoise water and held her down. Gaby's arms flailed, her desperate jabs never making contact with his body.

Kailyn screamed and pounded on the window with her fist. No one glanced up.

Some instinct caused Kailyn to hold the expensive phone to the window and without consciously meaning to, she snapped a photo. And then another. And another.

Gaby went still.

Kailyn couldn't take her finger off the button. She kept pressing, the camera phone clicking and whirring and warming up for yet one more. A sudden beam of light from the descending sun caught the plastic frame of the phone display. The beam sharpened and fragmented, bouncing off the polarized glasses of the men. Momentarily blinding Gaby's psycho husband—

All three jerked up at the same moment. Flores, his hand still cramming his dead wife's head into the water. As one, they shunted toward the house. The water streamed off Flores's ruined business attire as he mounted the pool steps.

Kailyn shrank back. But too late, they'd seen her. Her eyes ping-ponged, seeking a place to hide.

And then, the blessed sound of sirens.

The men froze, exchanging glances. Flores scowled. He motioned for the men to follow him. They disappeared through a gate at the rear of the property.

She wriggled under the massive mahogany desk in the corner, dragging the tote and the whimpering dog in after her. With her knees bunched to her chin, her teeth chattered. Still in her swimsuit, she hugged the tote and the dog to her chest as shock set in while she waited for the police to find her.

3

For the record, Miss Eudailey, state your full name and relate the events of last Wednesday." The federal prosecuting attorney positioned the mike toward her.

Had she ever been this tired in her life?

Kailyn contemplated laying her head upon the table separating her from the various law enforcement officials arrayed against her on the other side.

Yeah, arrayed against her.

Expecting rescue, she'd been treated like a criminal ever since the homicide detective had hauled her butt out from underneath the desk. Only her insistent pleas for them to check the photos on the cell prevented the police from Mirandizing her.

The dog became vicious when the officers attempted to remove the tote bag from her shoulder. When she threatened to tape her mouth shut before she'd help them if they didn't leave the dog alone, they backed off, and allowed her for now to keep Gaby's last gift to her.

She closed her eyes. Her laughing, bubbly friend couldn't be dead. But it wasn't a dream. More like a nightmare.

A nightmare her mind replayed every time she tried to sleep. She should've stopped Flores from hurting Gaby. Instead, she froze and took stupid pictures.

"If you'd attempted to come to her rescue, you'd be dead now, too."

The older of the two deputy U. S. marshals stared at her, his mouth set in a grim line, and she realized she'd spoken her guilt out loud.

So for the hundredth time—for the record—she restated her name and how the tragic events unfolded.

One of the agents snorted. DEA, FBI, or U.S. Marshal's Service. She forgot which. The men in black seemed to be cut from the same mold, blurring and blending in her mind.

"And you still maintain you had no idea you'd befriended the wife of one of the most notorious Mexican Mafia drug lords in the southeastern United States?"

She bit her lip. "We met at the gym, I told you. We had coffee twice a week. She attended church with me."

Her eyes filled with tears at the memory of Gaby's last words. She swallowed past the lump blocking her throat.

"Miss Eudailey?"

The kind tones of the older marshal penetrated the haze she'd sunk into these last few days. The gray-haired man in his late fifties opened a manila folder on the tabletop. He withdrew several color photos and fanned them out in front of her. "Esteban Enrique Flores."

He pointed to a picture of Gaby's husband. And murderer. "An American citizen like your friend, Gabriela. Federal agencies have been trying to nail him for drug trafficking for years. But he's a slippery one. The bastard son of a Mafia cartel boss."

Steve Matthews—she recalled his name—threw his colleagues a glance. "Esteban has spent a lifetime trying to measure up to his more legitimate half-brothers and their contributions, so to speak, to their father's drug empire. With an MBA from an American university—where we surmise he met Gabriela Mendoza, whose family appears to have no prior drug connection—Esteban runs the American arm of the family business much like your grandmother runs her corporation."

Kailyn winced. She'd not seen Carole Eudailey since the police took her into protective custody. Nothing infuriated her grandmother more than adverse media coverage.

Just as well. The FBI offered her a new life in exchange for her agreeing to testify against Esteban Flores. They couldn't nail him on trafficking, but with the help of the photos, she'd nail his hide to the wall for the murder of her friend.

A new life didn't sound so bad. Nothing about her old one evoked the least bit of regret in leaving any of it behind.

Matthews assessed her. "Are you sure this is what you want to do, Miss Eudailey?"

Assistant U.S. Attorney Rogers made a noise of protest.

Matthews frowned. "She's got to be sure about what she's agreeing to do, if you're going to have a solid case this time. How many other witnesses have bailed on you when it came time to testify against this sociopath?"

The other marshal, Whitten, shoved photos across the table of Gaby's death throes in the pool.

She flinched.

"You'll be in danger from his organization for the rest of your life." Whitten jabbed his finger at the figure of Flores. "His tentacles are far-reaching. He'll never give up the search for you to exact revenge while he draws breath."

His brow wrinkling, Matthews shot Whitten a look. "Long as she follows the rules, Miss Eudailey will be safe. New ID, new location, new Social, new job." He gave her an apologetic look.

She shrugged. "No great loss to the design world, Inspector."

A major she'd settled on when it became glaringly obvious during her five-year college plan she wasn't good at anything else. Good at anything which represented the proper image her grandmother expected her to portray, before she yielded to a lifelong pursuit of tennis, Kodak-worthy progeny, and being someone's arm candy.

Matthews withdrew documents from another folder. "The Marshal's Service has never lost a witness in its entire history yet, Rogers."

Whitten crossed his arms over his barrel chest. "Lost none who played by the rules."

Matthews handed the pen over to her. "You remember what I told you, don't you, Kailyn?"

She nodded and extended her index finger. "One—never return to any location in your former life." She ticked off another finger. "Two—never contact any person from your former life." She held up a third finger. "Three—never tell anyone about your past."

The marshal smiled. "Excellent. I'm sure after a period of adjustment, you will thrive in your new identity."

For perhaps the last time in her life, she scrawled the signature of her real name on the dotted line. She tossed the pen onto the paper and thrust them at Matthews. Signed her life away toward, hopefully, a better one.

The sympathy and unexpected compassion in his steady hazel eyes almost undid her.

"You're doing an incredibly brave, self-sacrificing thing, Kailyn."

Reaching for the turquoise tote beside her chair, she scooped the dog into her lap. She stroked the dog's almost hairless back. Partners in adversity, they'd arrived at a mutual tolerance of each other.

She hugged the dog. "I'm doing the only thing I can do and still live with myself after what he did to—"

Whitten scraped the office chair across the concrete floor. "Well, that's that."

The dog quivered at the sound.

Matthews offered his hand across the table to her. "Welcome, Kailyn Jones, to WITSEC, the federal witness protection program, and the first day of the rest of your new life."

One Month Later

"I'd been out of the country a month before I received your SOS."

Steve, his adoptive father, clapped him on the back. "Guatemala or Mexico this time? Or can't you tell me?"

Aaron gave him a hug. "Both. I hear through the clique the Feds have Flores for murder one." He stretched his legs in front of him. "For his wife. And you've drawn the protective service case for the eyewitness?"

"Sort of."

Aaron wrapped his hands around the mug of joe. "What do you mean?"

He perused Steve's new Atlanta digs. His first visit since Steve requested a transfer from the Dallas office to escape the bittersweet memories after Nancy's death. He understood how lonely Steve must have been minus his wife of thirty years. He missed her, too.

"Out of the blue, Whitten received the case. He's Kailyn's official inspector, but he's moved her already this last month. And now I have again."

Aaron took a long sip, enjoying the scalding burn down his throat. "Sounds like your star witness has been breaking some rules."

Steve shook his head. "I don't think so. Kailyn swears to me she's followed our protocols to the letter. Something else's going on."

Aaron raised his eyebrows at the man who'd been the only father he'd ever known. "A leak? In the Marshal's office?" He frowned. "Wait. You said this woman told you. But you're not her inspector."

Steve sighed. "It doesn't happen often, but there was the one situation in the Chicago office a few years ago where a marshal was convicted of corruption in an organized crime case. And yes, after her latest classified location was compromised, Kailyn called me, not Whitten."

"This Kailyn, how did she manage to contact you?" His eyes widened. "You didn't give her your personal cell number, did you?"

Steve bit the inside of his cheek.

Aaron placed the mug on the Formica with a solid thunk. "Man, are you trying to end your career four years out from retirement?" His eyes darted. "Tell me you didn't reveal the location of your personal space, too."

Steve shrugged. "I know it was unorthodox—"

"Try totally against the rules." Aaron leaned over the table. "Who is this chick? You've got to consider the criminal connections she's got. How she could change her mind about testifying, leveraging her life to her *hermanos* with information on how to silence a United States deputy marshal permanently."

"She's not a criminal."

Aaron made a face. "They're all criminals who've tried everything else first to save their necks."

"Most of our protected witnesses are criminals, but not her. She happened to be in the wrong place at the wrong time, an innocent bystander."

"There's no such thing as innocent."

"Son, I know after what you went through, your perspective is..."

Aaron gave a barking laugh. "Warped?"

Steve sighed, sadness written across his face.

Aaron shifted in the chair. He hated when Steve gave him his hangdog look. Steve and Nancy had spent tons of money to give him the counseling he'd needed when they'd found him and brought him into their lives.

"She's not like that."

Aaron snorted. "They—women in particular—are all like that. Except for Nancy, of course."

"This one's not."

Aaron cocked his eyebrow. "What makes this one so special?"

"She's a sister, a fellow believer. Good people as my pa would've said."

Aaron rolled his eyes. "Don't start with the religious claptrap. I sat on the pew between you and Nancy for years. I've heard it all. But you know how I feel about any sort of crut—"

He bit off his words as hurt flashed across Steve's face. Sometimes, after spending months undercover with the lowest dregs of humanity, he forgot how to be with normal people.

Aaron ran his hand over the bristly stubble of his chin-strap goatee. "I'm sorry. You know I don't mean to insult you. I'll grant that you and Nancy were never hypocrites. You live your religion."

"But you see my relationship with God as a crutch. Something for weaklings?"

He hadn't seen his father in four months and this is what his big mouth had done to derail what little time together they had? Time to make amends.

"I don't see it having any place in my life, Steve. It's fine for you. But I don't see much evidence of your God's existence on the streets where I've lived. And if He does exist, I think maybe He's got it in for me, anyways."

"Your Creator loves you more than you can imagine."

Aaron fought the urge to roll his eyes again. "Now you sound like my grandmother."

"You could learn a lot from her."

He held up his hand. "I didn't belong there, either. Less," he muttered, "than I belonged anywhere else."

"Aaron..."

He cleared his throat. "Why did you signal me to contact you? What's this witness problem got to do with me?"

Steve gazed at him a long moment, but thank God—if Aaron had been willing to believe one existed—he dropped the touchy subject of religion. For now. Steve and Nancy had been as persistent as a chigger on the issue with him over the years.

He briefed Aaron on the particulars of the case. "You didn't compromise your cover to meet me here, did you?"

"Nah, nobody knows my face in Atlanta. Your witness actually enabled me to switch my investigation from Flores's American operation to the more international aspects of his father's empire."

"You couldn't connect Flores with the drug shipments on U.S. soil?"

Aaron heaved a sigh. "What drug shipments? Like overnight, the shipments stopped. And you and I both know men like Flores and his crew don't intend to go out of business."

"Maybe he's trying to go legit?"

Aaron shook his head. "No way. His father and half-brothers rule portions of Mexico and Guatemala like little fiefdoms. No way would they relinquish their power and control. They've sunk their money into something more profitable than drugs, something more low-profile we suspect, but what exactly we don't know."

Steve grimaced. "Any leads?"

"Intel from DEA agents in Central America said the Flores crime family was on the verge of switching enterprises. From my meetings with Esteban, he was reaching out to the Latino gangs," he leaned forward. "Cliques, to bring them into the new operation. But then"—he locked his fingers behind his head—"word on the street is that, for the first time in his life, Flores lost his cool, murdered his wife, and the rest is history."

"But if Kailyn and her testimony were removed from the picture..."

Aaron nodded. "Life for Flores would pretty much return to normal."

"Big stakes."

Aaron eyed him. "Big guns hired to make sure she never testifies and ensure anyone else who gets in their way doesn't live to collect retirement checks."

Steve gave him a crooked half smile. "Which is where you come in. To keep me safe this time. I wondered if you could scout around the Flores operation, since you and he are such buddies, and give me a heads-up on how they keep locating my witness."

"I'll try. But you still haven't told me what the personal interest is in this woman. You got the hots for her or something?"

Steve flushed. "Not at all. She's a few years younger than you."

Aaron waved a hand. "Hey, man. The old man's darling thing is a sweet deal, so I've heard."

"She's not like that. It's"—Steve pointed to himself—"not like that. You know Nancy is—" He swallowed. "She was the love of my life. But Kailyn's alone and—"

Aaron bolted upright. "Don't tell me she's another one of those lost lambs you're so fond of rescuing? You should've never gone into law enforcement and instead followed Nancy into social work."

Steve stiffened. "She actually reminds me of you."

Aaron pursed his lips. "Don't give me the whole 'leave the ninety-nine and find the one lost lamb' crap. You know better than to get emotionally involved with a witness. It'll get you killed. It's why I never—"

"It's also why you're so alone."

Aaron clenched his jaw. "My choice, man. My choice."

Steve gave him a brittle smile. "As is everything in life, Son. One choice after the other. Will you help me keep Kailyn safe or not?"

Like Steve was giving *him* a choice?

He grabbed his knit cap off the table. "I'll help you. Not for her sake, but to keep you safe, I'll do whatever it takes."

Aaron paused at the door. "You've got her stashed somewhere?"

Steve nodded. "I chose not to include Whitten in the loop this time."

"You don't trust him."

"Kailyn doesn't trust him. Her last job as a barista here in Atlanta, she spotted suspicious characters casing the coffee-house. And when they spotted her, she delayed them and got away. Called me from a pay phone."

Aaron tilted his head. "Dare I ask how this upstanding citizen managed to delay and avoid two of Flores's thugs?"

"She upended two scalding coffee carafes in their laps."

Aaron whistled. "Gutsy and resourceful. Stupid, too, considering she had to get mighty close to them."

"Which is why it worked. They didn't expect her to walk right up to them in a crowded restaurant."

"I'll be in touch when I've got something."

Steve laid a hand on his shoulder. "Don't be too long about it. I suspect Kailyn's running out of time."

4

"This Aaron person is someone you trust, Steve?" Kailyn paused, the knife in her hand poised over the lemon.

He positioned his hand over his jacket pocket. "With my life."

She bent over the cutting board. "I don't understand how Flores's henchmen keep finding me."

He glanced out the window of the remote cabin rental in which he'd relocated her two hours ago. "I don't either. We've checked for electronic bugs, tracking devices, the works." The dog insinuated his head underneath Steve's hand and licked his fingers.

She considered the dog an excellent judge of human nature. The dog had hated Whitten from the get-go.

Proof enough for her to use the cell number Steve had slipped into her hand when they left the courthouse a month ago. She'd not hesitated to dial it when she raced out of the coffeehouse.

An inauspicious end to her barista career. She pondered where and what Steve would find for her to do next. Once they dodged the killers on her trail.

Wasn't like she was exactly overloaded with useful skills.

"Perhaps I'd better relegate the dog to the bedroom till our meeting ends."

Kailyn placed several store-bought cookies on a plate as the dog yawned. "He looks ready for a nap."

Steve laughed, scooped up the dog, and deposited him in the bedroom. "He's not the only one." He closed the bedroom door with a firm click and refocused on the driveway.

"You're sure about this guy?" She flushed. "I know I've asked before."

He smiled. "Twelve times already today. But it's okay. I'd be super-careful, too, if I'd survived what you've been through. He says he has intel on your situation."

She took a deep breath and perched the lemon slices on the rim of three tea glasses. She told herself to take a chill pill.

His hazel eyes twinkled. "Three things I believe beyond a shadow of a doubt, Kailyn."

She allowed a small smile to leak out of the corners of her mouth, recognizing his imitation of her performance at the courthouse. "Okay, Deputy Marshal Steve Matthews, I'll bite. What three things do you believe?"

He flipped his fingers one at a time, counting. "I believe in God and His unfailing love for me."

She held the cutting board under the running water of the faucet. "Go on."

"Two, I believe in the Constitution upon which this great nation was founded."

She inserted the cutting board in the draining rack. "I'd expect no less from a U.S. marshal. And three?"

At the sound of a motor, his attention swiveled to the window. He grinned. "My boy's right on time. Three, I'd trust my life with him." He flung open the plywood door and moved out onto the front porch.

Kailyn frowned. "Your boy? I thought you said..." Her gaze latched onto the man emerging from a silver Chevy sedan. She recoiled and put a hand to her throat.

Her eyes darted, searching for an avenue of escape. But the cabin had only one means of egress—the front door, where Steve and the hoodlum who'd almost molested her at the hotel party blocked her only way out.

She'd been betrayed. Again. She'd believed Steve was different. He'd reminded her of her dad.

The men shoulder-slapped each other, and the gangster said something to Steve she couldn't decipher. Steve headed for his own parked vehicle.

"Something I left in the car. Go on in, Aaron," he called with a wave of his hand. "I'll be right behind you."

Her heart pounded.

Once again, she'd chosen wrong. Or perhaps Flores had gotten to both marshals. No matter, yet once more she'd proven to be a rotten judge of character.

She had only moments to disarm Esteban's man before Steve returned. If she wasn't successful in disabling the gangster, she'd never be able to defend herself against them both.

Gripping her only weapon till her knuckles turned white, she positioned herself out of sight to the side of the open door. The creaking tread of the plank across the threshold alerted her. She tensed, her nerves aquiver and her senses on overdrive.

When the gangster's form crossed into the cabin, she took a deep breath. She raised her arm high above her head.

And lunged.

The knife in her hand slashed through the air.

Aaron caught her arm in midair, the knife gleaming. If he hadn't seen the split-second shadow, the arc aimed straight for his heart...?

Her forearm blocked, he spun her around, gripping her waist and trapping her free hand at her side. His other hand locked in a death grip on the arm wielding the knife.

One arm wrapped around her core, he immobilized her against his chest. She'd have to stab herself before she could stab him. She back-kicked at his shins. She writhed, trying to break out of his stranglehold.

"Drop the knife," he hissed in her ear.

"No way I'll let you kill me without taking one of you with me first."

Her stiletto made contact with his foot. He grunted, but knew better than to slacken his hold.

"Let it go, gringa."

Her body arched and twisted in a futile attempt to escape. Her momentum, the sheer strength of her adrenaline born out of desperation, carried them deeper into the cabin. A good five inches shorter than him, she almost knocked him off his feet.

And he probably outweighed her by fifty pounds. But she was tougher than she looked. A formidable opponent. She'd caught him by surprise.

He wouldn't make the same mistake again, of underestimating her. His fist slid down her arm.

"Drop it, or I will break your wrist."

She bit her lip. She'd have bitten him, he knew, if she could've snagged a piece of him.

"No…" She ground her teeth at him.

They stumbled past the table and they banged into the corner. He winced as the wood jabbed into his side.

"What in the world—?" Steve dashed into the cabin. "Aaron? Kailyn?"

Furious barking erupted from behind a closed door.

"I got this, man. This crazy, psycho gringa is going down."

"I trusted you, Steve," she shrieked. "You sold me out to this gangster scum."

"It's not what you think. Not what either of you—"

"For the last time, drop it," Aaron warned. He pressed his thumb into her wrist bone.

She cried out at the sudden, sharp pain he inflicted. From his view of her profile, he watched her eyes well with tears. But she didn't drop the knife.

He slammed her hand and the knife on the edge of the sink. "Drop it or I will break your hand and every finger one at a time until you let go."

Aaron banged her hand on the counter, once, twice.

Tears spilled down her cheek, but she didn't let go.

Steve tugged at his arms. "Let her go, Son. She's scared. I didn't realize she'd seen you undercover with Flores. I didn't know you two knew each other."

"If I let her go," Aaron rasped, "she'll stab me and kill you next."

He smashed her hand down one more time.

With a choking sob, her fingers flexed and the knife dropped into the sink. He shoved her toward Steve and took possession of the weapon.

"No, you're wrong," she shouted. Steve restrained her. "I'd have stabbed him, but I'd have slit your throat."

He wheeled, gripping the knife. "And, hung around to watch me bleed out. Sweet one, Steve. I can see why you've gone to such lengths to protect this b—"

"Enough, Aaron."

"What now, Steve?" She laughed, no mirth in the sound. "Shall I get down on my knees with my hands behind my back so you two can put a bullet into my skull? Or will you drown me in the pond out there like your boss drowned my friend? Tell me what comes next. I'm not up on the latest gangland-style executions."

"Kailyn," Steve growled. "Will you calm down and listen?"

He propelled her into one of the chairs. "This is my adopted son, whom I've known since he was a boy."

Aaron lobbed the knife at the kitchen island where it stuck point first into the butcher block. "Since he arrested me in a gang flop-house at the tender age of eleven."

Steve rolled his eyes. "You were never arrested. Nancy took one look at your scrawny self and made sure of it. You got caught up in a drug raid. Right place, right time."

"Unlike me," she spat. "What's this about?"

"It's what I was trying to tell you before you went ballistic." Steve squatted to her eye level. "Aaron here has been undercover in the Latino gangs for three years working on putting the gangs and their Flores connection behind bars."

Kailyn wilted. "He's a marshal?"

Steve gave a laugh. "No way. He's FBI. Not tough enough like his old man to have a hope of making it through marshal training. So he took the easy way and joined the Feds after his Ranger tour ended."

"Ha, ha, ha." Aaron grabbed the tea pitcher. "Mind if I get something to drink? Subduing hostile, *loca* females is thirsty work." He poured himself and Steve a glass. "Fooled you, didn't I? At the party in Charlotte. Saved your sorry life, in fact."

She wrapped her arms around herself and glared. "By pawing me?"

"Don't flatter yourself, Sweetheart." His chest heaved. "I saved you from probably being gang-raped in a room full of dopeheads, drunks, and thugs."

Kailyn bristled, hostility radiating from her like jalapeños on toast.

Steve raised his hands shoulder level. "Not sure I want to know what went down between the two of you. But Kailyn Jones, let me formally introduce you to my son Aaron, alias Rafael Chavez, whose earlier life in the barrios of Albuquerque gave him enough street cred to allow him to penetrate the highest level of the Latino gangs in the United States. And, gain access to the inner circle of Flores and the Mexican Mafia."

Aaron swung one of the chairs around and straddled it. He sipped at his tea. Had the debutante sitting across from him made it? Sweet like he liked it. Like Nancy had made it.

He studied the twenty-something woman across from him. Long, straight, blonde hair hung to her shoulders. Iris-blue eyes. Pretty, if you liked white women.

Which he didn't.

Like others of her social standing, she was the model of understated elegance. Pearl studs dotted her ears. A strand of pearls—he'd bet his last paycheck were real—encircled her slim throat.

The uniform of her elite class, very WASP. The navy-blue blouse and white crop pants accentuated the casual arrogance that growing up surrounded by material wealth provided. No rings, he noted.

Leaning his chin on his arms across the back of the chair, he detected a whiff of the fragrance he remembered from their unfortunate, up-close-and-personal encounter at the party. The scent brought his Fort Benning days in Georgia to mind.

She rounded her eyes at him, noting his perusal. She stuck her tongue out at him.

He laughed and threw back his head, chugging down the rest of the tea.

Magnolias, he decided. She smelled like the Southern belle she was.

One mystery solved. He perceived a scrabbling sound followed by whining. He frowned.

"Whatcha got for me?" Steve's question nudged him back to reality and the mystery of how the bad guys kept locating Kailyn Eudailey/Jones.

"No leak from Flores. He's getting info from someone inside the Marshals' office. Your suspicions about Whitten may be right on target. With her stashed here, without his knowledge, maybe you stand a chance of keeping her hidden until trial. Which is when, by the way?"

Her lips tightened. "After the indictment in front of the grand jury, Flores's lawyers, including Dex, successfully lobbied for a change of venue. They're stalling with every legal trick in the book, but right now the trial's set for January at the federal courthouse in Raleigh."

"Until then," Steve's gaze ping-ponged between the two of them. "I intend to do whatever it takes to keep her safe."

Frenzied yapping erupted from behind the closed door.

Aaron flicked a puzzled look at Steve. "What the—?"

"Her dog," Steve mouthed.

Aaron scowled. "You allowed a witness to bring a dog into WITSEC?"

Steve shrugged. "We needed her testimony and she insisted."

"Am I allowed to move now, Special Agent Whoever You Are?"

Aaron eyed her. "As long as you keep your distance from any lethal objects, I guess."

Keeping her hands high and shoulder width apart, she exaggerated with extreme caution her movements toward the rear door.

His lips twitched. Funny, in a sarcastic way. And gutsy, in a lost cause sort of way.

But then, as he recalled from his history textbooks, Southerners tended to specialize in lost causes.

Not the lay-down-and-die type he'd first taken her for. Which didn't exactly compute with what he knew—limited to be sure—of her former life in what Steve called the high-rent district.

He straightened and his shoulder twinged, reminding him of their struggle moments earlier. She'd certainly given him a cardio-vascular workout. If her fight instinct when backed into a corner was anything by which to judge, her chances of surviving and thriving in WITSEC had just risen a notch in his estimation.

The smile died when she turned the doorknob and a snarling dog—teeth bared and ears laid back—launched straight for his leg. The ugliest excuse for a hound he'd ever—

"You keep that mutt away from me," he glared. "Or I'll squash him like a cockroach." He lifted his boot to show her he was serious—and to remove his foot from harm's way.

"You would, you…" Kailyn scooped the dog into her arms. The dog growled.

This Rafael/Aaron dude affected her the same way. From the turquoise chips in his ears to his baggy black pants to the open short-sleeved shirt layered over a white tank top.

And his swagger…

Made her want to growl and gnash her teeth.

On his neck.

His deep-set eyes narrowed. "Is that mongrel wearing a Superman cape?"

She tossed her head. "Superdog cape. Nothing wrong with doggy fashion."

He cut his eyes to Steve. He made a whirling motion with his finger at his temple. "La chica es muy loca."

Kailyn sank into the chair and stationed the dog in her lap.

Steve grinned. "But muy *bonita*, too, don't you think?"

Aaron shuffled his two-hundred-dollar sneakers—if there was one thing she knew, it was fashion. "He's the butt-ugliest dog I've ever seen. Probably the ugliest dog in America."

She covered the dog's bat ears with both hands. "Hush. You'll hurt his feelings."

"He's so ugly he looks like roadkill that somehow survived." He chortled. "Like a cracked taco."

She jabbed a finger in his direction. "You're cracked."

"You're—"

Steve cleared his throat. "If the two of you don't mind?"

Kailyn squared her shoulders. "I'm not working with this moron."

Aaron pointed at the dog. "What's his name? No, let me guess. Death Warmed Over? Frankenstein? No, wait. I bet that's his Halloween costume."

She cocked an eyebrow. "Oh yeah, and you're wearing yours, too. Dr. Jekyll slash Mr. Hyde? No, wait. Zorro slash Jerk slash Punk."

His nostrils flared. "Overprivileged debutante..." The rest lost in a burst of rapid-fire Spanish. Which she doubted was Sunday-school-Steve-appropriate.

"Children..." Steve's gaze swung.

Aaron's brow furrowed. "Exactly what did you hope to accomplish with your little knife trick?"

Kailyn crossed her arms. "Other than gutting a gangster pig like you?" She tilted her head at Steve. "As a native Texan, I figured you'd appreciate a fight against superior odds like at the Alamo."

Steve chuckled. "Not so much Alamo. More like Custer's Last Stand, in his case."

Aaron rolled his eyes.

She frowned. "I don't get it."

"No reason you should." He made a face at Steve. "So long as we remember who came out on top of that one." He pushed back. "I've got some leads to check out. I'll get back to you and your friend Taco, here, ASAP if I receive any intel on your situation."

She rose, disliking having him tower over her. She refused to be intimidated any longer by this lowlife. "Please don't hurry back on my account."

Aaron sauntered to the door. "Sure thing, 'cause it's always such a blast being with you. As much fun as being roasted over a bonfire. Slowly."

5

Dawn's early light had scarcely cleared the tree line, when Steve snatched the phone from where it buzzed on the tabletop, exchanging glances with Kailyn. "Aaron?"

Kailyn tensed. "What's wrong?"

He signaled to her to be quiet. "What's your ETA? You're sure they're on their way?"

Steve slapped his thigh. "I don't understand how they keep—I never told Whitten or anyone else where I'd—"

He listened for a moment. "We'll meet you on the forestry trail." He clicked the cell off.

"Steve?" Her voice trembled.

He sighed. "Aaron overheard a phone call disclosing our current location to Flores's enforcers. They're already en route."

Kailyn put a hand to her throat. "When? How long?"

Steve grimaced. "Not long. Aaron said to get out of here pronto. He's on his way. He'll park his car on the trail and wait for us."

Kailyn pivoted in a slow circle. "I haven't unpacked anything much since you brought me here yesterday. I'll gather—"

Steve caught her arm. "Leave it. There's no time. We're getting out of here now."

Kailyn shrugged him off. "I'm not leaving my dog. Two seconds. Let me..." She raced toward the bedroom. Grabbing the tote off the bureau, she plucked the dog—chew toy clenched in his jowls—and deposited him into the bag.

Steve motioned. He thrust open the door as a black Mustang flew to a squealing stop at the edge of the forest. Two men she didn't recognize and Whitten leaped out of the vehicle, guns drawn.

Steve hustled her inside. "Too late. Change of plans."

A popping sound pinged into the doorframe. She cringed and ducked. The dog whimpered.

"Get back!" Steve yelled.

He shoved the door closed. Locked it. Jammed a chair under the knob.

Gunfire peppered the wall.

"Behind the island," he prodded her. "I'll hold them off."

Kailyn bit her lip. "For how long?" She tucked her hand inside the tote to soothe the agitated, whining dog.

Steve crouched beside the window. "For as long as it takes."

Kailyn scuttled toward the scant protection of the island. "All former kidding aside, don't tell me this is going to turn into an actual modern-day Alamo."

A bullet whizzed overhead. She hit the floor.

He cracked the window with the butt of his gun and returned fire. "Of course not. Our reinforcement is on his way."

She groaned over the sound of the gunplay. "Don't tell me my life depends on your very special agent gangster?"

He kept his back to her, his eyes trained for the slightest weakness of his opponents. "He's a good man. He'll come as soon as he hears gunshots. He'll take care of you."

She poked her head around the corner. "Wait. What do you mean he'll—?"

"I'll hold them off and give you two a chance to make a getaway."

She shook her head, as if Steve could see her, his attention focused on the threat outside. "I'm not going anywhere—"

"What you can do is pray." He fired off another shot. "For our situation. For Aaron. For getting to experience another dawn." He winced as a shot rained shards of glass upon him.

Steve half-rose, a combatant trained in his crosshairs. His finger tightened. He squeezed the trigger.

"One down," he crowed. "Now for the turncoat marshal. Gives all of us a bad—"

His eyes widened and he staggered against the coffee table as a high caliber, armor-piercing bullet penetrated his Kevlar vest. He clutched his abdomen.

"Steve!" She crab-walked to his location, lowering him to the floor, and out of range of the deadly barrage raking the cabin.

Outside, she detected the throttle of an engine. The spray of gravel. A lone gun fired closer to the cabin. A car door slammed. Feet pounded on the planks of the porch. Steve's breath came in gasps.

The door rattled as someone slammed into the doorframe. They rammed the plywood once more, vibrating the wall. She rested Steve's head in her lap.

Swallowing hard, she extricated the gun from his shaking fingers. She swung the pistol toward the methodical, violent thuds coming from the other side. The chair wobbled under the doorknob. Inched away.

Kailyn cocked the lever, steadying her aim. The wood frame splintered, exploding as the door crashed open. She averted her face from the flying debris, but the split-second hesitation cost her. A man hurtled through the space.

She locked the sights of the gun on his chest.

Aaron's breath hitched. "Kailyn, don't shoot. It's me."

He raised both hands, his gun pointed toward the ceiling. "I stopped the guy with the marshal vest. The other shooter's taken off to join the others who are by now probably turning off the highway. I've been made. They'll be back within minutes."

Aaron's eyes fastened on the teetering gun in her hand. Never breaking eye contact, keeping one hand at shoulder level, he stuffed his gun in the waistband of his jeans.

"Kailyn? Did you hear what I said? We've no time for you to try to end my sorry life again. Not today." He bit off a bitter laugh. "Maybe when we're not running out of time. After we're safe, I promise I'll give you another chance."

He extended his hand. "Please . . . put down the gun."

What he'd said finally penetrated. She lowered her weapon.

And without the barrel staring him in the face, Aaron's gaze dropped to Steve. "Dad?"

Her head shot up at the vulnerability in the gangster's voice. He dropped to his knees and cradled Steve in his arms. His hands covered Steve's wound, trying to stem the flow of blood.

Steve's eyes flickered open. "Go," he pushed out from quavering lips. "I-I'm gut shot, Son."

Aaron shook his head. Tendrils of black hair escaped the leather band and hung like a curtain obscuring his profile from Kailyn. "I'm not leaving you."

Steve grasped his arm. "Take her…Don't trust anyone in my office. We still don't know how—" He choked, a gurgle of blood issuing from his bluish-tinged lips.

"Dad, don't leave me. Hang on. I'll carry you to the car. We'll get out of here together or not at all."

Kailyn rocked on her heels, holding the dog and tote tight to her chest. He sounded less cocksure gangster, more teenage boy now.

Steve shook his head. "I'm done for, Son."

"No." Aaron gripped the man in his arms tighter as if by sheer force of will he could make him whole.

"I'm done, for this life. No matter. Better one to come. Been missing Nancy something fierce this week." He attempted a smile, which came out crooked and bloody. "Didn't realize my ticket home would be punched today."

"Dad…" Aaron groaned.

Something glazed over Steve's hazel eyes. "G-got to get her out of here. Stop Flores." He coughed. Aaron turned him, so he wouldn't gag and drown in the blood.

Kailyn bit her lip until she tasted the metallic tang of her own blood.

Steve wheezed. "Save yourself. Save her. She's worth saving."

His hand quivered as he reached to pat Aaron's cheek. "As were you. The child Nancy waited for her entire life. P-promise me, Aaron. Promise me on your mother's grave—cause I know you don't believe in much else—promise me you'll take care of this last lamb for me."

Kailyn made a sound in her throat.

Steve seized Aaron's T-shirt in his fist. "Pro-promise me, boy."

Aaron sniffed. "I will, Dad. I will."

Something softened in Steve's face. His eyes cleared. He dropped his hand. Aaron eased his father back.

"And, Son, th-think on what we tried to teach you, before it's too late. I know your mother," he rasped.

Steve's eyes widened as he peered at the wall over their shoulders. "Both your mothers would love to see you again one day."

"Dad, don't—"

With a long, protracted sigh, Steve arched. His spirit escaping his shattered body, he fell lifeless onto Aaron's lap.

"No..." Her shoulders shook.

Aaron bent over his father. A second, two seconds passed.

"Go in peace, my father," he whispered.

And then, he gently reclined Steve's head upon the floor.

With one swift, sudden motion, he swept his hair out of his face leaving a streak of crimson, Steve's blood, across his high-planed cheekbone. Giving him a wild, fierce look. All traces of grief wiped away, he rose.

His eyes narrowed into slits of flint. "Get up."

She scrambled to her feet, clasping the purse strap. She swayed.

He gripped her arm, towing her toward the door. "We're getting out of here if it's the last thing I ever do. Though I doubt you deserve a second chance any more than me. But for Steve..."

She shivered, resisting the tug of his hand.

"Move!" he shouted. "You're stuck with me now. Till death us do part or the trial—whichever comes first."

Aaron yanked her onto the porch. She stumbled. Catching her, he wrenched open the passenger-side door. "Get in." He propelled her inside and hurled her door closed.

Sprinting around the car, he tamped the memory of what had just happened—to him, to his father—into the far recesses of his mind. To a place he'd learned long ago kept the hurt and pain at bay. Or at least less hurtful, less painful. Stopping to dwell on it might get them both killed.

Taking a deep breath, he threw open the driver-side door as a pimped-out Camaro blasted through the opening in the lane. "Get down," Aaron yelled.

An arm, with a 9mm attached, snaked out the window, aimed at him and fired.

As he raised his gun, white-hot pain scorched his arm, flinging him upon the car frame. Somehow, he managed not to drop his own Glock. He returned fire as the Camaro roared closer.

The engine of his Chevy turned over, and Kailyn hauled him by his shirttail into the seat. Gritting his teeth, he swung his legs inside. She strained across him, almost climbing into his lap, and lugged the door shut. The car lurched as she smacked the gearshift into Drive.

"Go," she screamed. "Drive."

He jammed his foot on the accelerator, one hand wrapped around the pistol stock, one hand gripping the wheel. He trained the vehicle toward the forestry trail.

Shots careened and banged. One thwacked the roof.

Kailyn clung to the bag. "Can't you make this thing go any faster?"

"Sorry"—he fixed his eyes on the Camaro racing to catch them— "if it's not up to your NASCAR standards."

Kailyn gripped the handrest.

He completed a hairpin turn around a clump of trees. The Camaro didn't slacken its speed. She flung out her hands to the roof, to cushion the blows from the jolting and lurching as they flew over the trail at eighty miles an hour.

Seeing the gap ahead in the trees and the highway beyond, he punched it. "Hang on," he cautioned. "Might want to buckle up. It's now or—"

"Are you craz—?" She shrieked like an Irish banshee as the car catapulted from the forest and straight into the path of an oncoming Mack truck.

A horn blared.

The truck driver braked. The truck fishtailed. The tires skidded and screeched in a losing battle to grab traction from the asphalt.

She curled her body over the tote. He jerked the wheel and gunned it.

The Camaro, seconds behind them, wasn't so lucky. The front fender of the truck caught the side of the Camaro broadside, lifted it in its unstoppable momentum, and flipped the car, sending it and its murderous passengers into the ditch.

As they sped away, she pivoted, placing her knee in the seat. "The truck driver appears okay," she reported. "I hope those brutes don't hurt him."

She sank down, one leg folded under herself. "Do you think the crash disabled those men? You don't think they'll hurt the truck driver, do you?"

He flicked a glance in the rearview mirror. "Other motorists are stopping. Nobody's getting out of the Camaro so far."

Aaron cut his eyes at her. "And your overwhelming concern for me, by the way, is touching."

"You're bleeding on the seat."

He ground his teeth. "Yeah, all over the upholstery." He kept the nose of the car pointed in the direction of I-20 and the Alabama state line. "Looks like we lost them. For now."

"Are you always this optimistic? Mr. Glass Half-Empty. Mr. Merry Sunshine. Not."

The tote between them rustled. "Tell me you didn't br ㎎ Taco along for the ride."

"His name's not Taco. And, of course, I brought him." She sniffed. "I don't abandon creatures who need my help."

"What about this creature who could use some help?"

He gestured at the tote. "Got anything useful in there to wrap my arm?"

"We may be in luck. I haven't had time to unpack the essentials since Steve moved me yesterday to the cabin." She pried open the bag and removed the dog.

Bending over the seat, she installed him in the backseat. "Are you sure you don't want to pull over and let me drive?"

Pondering what she considered essential, he heard a seat belt click. His lip bulged as she tended to the stupid dog instead of him.

"Because speaking of NASCAR, I once dated a bona fide NASCAR legend."

Pain shot through his arm as he gripped the wheel. "I'm sure you did."

"And we spent a Saturday afternoon on his grandpa's farm ATVing. He taught me the tricks of the trade."

He stole a glance at her. "Again, I'm sure he did."

Good thing he'd parked the car so close to the cabin, no way she'd have been able to run any stretch of distance in those heels. A longer look scanned the pearl earrings and the strand at her throat.

And the summer-yellow sundress? Like a bull's eye painted on her back.

She rummaged in the bag. She extracted a bag of coffee beans, a toiletry case, and a Ziploc bag of doggie treats. The Pampered Pooch.

He rolled his eyes. "Do you own anything remotely useful? Including a sensible wardrobe?"

She stopped digging and tilted her head. "Sorry, I failed to pack appropriately. Didn't know the weekend in the woods involved running for my life. My bad."

He scowled. "Just so you know, deb . . ."

She frowned at him, rightly guessing at his nickname for her, debutante.

"Unlike Steve, I don't do the protector thing. I'm a hunter, a tracker, not some handholding, babysitting—"

"I get the picture. Here," she unscrewed a medicine bottle. "Take an aspirin for the pain." She jiggled two pills into her palm. "Oh, wait. I forgot. I'll need some, too. You are the pain."

"Ha, ha." He forced his fingers to loosen his death grip around the wheel. He winced, extending his arm and opening his palm.

"You want to give me the gun while you're at it?" She nudged her chin at the Glock.

One-handed, he opened a compartment between the seats, trans-ferred the gun to his free hand, and dropped it inside. Grunting, because he forgot for a moment about his injury, he closed the lid with his elbow.

"I'll take that as a no."

"A definite no. You going to give me those pills or what?"

She dumped them into his outstretched hand. "I've got a bottle of water…Or, maybe not," as he plopped the pills into his mouth and swallowed.

"You're welcome, by the way." She fondled the red Super-dog cape. "Look what I found to dress your wound." She tossed an exag-gerated, high-kilowatt smile in his direction.

"Great," he murmured. "What's Taco going to wear?"

"Don't you worry about Tac—Dog. He's sporting an Atlanta Braves jersey today, or haven't you noticed?"

He bit the inside of his cheek as she wound the cloth around his bicep and tied it off. With a bow. "Been too busy to monitor fashion trends today."

She settled into the passenger side. "Never be too busy to be styling. What's left then?" She cut her eyes at him. "The end of civilization?"

One thing to be said in her favor, he reckoned as they headed west past the Douglasville exit. At least she wasn't one of those hys-terical, sobbing females.

No…she was the knife-wielding, gun-toting type with homi-cidal tendencies. They rode in silence, blessed silence to his jangled nerves, for an hour.

Shifting his arm on the wheel, he flinched as his torn flesh screamed in silent, muscle-rending protest. "Would you do me one favor, though?"

Kailyn gave a deep, heartfelt sigh as if he tried all the patience in the world. "What?"

"Reach under the seat and pull out the packet I stashed there."

Her lips flatlined. "If you think I'm going to be a party to your drug-dealing—"

"Kailyn, por favor. For the love of Taco, sweet tea, and Georgia peaches, can you do nothing without arguing every step of the way?"

Stretching the seatbelt away from her, she groped under the bucket seat for the items he had brought to Georgia when he'd received Steve's message. Duct tape ripped as she pulled the package free.

"I've got a half a tank of gas," he explained, crossing into Alabama. "But as soon as we reach Birmingham—"

"Why Birmingham?"

He clamped his lips together, gazing at her in mock weariness. Not so mock at this point, with his shoulder tightening up.

"I really don't know, Kailyn. It seemed as good a place as any to regroup and make sure we truly ditched our tail."

"Fine." She unzipped the pouch. "There's," her eyes widened. "A lot of money in here."

"Yeah, I cleaned out my account before I hit Atlanta. I didn't know what I'd need, but I aimed to be prepared for any emergency."

Kailyn frowned, examining the documents secured in the bag. "And there's one, two, four," she gasped.

She flipped each of them open. "You have four American passports. Each with a different name. Rafael Chavez. Aaron Yazzie. Aaron Matthews. Ron Michaels."

Her eyebrows curved. "How is that possible?"

She gulped, slumping in the seat. "Taco and I—I-I mean..."

He managed to grin at her despite the pounding ache in his temples.

"Dog and I . . . We're running for our lives in the middle of a Bourne sequel." She lifted her eyes toward the suede-upholstered ceiling. "Dear God," she wailed, "help me."

He seconded the feeling.

6

He'd given her a wad of cash to purchase supplies when he parked outside a Birmingham pharmacy. "Stay out of the security camera's range," he warned. "FBI, Marshal's office, Flores—everybody's probably out looking for us now, deb."

"My name's not..." Kailyn pondered slugging him, in his bad arm, of course, but compassion—and the strict training of childhood—had its way.

Later—after trolling through parts of town she would've been afraid of from the inside of an armored tank—he drove into the shabbiest motel parking lot she'd ever seen.

Kailyn pressed her face to the window. "Is a drug deal going down over there?"

"Stop pointing, Kailyn. In-con-spic-u-ous. Can you wrap your society girl mind around the word?"

Kailyn arched an eyebrow. "No way I'm staying here."

He shifted the Chevy into park and switched off the ignition. "Oh, yes, you are. Until we have time to analyze our position and consider our next move."

Aaron forced open the door. She groped for the tote.

"Leave it. And the dog." He studied the dog. "I will grant you that Taco's the quietest dog I've ever seen."

"His name isn't—" she sputtered. "He's a smart dog. He's learned to assess situations around him before reacting." She stroked the sleeping dog. "He's had to make himself be as inconspicuous,"—her eyes flashed over to him in triumph—"as possible to survive."

A funny look crossed Aaron's face, gone so quick she might've imagined it. "In order to make himself less of a target, you mean?"

"Exactly."

He darted his eyes around the parking lot.

"What about your arm? Won't the motel manager be suspicious when he sees the blood oozing down your sleeve?"

"You mean my Superdog bandage?" He gave her a tight smile. His smile—her stomach lurched—boded no good for her. "That's where you come in. Since you apparently have a difficult time doing what you're told—like staying in a parked vehicle—"

Her brow furrowed.

"—you're going to be my cover. My girlfriend who's wrapped herself all over my bad side."

She crossed her arms. "So not happening."

"...while I secure a room..."

"A room? As in one room to share?" She pointed from herself to him. "As in the two of us? Overnight? Huh. In your fondest, delusional daydreams, mister."

"Nobody in this neighborhood's going to buy you and me," he gestured, imitating her, "in two separate rooms. Not all of us have trust funds to fall back on, either. Or perhaps you'd rather spend the night in the car and experience Birmingham's underbelly firsthand?"

Thrusting the door open, she flounced—yeah, flounced—out of the car.

"Spoiled, rich...," he muttered.

"Mush-brained, moronic," she jeered.

In a sudden move, he grabbed her, pulling her to his side. "Baby, you know how I love it when you sweet-talk me." He yanked open the glass-fronted office door and with a dip and a swagger, dragged her in with him.

She stiffened, but positioning herself catty-corner to him, she camouflaged his wounded arm.

"Don't hang on so hard," he hissed in her ear. "A little less body weight. A little more support." He pretended to nibble at her earlobe.

Her pulse skyrocketed.

Aaron veered toward the seedy, overripe man behind the counter. "We'd like a room."

The man, with effort, rotated from the rerun of *Charlie's Angels* and gave her the once-over. Up, down, and sideways. Made her skin crawl. Aaron threaded his hand into hers.

"Sure thing." The man grinned, apelike. "An hour? Or two?" He licked his bulging lips. "Maybe the special evening rate with this one?"

Kailyn convulsed.

Aaron squeezed her hand, warning her to be still. He put on a face to mirror the manager's. "You got that right, brother." And then he let loose with something in his rapid-fire street Spanish, sending the manager into gales of appreciative laughter.

Her face burned. She gave a not-so-gentle yank on Aaron's arm— his bad arm. He fought to control his breathing, but kept the smile painted on his face.

Aaron dug with his free hand into his jean pocket, plopped the cash on the counter. "With something extra for a man who understands how it is, brother," and received a key card in return.

The manager still chuckled at Aaron's ribald remarks when Aaron shunted them out the door. At the car, he released her. She staggered against the hood. Taco poked his head over the window frame as Aaron popped the lock.

"Got us a room around back. Better to keep the car out of sight."

"He rents rooms by the hour?" Choking on fury, she slid into the passenger seat. "You let him think…" She gripped the armrest as Aaron drove behind the motel. "…think I was a prostitute."

Aaron flicked a glance in the rearview mirror. "Would you prefer he believed he was renting a room to a federal witness on the run from Flores?"

She ground her teeth. "But a hooker?"

Aaron laughed as he pulled into the space. "Don't worry, Sweetheart. I let him know how high dollar you were."

Her mouth hung open.

Aaron grasped the pharmacy bag. "And I told him I'd let him know later if you proved worthy of the extra expense."

"You're the most..." Fuming, she released Taco from his seat harness and with the dog and tote in hand, followed him into the room.

She froze, crinkling her nose at the overwhelming stench of— she didn't want to contemplate what.

Flinging the bag on the dresser, he plodded toward the bed. "I realize this isn't exactly the five-star you're used to, but—"

"Stop!"

He halted mid-stride. "What?"

Stashing Taco on the bureau—afraid to put him on the rancid-smelling carpet—Kailyn scurried toward Aaron. "Don't sit down. There's probably bedbugs." She gulped. "Lice, fleas. Not to mention if they change the...After..." She shuddered.

He grinned and sank onto the sagging mattress. "Where's your faith? Live on the edge a little." His grin faded. "Besides, I need you to help me clean the wound." His face paled.

"Are you all right?" She propped her hand on his forehead.

He reared. "What are you...? You're not my mother."

"You've got a low-grade fever. Maybe you should take more aspirin."

He extended his arm instead. "Would you kindly release me from this cape?" He patted the mattress beside him.

Shaking her head, she fetched the bag and the straight-back chair under the desk. He cocked an eye at her.

"No upholstery, less germs."

"Ah," he nodded.

"Remove your shirt so I can examine the damage." She glanced at the feeble light emanating from the lone lightbulb in the ceiling. Dead bugs littered the incandescent globe. "Not exactly well-lit in here."

He shrugged out of one side of his shirt and flinched. "Lighting isn't a requirement with this particular clientele."

"Wait, your shirt's stuck to the wound where the blood dried."

His lips had taken on a whitish tinge. "Just rip it off like a Band-Aid."

"Let me try to moisten the area first before I ease it off." Retrieving a washcloth from the bathroom, she ran the cloth under the hottest setting. She cringed when a cockroach scuttled into a far corner. As yellowish water tumbled from the faucet, she prayed what she was about to do wouldn't infect him with a horrible disease.

She pulled the chair closer to the bed and dabbed at the shirt fibers. He swallowed and twisted his face to the wall. After a few minutes, satisfied she'd done what she could, she pried the shirt off the rest of the way.

Blood had seeped into the white tank top. "Take that off and I'll try to get the blood stains out in the sink."

He clamped his lips together. "No."

She frowned. "Why not?"

"Just clean me up and bandage my arm. I'll be fine."

She shook her head at his stubbornness and scrutinized the damage. "Looks like the bullet caught you in the fleshy underpart of your arm."

His face stoic, he held his arm to the light to examine it for himself. "Exit wound on the other side." He nodded. "Good, it'll make it easier to treat with no bullet lodged in there."

She rinsed out the washcloth and poured the rubbing alcohol over the cloth and her hands. "This is going to sting."

"I'm tough. I can take it."

She laid the cloth against the skin around his wound. He tensed. She paused, looked at him.

"I'm fine. Just burns. Get it over with."

"Okay, tough guy." With small, circular motions as gently as she could, she managed to clean away most of the blood around the two wound areas.

She slumped. "Oh, no. Some shirt threads are caught in the entry wound."

"Then you're going to have to clean it out before you bandage it."

Her eyes widened. "I can't…" She shook her head. "I'm not medical material. I flunked out of candy-striper training. I'm—"

"You're going to have to, Kailyn." His mouth tightened. "I can't do it for myself. And there's no way either of us need to show our faces at a hospital."

"But it's going to hurt."

He gave her a grim smile. "News flash. A lot of things in life hurt before they get better."

Chewing her lip, she rummaged through her cosmetic bag for a pair of tweezers. Holding them over the sink, she poured alcohol over them to disinfect them.

She glanced over at Taco, who lounged with his head on his paws watching them with big, dark eyes. "You're being such a good boy to wait for your supper. I promise as soon as I—"

"Do you mind?" He gritted his teeth. "Stop stalling."

Taking a steadying breath, she returned to his side. "This is going to hurt me more than it will hurt you."

He gave her a lopsided grin. "That's what I'm hoping."

Kailyn closed her eyes, uttered another prayer. She swallowed. When the metal touched his flayed skin, Aaron quivered, but he kept quiet. He gripped his knee with his one good hand till his knuckles turned white.

Probing the wound, she appreciated the effort it took him not to cry out. "I'm sorry. Sorry. Sorry." Bile rose in her throat.

"Just get it over—" He inspected her face. "You're not going to throw up on me, are you? Or faint?"

"Maybe." She pushed away from him. "I told you I was no good at this sort of thing. I have no useful skills to speak of. I...I don't want to hurt you."

She squeezed her eyes shut, willing the image of red, pockmarked flesh to fade.

"Kailyn."

She didn't respond, but concentrated on breathing in through her nostrils and blowing the air out through her lips.

"Look at me, Kailyn."

At the somberness of his voice, her eyes opened.

He gazed at her with the first hint of compassion she'd seen in his face. "You're stronger than you think. I've been hurt far worse than this. Worse than you could ever inflict."

Aaron smiled. "Where's the woman who wanted to slice me open with a paring knife? This, compared to that, should be a piece of cake."

She held her hand, palm out. "Don't talk about cake and intestines in the same sentence."

"You got it."

Kailyn took another deep breath. He tried to remain immobile, but he vibrated with the effort as she extracted two tiny threads. "Almost," she promised.

She heaved a sigh of relief when she had completed the operation. She fished the antibacterial ointment from the bag and slathered his arm. She wound long strands of gauze around his arm and taped the ends together.

"There. Not too tight." She reviewed her handiwork. "Not too bad, all things considered."

He exhaled, blowing the tension out through his lips. "You did fine."

While she tidied up, she sensed him watching her. When she set a bottle of water beside him on the nightstand, he caught hold of her arm. His gaze sharpened on her wrist. At the bluish thumbprint on the underside.

"I did this, didn't I?" He turned her hand over and winced at the greenish purple bruises. "I'm sorry. I don't make a habit of manhandling women." His finger, warm and gentle, brushed the darkened area.

She wondered, as her heartbeat accelerated, if he'd kiss it and make it better. She struggled with the realization that she wanted him to try.

Kailyn swallowed past the lump in her throat. "Wasn't your fault. My skin marks easy. And I don't blame you. You do what you have to do when a knife-wielding, crazed debutante attacks you."

His lips curved, an awareness of her in his eyes. "When you put it like that..."

What was happening here?

She jerked her hand free. Scooted the chair toward the desk and plunked herself down. Removed herself from his reach, out of harm's way.

Kailyn schooled herself to remember this Aaron-whoever was also Rafael Chavez. Not to be trusted. Trust could get her killed.

Like Gaby. Like Steve.

She didn't belong here. She didn't belong in the places, like this, he frequented. She must stay on her guard. Especially with this FBI agent whose three-year cover she'd managed to blow sky-high.

In the real world, becoming more and more real each day, debutantes and gangsters didn't mix. Much less become friends.

Or, more than friends.

Aaron watched the interplay of emotions across her face. What was going through her pretty head? She withdrew to a safer emotional distance for both of them. He wondered why he felt the loss so keenly. And what might've happened next had Kailyn not exercised good sense and moved away?

What was wrong with him? He knew better than to get emotionally invested with a witness. That kind of behavior would get them killed. Had gotten Steve killed.

Their survival depended on his continued objectivity and dispassionate reason.

He blamed his injury and the gouging pain of Steve's death. He wasn't feeling up to par. No one was at their best with a bullet wound.

Or when a beautiful blonde sat inches from his face.

He flushed. Get a grip, man.

She produced two bowls from the recesses of the cavernous tote. She filled one with bottled water and the other with dry dog food she acquired at the drugstore. Taco perked and whined, straining toward the food.

Bowls in hand, she surveyed the room and sighed. She positioned the bowls on the floor and deposited Taco near them.

"We're going to have to disinfect his paws." Her lip curled. "Not to mention ourselves after we leave this dump."

She avoided his eyes. He kept his chin tucked into his chest. He sagged, his eyelids drooping as weariness and pain took their toll.

"Don't."

He bolted upright. "Don't what?"

"Don't lay on that filthy bedspread."

He lolled against the headboard. "I promise you, Kailyn, I've been in far worse places."

She frowned, but retrieved a leash from the tote and snapped it onto the ridiculous ruby collar Taco wore.

He narrowed his eyes. "Where do you think you're going with Taco?"

"Taco—" She scowled at his grin. "The *dog* needs to take care of his business. I'll be right back."

He stiffened. "No, I don't think so. Not a good idea in this neighborhood. You're a robbery or worse waiting to happen, deb."

She fondled the pearl necklace at her throat. "I'm only going to take him behind the bush." She pointed out the window overlooking the parking lot. "You can monitor me every step of the way. We'll be back in a flash."

"Not a good idea. Let me—" Taco growled as he extended a hand in the dog's direction.

"A worse idea. You don't look so hot."

He gave her a crooked smile. "That's not what the ladies tell me."

She sniffed, rolled her eyes. "Suddenly, I'm feeling nauseous again."

He laughed out loud and wished he hadn't when he scraped his arm against the nightstand.

"Actually, you do look hot, as in feverish. Stay right where you are." She unclasped the pearl necklace and laid it on the desk. "Here. Will this satisfy you?"

He snorted. "If this is your idea of blending in the 'hood…" But truth be told, he was feeling woozy. "Uptown girl goes slumming. And all for…" He glowered at Taco's beady eyes. "All I can say is I hope you didn't pay much for this high-bred pooch."

She ambled toward the door with Taco. With a great deal of effort, Aaron swung his legs to the floor.

"Taco came from a rescue shelter. He'd been abused."

Aaron swayed. "Abused?" He placed a hand on the wall to steady himself, almost knocking over the ceramic lamp.

Opening the door, she paused. "Are you sure you should—?"

"I'm fine." He gave Taco a more sympathetic look. The mended cracks—scars—on the mongrel's hairless body made more sense.

She stepped outside. He staggered behind her, one hand using the wall as a crutch. He thought about his last conversation regarding crutches.

"Poor Taco, broken and marred." Like him.

Gliding off the curb, she gave him a funny look.

Had he said that out loud?

"But a survivor. Like you and me both." She gave a tremulous smile, sending his pulse zinging. Must be the fever.

She high-stepped behind a large, overgrown holly and disappeared. He closed his eyes...

And the next thing he knew the round steel imprint of a gun barrel pressed into his temple.

His eyes flew open.

"Don't move, Chavez, or I'll blow your brains out here on the sidewalk for the trouble you've caused me."

With a sinking realization, he remembered he'd left his gun on the dresser beside the tote.

"Get your hands in the air where I can see them."

He gulped, but obeyed.

Nicolas Villeda gave him an evil grin. "Thought you'd seen the last of your old pals, huh? Flores has put a bounty on your head, man..." He licked his chops. "Dead or alive. But after that little stunt with the eighteen-wheeler in Atlanta, I'm more than happy to save myself the trouble and settle for the lesser 'Dead' fee."

Villeda jabbed him in his wound. Sparks of flame spiraled in front of his eyes. He blinked and took a breath, trying to work through the pain.

"Get in the room and down on your knees."

He stumbled, hands raised, across the threshold. When he didn't go down fast enough, Villeda pistol-whipped him to the floor. He fell, but caught himself.

"I said to keep your hands up, *malinchista*, traitor."

Aaron got his first good look at the most notorious of Flores's enforcers in the mirror over the desk.

His back to the open door, Villeda's rattlesnake eyes cast left and right. "Where's the girl, amigo?"

Aaron clenched his jaw. He needed to stall, to buy time for her to escape. He hoped she'd see or hear something amiss and hightail it out of the vicinity.

He would've prayed, but having lived his life thus far without religion, he'd too much respect for Steve's God—if He indeed existed—to call on Him upon the occasion of his own demise.

Aaron's only hope now was to delay, distract, and wait for a chance to disarm the creep. "How did you find me?"

The gun at Aaron's temple, Villeda palmed the strand of pearls Kailyn had left on the desk. "More like find the girl, find you. Whitten,"—he stuffed the pearls in his blazer—"made sure before he placed her the first time." He cocked the hammer. "Where is she? I know she must be around here somewhere."

"I knew you were stupid, Villeda. But you don't expect me to tell you, do you?"

Which earned him a punch in his sore arm. But accomplished his larger goal of hastening Villeda into acting. Even if it meant his own death. A gunshot if nothing else would warn her not to return.

Villeda rapped the barrel into his skull. "So what're you? Cop? DEA? ATF? Let me show you how Flores deals with traitors."

He held his breath, shut his eyes, and reconsidered his previous stand on the Almighty.

"Taco, attack!"

His eyes popped open.

In the mirror, he beheld Taco, the snarling, vicious version, lunge at Villeda.

Okay, at Villeda's ankle.

"What the—?" Villeda yelled a stream of curses.

The gun pulled away from his skull as Villeda whirled. The elegant debutante jerked the table lamp off the nightstand, cord and all, and smashed it across Villeda's head. The shattered ceramic shards flew in every direction.

Villeda spun and toppled like a great oak felled. He landed face first on the carpet, knocked out cold. Blood dribbled the length of his hairline. Ears laid back, Taco howled, circling his bested opponent like David over Goliath.

She planted her hands on her hips and crinkled her nose. "Ooh. The germs on the carpet alone …" She sighed. "Couldn't be helped, I suppose." Slinging the tote over her shoulder, she patted the dog. "Good boy, Taco."

"Great boy," Aaron wheezed and sank onto his haunches, not sure what just happened.

Her arms underneath his shoulders, she hoisted him to his feet. "Are you okay? Did he hurt you?"

"I'm okay." His voice sounded strange to his own ears. "But Villeda's going to have a whopper of a headache when he wakes up. Sometime tomorrow or the next day."

"Aaron, your skin's so flushed. You're burning up. We need to get you to a doctor."

He shook his head.

At least, he thought he shook his head. The effort to do so, monumental. "We've got to get out of here. Villeda may not have been alone. Just help me get to the car."

"But—"

His head rolled. Too heavy for his neck. "Can you do nothing, *querida*, without arguing first?"

Biting her lip, she slung his good arm around her shoulder and trundled him out the door. "There's no way you're in any condition to drive. Taco, come."

Tiny, tapping toenails followed in their wake.

"It was the pearls, baby."

She ignored him, propping him against the hood.

"A tracking device in the pearls." He frowned, his brain fuzzy. "Why am I on the passenger side?"

She yanked open the car door and peeled him off the hood. Lips pursed, she shoved him into the seat. Leaning over him, she buckled him in place.

He lifted a shaky finger to touch one of her earlobes. "Pearls... *Hermosa*."

She retracted herself from the vehicle. "Oh, all right." She removed the earrings and held them for him to see. "Satisfied?" Making a fist, she sent them flying across the parking lot.

He smiled. "Gracias, mi *corazón*." His tongue thickened, slurring the words. "For everything. Kailyn and Taco to the rescue. Witness saves agent."

She strapped Taco in the backseat. Entering the driver's side, she positioned the tote between them and inserted the key into the ignition. "You're welcome."

His eyes drooped. He reclined on the headrest. "Maybe I will let you drive. Till I've rested."

She cranked the engine. "Whatever you say, boss." She snorted. "By the way, where are we going now?"

He took a deep breath. "Have I told you, by the way, you and the dog have a way of growing on people?"

A smile lifted the corners of her mouth. "Have I told you how I love it when you sweet-talk me... baby?"

He laughed. Or tried to. Her smile the last thing he remembered before he fell into the darkness.

7

He scared the living daylights out of Kailyn when he lost consciousness. He'd also managed to infect her with his sense of impending doom. So, offering a small prayer, she pulled out onto the interstate and drove.

Kailyn's prayers for guidance were answered less than a mile later when she spotted a billboard advertising New Orleans jazz.

Wending a quick thanksgiving skyward, she decided to break WITSEC rules number one and two—never revisit a place or person from your former life. CeCe would take them in. CeCe would know what to do with Aaron's fever. CeCe had skills, useful skills, like first-aid training.

Kailyn stayed on Interstate 59. But when she stopped for gas at Meridian, Mississippi, she bought a map. And a Spanish-English dictionary.

Making a slight detour in Laurel, she crushed more aspirin and forced them down his throat when he awoke after nine o'clock. She tried to get him to drink some water but after only a few sips, he sank back into the grips of the fever.

Six hours later, give or take, she pulled beside the curb behind CeCe's building in New Orleans. Exhausted beyond coherent thought, she laid her forehead upon the wheel.

A boom box shattered the early morning silence. Jerking upright, she observed several less than stellar figures in the park on the other side of the street. A genuine hooker, she guessed, and her pimp. Or a john—if she were using the correct terminology. Perhaps a drug dealer, maybe one of Flores's connections.

She sighed. Aaron would've known.

Glancing over to him sprawled in the seat, she bit her lip to keep from crying. She really wasn't up for this kind of stuff.

But crying was for sissies. She squared her shoulders and rehearsed every Pollyanna maxim as she released Taco from his harness, snagged the tote, and prepared to haul a man twice her size to CeCe's door.

'Cause when the going got tough, the debs went... shopping?

From her previous visits, she remembered four locks separated CeCe's apartment at the top floor of the mission house. The three-story brick building crouched squarely in the middle of the Irish Channel district. A working-class neighborhood that had never seen better days—before Katrina or since. She shut her eyes, trying to recall the code CeCe punched in at the outer iron-scrolled gate.

1-3-4-5-7. CeCe's birthday, favorite number, and the month and day they graduated college.

The gate buzzed and opened a few inches. She dragged a barely conscious Aaron through, Taco trotting at her heels. Careful to shut the gate behind them, she waited to hear the lock click. Gangs and criminals prowled these streets.

Her lips tightened. Gangs and criminals were stalking her. She faced the next hurdle across the Creole-styled courtyard. A padlock, but she knew where the key was hidden. She draped Aaron against the rusty chain-link fence and shifted the second green garbage can until she located the loose brick paver and removed the spare key.

Once behind the fence, she retrieved another key secreted on top of the doorjamb and penetrated the building. One plodding foot at a time, she lugged Aaron up the two flights of stairs to the loft apartment in which CeCe resided when not at her job at the free clinic or daycare program downstairs. Taco fought his own uphill battle up the steps. She knocked on the steel door.

No response.

She pounded harder this time.

Oh God, please don't let CeCe be on a mission trip to Haiti.

Silence.

Kailyn had lost feeling in her shoulder. If she didn't get them inside soon, she couldn't support his weight much longer. His skin scorched the bare flesh of her arm. Her hand grasping the doorknob, a sob caught in her throat.

The knob turned in her hand and the door fell open. As did she, Aaron, and Taco.

"CeCe?"

Her voice echoed the way sound reverberates in an empty dwelling.

"CeCe…?" she whimpered.

Taco abandoned her, sniffing and cataloguing the rooms with his nose.

Aaron moaned.

He was so hot. It almost burned her hand to touch his forehead. What little she remembered from her candy-striper days, she knew this wasn't good, recalling that, if fevers remained too high for too long, patients sometimes went into convulsions.

And died.

She had to get him cooled down. Fast. She revolved them in a half circle, considering the ice in CeCe's refrigerator freezer. And abandoned the idea as too slow.

Kailyn shuffled toward the tiny bathroom with Aaron. Desperate for a solution, any solution, she threw open the shower door. She helped him step over the threshold and propped him in the corner. Exiting the stall and standing an arm's length away, she cranked the faucet to its coldest setting.

His eyes flew open as a blast of bone-chilling water drenched him. He gasped as the water spilled into his mouth and down his bloody tank top, puddling in his sneakers. "Kailyn!"

Aaron shook the wet hair out of his eyes, resembling for a moment Taco after his own unwelcome encounter with water. "Let me out of here."

He stumbled forward. "What are you—?"

"No." She shoved him under the shower jets. "Your fever has to go down."

71

In one swift move, he yanked her underneath the spray with him.

She screamed, shuddering as the sudden ice-cold water soaked through her clothing, plastering it to her skin.

He tried to move past her, but she trapped him. Her arms locked around his waist, blocking his escape route, and she let the water fall on both of them.

"Stop, Kailyn."

He wrenched free but only succeeded in collapsing against the tiled wall. And he gazed at her, those dark eyes of his, with the hurt bewilderment of a child who doesn't understand why he's being punished.

"Kailyn..." He blinked the water out of his face, his teeth chattering. "Please...it's cold...Stop...I'm cold."

Huddling in the corner, he shivered and wrapped his arms around himself. "Please... *querida*."

She sighed. She'd looked up that particular word at the first rest stop when they crossed the Mississippi state line. A term of affection, meaning dear.

Or darling.

Shaking, she rotated the water valve to OFF. "I think we've both had enough." Positioning her arm around his waist, she helped him out of the stall, where they discovered CeCe, flanked by three teenage hoods framing the doorway.

CeCe planted her hands on her skinny hips, cocked her head, and poked out her lip. "What are you doing, girl, drenched to the skin, in my bathroom, with a Latino gangster?"

Kailyn shivered, a puddle of water draining from their clothes onto CeCe's hitherto spotless, if cracked, linoleum floor. "It's my fault, CeCe." Aaron's head rolled forward.

"I've almost killed him. You know I'm no good at these things. But he was shot protecting me. He's been unconscious since Birmingham—"

"Shot?" CeCe exchanged looks with the boys. "What were you doing in Birmingham?"

Tears poured down Kailyn's face. The accumulation of months of tension. The violence. Her own helplessness.

"After Steve died, we had to get out of Atlanta fast."

CeCe jerked her head to a closet. "Get towels, Shaquan. Who is Steve? Why were you in Atlanta? Last time I talked to you, you were home in Charlotte. Although," her eyes narrowed. "When I tried to call you about a month ago, the number was disconnected."

"His arm is infected, CeCe. He won't let me take him to a doctor. You've got to help him, please."

Snot ran down her nose. She couldn't even cry pretty. She swiped at her face with her free arm.

CeCe gave her a penetrating look. "We'll take care of your guy. Shaquan, Kendrick. Take the man from Miss Kailyn. She's about dead on her feet. Dry him off and bring him into the spare room. I'll take care of Miss Kailyn."

"Take care of him first. You, not them." Kailyn's voice wobbled, ending on a shrill note. The hysteria she'd kept at bay since the day Flores murdered Gaby crescendoed.

The boys gaped at each other and then CeCe.

CeCe held up her hand. "Calm down, Kailyn. You're not making any sense." She grasped Aaron's arm. "I got him. I didn't see any luggage, though."

"Just the crazy dog we shut in the bedroom," one of the boys reminded. "And the bag."

Kailyn closed her eyes, envisioning poor Taco going postal in an attempt to defend his humans. She'd not heard his warning barks due to the shower.

CeCe inspected her. "You need some dry clothes, too. Take whatever you find in my bedroom. I'll deal with your young man." She gestured. "Kendrick, Shaquan, Demetrius."

The boys hung back. "He's Conquistadores, Miss CeCe." One of the boys pointed to Aaron's hand where it trailed off Kailyn's shoulder, at the tat between his thumb and index finger.

"Yeah, Miss CeCe," another chimed in. "Those are bad dudes."

CeCe straightened. "He's hurt and Miss Kailyn is our friend." She arched a brow. "Or have you forgotten, Shaquan, how she helped your little sister learn to read?" CeCe swiveled her head. "Or how Kailyn took your grandma, Demetrius, downtown to file the paperwork to keep your little brother out of foster care?"

The boys scuffled their feet.

"Yo...this gangbanger swamping Miss Kailyn ain't getting any lighter."

The boys lumbered forward.

Once Aaron's weight transferred, Kailyn staggered. CeCe caught her arm.

"We've got to get his fever down, Ce. Get him out of those wet clothes." Hot tears pricked her eyelids. "I didn't know what else to do."

CeCe angled her toward the hall. "Leave him to me, hon. I'll take care of everything." She tugged Kailyn toward a bedroom. "When's the last time you ate?"

Her brow creased. "I-I don't remember."

"Or slept?"

Kailyn shook her head.

"I'll take care of your man, but I need you to tell me exactly what's going on."

She clutched CeCe's arm. She watched as the boys installed Aaron in the extra bedroom. "I probably should've never come here, endangering you and the children. But I was so scared." Kailyn gulped. "I'm still so scared."

CeCe steered her toward the chest of drawers and removed a pair of shorts and a cotton top. "Then I expect I'll be praying for you as well as tending your man, too."

She handed Kailyn a fluffy green towel. "What's his name?"

Her lips trembled. "I'm not sure. But Steve called him Aaron."

CeCe shook her head. "What trouble you done got yourself into now, girlfriend?"

She swallowed past the lump in her throat. "A world of trouble, Ce. A world of trouble."

The first thing Aaron beheld when he opened his eyes was Kailyn asleep, curled into a moss-green armchair, scooted next to the bed. Which was the next thing to register.

He was in bed in a room whose steel rafters rose to an incredible height. Sunlight slanted through the iron bars on the outside of a window.

Shifting, he found Taco lying prone on the mattress, his soulful dark eyes fixated on Aaron. He racked his brain to remember if he and Taco were currently on cordial terms. Or, if he needed to retract any digits from the vicinity of Taco's mouth. He must've clenched his fist because at the movement, Taco raised his head off his paws and gave a short woofing bark.

At the sound, Kailyn bolted upright and shot out of the chair. "Aaron?" A curtain of her hair brushed across his face. Her hand, palm down, rested against his forehead.

She smiled, crinkling her eyes. "Good, you've been fever-free for twenty-four hours. Welcome back to the land of the living."

"Living?" His voice sounded rusty. "What happened?" he croaked, then moistened his paper-dry lips and tried again. "Where are we?"

She sank, one leg folded under, into the chair. "You were shot. You had a high fever. So I took us to the one place where you'd receive help."

He scrunched his forehead, remembering as if in a dream Villeda's attack. "Where are we, Kailyn?"

She fidgeted. A sure sign, in his limited experience with her, that she was stalling. Or searching for the right spin to put on something he knew he was going to find unpalatable.

"We're in New Orleans at my college friend CeCe's apartment."

His eyes widened. "You violated protocol. You know—"

"She knew if she didn't get help, you were going to die." A voice, Southern and gravelly, sounded from the doorway.

Flat on his back, he struggled to rise. Kailyn eased him forward and plopped the cushion from her armchair behind his head. "Not so fast, tough guy. You're going to be weak as water for a few days."

Resting his head against the cushion, he was momentarily overcome by the sweet smell of magnolia, the sweet smell of Kailyn. He swallowed.

"Are you thirsty?" Kailyn reached for a glass of water on the bedside table and lifted the glass to his lips. He gulped the contents, grateful for the liquid on his parched tongue.

"Not too much at first, Kay-Kay." The voice edged to the foot of the bed. "His system may not be able to handle too much yet."

His eyes meandered to place a face with the voice. An attractive black woman, with milk-chocolate features and hair in tight black curls, folded her arms across her chest. "You're going to be out of commission for longer than a few days, I can promise you."

Aaron scanned the room, assessing the threat level. "We can't stay anywhere long."

Kailyn plunked down the glass. "It's okay. Aaron meet CeCe Johnson. CeCe, this is Aaron. I've explained the situation to CeCe."

His eyes widened. "You what?"

"Only the essentials. I didn't want to endanger CeCe and her mission any more than necessary." She patted his head.

Like he was a child. Or a dog.

He scowled at Taco, who inched closer. "What is the dog doing on the bed beside me?"

At a sudden realization, he stared at the sheet covering his bare chest. His voice rose an octave. "Did you undress me, Kailyn?"

She blushed—something of which the women he encountered in his line of work were incapable—averting her eyes. "No...CeCe and her boys...CeCe's a trained professional..."

His gaze tracked to CeCe. "You're a nurse? So then you've reported—"

"I'm not a nurse. Or you're right, you'd be explaining your gunshot wound to law enforcement right now."

"And Taco has refused to leave your side except for potty breaks and doggy treats." Kailyn feathered a strand of hair out of his face.

His pulse leaped. She'd become very hands-on, he noted, since his illness.

Not that he was complaining.

"CeCe works with the free clinic downstairs. She also coordinates the mission-funded daycare and after-school program next to the clinic."

He scrutinized the bandage expertly taped around his forearm. "How did you—?"

"Unfortunately, in this neighborhood," CeCe elaborated, "the grandmas and the staff at the school are all too familiar with treating the stab and gunshot wounds resulting from yet another gang war. We've learned to deal without unnecessarily involving the police."

Tensing, his eyes swung from her to Kailyn and back. "Gang? Which one?"

"Not the Conquistadores, if that's what's got you worried." CeCe's mouth quirked. "Around here, we're the wrong color. More like ghetto rats."

Conquistadores... He gave her credit for having the street smarts to recognize the gang tat identifying his allegiance.

"Inside these walls," CeCe gestured, "you're safe for now. Because the mission gives their younger siblings a better chance than they had and because we keep their grandmas supplied with insulin, the boys got our backs. They won't allow any within these walls to come to harm." She leveled a glance at him. "Including you."

Kailyn tilted her head. "So you see we're in the best possible place. Everything's worked out—"

"Here we go again, Little Miss Merry Sunshine," he growled.

"I was careful driving here. I checked the mirrors every few minutes like you do." She sniffed. "And just because I don't choose to walk around expecting the sky to fall doesn't mean I don't grasp the seriousness of our situation."

He stiffened. "We need to get out of here before those goons latch onto our trail again. I'm responsible for your safety or have you forgotten that? And why am I getting a foggy recollection of being half-frozen to death?"

Kailyn's face constricted.

"Freezing your skinny butt probably saved your sorry life." CeCe examined the bandage on his arm. "I know you're feeling better, if you're able to snap at each other."

His stomach rumbled.

CeCe's lips twitched. "And maybe well enough to eat something."

"She makes the best jambalaya in the world."

CeCe grinned at Kailyn. "Over a bowl of which you fell asleep last night. But not for him. Too soon. Clear broth, I think, for now."

Kailyn nodded. "She'll have you on your feet in no time." She hugged her friend. "Thanks, Ce, for everything."

"Got to get this lunkhead on his feet, so he can take care of my girl." CeCe patted him on the head.

Like he was a child. Or a dog.

"You're a real answer to my prayers."

His jaw dropped. First time he'd ever been the answer to anyone's prayers.

8

THE NEXT FEW DAYS PASSED IN A BLUR FOR AARON AS HE STRUGGLED TO regain his strength. The boundaries of his world shrank to the confines of the bedroom. With Kailyn's shoulder for support, he made his first foray to the window. Those few steps so completely exhausted him, he and Kailyn almost didn't make it to the bed before he collapsed.

A week later, they'd achieved a routine. His few tottering steps became enough to get him to the hall bath and back on his own steam. Days later, he'd memorized every nook and cranny of the tiny loft apartment. He took his meals at the dinette table with CeCe and Kailyn. He monitored CeCe's Internet connection and TV news for further intel on their situation.

With CeCe at work and Kailyn assisting at the Center—which he'd vehemently protested and been completely overruled by both women—he had time to think on the events of the last few weeks. And time to mourn Steve, giving way to the privacy of his grief alone in the apartment, except for Taco.

Who'd inexplicably attached himself like a leech to human skin. A burr to clothing. A mosquito to blood.

He pondered his next move to ensure Kailyn's safety until the trial. Thought about his last conversations with Steve. An idea, an escape plan, hatched. He mulled the possibilities over in his mind, weighed the chances of succeeding. Contemplated outcomes.

One restless afternoon, he knew if he didn't get out of the apartment he was in danger of losing what little brains hadn't been scrambled thus far. Throwing open the door, he thrust his head out and ventured onto the landing, not exactly sure what lay on the other side of CeCe's world. The bottom of the stairwell led to three doors. One to the clinic, he skirted past.

Another to the street, he had no recollection of traversing. A sudden thought struck him, causing him to wonder what Kailyn had done with the Chevy. The third door opened to a maze of hallways unfurling into a large recreation room.

Where Kailyn perched on a mat, her back to him, encircled by a bevy of small, dark children. She was singing—he grinned—not exactly Taylor Swift, but she was managing okay. Something about wheels on a bus.

She segued into an affected French rendition of "Are You Sleeping?" and sent them falling all over themselves in gales of laughter. She then switched to a heavy Southern hillbilly twang. He bit the inside of his cheek.

An accent which she further exchanged for mimicry of a refined, aristocratic drawl. The tone she'd used on him at the hotel in Charlotte.

"She's good with them, isn't she?"

He found CeCe at his elbow.

"Carole Eudailey—talk about ice water in her veins—did her level best to convince Kay-Kay she was pretty much useless. And worthless."

He studied CeCe.

She assessed him right back. "I spotted your scar."

His eyes dropped.

"I take it you know something about people who assault the body and soul. I'm thinking maybe you've been there, experienced that."

He kept silent.

"Kay-Kay has the biggest heart. She has what I call a natural affinity for the least of these." She flicked a look in his direction. "Don't know if you understand what I mean."

80

He straightened. "Despite appearances, CeCe, I have spent time on a church pew."

"She can't help herself. Kay-Kay just loves people." A hard look came his way this time. "Whether they deserve it or not. Whether she should trust them or not."

He folded his arms. "Kind of like how she got herself in this situation in the first place, you mean?"

CeCe set her jaw. "Kind of like why she's so easy to hurt in any situation, I mean."

He held both hands, palm up. "I'm here to make sure that doesn't happen. I'm her bodyguard, her babysitter, until—"

"Until somebody else takes her off your hands?"

He frowned. "I'm committed to doing whatever it takes to keep her safe, you have my word, CeCe."

She glanced to where Kailyn held court with the children. "Then why am I thinking your 'whatever' may be her undoing?"

"I don't know what you mean."

She snorted. "I'm thinking maybe you do."

"What're you trying to say, CeCe?"

She glared at him. "I'm saying whatever you do, wherever you end up with her, help her make a new start to be the Kailyn she was meant to be." She waved a hand. "Name, city don't matter. The only true skin you fit in is your own."

A concept he'd run from his whole life.

"We're going to have to leave soon."

"I know."

"I've had an idea, but I'm going to need help. Maybe help from your boys."

She poked her head around the doorframe. "Laneisha! Tell Shaquan Miss CeCe needs to talk to him right away."

A thin, teenage girl yanked open an exit door and hollered toward the park. Minutes later, Shaquan strolled inside.

He gave Aaron the once-over. "You still look like death warmed over, dude."

CeCe jerked her thumb at him. "The man needs your help." She pointed at the do-rag on his head. "And you know better than to wear that thing in front of me."

He shuffled his feet and affected a swagger, but removed the head covering. "What ya need, man?"

"Fake IDs, Socials, a new vehicle and..." He swallowed, glancing at Kailyn's back. "A little something else."

Shaquan shrugged. "Ask for something hard next time. I gotcha covered, bro. How soon?"

Aaron sighed. "Yesterday?"

Shaquan strutted. "I gotta man with connections to a chop shop."

"La, la, la." CeCe covered her ears with her hands. "I don't want to hear this." She ambled away.

"I got another dude who can fix you up with the rest." He paused, cocked his head. "For a price."

Aaron nodded.

The boy chuckled. "But any friend of Miss CeCe and Kay-Kay, I'll make sure gets a discount."

Aaron's lips curved. "I appreciate it, man."

"Hey, what're friends for? And what kind of wheels trip your trigger this week?"

The boys arranged to trade the hidden Chevy—plus a wad of his dwindling cash—for a two-year-old, fully loaded Ford F-250, complete with registration papers in the name Aaron planned to assume. Funny thing about the name. Sometimes life had a way of coming full circle.

Mid-morning, he lost track of Kailyn.

With Taco at his heels, he scoured the building, but she was nowhere to be found. In a state of unaccustomed panic, he spotted Kailyn out the window. On foot, with Kendrick, she crossed the length of the park and headed toward the building. Huge shopping bags from a discount chain store in each hand.

Fuming, he lay in wait for her in the apartment. Minutes later, her heels clip-clopped on the staircase. Taco's posterior jiggled in anticipation.

"Where have you been?"

Taco raced around them, barking and wagging his tail like a flag on the Fourth of July.

Aaron gestured to the bags. "Does the phrase 'Flores wants to kill you' mean anything to you?"

She rolled her eyes. "Chillax, dude."

He gritted his teeth. "What were you thinking? You got a death wish?"

"I was thinking while you're making plans for our next relocation, I needed to make preparations of my own." She plopped the bags on the sofa. "Like new clothes for our new identities."

She wrinkled her nose at him. "Aren't you getting tired of wearing the same old jeans, tank, and ripped shirt?"

He squinted at the shirt in question, at the bloodstains repeated scrubbings had failed to eradicate. He fiddled with the cross around his neck. "Okay, you might have a point."

"And look what I bought…" She extracted several jeans, shirts, and tees from one of the shopping bags.

His eyes bulged. "How did you…Why did you…Where did you get the money to pay for this?"

She folded her arms at the accusatory tone in his voice. "Kendrick took me to a pawn shop in the Vieux Carré and we took the bus out to the supercenter on Tchoupitoulas." She rolled the word around. "Don't you love the names in this city?"

"What I would love," he jabbed a finger, "is you not going off without telling me or getting yourself killed by doing something—"

He broke off at the dangerous glint in her eyes.

"You still haven't told me how you got the money for this shopping spree."

"Taco contributed." Her arm swept the couch. "And I got all this for less than a hundred bucks."

His gaze darted to where Taco lolled beside his bowl in the kitchen. He frowned. "You hocked the collar?"

She displayed a metal-studded collar and a camouflage dog vest. "Perfect for a dog traveling under the radar. A pooch going off the grid."

Kailyn sighed, surveying her purchases. "I'd never been to Walmart before. Who knew you could find so much in a store like that? Duffel bags, snacks for the road trip, socks, and unmentionables." She blushed and buried her face in one of the bags.

He rubbed the back of his neck to work out the kinks. "I can't believe you risked our cover for—"

"And look what I got for you…"

He closed his eyes, afraid to imagine.

"They're perfect for your color season."

His eyes flew open. "My what?"

She exhibited several shirts. "You're a winter with your dark skin tone, hair, and eyes."

His lip curled. "I'm not wearing a purple—"

"It's not purple. It's eggplant. And here's one in blue to make your skin tones pop. If there's one thing I know it's color." She sifted through the bag.

"Skin pop? I don't want my—"

"Look at this beautiful hunter green? And this turquoise…" She batted her eyes at him, clutching the shirt to her chest. "I love the color turquoise, don't you?" She brushed a finger against his cross.

Magnolia flooded his senses. "I guess…"

Her hand fell away. "You don't like what I picked out for you?"

Aaron remembered CeCe's words. "It's fine, Kailyn. Thanks. You thought of everything." Capturing her hand again, he rotated her wrist.

Good to see the bruises he'd made on her arm had faded away. It bothered him to think he'd marked her, marred her lovely, ivory skin.

She searched his face and her breath became uneven. She drew her brows together.

He retreated and ran a hand over the top of his head. "You bought a new wardrobe for yourself, too, I hope."

She gave him a tentative smile and followed his lead. "You said where we're going we need layers. Cool mornings. Cold nights. Temperate during the day."

"Yeah. I've got a meeting with Shaquan's contact this afternoon. I'll need to snap a picture of you with the camera the man sent so he can finalize our documents."

"Another reason I went to Walmart. Give me an hour."

"But—"

Kailyn shooed him away and headed for the bathroom. He spent the next hour packing the new wardrobe in the black duffel bag. No way was he traveling across the United States with the fuchsia bag she'd chosen for herself.

So Kailyn. She so didn't seem to get inconspicuous.

Halfway through his packing, his nose twitched at the pungent aroma, like ammonia, emanating from behind the closed bathroom door. He dared not contemplate what she had up her sleeve now. He'd slipped out of his seen-better-days jeans and into a new pair when the bathroom door squeaked behind him.

"Voilà!"

In the act of removing a navy blue tee from its packaging, he swiveled. His mouth fell open. The shirt in his hand dropped to the bed. "Who are you and what have you done with Kailyn?"

Her mouth pulled downward. She tugged on a strand of still wet, but copper-colored hair. "You don't like my hair?"

"It's red," he pointed out unnecessarily.

Her lip trembled. "It's actually my natural color. Like my mother's. Grandmother preferred me as a blonde, so I..." Her chin quivered. "You don't like redheads?"

"I-I..." He swallowed. "I don't have an opinion either way." He veered toward the duffel bag on the bed. "I was just surprised, that's all."

He cleared his throat. "Though the red explains so much..."

"I decided it might be a good idea to change my appearance." Her voice changed as she drifted closer. "To go with my new identity."

He kept his back to her, stuffing socks into one of the side pockets on the bag. To give himself time to get control of the unfamiliar surge of attraction he felt for this most beguiling of witnesses.

"What's the scar on your back?"

He shut his eyes. So stupid. He'd forgotten. He was usually so careful about keeping the brutal reminder of his former helplessness—forever etched into his skin and his soul—hidden from view.

"A war injury from Afghanistan? Conquistadores gang initiation?" Featherlight, her finger traced the shape of the thick, ropy scar tissue. He stiffened.

Her breath fanned his skin. "An old wound. A deep cut. Painful. A horseshoe with an E in the middle. Shaped like a…" She drew in a sharp breath.

Aaron flinched, unable to face her. He didn't think he could stomach the pity. Or the disgust. The usual reaction.

Some part of him dreaded it coming from her. Especially from her. To see him disfigured, the symbol of his humiliation. A vulnerability he'd spent a lifetime ensuring he'd never experience again.

He groped for the shirt and stuffed his head inside, jamming his arms through the holes.

"…like a…" she whispered.

Aaron fumbled with the folds of the shirt, bunching on him. "Like what it is. Was. A belt buckle on that particular day. Whatever he could lay his hands on at the time. Extension cords. A lit cigarette. You name it."

Silence.

He took a ragged breath, hunched his shoulders, and pivoted on his heel.

What he beheld in her eyes astonished him, coming from the Life-Ought-Always-to-be-a-Party Southern belle.

Rage. Consuming rage contorted her features. Sparks of fire glinted in her blue eyes.

He sank onto the mattress. Not what he'd expected.

"Who?" she spat and whirled, pacing like a caged lioness. "Who did that to you? When?" Her nostrils flared.

She clenched her fists. "He ought to be..." Her arms windmilled. "I'm going to..." Her eyes narrowed.

He stared at her, at what he believed Steve would've called a righteous, burning fury.

"Drawn and quartered. Disemboweled. No, wait." Her voice went deep. "Too quick. Maybe flayed first. Inch by—"

"Kailyn." This woman was like none other he'd ever known. Funny, smart, annoyingly optimistic.

And—remembering a certain knife incident and Villeda's unfortunate encounter with a lamp—frightening homicidal tendencies. Exercised on behalf of herself and others she chose to protect.

Cocking her head and wild-eyed, she stopped her ranting to look at him. "What?"

Her loyalty warmed him. Warmed places in his heart frozen almost as long as he could remember.

Aaron rose and captured each of her fisted hands in his. "Remind me to never get on your bad side."

"But, Aaron..."

Her loyalty deserved a few answers. Answers he'd only given to three people in his life. Steve, Nancy, and his grandmother.

"My stepfather. He married my mother when I was six. The abuse started a few months later."

"You were six?" Her mouth tightened. "Keel-hauled ...burned at the stake."

He rubbed a wisp of her hair between his thumb and forefinger before tucking the copper tendril behind her ear. "He died a long time ago, Steve later found out. In prison."

Now her eyes welled. "Oh, Aaron." She cupped his face in her hands.

A longing rose within him for this witness and everything she represented of what was good and right and true.

Broken long ago, marred and marked by what had been done to him, he was also tainted by the things he'd done in the line of duty. Darkness to her light.

He removed her hands from his face. "I think you had a good idea though."

She cut her eyes at him. "Which one? The stake or the plank?"

He smiled and moved himself away a few inches. For breathing purposes.

"Neither. I'm talking about the idea to change our appearance." He untied the leather band he wore to keep his hair pulled out of his face.

His hair tumbled onto his shoulders. "Think CeCe would do the honors?"

She tilted her head down and looked up at him with a sideways glance. "Don't need CeCe for this." She gave a strand of his hair a playful tug. "I got you."

Which was exactly what he already feared.

9

Lean your head back and trust me."

Kailyn cradled his head in her hand where he perched, the dinette chair jacked up to the kitchen sink.

"Make sure this time that the water's warm."

She made a face. "Ha, ha. I know what I'm doing."

Aaron rubbernecked the shears on the counter. "I'm not sure I should trust you with sharp objects in such close proximity to my throat."

"Be still," she commanded and proceeded to soak his hair. "Hold up a sec." She left his head hanging on the edge of the sink. "Let me suds you up."

"Do what?"

"Stop fidgeting." She poured a dollop of shampoo into her palm. "My mom was a hairdresser before she married the soon-to-be-disinherited Eudailey son. One of the things Grandmother especially hated about the, and I quote, 'redneck trailer trash' who married her son. But I watched Mom do this countless times."

He bit his lip but ceased squirming.

She rinsed out the shampoo using the spray nozzle. "Now for conditioner." She reached for a bottle. "To bring out the natural highlights in your hair."

He groaned.

She ignored him. "Make your mane shine."

"What am I, a horse?"

"Just close your eyes and try to imagine you're at an exclusive spa." She kneaded her fingers into his hair and deep massaged his scalp.

"Relax. Doesn't this feel good?"

"Hmm…"

But his shoulders loosened and his skull became putty in her hands. After rinsing, she draped a towel around his head and began a vigorous rubdown of his wet hair.

He straightened. "Hey…"

"There." She removed the towel and wiped her hands.

"Are we done?"

"Just the first act, *querido*."

He jerked, his eyes widening. "What did you say?"

She gave him a tiny smile. She worked her hands through the length of his hair, giving in to her urge to touch him. A pulse jumped in his jaw. His chest rose and fell.

Kailyn circled him, her hand in her chin. "I'll shape the top." She squinted. "And the sides?"

She slung the towel over her shoulder. "You won't recognize yourself when I'm done with you."

He grimaced. "That's what I'm afraid of."

She gripped the scissors. He eyeballed the instrument in her hand.

"We're friends now, right?"

She smirked and brandished the blades, imitating a pirate movie. "Sure we are."

He sighed. "Did I tell you how much I like your hair?"

"Flattery will get you nowhere," but the corners of her mouth lifted.

Thirty minutes later a swath of ebony hair covered the mat she'd placed underneath the chair. She laid aside the clippers she'd used to tidy the nape of his neck. "Okay."

He perked. "We're done?"

Kailyn's heart beat in triple time. Suppose he didn't like it? She glanced at the shorn locks at their feet. She swallowed. No going back now.

"Can I see?"

She nodded and followed him to the mirror in the bedroom. He took one look at himself—she held her breath—and favored her with a crooked smile.

Kailyn exhaled.

He touched a finger to the short-hair-on-the-top, close-cropped-on-the-sides cut she'd given him. "I wore it like this in the military. Full circle."

Relief washed through her. "It seemed to suit you."

Taco dashed around the corner and skidded to a stop as the front door opened. He greeted CeCe with three short barks.

"Ce," Aaron called. "Come take a gander at our new 'dos."

"You two have been busy this morning." CeCe tweaked a strand of Kailyn's hair. "Glad to see you return to being your own beautiful self."

CeCe pointed to his reflection in the mirror. "I like how you got rid of the length to draw the eye to those fabulous cheekbones of his."

Flushing, he shuffled his feet.

Kailyn grazed her fingertips across his now clean-shaven jawline. "Sets off his eyes better. His best feature."

He gulped and stuffed his hands in the pockets of his new jeans.

CeCe nodded. "Softens the sharp angles of the rest of his face. Not exactly GQ, but he'll do."

Kailyn frowned. "More rugged than classically handsome, I'll grant you. But he has an interesting face."

He planted his hands on his hips. "Do you two mind? I'm still in the room or had you forgotten?"

She and CeCe exchanged small smiles and giggled. CeCe veered toward the hall. "Finish up here and I'll have lunch on the table in a few."

He ducked his head, examining himself once more in the mirror. "Less Rafael for sure."

She pressed her shoulder against his. "More Aaron, less Rafael than you give yourself credit for." She peered at their reflection. "Rafe wouldn't have jeopardized his cover to rescue a clueless debutante from the party. But Aaron would and did."

Kailyn gave him a lopsided smile. "If Aaron is even your real name."

He searched her face, an intensity in his eyes. "My name is Aaron. The one I was born with."

She felt the extent of his trust in her, the lowering of his guard, to trust her with this most personal of things.

His name and true identity.

Acting upon impulse, she hugged him. "Have I thanked you for saving Taco and me? Told you how grateful I am?"

The strangest expression flickered across his face. "I don't want your gratitude, Kailyn."

Something electric vibrated between them.

"What do you—?" The color mounted from beneath the collar of her blouse.

She fluttered a hand. "Never mind. Let me go help Ce." She fled down the hall lest he tell her something she'd rather not hear.

Like the truth.

She was a yet-to-be-fulfilled obligation extracted from him at the dying side of his adoptive father. Come January, if they lived till the new year, they'd part company and never lay eyes on each other again.

But he was like no one she'd ever known.

"He's a complicated man." CeCe paused in the middle of putting napkins on the table.

She'd spoken her thoughts aloud. Kailyn's lips parted and she closed them, shaking her head and trying to clear her treacherous thoughts.

"We're night and day different. A deb and," Kailyn shrugged. "Whatever he is. Whoever he is."

Kailyn sighed. "Every time I'm near him, every conversation? Just when I think I've got a handle on him, I find new layers. Depth upon depth."

CeCe squeezed her hand. "Will I ever see you again, Kay-Kay? After you leave here?"

Kailyn stifled a sob.

CeCe took her in her arms. "I'm praying for you. Remember what we talked about these last few weeks."

Kailyn's mouth quivered. "I will. But what about him?" she whispered. "What am I going to do about him?"

"I'm praying for the both of you. For God to make smooth and straight your path toward safety. And perhaps to each other."

She shook her head. "There's no future there, Ce. I've accepted I'll never experience anything remotely resembling a normal life again. There's nothing but constant relocation and secrecy in my future."

"You've got a new source of strength to carry you through now."

She closed her eyes. "I'm still such a baby to this whole prayer and faith thing, Ce."

"Look at me, Kay."

She gazed into her friend's somber dark eyes.

"Your faith's only as good as the object in which you've entrusted faith. And in this case, your faith and trust are well placed in the Lord. 'Cause whatever happens, wherever you and Aaron end up, together or separate, my Jesus has promised you'll never be alone again."

Aaron punched the numbers into the keypad of the burner phone he'd bought at the supercenter Kailyn favored. Long past time to check in. Reilly, his contact for the Flores operation, answered on the first ring.

"Matthews? When you dropped off the grid three weeks ago, we figured you for dead. Especially after the Atlanta police found your dad—"

"He's why I'm calling." But he refused to rehash the terrible day he'd lost Steve. "I'm on the case, albeit from a different angle. Steve called me in at the last moment and entrusted me with his witness, a woman named—"

"She's with you?" Reilly exhaled. "Thank God. We didn't know what happened to her. Rogers, the federal attorney, has been going crazy. Flores's lawyer demanded Rogers drop the charges against his client. As if he knew we'd lost contact with the only witness we had to make a case against him."

"She's the other reason I called. Tell Rogers I got her. And I'm going to keep her off the radar until time for the trial. I'll have her at the courthouse, I promise—"

"Where are you, Matthews? I can send a team to extract the girl—"

"Oh, no, you won't." He pressed the phone to his ear. The thought of sending Kailyn into the unknown, into potentially untrustworthy hands, rocked him to his core. "She's safe with me. And she's going to stay that way. I'll see to it."

"It wasn't a suggestion, Matthews," Reilly growled. "More like an order. I'm telling you—"

"And I'm telling you, nobody knows her like me. Or the situation. At this point, after what Whitten pulled at the Marshal's office, I won't risk her life with anyone else. Who knows who else Flores has managed to corrupt?"

Reilly adopted a more conciliatory tone. "What's going on here, man? Flores has a contract out on Rafael Chavez, too. Your life's at risk. Come in and let us help you. Help you both."

He shook his head as if Reilly could see him across the miles. "My trust tank on a good day operates on a pretty low level, Reilly. And right now, it's burning on empty."

Aaron monitored his watch, keeping track of the minutes he'd used. Only a short amount of time before the Bureau pinpointed the location of this call. "Tell Rogers what I said. I'll do this my way. Or there won't be a way."

"I'm warning you…"

Time was up.

"Consider this my resignation then, Reilly. Either way, I'll see you in January."

"Matthews…"

He hit Off and chucked the phone into the dumpster behind the store. For better or worse, he'd sealed his fate and probably ended his career.

Better or worse?

He smiled thinking of the risky plan he'd concocted on the fly. And when Kailyn found out...?

The grin died on his face. He'd burned his bridges behind him. Now to face the next hurdle—and her wrath.

He'd not been back at the apartment five minutes when Demetrius burst through the door.

CeCe folded her arms across her chest. "You got a problem with knocking, boy?"

Demetrius leaned against the corner of the sofa, panting. "I r-ran all the way. Shaquan says I was to tell you. Warn you..."

Their New Orleans idyll had come to an end. "Flores?"

The boy nodded.

Kailyn tucked her arm in the crook of his elbow. "Aaron...?"

Demetrius's shoulders drooped. "Three men. Asking questions about a Latino and a blonde."

She quivered. "Maybe the FBI or the marshals?"

Demetrius shook his head. "Mixed their English with their Español." His eyes cut over to Aaron. "Suits, not Conquistadores."

"Thanks for the heads up. Tell the other guys how much I appreciate all they've done."

Demetrius sighed. "The dudes are flashing dollar bills. *Large* dollar bills. Not everybody in this hood's as trustworthy as us."

Aaron nodded. "Only a matter of time before they encounter the right person, needing the next high."

"Or drunk, staring at the bottom of another empty bottle."

He cupped Kailyn's ear. "Get your stuff, baby. It's time to blow this joint for good."

She reached for her friend. "CeCe..."

"Come on, sugar. I'll help you with the bags."

Demetrius straightened. "I know a shortcut through the alleys to where we stashed your wheels. You'll be gone before they realize you were here."

Turquoise tote on her shoulder, Kailyn and CeCe emerged with the fuchsia and black duffels in their hands. Taco trotted at their heels.

"Uh, Kailyn…" Aaron gestured. "Don't you think it'd be kinder to Taco to leave him with Ce?"

She rounded on him. "Absolutely not. Where I go, he goes." She flung the pinkish bag at the floor between them. Like a gauntlet. "Or not at all."

"Taco makes us too conspicuous. Villeda hasn't forgotten about him. I promise I'll get you a new dog when we arrive at our destination."

"I don't want another dog." Her eyes blazed blue fire. "After all Taco's done for us?" She jabbed the air with her finger. "For you?"

She lifted her chin. "I figured you to be more loyal than this."

He leaned over the bag and got in her face. "My main allegiance has always been and always will be taking care of my own skin first. Taco puts a target on both our backs."

"I hate…" She pushed her lips forward. "I intensely dislike you, Rafael."

Aaron's chest tightened, but he refused to back down. "At the moment, I'm not so fond of you, either, deb."

Her eyes, the same eyes which survived several brutal attempts to end her life without losing her composure, now teared.

And undid him.

Which had probably been her intention. Part and parcel of the bag of tricks belles like her came equipped with from birth.

He threw his hands in the air. "You make me crazy." He snatched the girly bag off the floor and procured the black one from CeCe. "He's your responsibility. Coyote food."

She blinked at him. "What?"

"Nothing," he mumbled. "But let my subsequent demise also be on your head, chiquita."

And his reward for total, unconditional surrender?

She gave him a quick, chaste kiss on the cheek. Taking all the beans from his burrito. She scooped Taco into the tote carrier. He gave CeCe a fierce hug.

"My prayers go with you both," CeCe whispered in his ear.

"Good," he growled. "With her," he jerked a thumb in Kailyn's direction, "I need all the help I can get."

He swiveled to Demetrius. "Keep Miss CeCe safe from those thugs, you hear?"

"No worries." Demetrius hitched his sagging britches. "We always got her back."

"Wish somebody had mine," Aaron muttered. "Are you coming?" he called over his shoulder.

She smiled. "Right behind you. Right where God and I will watch your back."

As the truck ate the miles across the bridge spanning Lake Pontchartrain, Aaron mulled over what he had to tell her. She wasn't going to like it. But what he feared most was she'd laugh right in his face.

Bruising his ego, not his heart. Or so he told himself.

Strapped in the middle between them, Taco fastened his eyes on the road. Aaron checked the rearview mirror at the receding city. He took a surreptitious look at Kailyn, taking pleasure in the way her lips quirked at the corners.

She'd flipped on the radio and hummed a tune from the oldies station. Her shoulder-length copper curls waved in the breeze of the half-open window. She wore the light blue cotton blouse and jean skirt from the discount store like haute couture. To look at her, you'd assume she hadn't a care in the world.

It was all he could do not to keep looking at her, all he could do not to give in to his desire to caress the contours of her face. He forced his attention to the road. Several hours later, at Alexandria, he merged onto I-20 and pointed the nose of the truck toward Texas.

She twiddled the radio dial and cranked the volume. "I love this song." And proceeded to gyrate to the Beach Boys rendition of a trip to Kokomo, her hands making motions like she rode the surf.

"That's where I wanna go—oh—oh," she warbled.

He grinned, loving that about her. How no matter how grim the circumstance, she managed to seize every possible moment and infuse it with her own unique joy of life. "I didn't realize you liked to dance. I do a mean Texas two-step."

She arched her brow. "I've seen what you call dancing."

The heat rose in his cheeks. "That wasn't me."

She huffed. "Don't you dare say it was Rafael. Talking to you is like talking to a schizophrenic."

He tilted his head. "Takes one to know one, babe." Taco moaned in his sleep. "Do I rightly remember in the midst of my delirium and Villeda's attack you said Taco was once abused?"

She nodded and stroked Taco's small, ratlike head. The whimpering ceased and Taco settled into a more peaceful sleep. "Born in a puppy mill, Gaby said."

Gaby?

"I thought—"

"With cases of abuse, it requires slow, steady, never-quit patience beginning with only as much physical contact as he can stand. Proceeding at a pace in keeping with his comfort level."

Losing his train of thought, he had the sudden uncomfortable feeling she wasn't only talking about abused canines.

"Abused creatures need a safe place to return to, a quiet place in which to de-stress. I've learned to read him and use what I know to bring him out of his shell."

He recalled several occasions when he suspected she had used an equivalent brand of therapy on him.

She smiled at him. "He doesn't take to everyone, you know. You can't pressure a victim of abuse to warm up to you. They'll come when they're ready. But Taco likes you. You make him feel safe."

Kailyn smoothed a puff of white hair fringing Taco's head, dropping her eyes. "Like you make me feel."

His heart thudded in his chest. He kept his eyes on the highway and his hands wrapped tight around the wheel. Best to get this over with.

"Aren't you going to ask me where we're headed?"

"I figured you'd tell me when you're ready."

"Aren't you the least bit curious?"

She shrugged. "I trust you."

He scowled. "You shouldn't trust anybody so completely. So blindly. Not even me." He shuddered to think of how close she'd already come to falling prey to someone as unscrupulous as Flores.

"You could stand to be more open in the trust department."

He rolled his eyes. "Thank you for the psychoanalysis, Dr. Kailyn. Trust can get you killed."

"What's life without some risk?"

"Says the witness on the run from the Mexican Mafia."

Kailyn laughed.

He sighed, sidetracked again. He'd never met anyone who could get him so...

"Look in the glove compartment," he pointed. "Welcome to your new identity. Till January at least."

Kailyn removed the pouch of papers supplied by Shaquan's source. He held his breath and waited for the explosion.

Silence ticked.

Gathering his courage, he took his eyes off the road and watched her shuffle past the IDs, withdraw the license from the stack, unfold and peruse it.

Kailyn read the forged certificate aloud. "This certifies Aaron Jacob Yazzie and Kailyn Nolie Jones were united in holy matrimony...In the year of our Lord...And the State of Georgia..."

She scanned to the bottom of the page. "Last week?" The paper fluttered to her lap.

He searched her face, finding not anger, but shock. Time for the risk-taking she'd talked about. He swallowed past the lump in his throat.

"By the way, Kailyn, will you marry me?"

10

"EXCUSE ME?" KAILYN GAPED AT HIM. "DID YOU JUST—?"

Aaron avoided her eyes and kept his gaze trained on the road. "We'll bypass Albuquerque. I know too many people there. We'll make a stop at Santa Fe and then head for the eastern half of the Navajo Nation, where I was born."

Her mouth fell open.

Aaron cut his eyes over to her. He gripped the steering wheel and went on in a smatter of words. As if he couldn't rid himself of them fast enough.

"Prepare yourself, though. It's like a Third World country. Poverty, unemployment, crime, alcoholism. Nothing but sky, mesas, and canyons. Not going to be a stay at the Hilton. Nobody goes there."

He snorted. "Nobody lives there who doesn't have to. My grandmother and I don't see eye to eye on most things, but I think she'll let us stay at the house—"

"You have a grandmother?"

His mouth closed with a snap, biting off the rest of his—and she could tell—well-rehearsed presentation. A muscle ticked in his jaw.

"All that," he gestured. "And all you got out of it was I have a grandmother?"

She shifted in the seat. Taco stirred. "You're Navajo?" Her eyebrow rose into a question mark. "Like an Indian kind of Navajo?"

His lips thinned. "Is there another kind I don't know about?"

She reclined against the upholstery and folded her arms. "Let me get this straight. You're not Latino. You are a Navajo FBI agent?"

"My birth name's Aaron Yazzie." He bristled. "And I am an FBI agent who happens to be Navajo."

He extended the bronzed skin of his forearm. "Which turns out offers a few advantages in my line of work. A few adjustments and I'm Rafael. A few more and I can become your least favorite jihadist trying to cross the border, who may or may not bear a strong resemblance to Rafe's Uncle José."

She threw her hands in the air. "Do you mean to tell me I've been studying Spanish for nothing?" Taco yawned.

He frowned. "Why were—?"

"I can't believe you didn't tell me something so important about yourself."

"Not important." He shook his head, turning his eyes back to the road. "I'm an apple. White on the inside, red on the outside."

He grimaced. "And if adoption could've changed the color of my skin, I'd have already been there, done that. As a condition of relinquishing her familial rights, my grandmother insisted I spend every summer with her. Where I chopped wood. Herded her sheep. Hauled water 'cause the stupid hogan has neither running water or electricity."

Aaron snorted. "Reclaiming my heritage. Like there's any future for anyone there? Living in the past. Bound by traditions as alien and foreign as..." He sputtered to a stop.

"But you were born there."

"An accident of birth. A mistake of—"

She pressed his arm. "There are no accidents. No mistakes in God's—"

"Oh, she's gonna love you," he growled. "Both of you with your dewy-eyed faith in something and someone who probably doesn't exist. Once she gets over the fact you're a *bilagaana*." His mouth worked over the word.

"Bila—?"

"White person. I don't know much Navajo. My mother left the Rez when my deadbeat dad deserted us. She got a job in Albuquerque, fell into the clutches of my stepfather. And the rest is history. Or at least my history. Is this synopsis of my sordid life story complete enough for you?"

She sighed, thinking of his scar. Her first reaction had been anger. She'd never tell him her second.

After he left the apartment that day, she'd gone into the bathroom, turned on the faucet, and cried her eyes out for the hurt and pain of the little boy he'd been.

Kailyn squared her shoulders. "So we'll blend in and—"

He gave her a wry smile. "*Dzani*—woman," he explained. "Only place you'd ever blend in with your hair," which he tweaked. "Might be Ireland."

She stiffened.

"And only then till you opened your Southern mouth."

"How is us marrying each other part of this plan to fly under the radar till January?"

"My grandmother's told everyone I'm a Ranger. She's not been so forthcoming about the last five years of my life. Nobody much cares for the Bureau on tribal land. Our cover story will be I met you while stationed in Georgia and after a brief courtship—"

"Whirlwind."

A smile touched his lips. "Tempestuous courtship during which we fell madly in love…" He stroked his chin. "Fiction, of course."

Her stomach knotted. "Of course."

Aaron glared. "We decided to spend our honeymoon getting to know my Navajo family."

"Oh, yeah. About the honeymoon thing? I'm not like the women with whom Rafael"—she pursed her lips—"fraternizes."

"You're just not going to let that go, are you? I've explained—"

She held up a hand. "I think we need to establish some ground rules for this fake marriage."

"Marriage of necessity." He gritted his teeth. "Is this how marriage is going to be with you, Sweetheart? Nag. Nag. Nag. Offering all the headaches and none of the privileges?"

Kailyn flipped her hair over her shoulder. "You got that right." She sniffed. "And your idea of a proposal is driving north and popping the question in a truck?"

She wiggled in the seat. "To the strains of Kenny Chesney on the radio?" She wrinkled her nose. "What sort of memory is this for us to tell our children later?"

"Hey," he barked, "it's the closest I ever intend to get to that particular form of legalized torture."

"What have you got against marriage? My parents were wildly in love until the day they died."

"Glad to know somebody had a good experience. Two out of the three marriages I've been acquainted with have proven less than stellar choices. My mom and alcoholic father, a disaster. My mom and stepdad? A worse idea."

"But Steve and Nancy…"

"Are the exception to the rule. Trust me. I'd have tried something else—anything else rather than—"

"Rather than marry me," she spat. "Because being married to me is your idea of—"

He slapped his palm on the wheel. Taco jerked and buried his nose in Kailyn's lap. "I'm out of options, Kailyn, until January. When you can rid yourself of me and everything else that's happened the last month."

That stung. As if what they'd been through had been nothing but a royal pain…for him.

His eyes narrowed. "Until we can both get on with our lives. Unless you don't think you're up to playing the game."

She twisted her face to the window. "I'm up to any game you want to play."

But she wasn't really. She was in way over her head, out of her league. A gazillion miles outside her comfort zone since…Since the elevator doors opened and Rafael Chavez backed her into a wall.

Tears burned her eyes, but she'd be tarred and feathered—maybe make that scalped and feathered after his latest revelation—before she'd let him see.

They took turns driving, allowing the other to catch some shut-eye. It was all Aaron could do not to take the exit into Dallas and verify for himself if the Marshal's office had laid Steve to rest next to Nancy. But he knew better than to veer into what could be a trap. The Bureau would stake out the gravesite, hoping he'd pay his respects.

And if somehow Flores discovered his connection to Steve, an ambush of a deadlier sort awaited.

The Mouth of the South as he liked to refer to Kailyn—behind her back, because he'd learned the hard way about her right hook—spent a lot of time babying Taco. And avoiding conversation with him.

Leaving him wondering what she was thinking.

He'd been relieved she'd taken the news of their so-called marriage in stride—translation, she'd neither slapped him or laughed herself silly at the notion. He'd amused himself the next one hundred miles imagining Miss Deb of the Year in the primitive conditions of the Rez.

But she'd grown hard to read, keeping her thoughts and opinions to herself. He steered into a side alley a few blocks off the main plaza and parked the truck.

"We're here." He switched off the engine. And decided he couldn't take the silence anymore. "Are you mad?"

She swiveled, her face purposefully blank.

Aaron never believed he'd live long enough to miss her usual chatterbox, nonstop commentary on life.

He took a deep breath. "Disgusted?"

Again with the inscrutable features.

So not Kailyn, whose every thought upon entering her brain—as far as he could tell—either came out of her mouth or appeared on her face. Usually both at the same time.

"Ticked? Fried? Nauseous?"

She arched an eyebrow, but finally an emotion. "I'm trying to accommodate your express wishes. Seen, but not heard. Your perfect, docile witness."

In her oh-so-polite, upper-crust tone copied straight from her grandmother.

Which pushed a button. As she'd meant it to, rasping over his last nerve.

"Don't do me any favors. Be yourself."

She crossed her arms. "I thought you disliked my true self."

"I like the old Kailyn just fine."

She lifted her chin.

He raked his hand through his hair. "No wonder my father drank."

That earned him a haughty look.

"Sure, blame the victim."

He gritted his teeth. "So you feel victimized having to marry me? A fate worse than death? You let Flores's men catch you and they'll show you what real victimization is, *dzani*."

She gulped and hugged Taco. "It's only pretend. I don't know why we're even arguing. I just hate to lie to your grandmother."

He blew out a breath, letting the air and his anger trickle out. "It bothers me, too. But a small price to pay to save your life." He darted his eyes around the alley. "Not to mention saving mine, too."

A tight smile. "Glad to know when push comes to shove you'd choose marrying me over death."

"Kailyn..." He bit the inside of his cheek.

How did he fall into these verbal land mines she laid for him?

"I drove to Santa Fe to get wedding rings. Cheap."

Kailyn's eyes lit. "We're going shopping?"

"Cheap, I said."

"We need to buy a camera, too. Take photos."

He released Taco from his harness and grabbed the leash behind the seat. "What for? Come on, boy."

Opening the door, he slid out and patted his thigh. Taco jumped to the pavement where Aaron clipped the leash onto his collar.

"Play the game, Yazzie." She unfolded herself from the truck cab, smoothing her khaki skirt. "We'll need pictures to show your grandma how happily we've spent our honeymoon thus far."

He rolled his eyes. "Yeah, that's us. The happy, happy newlyweds."

Upon merging into the pedestrian tourist traffic at the Palace of Spanish Governors, her head rotated, taking in the Southwestern charm of Santa Fe.

"Would you look at the colonial Spanish architecture?" Her lips parted. "The pink terra-cotta tiles." She pivoted in the middle of the street. "Orange-red adobe walls." She pointed at a turquoise-painted door.

"Like the sky," he explained. "Very Santa Fe. Very Southwest. Land of Enchantment."

Clasping her hands under her chin, she grinned. "I'm starting to be enchanted."

Yeah, him, too.

He tugged her toward the Native American vendors arrayed with their wares under the arcade of the Palace. "Knock yourself out. Get us some wedding rings. Best deal in New Mexico." He squeezed her arm. "But stay within our budget."

"I didn't know we had a budget."

"Exactly."

Hanging back, he allowed her to study the intricate silver jewelry, displayed on boldly striped blankets and rugs. "Earrings. Necklaces. Bracelets."

"Squash blossom," he pointed. "Highly prized among the Navajo." She strolled a few paces ahead, head bent, perusing each vendor. "But we're only in the market for—"

"Turquoise…" she breathed. She gazed at him, the blue irises of her eyes larger. "I've never seen so much turquoise."

Aaron nodded. "Right. I forgot you liked turquoise. Well, baby, have you come to the right place for turquoise."

Her eyes tracked downward and thirty minutes later his feet were tired and his belly hungry for the breakfast they'd not yet eaten. He should've known there was no such thing as a quick shopping expedition involving a deb.

"Just pick something. Taco and I need to eat before we head to the mountains."

She fluttered her hand. "I'm trying to find the perfect bands for us. They must say Aaron and Kailyn Yazzie."

Which sounded weird. But in an unexpected way, it pleased him.

Realizing what she'd said, Kailyn gave him a funny, uncertain smile before turning back to the jewelry.

"I've found the ones." Her eyes shone as she held her treasures in the palm of her hand. "See? Not too feminine. Masculine touches. Just right."

Her smile faded. "Or don't you like them?"

CeCe was right. That Dracumother of hers had done a number on Kailyn's self-confidence.

He examined the worked silver with the triangular inlaid pieces of turquoise circling each band. He smiled. "I think my grandmother would approve. Actually, very traditional."

She preened. "Okay," she gestured. "Then pay the artisan man."

He scowled.

The elderly Navajo cackled. "Get used to it, man." He named his price.

His eyes widening, Aaron seized her arm. "Would you give us a minute?" he said to the vendor.

Edging closer, his breath ruffled the tendrils of hair curling around her ear. "When I said cheap..."

He'd botched the proposal thing. He was struck by an irrelevant thought, wondering if she'd been engaged to dirtbag Dex—his gut clenched—or anyone else? Pondered how smooth-tongued Dex might've popped the question. He clamped his jaws together.

Like Aaron Yazzie couldn't do better than some sorry excuse like Pretty Boy Dexter any day of the week. He'd be hogtied and put out to pasture before he messed up this time with Steve's witness.

She looked ready to cry. "Oh. I'm sorry." She palmed the rings. "I'll find something less expensive."

"No." He pulled her against his side. "That's not what I meant. You don't have to get the cheapest thing you see. I know it's not the wedding you dreamed of, but I can do better than this."

"I thought you said this was pretend," she whispered.

He blinked. "It is, but—"

"I like these rings. I don't want any other wedding rings."

Shades of the dog debate all over again. There was no understanding this woman. She'd try the patience of a saint.

Which he most definitely was not.

"If you're sure these are the ones you want, then—"

"Oh, yes. Yes. Yes." She teetered on the tips of those ridiculous heels she wore, clutching his arm. "This is exactly what I want."

Music to his ears?

He extricated the bills from his wallet.

"Good luck on your marriage," the man called.

He sighed. "Thanks, we'll need it."

Buying a camera at the visitor center, Kailyn, her face buried in a tourist map, conducted them from colorful side street to colorful side street. His chances for getting breakfast were fading fast.

"At four hundred years plus," she read aloud, "Santa Fe is America's oldest capital city."

She insisted they pause beside a bubbling fountain for a photo op. Upon learning they were on their "honeymoon," a nice couple from Kansas offered to snap several photos of them.

"A little closer," the man waved, one eye pressed to the lens. "You on your honeymoon or what? Put your arm around her or something."

He and Kailyn exchanged wary looks. Wondering if he'd lose an appendage, he crooked his arm across her shoulders.

She wrapped her arm around his waist. "I don't bite," she hissed.

"Everything but biting is how I remember Georgia."

Taco perched on his hindquarters as if sitting for a formal portrait.

"Smile, the two of you," the Kansas man admonished. "You couldn't have pried me off the missus with a—"

The sixty-something matron rapped his shoulder. "Now, Buck, no need to tell all our secrets." She giggled. Her husband chuckled.

He and Kailyn got out of there as fast as they could.

"Are we ever going to eat?"

She tilted her head. "Aren't I worth the wait?"

"That remains to be seen. But there's one more place I think you'd like."

She smiled. "Okay. You lead the way."

They peered at the miraculous staircase at the Loretto Chapel. He rubbed his hand along a section of one of the treads. "Legend has it Saint Joseph himself was the mysterious carpenter who answered the prayers of the nuns. Nobody understands how the carpenter managed to produce such angles with no visible means of support for the structure."

"I'm impressed by your knowledge."

He shrugged. "Mechanical engineering degree. Had to get an undergraduate in something. I'm good with my hands." He gave her a smug smile.

"Good thing we haven't eaten breakfast yet or I might lose mine."

"I'll have you know I've brought you to the premier wedding venue of Santa Fe."

She gazed at the stained glass windows and Gothic altar. The corners of her lips curved. "Oh…"

He caught hold of her hand. "Come outside."

Finding the small courtyard deserted, he fished the rings out of his jean pocket. He drew her left hand toward him. Holding her ring poised over her third finger, he waited while her eyes traveled from her hand in his to his face.

He slid the ring onto her finger and handed her the ring she had picked for him. After she pushed it on his finger, he clasped her hands.

"For better or worse. For poorer more than rich. In the good times and the bad. I promise to do everything within my power to honor, protect, and defend you until…" His throat constricted.

Kailyn twined her fingers in his. "From this day forth, until the Lord sees fit to part us."

Something tore in his chest. "Amen."

Tears welled in her eyes, painting them a liquid blue. She laughed, letting go of his hand to wipe her face.

Her hand trembled. "Well, that was lovely. Not legal or real. But lovely."

She surveyed Taco, who cocked his head, his big eyes gazing at them. "Are you guys ready for breakfast now?"

He brushed his finger across her cheek, catching a tear on his fingertip. "Isn't this the part where the groom gets to kiss the bride?" he whispered.

Rising on her tiptoes, she leaned forward, aiming for his cheek as he shifted position.

"Or is this more of the headaches without any of the—?"

And their lips met.

The touch of her mouth, cool and sweet, jackhammered his pulse. He pressed his lips against her. She inhaled.

And wobbled. He caught hold of her, his palms cupping her elbows. She quivered like an aspen in a meadow breeze. And truth be told, he didn't feel too steady, either.

Her hands splayed against his chest, the warmth of her skin soaking through the fabric of his shirt. He refused to rush her. Allowed her to proceed at her own pace, at her own comfort level.

And he waited, waited for her to push him away.

But she didn't.

Instead, her hands drifted and locked behind his neck. She stared at him, hard for a second, her brow creased, her lower lip caught between her teeth. He folded his hands over the small of her back, tightened his hold.

Held his breath.

Stretching, she brushed her lips across his, placing a kiss in the corner of his mouth. "Now we are official." She released him, her heels lowering to the ground. "Our officially pretend marriage."

Red patches splotched her cheeks. "Guess we—I—got carried away. Sorry."

Many more kisses like this one and she wouldn't be the only one having a hard time distinguishing between make-believe and reality.

Aaron swallowed. "Probably good for our cover."

Her eyes riveted on Taco, she nodded, chewing her lower lip again.

Aaron fingered the cross at his throat. "I have a wedding present for you."

"You don't have—"

"I want to." He untied the rawhide band he'd strung through the loop. "My mother gave it to me. Don't know if she believed in the object itself or Who it represented. But she gave it to me to protect me. The Navajo believe the sky stone is a protector. She said it'd keep me safe in the dark."

He grunted. "And I guess, so far she's been right."

"You shouldn't—"

"I want to give this to you." He draped it around her neck, where it hung in the hollow of her throat above the V-neck of her blouse. She positioned her hand over the turquoise-studded silver cross to hold it in place.

He circled behind her to fasten the clasp, sweeping her hair off her shoulders. "There." He stationed both hands atop her shoulders. Closing his eyes, he placed a light kiss on the delicate skin at the nape of her neck.

"Thank you, Aaron. But I'll only keep it until…" She rested her head against the contour of his shoulder. "Till January."

He drank in the intoxicating magnolia scent of her, filling his senses. The pit of his stomach knotted. And suddenly, January loomed far too close for comfort.

11

KAILYN HAD NEVER SEEN HIM SO NERVOUS. SINCE LEAVING SANTA FE, AARON fidgeted in the seat. His hands clenched and unclenched around the steering wheel.

He'd taken them to the Tecolote Café on Cerrillos Road after they left the plaza. "A local institution," he informed her.

"Teco—" she practiced the word.

"Not Navajo. But it means the owl." He snorted. "To a traditional Navajo an owl is a harbinger of death. But to an *álni* like me, Tecolote's *desayunos* are to die for."

Before the waitress escorted them to a table, Kailyn stashed Taco inside the tote and out of sight.

"*Álni?*"

He nodded, scanning the menu. "I learned the word the hard way."

She raised her eyebrow into a question mark.

"It means split in half. Between two cultures. My grandmother's neighbors didn't say it to be polite." He fiddled with the utensils. "And you know what happens to creatures who try to straddle the middle of the road."

She flicked her gaze toward Taco's wet nose poking out of the tote. "Roadkill?"

"You got it." He shrugged. "So I chose the dominant side. Where I'd have the most opportunity to never have to live in that stark, tradition-bound place ever again."

"Until taking care of Steve's witness forced you to return. I'm sorry."

"Don't be. It's proving to have its..." he reddened, "compensations."

She twisted the wedding ring on her finger. The waitress returned bearing a coffeepot.

Aaron extended his cup. "Black. And I hope it's strong. Ma'am," he smiled at the waitress, "you have no idea what I've already been through this morning."

Kailyn kicked him under the table.

"Ow. Give us a minute, please." He massaged his leg. "Only thing to know about New Mexico is to be able to answer the question, 'Green or red?'"

"What?"

"Chile. Do you want green or red chili peppers in your food?"

She drew back. "In your breakfast?"

"In every meal, *dzani*. Breakfast, noon, and night. Oh, and," he cracked a smile, "whether you prefer hot like you Southerners favor it or very hot like me."

"Please," she crossed her arms. "You're making me queasy."

He laughed and signaled the waitress. The last time he'd laughed or joked or smiled.

Four hours ago.

She cut her eyes over to him in the bouncing, bone-jarring cab. They'd stopped for gas and lunch in Farmington and turned off onto Highway 491. Somewhere beyond the towering mesas and sandstone cliffs, he pulled onto a secondary road, more ruts than pavement. She scrabbled for the ceiling to steady herself. Her teeth rattled.

Fondling her necklace, Kailyn pointed at the striations of purple, red, orange, and pink banding the flat-topped buttes. "It's beautiful here."

Mountains stretched in every direction. A cluster of trees, wreathed in the golden yellow of late September, ribboned the wooded grove alongside a desultory riverbed.

"It's barren." He cleared his throat. "And I'd better warn you about my grandmother, Delores Yazzie. She'll probably let us use the spare bedroom. If she lets us in the house."

Kailyn shifted position. "Spare bedroom? And where are you planning to sleep?" She tensed. "And what do you mean if she lets us in the house?"

"She doesn't exactly approve of the lifestyle choices I've made." His lips thinned. "She doesn't approve of anything about me. I'm nothing but a disappointment to her. But she'll feel obligated due to Navajo hospitality to let us camp out for the night in the hogan, if nothing else."

"The one with no indoor toilet facilities or running water?"

And as she'd intended, his lips curved.

His shoulders relaxed a notch. "Yeah, deb. Think you can handle it?"

Kailyn lifted her chin. "I can handle anything you dish out and more."

"So I saw." He grinned. A wolfish grin. "Back in Santa Fe."

Blushing, she cursed her redheaded skin tone. Showed every emotion when she longed to...

Her eyes flickered to the desert, painted in broad strokes of brown and tan with the occasional green of sagebrush. Best not to dwell on what she'd longed for in Santa Fe.

She was so stupid. So everything Rafael accused her of being. But Aaron's mouth on hers had been like a bow brushing across her strings, vibrating her to life. To impossible outcomes.

Aaron made her feel things she'd never felt. Made her believe she could do things she'd never tried before. Stupid, stupid, stupid.

He was a born actor. It's what kept him alive undercover. And she and he were just acting their parts in a well-crafted play designed to keep her alive. This façade would come to an end in January.

A wood-framed house appeared in the distance. Behind the house, an octagon-shaped hogan of fitted pine logs nestled in the far shadow of a red rock canyon. Between the two structures and underneath a cottonwood arbor, brightly colored fibers laced a wooden loom.

"I don't see a vehicle." She swiveled to find Aaron mauling the wheel again. "Perhaps she's not at home."

"Grandmother doesn't drive," he muttered. "She's home." He jerked the truck to a standstill beside a gnarled, stunted juniper. "Welcome to the dead end of nowhere."

She reached for the door handle.

"Don't."

She dropped her hand.

"With a traditional like my grandmother, it's polite to wait until you're invited to come closer."

So they waited fifteen minutes.

"Maybe she doesn't know we're out here," she gestured at the darkened interior of the house.

"She knows. Sound travels for miles in this desert climate. She heard somebody coming before we ever turned off the main road. Not to mention the dust trail we kicked up."

In the gathering dusk, the planked door to the hogan opened and an elderly woman ventured out.

His breath caught. "Don't tell me after what I went through to get a brand-new house built for her, she's still living in..." He raked a hand across the top of his newly-shorn hair.

The old woman, her white hair bound in a bun, strolled toward the arbor. In her seventies, Kailyn guessed, although with the dark, lined faces of the Navajo women she'd seen in Farmington it was often hard to tell.

But the old lady, clad in a bright pink long-sleeved silk blouse and purple velvet skirt, moved with slow, sure motions. She lowered herself to the loom. Her gnarled hands tamped the fibers with a quick, gliding swish.

"Maybe she doesn't know it's you," Kailyn offered when the woman made no attempt to communicate.

"She knows. Probably why she's keeping her distance." But he shoved open the truck door and swung his boots to the dusty ground. The dinging of the door seemed out of place in this remote, tranquil corner. "Stay there. I'll come get you." He slammed the truck door.

He helped her down. "Stay, Taco," she commanded. The dog rested his front paws on the window jamb, his fluffy white pompadour waving in the evening breeze.

Aaron leaned on the hood of the truck. He pressed her to his side. Nothing stirred. No sound except for the clicking cooling of the engine.

He pushed back the brim of the cowboy hat they'd purchased in Farmington. "Stubborn old woman…"

Kailyn shivered.

Enfolding her in the circle of his arms, he sheltered her from the wind. "Night falls quickly here and cools the earth." Tucking her head into the curve of his neck, she felt his breath rustle the tendrils of hair against her ears. She savored the scent of the Big Red gum he liked to chew.

Kailyn huddled into the heat of his body, warming hers, through his Western-cut shirt. She nestled into the musk cologne he favored and the indefinable essence of Aaron Yazzie.

With great dignity, the old woman lumbered to her feet, the turquoise-studded concha belt banding her waist gleaming in the shafts of the setting sun. She halted by the porch of the wood-framed house. "Grandson, you have returned to reclaim your heritage."

Aaron straightened, his arms falling to his sides. "*Shinali*, I have come to introduce my…" He moistened his lips. "My wife to you." His hand in the small of her back, he nudged Kailyn forward.

She smiled at his grandmother, extended her hand. "Mrs. Yazzie, so good to meet you. I'm Kailyn. Kailyn…Yazzie." So funny to say it. Funny and inexplicably pleasurable.

The old woman sized her up and down, her face as impassive as slate. Kailyn's smile faltered.

Frowning, he grasped her hand, weaving his fingers through hers. "The Navajo don't like to be touched by strangers. I should've warned…"

"I dreamed you'd return this week and bring a bride with you." The old woman's voice rang clear and steady through the space between them. "The Creator did not reveal to me you'd choose an Anglo." Her full lips bulged. "Though I suppose I should've guessed."

Kailyn's face fell. Of course the old woman would've wanted him to marry within the tribe.

He scowled at his grandmother. "In respect, I bring my bride to meet you and you scorn her—you scorn me—the way you scorn the home I built for you in your old age."

The old woman bristled. "I will die in the home I was born in and raised my son, your father, within." She gestured at the modern dwelling behind her. "I save this for the day you return to your people."

He thrust Kailyn behind him. She clutched the back of his shirt with her fists, caught in the battle of two strong wills. He quivered with outrage.

Shades of love me, love my wife?

Kailyn tugged at his shirttail. The old woman might be his grandmother, but she'd be dipped in hot oil before she'd allow anyone to bully him. "It's okay, Aaron. We'll go back to Farmington." She placed the palm of her hand across the breadth of his hard-muscled shoulders, where the buckle had scored his flesh.

The old woman's dark, deep-set eyes followed her gesture. Something softened in her face. "No need to return to the city. What's done is done."

Hardly the reception she'd hoped for. Nor Aaron, apparently. He didn't move a muscle.

The old woman pursed her lips and jutted them toward the truck. A gesture Kailyn found reminiscent of Aaron. Something she had also observed in Farmington. A distinctive cultural habit of the Navajo.

"What's the creature in the vehicle?"

He clenched his jaw. "My dog, Taco."

The old woman ambled to the porch. "I prepared the bed with fresh sheets. Towels in the bathroom. Stew's on the stovetop."

Nostrils flaring, he swept Kailyn off her feet, gathering her in his arms. Her heart thundered.

She locked her arms around his neck as he strode toward the porch and past his grandmother. "Aaron...?"

He threw open the door. "My name's on the deed, too."

Aaron carried her over the threshold and settled her on the other side. With a swish of her skirt, Delores Yazzie followed them inside. His hands cupping Kailyn's cheeks, he planted a quick kiss on her forehead.

Kailyn's skin tingled at the feel of his smooth lips against her skin. Delores's eyes narrowed.

He draped an arm across Kailyn's shoulders. "Maybe we'll paint the door like those turquoise ones you loved in Santa Fe, my wife."

Delores's gaze dropped to the turquoise cross around Kailyn's neck. She nodded, as if satisfied. "Congratulations, Grandson, on your new wife."

A smile creased the contours of her hawkish features. Her eyes glinted. "What beautiful children the two of you will make."

He coughed, shuffling his feet. Kailyn's face flamed.

Aaron watched as Kailyn settled Taco into his cushy navy-striped bed in the corner of the kitchen. Taco had sniffed at Aaron's grandmother's hand while the old woman's face remained stoic. Taco retreated to his water and food bowl, never taking his sharp eyes off her.

Smart dog.

Aaron knew the feeling. He yanked the ladder-back chair from under the farmhouse-style table.

Delores stirred the pot on the range. "What's wrong with your dog? He looks like a lamb plucked and sheared of his wool."

Her eyes blazing, Kailyn opened her mouth.

Aaron set the chair with a thud on the piñon pine floors. "There's nothing wrong with Taco. Best guard dog in a handful of states. Tough like rawhide. Reflexes of a cougar. Instincts as honed as a grizzly's."

Kailyn's mouth closed with a snap. She brushed her hands against her denim skirt. She'd changed for dinner.

His mouth quirked. In Kailyn's world, everyone changed for dinner.

Plopping into the chair, the cane bottom creaked at his weight. Leastways with his grandmother determined to live out her days in the hogan, they'd have the house to themselves. Save some explaining. Kailyn would have the master bedroom to herself.

Saving him from having to endure the Southern-sized hissy fit she'd have thrown otherwise.

He studied his grandmother's back. Hadn't seen her in a dozen years, but she'd not changed other than her shoulders appearing more stooped. "Still got a boulder-sized chip on her shoulder," he muttered under his breath.

Kailyn placed a mat and utensils in front of him. "She's not the only one," she whispered.

His grandmother stirred harder, the only sign she'd heard. But the old woman, he recalled from unfortunate experience, possessed the ears of a bat.

Aaron hooked Kailyn around the waist and hauled her onto his lap.

With a gasp, she punched him on the arm. "What're you doing?"

He leaned into her space, his lips inches from her earlobe. "We're newlyweds, remember. You got to start laying some loving on me, *dzani.*"

She batted her eyes. "Pretend, you mean?" She trailed a row of kisses across his jawline, her lips petal soft.

He went rigid with shock. And delight.

Laughing, she removed herself from his lap. "Grandmother"— she addressed Delores the way he'd instructed—"let me help you with dinner."

Over the steaming pottery bowls of mutton stew, he watched his grandmother watch them.

"How long will you stay?"

Kailyn's eyes darted to him.

He rested his elbows on the table. "We're on our honeymoon. A few months. Through Christmas?" He shrugged. "We'll see how it goes."

"You can leave your 'job,'"—Delores said the last word like one might verbalize 'excrement'—"for so long?" Her unreadable eyes cut to Kailyn. "Does *she* know what you do?"

"I've," he swallowed, "sort of resigned."

Kailyn's spoon clanged against the bowl.

"Good news," his grandmother smirked.

Kailyn flipped her hair over her shoulder, her lips tightening. "We met during his last assignment." She'd taken on her haughty Carole Eudailey tone.

He gave Kailyn a tiny shake of his head.

She ignored him. "He's brilliant at what he does. Brave. Brings light into darkness like his name."

He rolled his eyes. Great. No telling what secrets she'd spill now that his grandmother had succeeded in riling Kailyn's Irish.

Delores Yazzie was on a fishing expedition in the middle of a bone-dry desert. She excelled at pushing other people's buttons.

He'd informed Kailyn of the Navajo beliefs regarding speaking names too much, robbing them of their supposed power. Hence, the Grandson and Grandmother.

The old lady laid down her spoon. "What assignment?"

Kailyn's eyes widened.

Yeah, caught and snared by a professional. Another one bites the dust, thanks to Delores Yazzie.

"We actually met at a party," he interjected.

Kailyn's eyes slid over to his. "He was…" A smile teased at the corners of her mouth.

Aaron held his breath.

"…dancing…"—She lifted the tea glass to her lips—"with someone else."

He accepted her challenge and tossed it back. "We were both there with other…"—he picked up his glass—"dates."

She positioned her hands flat against the tabletop. "I saw him across a crowded room." She allowed a small sigh to escape from between her lips.

He cocked his head, his gaze connecting with hers. "Love at first sight."

Kailyn's lips twitched. "And the next time we were together?"

He bit the inside of his cheek. "Fireworks. Everywhere."

They grinned at each other.

"And this must be the way"—his grandmother glanced out the window at the sound of tires on the gravel—"you tell the story to your children."

Sucker-punched, his mouth hung ajar. Kailyn blinked and flushed. He scooted his chair across the floor. "Who has come this late, *Shinali*?"

Delores avoided his eyes, scraped back her own chair and busied herself clearing the table.

He hastened to the living room and peered out the picture window. Taco's paws pitter-patted alongside. He scrutinized the blue Dodge truck, trying to scope out the lone occupant. His hand went to his hip, before he remembered he'd unholstered the pistol and left it in the duffel.

Kailyn drifted toward the door.

"Wait," he called, his voice gruff. "I can't make out yet—"

"It's your father," Delores spoke from the kitchen. "I called him earlier from that newfangled cell phone you sent me," she sniffed. "While you retrieved your bags from the vehicle."

Aaron whirled.

"He," Aaron jabbed his finger toward the Dodge, "is not my father. A sperm donor I'd just as soon never lay eyes on again. What's he doing here? Why did you call that stinking drunk? I didn't know he was alive, much less on the Rez."

Delores's eyes narrowed to slits. "There's much you've not bothered to find out. He's been back almost as long as you've been gone."

She planted her hands on her hips. "He's my son and whether you want to admit it or not, he is your father. And he's here because I asked him to help you."

He reared. "Help me? I don't need his help. His help I needed twenty-five years ago. Where was he when we needed food? Where was he when my mother found an Anglo to put a roof over our heads? For a price..." he snarled.

Delores shuffled toward the door. For the first time, he noticed a hitch in her step. "He's been sober for twelve years. Found harmony and balance. Tries to make a difference in other people's lives."

"He's not stepping foot in my house."

She threw open the door. A stocky man emerged from the truck cab, remaining in the shadow of the juniper. Gideon Yazzie.

Older than he remembered. More shrunken than he recalled. More worn than he'd imagined.

"How do you think you will support this *bilagaana* wife of yours without a job?" Delores crossed her arms. "Heard about the Great Recession? It's ten times worse, as in all things, here. Your father has established a successful construction business. He received a big grant funded through the Tribal Council to build tribal houses on a piece of land near Blue Corn Springs."

She edged onto the porch. Aaron followed with Kailyn.

"My son has long wished to speak to you from his heart. Unless you think you're too good to work a blue-collar job." Delores grasped the railing. "No one will hire you unless your own father does. No one knows you."

"No one trusts an outsider like me, you mean?" he growled.

Kailyn tucked her hand in the crook of his arm.

The gentle pressure of her hand calmed the wild hammering of his heart in coming face-to-face with the man he hated more than his abusive, but dead, stepfather. He despised having to go to this man, hat in hand, for work. But he'd not fully appreciated his dire prospects for finding a job until now.

The money he'd emptied out of his account had long since dwindled to near nothing.

Aaron couldn't afford his pride. He had Kailyn's welfare to consider. "Tell him to come." He swallowed past the bitter clump in his throat. "Tell him we have much to discuss."

Kailyn's fingers stroked the mark of his worst nightmare. The heat radiated off her hand, covering, encouraging, healing. He took a steadying breath.

"Tell him I will listen to what he has to say."

12

AARON AWOKE THE NEXT MORNING TO THE AROMA OF PERCOLATING COFFEE. He glanced out the curtain-less window and groaned at the dark face of the predawn sky. At the gentle tapping on his door, he hauled himself, shivering in the cold New Mexico morning temperatures, out of bed.

"Are you up yet? I've brought you something. Are you decent?"

Stretching, he pried open the door a crack. "That's debatable at any time of the day or night."

A sliver of Kailyn's face appeared in the opening. "That's why I asked. Here."

She thrust a blue pottery mug at him. "One of the few things I *can* do is make a decent cup of coffee."

Warming his hands around the cup, he closed his eyes, inhaling the rich fragrance of the gourmet stuff she somehow managed to carry all the way from Carolina in Taco's tote.

"You're a lifesaver," he breathed, taking a sip.

"I've got sandwiches ready for your lunch when your father—"

He tensed.

"—when Gid swings by to pick you up."

He squinted at the bedside clock. Five-ten a.m. His eyes skimmed to Kailyn, scanning her jeans and long-sleeved blue-green flannel shirt—one of his—the ends bunched and tied over her tank top in a pretty bow.

The cross looked good against the delicate skin at her throat. "What time did you get up, Kailyn? I told you to sleep in. You didn't have to—"

"I wanted to make sure you had a good start before your first day on a new job." She chewed her lip. "I know how hard it was to be in the same room with Gid, much less listen to him apolo—"

"Attempt to explain," he scowled, jerking the door wide, "what can neither be explained or excused."

She frowned at him.

"Don't start with me on forgiveness is the Jesus Way like *Shinali*."

"Would it help if I told you I've tried the other way with my grandmother, and forgiveness was the only thing that helped? Helped me. Not her. I'm talking about you here."

He raised the cup to his lips, gulped, and swallowed. "Where's Taco?"

"I'm letting *him* sleep in. He and your—Gid hit it off last night."

He grimaced. "And here I was thinking Taco was a good judge of character."

"Take your shower and get dressed. I'm fixing you a Tecolote-style breakfast." She glided toward the kitchen.

He grabbed a red-patterned flannel and a clean pair of jeans before heading into the hall shower. He'd been surprised at the hourly wage Gid proposed to pay him. Charity, he suspected, another attempt to make up for what Gid hadn't done earlier in his life.

Not enough dust on the Rez for that. He gritted his teeth. But he'd ensure Gid got his money's worth and more out of his labor today.

He'd shrugged into his shirt, his feet still bare, when the smoke alarm went off. Yanking open the bathroom door, he tore off down the hall toward the kitchen.

Where a cloud of smoke obscured his vision, watering his eyes. He coughed. "Kailyn?"

She wrestled with a flaming skillet. Taco raced around the table, barking. "I was..."

He swiped a potholder off the counter and grabbed the pan. "Let me."

She stepped back, wringing her hands in an apron. He clanged the lid onto the skillet, extinguishing the flames. Heaving the iron skillet, he chucked it into the sink.

Taco yowled. The back door opened. Delores, her hair streaming down her back, hustled inside. "What happened? What's going on?"

Kailyn's lower lip wobbled. "I was trying to make breakfast." Taco darted between and around them.

"Taco," he commanded. "Enough." The little dog scampered into his bed, placing his front paws over his snout. The smell of burned eggs permeated the air.

Dragging a chair, he climbed atop and pressed the Off switch on the smoke detector. His ears continued to ring for a few seconds, phantom pain he supposed.

But blessed silence.

Delores posed a hand over her heart. "All this racket over breakfast?"

"I was trying..." Kailyn's voice wavered. "All I ever learned to make was coffee."

Her mouth pulled downward. "And sweet tea."

Aaron combed a hand over his head. "Well, there's always McDonald's."

Her face constricted. She made a sound in her throat. She clamped a hand over her mouth as tears welled and spilled down her cheeks.

"I'm sorry." She wheeled. "I'm—" and dashed down the hallway.

"Kailyn...I didn't mean—"

"The girl's trying her best to please you."

He turned toward his grandmother to find both her hands planted on her skinny hips. "Please me?" He reared. "She pleases me just the way she is."

Delores glared at him. "Wouldn't kill you to tell her so sometime." And then she muttered something about dumbheads in the *Diné bizaad*, language of the Navajo.

Which she translated into English in case he hadn't caught it the first time. "You don't learn to button your lip, you'll not stay married come Christmas." She stalked out the door.

He slumped against the countertop. The skillet smoldered in the sink. All this and it wasn't even light outside yet.

"Taco, my man," he sighed, "this marriage thing ain't for sissies."

Kailyn glanced out the window at the shawl-wrapped figure of Delores sitting under the lattice boughs of the arbor. She'd made a right fool of herself in front of the old lady this morning.

She ran a dishcloth over the tiled countertop. Once Delores exited the house, she'd slunk into the kitchen to find Aaron—bless his heart—scrubbing at the blackened skillet. She plucked the pan from his hand, and without a word handed him a box of cereal.

Without a word, he'd eaten it. She swiveled from scouring the residue of what had been an optimistic omelet to find merriment dancing in his eyes.

She jabbed the sharp end of a spatula at him. "If you dare laugh, Aaron Jacob Yazzie, you won't live long enough to regret it."

He scraped back his chair, shuffled beside her to rinse out his bowl. Tires spun outside.

Gid's voice called from the porch. "*Ya'at'eeh,* Aaron?"

"*Ya'at'eeh,*" Aaron called in the traditional Diné greeting. "Be right there."

She handed him the bag containing his lunch. Frost glistened like diamonds on the windowpane. "Wait. You don't have a coat. I didn't realize it'd be this cold here. You can't go out in your shirtsleeves."

With a lazy grin, he planted a kiss on her cheek. "I've got your love to keep me warm." He snatched the Thermos. "And the best coffee this side of the Mississippi." He laughed all the way to the front door.

Kailyn put a hand to her cheek, covering the spot where the feel of his kiss lingered. And she spent the next hour smiling as she finished cleaning in her first attempt to be the perfect, pretend wife.

She quailed at the prospect of the long day ahead alone, except for the disapproval of Delores Yazzie. "What can't be cured, must be endured." Her mother had oft-quoted it in the months after her diagnosis.

Gathering her courage, she edged out the back door and headed toward Delores's erect carriage. A posture with which Carole Eudailey could've found no fault. Sighting her, Delores stiffened.

Kailyn squatted on her heels, watching Delores insert the yarn into the loom. "I like how you've chosen to weave the gray next to the black, grading the tones."

Delores brushed her hand across the length of the yarn.

"Is this a pattern you created? Where did you learn to weave?"

Aaron's grandmother beat the wool down on the warp. "From my *shima*." Whoomp. Whoomp. Whoomp.

The silence stretched out, broken only by the slither of a lizard.

"*Shima* means mother."

"And *Shinali* means grandmother?"

Delores trained her eyes on the yarn. "Paternal grandmother. I am the mother of your husband's father. *Shimasani* would be his maternal grandmother, but their side passed from this earth a long time ago. Red lung from the uranium mines."

Kailyn sank onto the sheepskin rug, drawing her knees to her chin. Delores spoke English in the way a person does whose first language had been anything but English. There was a rhythm to the way the Navajo spoke English. They started; they stopped. They continued with long intervals between words.

Delores pointed her lips at the necklace around Kailyn's throat. "His mother's father crafted the cross. Good silversmith. Given to his daughter and then passed to her son. I don't believe I've ever seen him not wearing it before."

Kailyn fingered the cross. "His wedding present to me."

Silence as Delores mulled on it.

"His other grandmother belonged to my church." Delores's hands stilled. "You go to church?"

"If that's an invitation, I'd love to go to church with you."

Delores sniffed. "You get my grandson to go, it'll be a miracle."

"God's still in the miracle business, I believe."

And for the first time in their acquaintance, Delores favored her with a smile. "Yes, he is. I've been praying long years for the boy to come home. And God has answered my prayers."

She paused to make sure Kailyn paid attention. "His mother left the Rez to find work when my son tried to fill the emptiness of his soul at the end of a bottle."

Delores hunched her shoulders. "I learned the hard way only Christ fills the emptiness. After my son became a drunk. After my husband died. When drought destroyed our crops. When the sheep died."

Her eyes took on a faraway look. "My grandson's mother had already gone, taking the boy with her. She always wanted more than one can expect here on the Rez. But the city didn't fill the empty spaces inside her. The pursuit only made life worse for her and the boy."

Delores crossed her arms. "You, I can see, are used to finer things."

Kailyn bit her lip. "Grandmother, I, too, have learned the hard way money doesn't fill the emptiness. Neither does success or relationships. Only Jesus."

The old woman rose in one fluid motion. Kailyn doubted she'd be so limber in her seventies. "You know how to drive?"

Kailyn nodded and scrambled to her feet.

"I need to make a stop at the trading post where I consign my hand-dyed yarn. I'm thinking you might need to purchase supplies at the stores in Farmington?"

"Yes, ma'am. I'd like to."

"We go then." Delores meandered toward the hogan. "I'll get my purse and meet you at the truck."

Kailyn rushed to the house and scooped Aaron's keys off his dresser. Delores had only furnished the house with the necessities. In fact, Aaron had slept on the bare mattress in the spare bedroom last night with only a handwoven blanket for covering.

Delores waited on the porch, a shopping bag over her arm. Taco stutter-stepped out the door behind Kailyn. Delores frowned.

"Better shut him in the house or he might be coyote food before we return."

Kailyn's eyebrows lifted. She glanced side to side. "For real? Aaron mentioned that, but I thought—"

"And better lock the door." Delores snorted. "Was a time no one locked their doors on the Rez. That time has come and gone."

"Yes, ma'am." She coaxed Taco into the house, making sure he had water and food in his bowl. Plus a few of his fancy doggy treats.

She handed him the little rag monkey he liked to gnaw. "I promise, Taco, we'll be back before long."

Once in the car, she adjusted the seat to her height and cranked the engine. Delores watched the passing scenery and didn't speak until they left the teeth-rattling side road and entered the paved portion.

"It is good..." Delores began.

Kailyn cut her eyes to the right.

"...good you've brought the boy home." Delores nodded. "His mother took them outside the *Dinétah*, the ancestral homeland. It is here," she gestured out the window. "Between the four sacred mountains we find our strength, our balance, our harmony."

"Aaron—"

The old woman winced.

"My husband," Kailyn corrected. "He spent summers with you after the Matthews adopted him?" A tumbleweed blew past the tire. She gripped the wheel and focused her attention on the road.

"I wanted him to know The People, the Diné. He left here when he was five. He didn't return until he was twelve." Delores shook her head. "He'd become more Anglo than Diné."

Kailyn darted her eyes at the old woman gazing at the juniper-studded hills.

"Diné children belong to the maternal side of their families." Delores folded her hands in her lap. "His were no longer living when his trouble came. I fought the Anglos at first until I saw him with the woman who wanted to adopt him. He was everything to her, the way a good mother feels about her own flesh and blood."

Kailyn nodded.

"More important, she was everything to him. She gave him a sense of safety, the protection he would've gained if he'd been open to it from the *Dinétah*."

Delores sighed. "He came every summer until his adoptive mother died. But afterward, in his sorrow, he stopped coming. He joined the White-B-I agency and shut himself off from The People."

She closed her lips when she finished everything she intended to say.

"Thank you, Grandmother, for telling me this."

Delores waved at a flat-roofed adobe coming into view. "The trading post. We stop here. I'll restock my yarn and pick up my commission check for any rugs of mine they've sold."

Kailyn parked alongside a Jeep. "You do beautiful work."

"Sheep belong to the Diné women. Many a family has survived the hard times through the work of the mother's hands." Delores hopped down and retrieved the shopping bag. "Women have considerable status among the Diné."

Kailyn joined her as they mounted the planked steps to the interior. "I think I could learn to love it here," she teased.

Inside, she oohed and aahed over the assortment of yarn colors hanging from the rafters and the rugs on display. Boldly patterned pottery lined the shelves. Delores dickered with the proprietor. The owner handed Delores a brown parcel.

"I am ready to go now," Delores announced.

Kailyn followed her out to the truck.

Delores stowed the package behind the seat. "Where do you want to go in Farmington?"

"I'm looking for a few items," she needed to phrase this delicately, "to make the house more..."

"Like your home?"

Kailyn nodded.

"It is good." Delores fluttered her hand. "I know a place—a cheap place—to buy furniture and lamps and stuff."

Once she found out Kailyn liked to sew and after combing through the thrift and consignment stores, Delores suggested a fabric store as their final stop of the day.

Kailyn pulled into the crowded parking lot of an all-purpose quilt and upholstery center. "My degree required me to take sewing classes, textile classes, you name it, in the decorative arts."

"Huh..." Delores sniffed. "You are very traditional girl to be Anglo."

And it might've been her imagination, but she detected the tiniest bit of approval in the old woman's voice.

Just a speck.

She fell in love with several showcase fabrics from which she planned to assemble a quilt for the master bedroom. She buzzed around the warehouse, waiting for cutting assistance from the swamped staff, gathering accent fabrics for cushions for the living room.

Delores flipped through a magazine in the seating area until a young couple entered the store. The woman, a brunette with soft green eyes, hurried over and hugged Delores.

So... Delores was not above touching all Anglos. Just her.

The man, Nav—Diné, she repeated to herself—was heart-stompingly handsome. He, too, gave the old woman a hug.

"My grandson's new bride," Delores jutted her lips toward Kailyn. "He brought her home last night." She raised her chin. "They plan to stay till Christmas and his wife will attend church with me on Sunday."

The young woman extended her hand, a smile on her face. "I'm Erin Silverhorn." She took her husband's arm. "And my husband, Adam."

Kailyn introduced herself when Delores didn't.

He offered his hand to Kailyn. "We still consider ourselves even after four years to be newlyweds, too." His eyes sparkled in his wife's direction.

Erin stroked her stomach. "Hardly newlyweds."

Kailyn realized that underneath the lilac silk overblouse, Erin Silverhorn was probably six months pregnant.

Adam Silverhorn draped his arm around his wife's shoulder. "We'll always be newlyweds." He whispered something in Erin's ear, causing her mouth to quirk at the corners.

Swallowing past a sudden lump in her throat, Kailyn found herself overwhelmed with longing, a longing for something she couldn't define.

Erin squeezed Delores's hand. "I've heard so much about the mysterious Aaron Yazzie from his proud *shinali*..."

Kailyn flicked a glance at the old woman to make sure they were talking about the same person.

"...I can't wait to finally meet him."

Delores smiled. "These friends live on the Arizona side of the Rez. Their uncle pastors a church in Cedar Canyon."

Erin peered around the crowded store. She sagged against her husband. "We chose the wrong day to visit the fabric outlet. We'll never be able to pick out the fabric for the baby's layette and nursery."

"I'll help," Kailyn offered. "I'm pretty good with colors and coordinating fabrics."

Erin's eyes widened. "Oh, Kailyn, would you?" She clasped her hands together. "I'm terrible at these sorts of things."

"Sure. Are you planning for a boy or girl?"

Adam and Erin exchanged looks.

Erin moistened her lips. "We don't want to find out, so we're hoping to create something to work for either. Something to reflect the baby's Diné homeland."

Adam nodded. "Something without color. Like the browns and tans of the landscape." He eyed his wife.

They shared a long look of remembrance and laughed.

"Sorry," Erin patted Kailyn's arm. "Old joke."

Kailyn shook her head. "But the desert's full of color. The turquoise of the sky. The red chile peppers. The orange adobe walls. The smudged blues and purples at sunset."

Delores's brow arched.

"You're in good hands, Wife." Adam plopped himself onto the sofa and seized a *Sports Illustrated*. "I consider my work done. Until you need me to write a check."

Kailyn found herself pulling bolts of fabric off the shelves, getting permission to cut a color swatch and giving Erin her ideas for the perfect Southwest nursery. Their friendship solidified when they discovered their mutual Carolina roots, love of sweet tea and Carolina-style BBQ.

Which Aaron would have her head for revealing if he caught wind of it.

"So," Erin rested her hip against the counter as they waited for the owner to cut the yardage Kailyn recommended for making the crib layette. "Would you consider assembling the other touches in the baby's nursery for me? I'd pay you, of course," Erin hastened to add. "Not as much as you're probably used to getting off-Rez with your talent, but with Adam working alongside his uncle mentoring former gang members finishing out their sentences—"

Kailyn jerked.

"…and my work at the Cultural Center, I promise we'd make it worth your while if you'd help me pull everything together. My friend, Nia, is helping me sew the layette. The ladies at our church are making a quilt for the baby, but my decorating skills leave much to be desired. Besides"—she averted her eyes, fingering the cloth—"it'd be fun to hang out with someone from my own cultural heritage."

Kailyn smiled. "I know exactly what you mean. We Southerners need to stick together."

Erin laughed. "And us new brides, too. Have you been married long?"

Kailyn's lips parted. She closed them. What kind of friendship could be maintained based upon lies?

She hated this. Absolutely hated this lying. It rankled something deep in her spirit. "Not long." She dropped her eyes to her flats.

"Would you? Help me? Be my friend?"

She took a deep breath. "I'd love to, be honored to do both."

"Delores mentioned you'd be visiting her church in Blue Corn Springs. Does your Aaron follow the Jesus Way or the Navajo Way?" Erin smiled. "Or manage to do both without compromising either like my Adam?"

Kailyn rolled her eyes. "Aaron follows more like his own way. But Delores and I are going to work on him."

"Girl," Erin chuckled, "you and I definitely need to talk."

Kailyn grinned.

Erin waited while the shop owner cut the prescribed yards for Kailyn's order, too. When the owner totaled the bill, Kailyn almost went into coronary arrest.

And then the owner made her an offer she couldn't refuse.

Venturing home with their purchases, she hummed a praise tune— "My Arizona friend is one handsome man, no?"

Kailyn's eyes narrowed at Delores, but she finished humming the chorus.

Delores smacked her lips together. "Anglos and Diné mucho appreciation for his fine self."

Kailyn bristled. "He seems nice enough."

"Best-looking man I ever see among the Diné. Like a movie star."

Kailyn raised her shoulders and let them drop. "If you're into that sort of thing." She blew a strand of hair from her face. "Which I'm not. I prefer a man with more depth to his face. Like Aaron, who's handsome just as he is."

The old woman cackled and fell onto the side door, her eyes turning to half-moons.

Kailyn's cheeks burned. What had she said now?

One hand clutching the three-stranded cord of turquoise hanging down the front of her velveteen blouse, Delores laid her other hand on Kailyn.

She shifted to find the old woman's eyes moist. Delores cupped Kailyn's cheek in her gnarled hand. *"Ayóó ániíníshní.* I love you, my grandson's wife."

And Kailyn realized she'd passed some unspoken test. She whispered back the tonally inflected Diné words to Delores. "Is that right, *Shin—*" she stammered, *"Shinali?"*

Delores thumped her chest. "I will teach you to cook and weave. The True God is good." She cocked her head like a small, brown wren. "Is He not?"

"He is, *Shinali.* All the time."

But all was not good when they returned to the house. They arrived, arms laden with shopping bags, to find Aaron wearing a hole in the wooden planks of the porch. Taco strutted beside him. Aaron appeared to be in full-fledged panic mode.

Fury bounced off him like heat off a hot tamale.

13

I CANNOT BELIEVE YOU." AARON JABBED HIS FINGER IN KAILYN'S DIRECTION. Her eyebrows arched. "I can't believe you went off without telling me."

He raked his hand across the top of his head, leaving it standing on its short ends, resembling a Mohawk.

Delores snorted and plodded past him. "Granddaughter does not have to inform you of her every move. And I'm certainly past the age where I'll answer to anyone but God."

He whirled. "And I can't believe you," he gestured at the bag in his grandmother's hand. "You told her about the Walmart in Farmington. Took her there."

Delores held the door open for Kailyn, who rolled her eyes, and followed his grandmother inside.

He found himself alone on the porch. Taco deserted him, too, probably thinking Kailyn good for another round of treats.

"Kailyn can't be trusted in that place," he grumbled, stomping across the threshold.

Shopping bags lay scattered across the living room. Talking to empty air, he stalked into the kitchen.

Delores paused from unloading a grocery sack. "His fear makes him harsh, Granddaughter. What put such fear into you, Grandson?" She deposited a quart of milk in the fridge. "Did you imagine your wife had already left you? Before Halloween?"

Kneeling beside Taco's bowl, Kailyn placed her hands on her thighs and pushed herself upright. "I'm sorry, Aaron." She touched his sleeve. "I didn't think about..." She glanced over to where Delores opened a can of kidney beans.

"But I've got great news." She extracted a plastic card from her jeans. "I got my library card and I got a job. Ow!" She yelped as he seized her elbow.

"Excuse us, *Shinali*." He clenched his teeth. "My wife and I need to have a conversation."

Aaron dragged her out to the porch. "Four-thirty Gid brings me home. I'm expecting to see my wife. And what do I find? An empty house." His chest heaved. "I was—Taco and I were—sick with worry, Kailyn."

Her face gentled. She brushed her finger along the hollow of his cheekbone. "Oh, Aaron, how was your first—?"

"And you..." he growled.

Her face fell.

"You got a library card? Where, I presume, you had to show your ID? And accepted a job," his voice rose. "A job I did not check out first?"

"I think you'll feel better after you've eaten." She patted his shoulder. "It's the perfect job for me. A fabric outlet full of textiles and"—she waved her arms—"color. I'll wait on customers and do decorating consultations. Definitely a God-thing."

She tilted her head, looking up at him. "*Shinali's* teaching me her famous chili recipe." She gave him the full benefit of her megawatt-age smile.

A smile he'd not seen from her since...since ever?

His justifiable anger weakened, distracted. For a sec.

"Does hiding from the Mexican Mafia mean anything to you, Kailyn?"

She responded by wrapping her arms around his shoulders. The familiar magnolia scent caused his senses—and his good sense—to reel.

"Mmm..." Her lips grazed his earlobe. "You've already taken your shower."

His heart jolted into overdrive.

"*Shinali* tells me we're only an hour away from dinner, so I better get in there and earn my cooking stripes."

Shinali? Since when were his grandmother and his wife on such cordial terms?

His nerve endings sizzled like rain on a hot Carolina pavement when the soft curve of her lips brushed his chin, but she stepped out of the circle of his arms. "I've got so much to show you. You'll never believe the bargains I found. Didn't spend one dime over our budget. You'll be amazed." She disappeared into the house.

His pulse went into staccato mode. His mouth went dry as desert sand.

Amazed?

He already was.

Kailyn spent the evening cutting squares and rectangles out of the fabric for the pillow cushions. Aaron, mollified after the meal, took out the knife he kept strapped to his leg, and whittled away on a weathered branch of ponderosa pine he and Taco had discovered on one of their rambles.

Grandmother departed after dinner. "Newlyweds need their alone time."

"If you leave us too much alone, Aaron could starve to death," Kailyn only half-joked.

Grandmother smiled, bearing a strong resemblance to the Sphinx. "I'll come for dinner. Breakfast is a time for husbands and their wives."

A remark that brought flaming heat to Kailyn's cheeks and caused Aaron to twist his lips in a funny way.

The next evening after work, he returned with purchases of his own. Two cell phones and a used sewing machine.

"How did you think you were going to sew these creations of yours?"

She shrugged. "I planned on sewing the old-fashioned way, by hand. Not as quick, but it works, too."

He installed her workstation near the picture window in the living room. "Gid and I checked it out during lunch to make sure everything functioned." He gave her a wry smile. "Finally, the mechanical engineering degree put to good use."

She responded by grabbing his arms and dancing them both around the room. Laughing, he tugged a tendril of her hair. "*Dzani*, I told you I could teach you a mean two-step."

Dzani, woman.

Unlike the Latinos, the Diné weren't big on terms of endearment. And the way he said it, that's what it was. That and the look in his eyes.

He programmed her phone with Gid's telephone number and his own cell number. "I want to know your location at all times, *dzani*."

She saluted. "Aye, aye." And returned to her testing of each lever and knob on her machine.

Over the next few weeks, they achieved a measure of normalcy, a routine. After getting him off to work, she worked mornings at the store. It was a proud moment when she fixed Aaron a proper Diné breakfast, a fry bread burrito stuffed with scrambled eggs, chiles, and bacon. Fry bread had been one of the first skills Grandmother insisted she master. And fry bread was used for breakfast, lunch, and dinner.

Under Grandmother's direction, she learned to distinguish local landmarks and the turn-offs to neighbors. Taking a loaf of homemade bread or a jar of her famous prickly pear cactus jelly, Grandmother made sure each of her friends received a proper introduction to "my grandson's bride." Always chaperoned on their outings by Taco.

Grandmother won the little dog's heart with bits of chicken she slipped him underneath the table. He'd taken to greeting *Shinali* first, sniffing her hand for treats. Which was just as well with his gourmet treats running low. And until Kailyn figured out how to order them online without a credit card, she had to ration Taco's Pampered Pooch snacks.

Once a week, she visited the library in Farmington. She'd made a friend with one of the volunteers, an older Anglo man. He became an ally in her quest for books on the Diné.

When Grandmother beheld the stack of books and their subject matter, she sniffed. "I can teach you more than those books ever can." And henceforth, Grandmother made it her business to instruct Kailyn in all matters pertaining to the Diné.

Aaron refused—point-blank, once he discovered Gid was a member—to attend Faith Community Fellowship with them. But in a way, Grandmother had been right about breakfast. Kailyn looked forward to their bright-start mornings together. She'd fix their coffee, and while waiting for Gid, she and Aaron enjoyed the warmth and flavor side by side as they gazed over the hogan toward the cinnamon-red mesa and the glow of the sun in its glorious display of pink, terra-cotta, and gold.

She'd also spent her first paycheck making sure he had a suitable coat for the cold October mornings. A barely used Carhartt she found at a Farmington thrift store. She painted the dining room table and chairs a weathered green, setting off the white kitchen cabinets. Painting the walls a dusty gold, she accessorized in chile red accents with the clock she found at Walmart and by making cushions for the chairs.

"I had a dream last night from the Dream-Giver," Grandmother told her one afternoon on their way to meet a special friend of hers.

Chugging along on 491, Kailyn smiled. The Navajo, she'd learned, were big on dreams. The difference between the traditional Navajo and the converted Navajo, as in faith, lay only in the source of their dreams.

The silence stretched. Unlike the Anglos, the Diné were comfortable with—preferred—the quiet.

"Okay, I'll bite. What was your dream about?"

Grandmother's lips lifted in a satisfied smile. "I think my grandson made a mistake when he built the house."

Kailyn frowned. She'd hoped they'd gone beyond Grandmother's disapproval.

Grandmother cut her eyes at Kailyn. "I think my grandson didn't make enough bedrooms for the many children in my dream playing outside the house."

Kailyn tightened her grip on the vibrating steering wheel. She flinched at the hurt Grandmother would feel come January. Something she tried not to dwell upon. Aaron was better than she was at pretending to be something he wasn't.

Today's outing carried them to a wood-and-stucco house on the edge of Shiprock in the shadow of the gray-brown Chuska Mountains. A Diné woman in her mid-thirties emerged from the house when they pulled into the driveway. She wore slacks and a sweater set. Her hair, though, was skimmed tight in the traditional bun like Grandmother's. The younger woman waved at the sight of the old woman.

Grandmother bustled to the front steps and the two women embraced. "*Ya'at'eeh*, my young friend."

The woman laughed, easing the life lines marking her otherwise beautiful, round face. "*Ya'at'eeh*, Auntie."

A term of respect for an elder. Not necessarily Grandmother's actual relative, Kailyn had learned after opening her mouth and inserting her proverbial stiletto.

"I brought my grandson's bride." Grandmother pointed her lips at Kailyn poised on the bottom step. "And," she rattled the bag in her hand, "the clothing my weaving group collected for your girls."

The woman stepped forward, her hand outstretched. "Let me introduce myself since Auntie hesitates to use my name. It's Willa. Willa Littlefeather."

Kailyn smiled and shook her hand. "I'm Kailyn. Kailyn Yazzie." A name becoming easier to say every day.

Too easy? Too comfortable?

"Come inside," Willa held the door. "The girls are at school. Otherwise," she led the way into the living room, "it wouldn't be so quiet."

While Willa, with traditional Diné hospitality, fixed herbal tea, Grandmother leaned over to Kailyn. "My friend trained as a social worker, but works full-time in ministry to the girls here at Grace House."

Willa entered, carrying a serving tray with steaming mugs. "Streams in the Desert Ministry."

Grandmother nodded. "A nonprofit mission many area churches support, ours," she patted Kailyn's arm, "included."

Willa handed round the cups. "It's so nice to finally meet Auntie's family. I'd begun to believe her grandson was a myth, a Rez legend."

Kailyn took a sip. "Only in his own mind."

Grandmother laughed, almost spilling her tea. "And my granddaughter has been to him and to me like streams of water in a parched land."

Willa settled onto the sofa beside Kailyn. "Isaiah."

Grandmother's eyes twinkled. She nodded. "My favorite."

"A home? What kind of... ? Never mind, I don't want to pry." Kailyn clamped her lips together.

Willa fluttered long, slender fingers. On her wrist, silver bracelets of turquoise jingled. "It's no secret. The foundation houses four girls at a time. I wish we could support more."

"One day," Grandmother tapped her temple. "I believe. Faith, friend."

"The girls were..." Willa sighed, "rescued from a life of addiction and prostitution."

Willa smoothed her trousers. "Our focus is to help the girls find God's love and to experience His power in healing the hurts of their abuse. In Christ there's peace, comfort, and hope to overcome. My girls range in age from eleven—"

Kailyn's heart seized.

"—to eighteen. Some of my girls fled abusive homes and fell into the hands of child predators. They were told they were nothing, lower than nothing. In Christ we show them that, although the effects of abuse are far-reaching, God's love is life-changing and can penetrate any darkness. They remain with us to finish their education and receive counseling until they graduate. But they will always have a base of support here with us."

Grandmother folded her hands in her lap. "My friend's already seen much fruit. Several girls graduated from the program and are pursuing degrees at the community college."

Willa set her mug onto the coffee table, her face alight. "It's only to Him that I can point them. In Him to find newness of life, to rid themselves of the fear and self-loathing. To embrace the new heart and new spirit with which He longs to shower them."

Grandmother nodded. "My friend rescues doves."

"Soiled doves whose own Diné relatives are too ashamed of what they've become to open their homes or their hearts once the staff and I have managed to convince a girl to leave the streets of Albuquerque and her pimp behind."

Willa's hands gripped her knees. "Did you know Native American girls are especially prone to victimization? Poverty, drugs, and alcohol abuse. Domestic violence. All are endemic on the Rez. And one in three women will experience sexual molestation."

Kailyn lowered the mug from her lips. "One in three?"

Willa's eyes dropped. "The average age for a girl to become caught in the web of trafficking is between twelve and fourteen. Runaways are especially vulnerable. Pimps excel in pinpointing what the girl longs for and temporarily becoming what they need. Until she's hooked on drugs and/or working for him. Doing whatever he asks, to please him."

Kailyn winced, her mind unable to fully comprehend the horrors Willa described. And for once grateful to Carole Eudailey, saving her from such grim realities after her parents died. But for the grace of God…

"How do you do what you do, Willa? How do you stand their pain?"

Willa raised her eyes to meet Kailyn's. "Because I must. Their pain is my pain. I teach them to believe God loved them enough to die for them. That they're of much worth and value in His sight."

Her voice quavered. Willa reached over and squeezed Grandmother's hand. "And I am refreshed by the prayers of His people, Diné and Anglo."

Kailyn cleared her throat. "I'd count it an honor and a privilege to minister alongside you in any way. I'm not skilled at anything important—"

"Pshaw," Grandmother flicked her hand. "My granddaughter's gifted in nurturing the creative life force of the spirit. In loving what to some is unlovely. She offers order and harmony. She walks in beauty."

Kailyn blushed, but Grandmother's praise warmed her heart. She fingered the cross at her throat.

Willa's eyes narrowed as she followed the movement of Kailyn's hand. But with a tiny shake of her head, she smiled, erasing her frown lines. "I'm sure if we put our heads together we can find something for you to do to bring beauty into those whose lives are sorely lacking in those areas."

Driving home later, Kailyn sighed. Grandmother, who'd remained pensive since leaving the home, turned from her contemplation of the *Dinétah*.

"She's something, isn't she?" Grandmother said, correctly guessing Kailyn's thoughts.

"I'm in awe of her strength and faith."

Grandmother nodded. "A warrior."

"On behalf of those with no voice or power of their own." Kailyn leaned against the truck seat, one hand resting on the steering wheel. They rode in companionable silence, passing the apple orchards, barren of fruit in autumn.

After supper, Aaron handed Kailyn her coat. "Let's take a walk."

"I'll get Taco's leash."

He shook his head. "Too many dangers in the dark for my man. Coyote food."

Slipping her arms into her coat, her eyes rounded. "What about me if it's so dangerous out there?"

He broadened his chest. "That's my job. To protect you."

Taking her hand, he led her past the hogan where through a window he watched *Shinali* enjoy a late-night cup of coffee from the pot on her cast-iron stove. She'd become addicted to Kailyn's Eastern blend, too.

In the blue velvet of the gloaming, they picked their way across an arroyo, skirted a large sandstone formation, and climbed the path his family's sheep had taken since the Tribe had given them this allotment decades ago.

Once on top of the mesa, he drew her closer to the edge. She hung back, pressing against his chest.

"Don't you like heights, Kailyn?"

She shook her head. "Not so much."

"Then don't look down, look up." He wrapped his arms around her. This mother's son wasn't as dumb as he looked. "I'll keep you safe."

Her cheek nuzzled the canvas of his jacket. "A statement which almost sounds half-full from the poster boy for half-empty."

Aaron chuckled. "What can I say? You've had a curiously uplifting effect on me." Placing his index finger under her chin, he tilted her head. "Now, lift your eyes and look."

She rested the back of her head against his chest. "Okay, what am I looking at? Or for?"

"Patience, Kailyn, isn't one of your gifts."

She jabbed him in the ribs with her elbow.

"Like all good things, you must wait for it. Let the darkness deepen and then you will see the lights."

"A statement worthy of a preacher."

"Kailyn..." He sighed. "Just keep looking up."

"I'm teasing." She nestled into the warmth of his coat.

Again, this mother's son wasn't as stupid as he looked. But he knew she was teasing. He appreciated how she didn't push her beliefs on him.

Just lived them.

The Diné life lessons *Shinali* taught her each day, Kailyn in turn shared with him each evening. In her own way, he supposed, helping him reconnect with his lost heritage. But as the weeks wore on, he remembered more of the words and customs from his early years. He, like many children on the Rez, had spoken the *Diné bizaad*, Grandmother said, before he spoke English.

He drew her gaze to the gauzy, starry brilliance of the Milky Way. "*Yikáísídáhí*. It waits for dawn."

She sighed. "I've never seen it before. Pictures…"

He rested his chin on top of her head. "Photos don't do it justice. The high desert air is crystal clear on a night like this. Unlike your humid, thick Southern air."

She twisted her torso. "Did you just use words like 'thick' and 'hot air' to describe my people, Yazzie?"

"I said humid, but if the stiletto fits…?"

She extended her sensible hiking boot for his inspection. "I've gone native."

He peered down the length of his nose at the glow-in-the-dark neon shoelaces lacing her boots. Only Kailyn. "You've gone something."

The girly-girl he brought onto the Rez only existed in snatches of color now. Instead of assuming the fetal position in the rugged world of the Diné, she'd opened her heart to it. He suspected she blended in far better than he in the ways that count.

Instead of wilting like a magnolia blossom in the desert heat, she'd blossomed, her confidence growing.

Without even trying, she was so beguilingly feminine, he had to remind himself forty times a day theirs was a cover. She wasn't really his wife. This wasn't their life.

They didn't have a life, not together.

She was nothing more than Steve's witness.

But like tonight's adventure, he rationalized, no reason their cover couldn't provide a little pleasure.

Like how she clung to his arm when coyotes howled.

A guy could get used to it. Even a guy who didn't do permanent.

The next day, he unclasped the tool belt he wore and dumped it beside Gid's tools in the bed of the truck. Quitting time. He slapped his work gloves together in a vain attempt to clear them of the ubiquitous red dust covering the Rez.

He had bought the gloves at Kailyn's favorite store after his first week's paycheck. The tools he'd been forced to borrow. He slid into the passenger seat beside Gid.

After three weeks, the twenty-minute round-trip had become marginally better than those first tense days together. But pals they were not. He tolerated Gid as a means to putting food on the table.

Buddies wasn't going to happen. Gid respected his need for distance and made few personal remarks once away from the job site and crew.

He grimaced.

Another little surprise—Gid's crew. Former alcoholics or drug addicts. Who'd graduated from a twenty-week program that had saved Gid's life twelve years ago. A residential program out of Shiprock. The support group for graduates met weekly, so he'd heard, in the fellowship hall of the Blue Corn Springs church Kailyn and *Shinali* attended.

Not the kind of help he needed. For weaklings like his drunk father. A help he'd not received in time to save his mother. A help he sure didn't need now.

"I'll always be an alcoholic, Aaron."

He half-turned in the seat. Did Gid read his mind?

Gid's knuckles whitened on the steering wheel as they traveled a back road out of town toward the house. Despite the lines of dissipation carved upon his face and the salt-and-pepper hair neatly braided down his back, Aaron could still make out the jutting cheekbones, the hooded dark eyes that caused his teenaged mother to fall in love with Gid.

"I'll always be an alcoholic," Gid repeated, his gaze fixed straight ahead. "But by the grace of God, I'm a recovering alcoholic. You returning to the *Dinétah* is the answer to many prayers I've prayed since God freed me from the shackles of my disease."

Aaron crossed his arms. "Is there a point to this?"

Gid's lips wavered, then tightened. "I have much to atone for. Your mother—"

"I'm not having this conversation with you." He glared. "I will not discuss my mother with you."

Gid's Adam's apple bobbed. "I share in the blame for her death. For what happened to you."

"Stop the truck." He grasped the door handle.

Gid jerked his head.

"I'm not going there with you. Anywhere with you. I'll walk home."

Gid's foot eased off the accelerator. "We're still miles from—"

"I don't care. I'd rather walk. Be eaten by wolves. Be alone as the day you deserted us for a bottle of Jack Daniels. You made your choice. An unforgivable choice."

Gid's face blanched.

"I've made it this far alone. I can make it the rest of the way alone."

Gid shook his head. "Stay in the vehicle. I'll return you to your wife. I'll not speak of these matters again unless you wish me to."

"Don't hold your breath, old man." But exhaling, he slammed the door shut. It'd be dark before he'd reach home. And once the sun set, the temps would plunge.

Rounding the curve in the rutted road passing for his driveway, the first thing he observed was a Navajo Nation Tribal SUV parked beside the juniper. At the hogan, a police officer in a khaki uniform shadowed Kailyn.

His stomach lurched. He'd gotten complacent, too comfortable. Bounding out of the truck before Gid brought it to a standstill, he barreled across the distance separating him from Kailyn.

14

At a run, Aaron beheld the thirty-something policeman standing a little too close to Kailyn for Diné courtesy. A little too close for Aaron's comfort. Kailyn extended a tea glass and the man, tall with hawkish features, accepted it from her.

His fingers lingered against her hand. And she smiled at the man, whom women probably found broodingly handsome.

When the man said something, Kailyn tilted her head to listen, laughed, and touched his sleeve, in her never-met-a-stranger way. The man stroked his chin.

Hearing his boots strike the hard earth, Kailyn, peering over the man's shoulder, smiled. The smile wavered when she took stock of the thundercloud brewing on his face. He inserted himself between them, blocking the man's view of his wife.

"Aaron..." A tinge of annoyance in her voice, she stepped around him.

He planted his hands on his hips and broadened his stance. "What does he want?"

"Aaron." This time there was no mistaking the disapproval in her tone. "I want you to meet my friend from church, Jace Runninghawk. He's with—"

"I'm with the tribal police." Jace mirrored Aaron's own stance, his feet a hip's width apart.

"So I see."

Jace assessed him, like a coyote sights and tracks his prey, before extending his hand.

He let Jace's arm hang in space.

"Aaron…" She nudged him. "Jace, I'd like you to meet Aaron—"

"Her husband." Aaron stuck out his hand. But glancing at Aaron's hand, Jace's eyes narrowed.

Jace crushed his hand and Aaron returned pressure for pressure.

Kailyn's gaze ping-ponged between the two men. "What's going—?"

"Jace, my boy."

His boy?

At Gid's voice, Jace turned. "*Ya'at'eeh*, Uncle."

Jace gave Gid a bear hug. Chummy, weren't they? His mouth flattened.

Taco pranced between Gid and Delores. The man embraced his grandmother, too. Like a long-lost, much-beloved member of the family. Roosting on the ground beside Aaron, Taco scratched his ear with his hind leg.

Jace pointed. "That's the funniest looking—"

"He's trained to attack intruders." Aaron folded his arms.

"Where you been keeping yourself this week, Son?" Gid's voice was gruff, but laced with affection. "Missed our weekly green chile burger at the Blue Corn Cafe."

Son?

Seriously?

Jace propped his black leather boot on the woodpile adjacent to the hogan. "Well, you know how it is, Uncle."

Gid laughed. "Still trying to wear down the sweet thang in Shiprock?"

Jace rolled his eyes. "And about as effective as water, one drop at a time, against a canyon wall."

Delores patted his cheek. "Erosion can take a millennium. But you never know when a flash flood's liable to carve a river."

Jace cut his eyes at Kailyn. "Anyway, I've decided to turn my attention to other projects."

Aaron balled his fists.

"Had a case arise this week near Gallup that's kept me busy. But when our mutual friend mentioned the return of the prodigal…"

Aaron leaned forward on his toes, tensing.

"…I decided I'd better take myself over here and get to know the pretty lady."

Aaron's nostrils flared. "The pretty much-married lady."

Jace's eyes widened and he rocked on his heels.

Frowning, Kailyn twined her arm through Aaron's. "Jace was just telling me about the Adopt-an-Elder program he, your—Gid—and the men from church are involved with every Saturday this time of year."

The Cheshire-cat smile returned to Jace's face. "Yeah, some of us regard it as a tribal duty and honor to take care of the Old Ones, those whose family have forsaken our ways and left them to fend through a winter on their own."

Aaron bristled.

"We head for the mountains." Jace jerked his head in the direction of the Chuska. "Spend the day collecting and cutting the wood and make sure each of the Old Ones has enough cords of firewood to get them through the winter."

Gid draped an arm across Jace's broad shoulders. "Jace and his fellow officers at the Shiprock station head it up. They find some of The People every year who've frozen to death trapped by snow in the remote canyons. Less now since he's galvanized the rest of the community."

A regular Lancelot. Something sour rose in Aaron's throat.

Jace's long, narrow face sharpened. "I also came by today to make sure Grandmother…"

His grandmother.

"… had her loom moved inside now the weather's turned cold." Jace gave Gid a fond look. "A two-man job."

"I'm sure my father and I can handle it after you leave."

Gid's head snapped around.

Kailyn rounded her eyes at him. "Aaron." She pivoted to Jace. "I'm sure what Aaron's trying to—"

"I'm sure Aaron said exactly what he meant." Jace smirked. "But even the Anglos feel something for their kin, I guess."

Aaron's blood boiled. This coyote dared to question his manhood? Challenge his loyalty to his family?

He clenched his jaw. "What time, Gid, did you say you'd be leaving for the mountains tomorrow morning?"

Gid's face lit. "I'd be glad to swing by and pick you up. Six too early?"

He never took his eyes off Jace. "I'll be ready."

A satisfied smile played about Jace's thin lips.

Leaving Aaron uneasy, wondering if perhaps in his less than keep-it-objective reaction, he'd fallen right into the very snare Jace had intended for him all along.

Kailyn scurried, Taco underfoot, between the table and the stovetop, setting a plate of steaming enchiladas in front of Aaron, who hunched over the table. They were alone for dinner for once. Jace invited Gid for a rain check supper in Blue Corn Springs and teased "his best girl" Delores into going with them.

Jace extended the invitation to her and Aaron, but one look at Aaron's face and she'd declined.

"No wonder you return from church so bubbly and..." Aaron made a face. "Now I'm wondering how much of your good mood has to do with your Jesus and how much is due to Jace Runninghawk."

"Excuse me?" Raising her eyebrows, she paused, the platter of fry bread in her hand. "What did you just say?"

He gripped the fork in one hand and his knife in the other. "Don't take your haughty tone with me, Kailyn."

"I don't know what you're talking about." She dropped the platter onto the table with a thud. "After I met Jace, I thought perhaps you could become friends since you two have so much in common."

"Only thing I see that coyote and I have in common is an appreciation for my fine wife." He stuffed a large piece of fry bread into his mouth.

She stared at him.

Had he said what she thought he'd said? Like he was...?

Aaron poked out his lips, chewing, and avoided her eyes.

She shook her head.

Her overactive, wishful imagination.

She cleared her throat and tried again. "You two have a lot in common." She held up her index finger. "Your law enforcement background..."

"Which no one's supposed to know anything about on my end," Aaron growled.

Undeterred, she extended her thumb. "Your shared Anglo background." At his frown, she continued. "He's one of the Lost Birds."

"The what?"

"One of those Diné children separated from their family by Social Services and a misguided government policy before the Child Welfare Act in the seventies. A childless white couple from Santa Monica adopted him out of the tribe."

"Lost Birds?"

She nodded. "Hundreds of children. Not all as fortunate in their placement as he was, so Jace tells me. A good, Christian family who helped him reconnect with his Diné roots as a young man. He dropped out of law school when he found his grandparents and father still living and returned to the Rez to better serve The People."

"Another lawyer." Aaron speared a bean. "You seem to have a thing for lawyers, don't you, Kailyn?"

She pulled her chair across from him and plopped down. "You're being ridiculous." She unfolded her napkin.

He pointed his fork at her. "You're being incredibly naive. Or have you forgotten about Deputy Marshal Whitten?"

She fought against the tide of disappointment welling up. This was about the case. Stupid to allow herself to imagine his concern was of a more personal nature.

"I haven't forgotten anything. But why must you approach every new relationship with such distrust? Why must you always assume the worst about people?"

His eyes went dark, unreadable. "Is this what's between you and Runninghawk? A relationship?"

She heaved a sigh. "Are you hearing anything I'm saying? Jace is exactly who he appears to be. Not everyone feels the need to resort to subterfuge, to hide from who they really are."

Aaron stiffened. "I'm not…And I'll tell you why I assume the worst. Because then, I'm seldom disappointed."

He clenched his fists. "Runninghawk's got hidden agenda written all over him. Your speech may be slow, but I know there's nothing wrong with your brain. Use your eyes and your wits, woman. He's playing you. Flores has dirty cops throughout this country."

She scraped back her chair. "Because no one in their right mind could possibly find me interesting for my own sake."

He glowered at her. "Don't put words in my mouth."

She rose. "Are you worried Jace will compromise my virtue?" She crossed her arms, leaned across the table, and got in his face. "Or more concerned about Jace trying to ice your star witness in bringing Flores down?"

"I have an obligation to fulfill." He stood and glared at her, eyeball to eyeball. "Why do you have to make everything so difficult?"

An obligation? Her stomach twisted. Just like her grandmother Eudailey.

She tossed her head. "I don't know who stomped all over your tortilla, but I can't talk to you when you act this way." She grabbed the leash. "Come, Taco. Let's get some air."

"Kailyn…" He slammed his fist against the table. The dishes rattled.

Yanking open the door, she fled before she lost whatever small thread of control she possessed over her emotions. She hurried toward the rock outcropping she'd discovered when she wanted to be alone. Taco's little legs pounded with the effort to keep pace with her.

She slowed her steps, striving to slow her erratic heartbeat. She meant nothing to Aaron. To him, she was a case, plain and simple.

But, with increasing disquiet, she knew there was nothing plain and simple about her feelings for him.

Aaron kept his gaze trained on the orange glow lighting the distant horizon. A dawn for the first time in weeks he wasn't sharing with Kailyn. He glanced at the men in Gid's truck. Poor substitutes for her.

Last night in the gathering dusk, he'd watched her go to her favorite prayer spot. She'd lifted her face to the sky and closed her eyes.

And he'd also observed the peace etched across her features when she returned to the house. A peace unknown to the turmoil of his spirit. In strained silence, they avoided each other the rest of the night.

He'd put away his carving, secured the doors, and turned out the lights. And sprawled in the darkness of the living room, wondering how he, usually so proficient in avoiding emotional entanglements like this, had gotten himself into such a mess. She made him so mad with her disregard for her personal safety. With her blind-to-human-fault nature. He wanted to shake some sense into her at the same time he wanted to—

He released a deep breath. Don't go there.

Agents lost their edge when they became emotionally involved with a witness. Here today, she'd be gone to a new life in January. He must maintain his focus on what was truly at stake—bringing down Flores.

So he found himself this morning on a wood-chopping, intel-gathering expedition. He frowned at Runninghawk seated between him and Gid. The two of them chattered, at this disgusting hour, like a pair of western jays.

Annoying birds. And those jays, if he remembered rightly, would steal everything you possessed if you turned your back.

Forty minutes and a steep climb into the forested hills, Gid drew the truck to a stop beside other dust-coated Rez vehicles. A crowd of men hunkered under the boughs of a giant cottonwood. At the sight of Aaron and Gid, one of the men threw up a hand.

He grimaced at the easy camaraderie among the men and Runninghawk, the rattlesnake. He snorted.

Gid wrinkled his forehead. "Getting a cold? Your sweet bride slipped me a Thermos if you need something hot to take off the chill."

He'd not seen her this morning. She must've met Gid at the door while he'd been in the shower. His lips twisted as he followed Gid to the throng of men. More likely, she'd hoped to catch a glimpse of Runninghawk.

Dividing into pairs, the men set off in opposite directions. He ended up paired with Runninghawk. Which suited his purposes, and he'd use the opportunity to his advantage.

"We got permission from the landowner to chop this wood?" he growled as Runninghawk wrested a half-dead branch from a nearby cottonwood.

Runninghawk flicked a glance at him. "Yeah, we work out an agreement each autumn with the tribe. The forestry dudes do a survey first. Don't touch anything if it hasn't been marked." He pointed to a red slash of paint against the trunk.

Aaron hurled the branches he'd gathered into a bigger pile awaiting pickup by one of the older guys like Gid who collected the fruits of their labor.

"I figured you'd understand about markings."

Aaron froze, half-bent over a sun-bleached log.

He gave Runninghawk an unfriendly smile. "But the real question is do you understand about territories?"

Runninghawk poked out his lips but didn't respond to his bait. Tackling a large piñon, Runninghawk made a cut and placed the double-handled handsaw in the groove of the trunk. "Think you could put your back into it and give me a hand?"

Aaron moved to grasp one end of the saw. Runninghawk pushed, he pulled and thrust back.

"Interesting case I've been working this week."

Push, pull.

"Dead man in a shallow grave. The M.E.—medical examiner—fixes his time of death around two or three weeks past. 'Course the Feds, him being found on tribal land, are all over it."

Push, pull. Aaron fixed his eyes on the teeth of the blade.

"'Bout the time you and the missus hit the Rez, wasn't it?"

Push, pull.

Aaron sucked in his cheeks and kept his head down, thrusting back. "And what does this have to do with me?"

Push, pull.

"The man, a Latino, died of a gunshot wound to the skull." Runninghawk wiped the sweat off his forehead with his arm. "Execution-style."

"Fascinating." Keeping his face blank, Aaron took care to continue taking even, steady breaths. "And you're sharing this why?"

Runninghawk cocked his head. "'Cause funny thing?" He let go of the saw. "The vic had the exact same tat on his hand..." his tone changed.

Aaron looked up.

"...that you, Aaron Yazzie, also sport." Runninghawk licked his lips, a caricature of a smile flitting across his hard features. "A tat worn, so the tribal gang task force informs me, by the mucho bad Conquistadores."

Runninghawk laughed, a sound devoid of mirth. "Funny coincidence, wouldn't you say, Aaron Yazzie?"

Villeda? How had he—?

"We've got a problem here on the Rez," Runninghawk hitched his jeans. "With the gangs in cahoots with big-time cartels, running guns, drugs, and illegal aliens. Figured you might know something about it, Yazzie."

"I don't know anything about your dead man, Runninghawk. I just got home."

Runninghawk's eyes darkened. "Since you mentioned territories, another interesting factoid I'll throw your way. This side of the Rez hasn't been frequented much by the Conquistadores. I'm wondering if you and your buddies are moving in on our Native gangs' territory to wage a turf war over supply routes."

Aaron's hand dropped to his side. "I'm sure you've already ferreted out enough gossip to know I belonged to a gang once, but I went clean. Joined the army."

"The latest gang personnel tactic," Runninghawk snarled. "To hone their skills, gang ties intact, on Uncle Sam's dime."

Aaron shook his head. "I'm here, like I told you, with my wife. Trying to reconnect with my heritage." Two could play at this game of cat and mouse. "Like you, too long among the Anglos."

Runninghawk reared. "I'm not Anglo anymore."

"You and I will always be Anglo in the deep places where it counts, in the eyes of The People." He eyed Runninghawk. "When push comes to shove, we'll always be on the outside looking in. Don't kid yourself."

Runninghawk's mouth tightened. "You may not belong, may not desire to belong, but I've got a community." He jabbed his thumb in the direction of town. "I share a bond of faith with many of The People, a tribe you know nothing about."

His lip curled. "A tribe and bond with Kailyn to which you remain clueless."

"Stay away from my wife, Runninghawk."

"I'm not letting your dirty dealings destroy your grandmother and father. I'd be willing to bet a month's salary that Kailyn doesn't know what you do for a living, does she?"

"Back off from my family." Aaron narrowed his eyes to slits. "Two fathers, Diné and Anglo, aren't enough for you, Runninghawk? You got to take mine, too?"

Runninghawk looked as surprised as Aaron felt. "Is that right? 'Cause the way I heard it, your father was available."

Aaron spun on his heel, striding toward the rendezvous spot. He'd not spend another moment with this coyote, this trickster who stole what belonged by rights to others. He found Gid halfway down the slope, tossing logs into the bed of the pickup.

Gid's face lifted. "You and Jace getting acquainted?"

Aaron scowled.

Gid's face fell.

"I thought I'd come help you load the truck." Aaron faltered and took a breath. "Maybe get you to introduce me to some of the elders when we deliver the first load."

A smile lit Gid's face and threatened to split his countenance from ear to ear. "That'd be right fine, Son, I mean, Aaron. I'm almost ready to shove off."

Aaron swallowed. "Good." He worked alongside his father for a few minutes.

"You done good, boy."

Aaron paused, his hand on a chunk of wood on the tailgate.

"Your bride," Gid nodded. "A real, sweet girl."

Aaron sighed, the sound welling from deep within. "Sweet as agave on fry bread."

Gid laughed and heaved another log into the truck bed where it collided with a thunk against the others.

Aaron missed the sunshine of her presence with a fierceness that took his breath. He lifted his eyes toward the overcast, leaden sky. How had he failed to notice how dreary the day had become without the sun to warm it?

"Uh, Gid...?"

His father turned.

"You got anything left of the coffee Kailyn sent?"

15

AARON EYED THE THREE-LAYER CHOCOLATE CAKE PLATED IN THE MIDDLE OF the kitchen table.

"Surprise!" Kailyn clapped her hands. "Happy birthday."

"How did you—?"

Grandmother and Gid exchanged amused glances.

"It's a chili-chocolate recipe from *Shinali*. I made it myself."

"That's what I was afraid of."

Her face constricted. Like he'd bashed her burritos.

"Grandson, you keep it up and the girl will have left you by Thanksgiving."

He frowned, reaching across the table for Kailyn's hand. "I meant I didn't know if after…"

She glowered at him.

"…what with your predilection for knives, lamps, etc.…. You might be trying to poison—"

She sucked in a breath, her eyes widening.

He snagged her hand. "Not coming out the way I meant. I mean I'd deserve it if you did."

Gid took a sip of tea. "You two lovebirds have a disagreement?"

Aaron focused on Kailyn. "My fault entirely. Forgive me?"

Her shoulders eased and he drank in the first smile he'd received from her in twenty-four hours—like the parched desert soil after a summer rain shower. His pulse thumped.

"I love birthday parties. Let me get the candles." She let loose of his hand long before he was prepared to let go. Tail wagging, Taco trotted at her heels, begging for his share.

There were a lot of things Kailyn loved, he'd discovered. A lot of things to love about Kailyn.

"No one can meet her and not fall in love," *Shinali* had said to him.

And she was right. So easy to love. He'd be tempted to allow himself to love her, too, except he carried more than just scars from his past.

In a way, he couldn't blame Runninghawk for appreciating the obvious. Until January, she was Aaron's to protect.

But after she testified…?

He swallowed. "You didn't have to go to all this trouble for me."

Kailyn spaced out the candles. "Thirty-two, right?"

He nodded, watching her strike a match. She managed to light three before dropping the match onto a saucer, her fingers burning. He scraped back his chair, leaned over and lit another one. "Here, let me help."

She swatted at him. "The birthday boy's not supposed to help. Let somebody do something for you for a change." She glanced around as the candle flames swayed. "Is there a draft in here?"

He cupped his hands around one side of the cake to block air movement while she lit the rest of the candles. "This is so sweet of you, Kailyn. Having a November 1 birthday usually meant my birthday got lost in the shuffle of Halloween."

Kailyn straightened, blowing out the match. "Not on my watch it doesn't. Let's sing."

After a hearty, if not exactly musical, rendition of the traditional song, Kailyn extracted a knife from the butcher block. "I'll do the honors," she announced with a coy look. "Since I'm so good with knives."

Their eyes locked across the diameter of the cake.

His insides flip-flopped. "Too much experience."

They grinned at each other.

"Did you two have a cake at your wedding?"

Both their heads swiveled toward Grandmother. He didn't like the glint in her eye.

"Uh…"

"Actually…"

Grandmother rested her chin on her folded hands, elbows on the table. "My son and I'd sure love for you to show us how you did it. Reenact what you did with the cake at the wedding reception." Her eyes narrowed. "As the bride and groom."

Kailyn's lips parted, the knife poised in midair. He closed his eyes, fearing what the old lady was up to now. Nothing to do but call her bluff. It wouldn't do to rouse the old woman's suspicious nature.

He flashed Kailyn a wide smile. "Sure, we can, can't we, Sweetheart?"

She blinked.

He rounded his eyes and shifted them to his grandmother.

She snapped to attention. "Of course, *Shinali*." Averting her face, Kailyn concentrated on slicing a wedge of cake. She handed him the saucer.

Kailyn played with the cross at her neck. "Who goes first? I forget."

"Shoot." Gid slapped his leg. "If I'd have known we were going formal I would've brought my camera."

"Why don't you go first, Grandson?" His grandmother's eyes challenged.

He gulped, broke off a small piece with his thumb and forefinger. Kailyn gave him a wary look and remained on her side of the divide.

"Better get closer to him, Granddaughter," Grandmother motioned. "Or he'll have cake all over your clean floors."

Kailyn edged around the table to where he held out the morsel of cake.

"For the love of turquoise, Granddaughter, closer, and open your mouth. He doesn't bite."

Like an obedient bird, her mouth popped open.

He slipped the tidbit between her teeth, his mouth near her ear. "Not much anyway," he whispered.

She blushed as red as a cactus rose. She snatched the plate and backed off.

"Your turn," Grandmother cawed.

He fluttered his eyelashes at Kailyn, putting on his version of her Southern flirt. "I'm ready. Lay it on me, *dzani*."

And too late detected the wicked gleam erupt in her iris-blue eyes.

Wadding the rest of the cake into her fist, she opened her palm and smeared it across the width of his face. He sputtered. Grandmother cackled. Gid hid a smile behind his tea glass.

"*Dzani*..." He rocked back.

Aaron pointed at his face. "Now clean up the mess you've made."

She arched a look at him over her shoulder. "Only Jesus could clean up a mess like you and me."

Despite himself, he laughed. Licked the icing off his lips. "You're probably right."

He could tell from the look on her face that his words surprised her.

Kailyn brushed against his arm. His heart pounded.

"But maybe I can help. A little." She ran her finger around the circle of his mouth, clearing a path. Kailyn held up her finger, making sure she had his attention.

She had his attention, all right.

And then, she stuck her finger in her own mouth.

His breath caught.

"You are evil, Kailyn Yazzie..." he muttered when his breathing resumed something resembling normal.

She angled toward the others—goggle-eyed at their antics—but her shoulders twitched with repressed laughter. "Too much chili, *Shinali*?"

The old woman winked at him. "Can't get too hot in my opinion."

"Gid?" He appealed to his father, but Gid was busy shoveling cake in his own pie hole and handing bits under the table to Taco.

His father rose, carrying his plate to the sink. "Let me help you ladies with the dishes. Speaking of Jesus," his lips curved, "Sunday morning comes mighty early."

Kailyn moved away, clearing the table.

His grandmother handed him a wet paper towel. "I was as stubborn as you a lifetime ago. But our mutual tribal cop friend..."

Runninghawk.

Wiping the icing off his cheek, Aaron watched her like a prairie dog monitored a circling hawk.

"...he hasn't missed church," she cut her eyes over to Kailyn at the sink, "in a month of Sundays." She patted his cheek.

"Point taken, Grandma."

He gritted his teeth as his grandmother took the paper towel from him and scrubbed at his face like he was a boy.

"Good. Neither your mother, your adopted mother, or I raised any stupid children."

The next morning, outfitted in a crisp white shirt, pressed jeans, a bolo string tie, and his Sunday-best Stetson, Aaron waited at the door for Kailyn to emerge from her bedroom. The delighted grin she bestowed on him compensated for burning his fingers on the iron. He contemplated her elegant figure—all from her thrift-store finds. Kailyn didn't do mediocre.

She wore a simple gray wool sheath, his cross at her slender neck. Despite the severe copper bun she'd fashioned at the nape of her neck, she was all too easy on the eyes.

His grandmother ambled to the porch. "If you two are done admiring each other, we'd best be on our way before we miss the preaching."

At Faith Community, located in the former Anglo-run boarding school, he parked beside a handful of cars and trucks. The pulsating pounding of drums greeted them at the door.

Once inside the school's former cafeteria, he spotted something he hadn't expected—a circle of chairs in the center of the room occupied by a group of men, some he recognized from Gid's crew. They surrounded a huge drum and with mallets in each hand they pounded out a distinctly Diné rhythm. Women, young and old, did a shuffle step around them in a larger circle. With their hands raised in worship, their moccasin feet kept time to the beat in an age-old sequence of steps.

Not what he'd expected.

But what surprised him the most were the words they sang. Words from Anglo hymns of praise to the Creator. First in English, they soon switched to the language of his birth. Reverent, worshipful, hauntingly beautiful, full of harmony. Completely Diné.

Kailyn sailed off to greet an elder. His grandmother favored him with a smile. "Culturally relevant. God's the Creator of every culture. From Him we received our language, our dress, our food, our land. And we give it back to Him in worship. The drums are the heartbeat of our people."

This church was much more casual than the churches he'd encountered during his time with the Matthews. He took a seat on the outer fringes and watched Kailyn flit from one Diné friend to another. His grandmother strolled in another direction. Kailyn greeted an old man who wore his Code Talker insignia with pride. In amazement, he observed one Diné after another pat her hand and touch her cheek—those to whom physical contact with a stranger was a cultural taboo.

But then again, it was him, as he'd suspected, who was the stranger here. Runninghawk had been right. These people—a handful compared to the prosperous Anglo congregations—belonged to a tribe he knew not of.

Speaking of Runninghawk…

He grimaced when Runninghawk sauntered through the door. Kailyn's eyes lit up and Runninghawk latched to her side like a hummingbird to a cactus flower. Runninghawk cut as fine a figure as Kailyn with his smooth talk and sophisticated ways. A credit to his Anglo upbringing.

Delores rejoined him as a Diné man in his mid-forties called the group to attention. "Preacher's ready to talk now." She waved for Gid to join them. Gid gave Aaron a hesitant smile.

Aaron scrutinized the preacher, who, like most, wore jeans, western-cut shirts and pointy-toe boots. He'd expected an Anglo preacher.

Delores patted his arm. "I'll introduce you to my friends after the service." She followed his gaze to the preacher's wide rodeo belt buckle as it gleamed under the fluorescent lights. "Diné are best shepherded by their own. Not many Anglos, like not many of our children, stick it out long these days with the world Outside having so much more to offer."

Kailyn finally, he noted with irritation, plucked herself from Jace's side and settled beside him.

Grandmother steepled her hands in her lap. "Not many willing to live in the poverty of their flock, so thereby they may win a few."

Gid nodded. "It takes years, decades, of someone willing to show respect and God's love, like Pastor Johnny Silverhorn in Cedar Canyon showed me."

The preacher—"Pastor Nez," Kailyn whispered—opened his large black Bible and read in the *Diné bizaad*. Aaron pursed his lips. He'd not known the Bible came in their language.

Pastor Nez flipped to an English version. Aaron glanced around, wondering how many of the younger ones, like him, spoke only English.

"From Luke, 'Suppose someone among you had one hundred sheep and lost one of them. Wouldn't he leave the other ninety-nine in the pasture and search for the lost one until he finds it?'"

Aaron's head snapped upright. Steve's favorite passage. His heart pinged anew with grief. Like Steve, if Aaron lost a witness, he'd go after his sheep.

But thinking of Kailyn, unlike Steve he'd hunt down and kill any wolf who breached his defenses. He flicked a snarky look at Runninghawk.

The preacher went on to speak of the beautiful work many of the women in the congregation created on looms. His gaze twinkled at Grandmother before moving on to several others.

"And as the gifted weaver creates order and harmony out of tangled skeins of disorder and chaos, so too the Creator's hand weaves the events of our lives with love and mercy into the warped strings of our hearts. Transforming us into a creation of beauty. So we may walk in beauty all the days of our lives."

Nez continued the story of a great Lamb who died for the sins of mankind, a tale Aaron had been subjected to before. He never got the part about someone supposedly as great as the Son of the True God allowing Himself to be captured and killed. Some greatness there, if He couldn't even prevent His own murder.

He stopped listening and, instead, focused his eyes on Kailyn's rapt face.

"Mankind faces trials and tribulations," Nez elaborated. "But we who know the True God have the power He alone gives, the power to walk through the arroyos and canyons of our difficulty."

Kailyn nodded. Amens peppered the air, sprinkled throughout the room. Aaron hunched his shoulders.

"Do you know Him today, my friends? Have you trusted Him to save you?"

Aaron shifted in his seat. Thanks, but no thanks. No need to bother on his account. He'd save himself.

Let the True God take care of those who needed His help. Like Gid or...He scanned the bowed heads.

Something stirred within him. These people possessed the same inner core of resilience, steel, and yet gentleness he'd witnessed in Steve and Nancy. He fidgeted.

With a considerable amount of relief, he watched the preacher close the prayer service and gesture for everyone to sing a final hymn. Afterward, he squired his grandmother around the assembly as she made her round of introductions. And at the look of sheer happiness and familial pride on his grandmother's features, her hand tucked in the crook of his arm, he mused this once—at last—in coming to church with her, he'd finally succeeded in gaining her approval.

Don't blink, he cautioned himself, or it'll pass.

Basking in the glow of her affirmation and with Kailyn secured onto his other arm and out of Runninghawk's reach, he failed to see the next curveball until he found himself roped into a committee by Gid to build a life-size crèche for the live nativity the children of the church planned for Christmas. Kailyn, he discovered, was sewing the costumes with help from her Anglo friends at the fabric store.

"All I said was I'd go to church. One time," he grumbled as she put dinner on the table later.

From the kitchen windowsill, Kailyn selected the tiny figurine of a jackrabbit he'd carved for her. "Your father knows how talented you are with wood." She replaced the rabbit to examine a butterfly he'd also made.

She cocked her head. "Unless you'd prefer I take your place and learn how to operate power tools?"

He rolled his eyes. "God forbid I put more potential weapons of destruction in your homicidal hands. I'll do it already."

She gave him an endearing, lopsided grin. "That's what I hoped you'd say."

Like the outcome had ever been in doubt when she turned those baby blues on him?

Putty in her hands is what he was and she knew it. Warrior becomes wimp, courtesy of one honey-tongued woman.

Kailyn watched Delores wend her way toward the house with the brown package she'd purchased weeks ago at the trading post clasped in her arms.

"What ya looking at?"

She whirled to find Aaron's hands planted palm down on either side of her against the sink.

His eyes beckoned. "Such passion, *dzani*. Perhaps we could work out a satisfactory relationship."

She blew a strand of hair out of her eyes. "Isn't this the part where you told me to run not walk?"

He laughed.

She lifted her hand to his cheek. He tensed, his dark eyes going opaque. Remembering how she'd once tried to hit him? Instead, she cupped his jaw.

He melted into her palm. "Now you've had time to consider the advantages of—"

"Your grandmother's seconds away from entering this house through the door behind you."

Releasing her, he jumped back. A good foot or more.

Still laughing, she threw open the door and greeted Delores. *"Ya'at'eeh, Shinali."*

Her eyes darted between them. He shuffled his feet and flushed. Taco insinuated his head underneath Delores's hand and licked her fingers. "I come with a wedding gift."

"Oh, *Shinali*..." Kailyn signaled at him behind Delores's back.

Delores pivoted. Kailyn froze mid-motion. His shoulders rose and dropped.

She bit her lip. "It's so thoughtful of you, *Shinali*."

Delores deposited the package and folded her hands at her concha-draped waist. "Go ahead. Open it."

Aaron jerked his head at Kailyn. She unfolded one edge of the paper.

"Don't tell me you're one of them?" He sidled next to her. "If you're going to open a gift, act like you mean to open it." He ripped at the package. "Christmas with you will evolve into Easter by the time you unwrap your gifts."

She stuck her tongue out at him and yanked open the other side. The gift stole her breath.

Delores sighed. "I was waiting until the right moment... I can see I've surprised you. Do you know what it is?"

Kailyn lifted the two-spouted vessel for Aaron's inspection. "It's beautiful. The design..."

"I got a funny feeling about this, Kay-Kay," he crooned in her ear.

She nudged him. "Thank you, Grandmother, for the...for the vase."

"It's a bridal jar."

Kailyn traced the delicate bits of turquoise embedded within the flower superimposed on the brown and white jar. "A what?"

He retreated to the other side of the table. "Uh...*Shinali*. You shouldn't have."

"It's part of a cherished Diné ritual usually taking place right before a couple's wedding. In your case," Delores shrugged, "I figured better late than never."

"Really, Grandmother..." His chest heaved. "You shouldn't have."

"Nonsense." Delores removed the jar from Kailyn's hands. "In the old days, the parents of both sides dug the clay, fired it, and presented it to the couple." She shooed them toward the living room.

"I've one more adjustment to make and we'll do this marriage thing of yours proper."

Kailyn gaped at him.

He shook his head. "*Shinali*—"

"Go," Delores fluttered her hand. "Take your bride and wait for me."

Taking Kailyn's elbow, he steered her into the living room, where they huddled against the front door as far out of Delores's earshot as possible. Taco burrowed into his favorite cushion on the couch.

"What're we going to do, Aaron? We're going to desecrate some sacred ritual. We can't keep lying..."

He scrubbed his hand over his face. "What do you want me to tell her? How we're both on a Mafia drug lord's most wanted list? Or how we're only—surprise, surprise, Grandma!—only faking our marriage?"

She stamped her foot. "I don't know, but we've got to do something. It's wrong."

He hooked his thumbs in the belt loops of his jeans. "You make it sound like we're living in sin or something." He curled a copper coil of her hair around his index finger. "Last time I checked, definitely not what was going on between us. Unless I missed something, somewhere…"

"This is not a joke, Aaron."

"Neither is a bullet in the back of your brain, Kailyn. I have a sneaking suspicion the old lady already suspects something's amiss. Don't let her fool you. She's as sharp as the spikes on a saguaro. You and I'd be lucky to be half as alert at her age."

"What about my age?"

Aaron fell into the wall. Kailyn whirled as Delores strolled toward them, jar in hand.

"Traditionally, the *hataalii*, medicine man, filled the jar with a nectar. Most couples today on the Rez supply their own concoction." She thrust the jar at Aaron.

"What did you—?"

"I made minor changes to reflect your shared backgrounds. You offer it to your bride first." She tapped one spout.

Bug-eyed, he handed it over to Kailyn.

"Drink it," the old woman commanded.

Steeling herself, mouth atremble, she lifted the jar to her lips, tipped, and swallowed as the liquid rolled around in her mouth.

"Tea," she answered his fearful look.

"Sweet tea," corrected Grandmother. "Now you turn it." She made a clockwise motion with her hand. "And the groom drinks from the same spout."

"Yes, ma'am." Kailyn followed her instructions before pushing the jar at him.

He complied.

"Now, you drink from the opposite side."

Which he did.

"Her," she nudged Kailyn. "Opposite again."

Kailyn followed suit.

"Now comes the tricky part."

Kailyn cut her eyes around the jar at Aaron.

171

"In culmination, you both must drink from the vase together."

Aaron chewed his lower lip. "At the same time?"

Kailyn placed her hand on one handle. Aaron wrapped his around the other.

Grandmother crossed her arms. "Without spilling a drop." She smiled, amusement and something mischievous glittering in her eyes. "It is said if a couple manages this feat without spilling a drop, their marriage will always be strong. As sweet as the nectar, as deep as the reservoir of their shared lives."

Kailyn released a tiny breath.

Aaron hefted the jar. "Ready?"

She nodded.

And in a quirky contortion of the limbo, both managed to drink from the jar without spilling a single drop.

Shinali clapped. "Now the jar becomes a cherished piece in your home. You must take great care of this vessel, symbolic of the vessel of your marriage. Placing the jar in a position of great honor. Making sure," she wagged her finger, "the vessel is never damaged or broken."

Grandmother raised her eyebrow like a question mark.

"Yes, *Shinali*," they answered in chorus.

"It is good," Grandmother rocked back. "It is good you do this in the sight of God." She waved a hand. "And what God hath joined together, let no one put asunder."

16

Kailyn accepted the herbal tea from Willa and sank onto the couch. The lively chatter of four girls echoed throughout Grace House.

Willa's cheeks lifted. "You made the girls so happy."

Kailyn shrugged. "I didn't do much. A little of this and a little of that."

"You helped them decorate their bedrooms to reflect their own tastes. You inspired them. Helping restore their confidence, showing them they were created with value, that they're deserving of love and goodness. That they can learn to walk in beauty."

Kailyn shook off her words. "I just brought some color into their lives."

She enjoyed coming to the home once a week and getting to know the girls. Each of them carried within themselves horrific hurts. Hurts she couldn't begin to fathom, didn't want to imagine.

But she envisioned, like Willa, the bright possibilities within each. And the more she got to know Willa, the more she admired how Willa lived her life. How she made a difference.

Kailyn took another sip. "Is there somebody special in your life?"

Willa ran the tip of her finger around the rim of the mug. "There is someone . . . But I don't encourage his interest."

Kailyn leaned forward. "Why not? What's wrong with him?"

Willa shook her head. "There's nothing wrong with him. I'm the problem. He'd be the perfect husband for someone. Someone besides me."

"I don't understand. I think you're pretty perfect."

Willa squeezed her arm. "You're sweet." Her mouth pulled downward. "But he's lived this privileged life before coming to the Rez. There's talk that, with his particular skill set, one day he'll be elected to the Tribal Council and perhaps even be Chairman."

Sighing, Willa glanced around the small but cozy room. "This is my world. These girls are my world. My world, my past, has far too much grime to fit with his. I'd hold him back, be a disappointment to his career in the end. I'm not the woman he needs—the pure, perfect Christian woman he deserves."

Kailyn set down her mug with a thud. "And he has a problem with what you do? Perhaps you're better off without him."

"Actually, I've laid every disgusting, perverse detail on him. To scare him away." Willa knotted her fingers. "But he continues to call. He continues to press me to give us a chance."

Kailyn gripped her friend's hand. "Are you sure it's an offer you want to refuse? Somebody who cares about you so much?"

Willa's eyes dropped to Kailyn's cross as it swung from her forward movement. "Once, a long time ago, when I wasn't much older than the girls, I fell in love. When he was gone…"

Her lips tightened. "I wasn't sure I'd make it. I wasn't sure I wanted to go on." Willa swallowed hard, wrenching her eyes from the cross. "To love in such a way, one must be so vulnerable. Open one's heart to such risk of pain."

With Thanksgiving behind them, and the holidays ahead, Kailyn had caught Aaron studying a road map. The route back to North Carolina. Perhaps Willa was indeed wise to hold back her heart.

Problem was, Kailyn didn't know how to safeguard her own heart. Feared she was well beyond the point of no return.

When Kailyn Eudailey left Charlotte, she'd left behind only bank accounts. When Kailyn Yazzie left the Rez behind for good in less than a month, she'd be leaving something far more precious than a trust fund.

So she refused to think about it. And resolved to enjoy her last weeks and Christmas with those she'd come to love.

Kailyn glanced at her watch. She scrambled to her feet. "My friend from the library is meeting me at the thrift store. I bought some furniture and he's going to help me load it into my truck."

Ten minutes later, she parked in front of the store, next to her Anglo friend, Burke Shepherd. His face lit at the sight of her, and she waved. They shared a love of books. And good coffee. Sometimes he'd take off early from his volunteer shift, and they'd gather at a nearby cafe before Kailyn headed home.

He was a lonely man in his early sixties. His wife died years ago, and his only child was estranged from him. He owned a prosperous ranch just outside the Rez on the other side of Farmington.

Clapping a Stetson atop his short white hair, Burke bounced out of his truck and around to Kailyn before she could switch off the ignition.

His blue eyes twinkling underneath bushy brows, he threw open her door and offered his hand. "My lady..."

"Such a gentleman," she laughed and stepped outside the truck. "I can't thank you enough for helping me load the entertainment center. My husband's going to be so surprised."

He laughed. "Glad to be of service. Anything to surprise your husband."

Putting his back into it, Burke loaded the Mission-style armoire and tied it down in the bed of her truck.

He removed his hat and swiped his forehead with the sleeve of his green denim jacket. "Good thing you brought those rugs to pad it with."

Burke gazed toward the distant Chuska. "Mountains got snow last night." He pointed. "Can't believe how late it is in the year and we've yet to see our first snow of the season."

He scuffed his boot in the gravel. "After the drought this summer, we need the moisture."

She hugged herself, thrusting her hands in the pockets of her coat.

He straightened. "Have you and the mister gotten your Christmas tree yet?"

She shook her head. "We keep meaning to but," she shrugged. "It's been one thing after another."

"Why don't you and I go pick one out right now? I could load it into my truck and follow you home."

"Oh, Mr. Shepherd, that's so sweet of you. But out of your way. The opposite direction from your ranch."

He rubbed his gloved hands. "It'd be fun. Not like I got much to go home to." His eyes dropped. "Unless this is one of those newly-wed traditions I'd be butting into... Your first Christmas together and all." He kicked at a stone.

Their first, last, and only Christmas. Her heart lurched.

But Burke looked so sad...

Aaron had been funny since what they'd come to refer to as the "bridal jar incident." Funny as in more aloof, closed off.

Reality until then had begun to blur, merging with the pretend. But afterward, with his manner distant, Aaron had been absent a lot. Working longer hours to finish a job, he said, less daylight this time of year. Before it snowed.

Pulling back in preparation for January? Guarding his heart? A smart move she couldn't duplicate.

"I think you may be on to something, Mr. Shepherd." She patted his arm. "A brilliant idea." She smiled. "And think how surprised Aaron will be."

He chuckled. "There's the spirit. And I know where to find the best piñon pine in town. You follow me and then I'll follow you home."

Good as his word, he helped her select a beautiful tree—and paid for it before she could stop him.

"My Christmas gift to you and the lucky son-of-a-gun husband of yours, missy."

He wouldn't hear of her paying him back. Thirty minutes later the two trucks arrived at the house. *Shinali* had gone to a weaver's meeting. Her good friend and fellow weaver, Gladys Begay, had promised to bring her home.

No telling these days when she'd lay eyes on Aaron. He'd return in time for supper, though, if nothing else. Aaron didn't miss many meals.

A smile teased her lips as she helped Burke unstrap the armoire. Sliding it forward off the tailgate, they managed to hoist and heave it to the ground. Burke took most of the weight, negotiating the steps. When Burke wheezed, she glanced with concern at his reddened face.

He wasn't exactly a spring chicken. What in the world would she do way out here if the kind man went into cardiac arrest? She gulped.

"Burke, are you sure—?"

"Step lively, missy." He shifted the weight between them. "I got just enough energy and strength to get this thing in the house before I give plumb slam out."

Kailyn shouldered her end of the armoire. And prayed he wouldn't fall dead of a stroke or heart attack.

They wrestled the thing across the threshold and shoved it into place on the wall opposite the couch. Taco skidded to a stop on the hardwood floor. His lips curled, he growled low in his throat.

She stepped between Taco and the shrinking Mr. Shepherd. "Taco...hush."

Burke's eyes bulged. "Didn't know you had a dog, Mrs. Yazzie."

"Kailyn," she corrected and bent to fluff Taco's 'do. Aaron had taken mousse and shaped it into a Mohawk. His idea of Indian humor.

Taking his guard dog duties seriously, Taco refused to be placated, yapping and snarling. Shushing him, she closed him in her bedroom.

Burke's eyes darted around, giving his breath a chance to steady. "Where's your TV? I'm not too bad with wires and cables if you want to get it operational before your man gets home."

She smiled. "The armoire was a steal. I'll have to save a bit more to actually put something expensive inside it."

He stared at her. "You mean to tell me, gal, you bought an entertainment center without any entertainment to go with it?"

She laughed. "Well, when you put it that way, it does sound ridiculous." She reached over to the bridal jar she'd deposited on a side table. She arranged it on one of the armoire's shelves.

"There." She stood back, chin in hand, surveying her handiwork. "Already filling up."

He shook his head, slapping his hat against his thigh. "One of them half-full people, aren't you?"

"Beats half-empty every time."

"Let me go wrastle the pine tree into your house."

She started forward. "Right."

He held up a brown-speckled hand. "I can handle it. But a glass of the sweet ice tea I've heard you talk about would sure hit the spot. Wet my whistle."

"You got it."

He was gone awhile. She had time to fix their glasses and plate some cookies. And then realized that, while she had a tree, she had nothing with which to adorn it.

Kailyn's eyes fell on the assortment of tiny carved figurines Aaron added to her collection each week. A little wire. Bits of string and she'd have a beautiful Navajo Christmas tree.

The front door crashed open. She hurried to help Burke lug the tree to the spot in the corner near her sewing station. Visible from every perspective in the room.

"Had to fit in a nicotine break while outside," he panted.

"I can't thank you enough, Mr. Shepherd." She breathed in the pine-scented air permeating the room. "You've brought much-needed Christmas cheer to my life."

Hat in hand, he tilted his head. "And you've brought some to mine, too, missy." His ice-blue eyes welled.

Burke gulped the tea and snagged three cookies before clamping his hat upon his head. "Best get on the road. You've got supper to cook and I've got animals to tend."

She laid a hand on his arm. "Why don't you stay for supper? My husband would love to—"

"No, ma'am." He yanked open the door. "Work to do. Maybe another time. A better time."

He'd not been gone five minutes when Gid's truck pulled up outside. The truck door slammed and the front steps creaked. Aaron bounded into the house.

She leaned against the kitchen doorway, wiping her hands on a dishtowel, admiring the breadth of his shoulders, which tapered to the lean, hard lines of his waist. Released from confinement, Taco gamboled, banging against Aaron's knees.

"Taco, my man." He bent and ruffled Taco's tiny white head. "What happened to your 'do? I had you stylin'."

His brow furrowed, his nose sniffing the air. "I smell cigarettes." His eyes widened, seizing first on the armoire and then on the tree. "Kailyn...What did you do?"

"Christmas, Aaron Yazzie. Ever hear of a little celebration called Christmas?" She'd only had time to string her favorite of his carvings, the butterfly, on one of the branches.

"How did you—?" His head swiveled between the armoire and the tree. "No way you fit both of those in the truck." His eyes narrowed. "Who helped you? Jace Runninghawk?"

She rolled her eyes. "No. As a matter of fact, you just missed Santa's helper. You probably passed him heading home in his truck."

"Him?" Aaron rose so quickly, Taco stutter-stepped and whined. "Him who, Kailyn?"

"Stop looking for a gangster behind every cactus, Aaron. He's all of sixty. A volunteer at the library. He offered to help me haul my loot home."

He glared. "Stop playing house, Kailyn. I don't like you knowing people I don't."

She crossed her arms. "Do you know how paranoid you sound?"

"Justifiable paranoia or have you forgotten about the dead man Runninghawk unearthed?"

"Not Villeda as you feared," she pointed out.

"Still a Conquistador, though." He raked his hand over his head. "We should've pulled out of here as soon as we heard about the man. Flores always sends two to three men per hit squad."

Kailyn flicked the dishtowel at him. "We couldn't disappoint your grandmother and father. They're both so excited about celebrating Christmas with us. Besides, nothing else has happened. False alarm. Unconnected to our situation."

She flicked the towel again. His hand shot out, catching the end of it.

Crinkling her eyes at him, she pulled herself hand over hand closer. "Must you always be so serious, Aaron Yazzie?"

A muscle ticked in his jaw. His hand, hard with calluses, gripped hers. His chest rose and fell.

"I'm"—swallowing, his face clouded and he drew back—"I'm dirty, Kailyn." He dropped his eyes to his boots. "When's dinner?"

Tears stung her eyes. He probably counted the hours and days until his duty to her and Steve was done. She'd lost her touch with Aaron, her ability to tease him into a lighter mood.

If she'd ever possessed anything to charm him with in the first place. Aaron Yazzie—the most unreadable, frustrating human being she'd ever known.

And what was she? A glutton for punishment.

How often did she have to be told he wasn't interested? Apparently, five hundred times a day wasn't sufficient to pound it into her thick skull. She was so incredibly stupid—as naïve as he'd asserted—to think, to believe, to hope...

Time to dial it back. "Get your shower. I'm reheating leftovers. I've got to take Taco to do his business and then I'll get dinner on the table."

He nodded and moved toward the hall. She unhooked Taco's leash and exited through the kitchen door. Taco strained at the leash, almost choking himself in his hurry to finish his business and explore.

At the edge of the fallow alfalfa field, she let him off the leash, allowing him to romp and play. She shaded her hand against the rays of sun disappearing over the horizon behind the mesa. A cloud of dust from a vehicle jostling along the fortresslike plateau floated in the air. The dust of the *Dinétah* created such fiery, orange-red sunsets.

With Taco engaged in his daily, fruitless battle to capture a rabbit or gopher, she drew a deep breath, taking in the beauty of the place she'd come to love.

A lot of things to love on the Rez. The simplicity of the life suited her far better than the stress of her former high-society existence. She noticed that the woodbin outside Grandmother's hogan was almost empty. She hated for her to return to a stove gone cold and no wood to rebuild the fire.

Kailyn headed to the woodpile Aaron kept stacked under the cottonwood arbor between the two dwellings. She'd gather a few armfuls and send him out to finish the rest after dinner. She shivered, having forgotten her coat. She wouldn't be on the Rez long enough to build up her thin Southern blood.

She grimaced. From Aaron's perspective, she wouldn't be leaving soon enough.

As she reached for the topmost log, Taco dashed from behind in a frenzy of barking. He caught the cuff of her jeans between his teeth and yanked.

"What in the—? Let go of me, Taco. You're going to rip my…"

Taco bolted in front of her, snapping his teeth. At her.

Kailyn posed a hand over her heart. "*Et tu*, Taco? What's wrong with you?"

She sidestepped him and gripped the log. Something rustled in the pile, shifting and dislodging the smaller branches.

He lunged and butted the log out of her hand. Flying through the air, the log landed with a thwack against the woodpile, sending the cord toppling. A light brown scorpion crawled from underneath the log she'd held. Two more advanced from the woodpile.

Taco pawed the ground. Five creatures emerged from the displaced logs. She stepped back. Taco inserted himself between her and the wood. She caught hold of his collar and tugged.

But before she realized what was happening, an army—or so it seemed—skittered from the pile, scattering in all directions, ringing her and Taco.

She let go of Taco when something crawled on her shoe. She screamed, kicking her foot, trying to fling off the creature. Taco pounced. The creature arched its tail and pincers drilled into Taco's leg.

His barking cut short into a high-pitched cry of pain.

"Taco!"

He wobbled on three legs toward her, but whimpering, he collapsed into a heap.

17

When Kailyn screamed, Aaron barreled from the house. The sun-baked earth crawled with scorpions.

"Don't touch Taco," he yelled. "The stinger's still in his leg. If you come into contact with it, it'll injure you, too."

Her eyes overflowed. "But he's hurting..."

"I'll get him. He needs a vet fast." He dragged her away to a safer distance. "Those are bark scorpions..."

"Poisonous?" she whispered.

He nodded, yanking his thick work gloves from his back pocket. "I've never seen so many in one place."

Aaron cleared the area around Taco, stomping a few remaining scorpions with his work boot. "Taco, my man." He squatted beside the whimpering dog.

Taco lifted his head and licked Aaron's arm.

Carrying him to the porch, he examined Taco's legs and tail. "What tangle did you get yourself into this time, mi amigo?"

She hovered at his elbow. "How bad has he been stung?"

"Multiple times."

"Oh, Aaron..."

"Injection amounts differ according to the scorpion's inclination, but I'm going to try and remove the stingers."

She wrung her hands. "What should I do?"

"It's like being electrocuted, a white-hot pain. We need to keep Taco immobile."

"Like a snakebite? Activity speeds circulation and spreads the poison?"

"Exactly. Get me something cold from the freezer to place on the sting area. And the tweezers out of your cosmetic bag."

By the time she returned with a bag of frozen peas and the tweezers, Taco's leg had swollen to double its normal size. His big brown eyes dilated as Aaron removed as many of the hypodermic-like stingers as he could locate on the little dog's body.

He enfolded Taco in his arms. "Kailyn, you need to drive us to Shiprock to the vet clinic."

"I'll hold Taco. You—"

He shook his head. "He's having trouble breathing."

Taco's leg muscles contracted.

Aaron's heart skipped a beat as Taco's hairless body quivered with tremor after tremor.

Kailyn's chin wobbled. "Aaron…"

"Come on," he called over his shoulder. "We don't have long to counteract the venom."

Once inside the truck, he rigged a pseudo-tourniquet around Taco's leg from a blue bandanna in the glove compartment. "To keep the poison from spreading to his heart."

Her face paled, but Kailyn shifted into gear and sped down the bumpy road. At every jostle, Taco fretted. She winced, biting her lip.

"Don't slow down," he urged. "Faster's better."

She gripped the wheel.

Aaron busied himself, trying to remember the first aid training he'd received in the army and the folk medicine *Shinali* had imparted to him over the years for dealing with the natural enemies on the Rez. He left the frozen peas on Taco's leg for ten minutes and then removed them before repeating the cycle.

His breathing raspy, Taco's drool soaked through Aaron's jeans.

And then Taco stilled.

Her face constricted at the sudden quiet. "Is he—?"

She cut her eyes over to him. "Did he—?"

"Keep your eyes on the road, Kailyn. Just drive." He swallowed. "And if you think your God still possesses any resurrection power you people sing about, now'd be a good time for Him to show up. If He even cares about any of us in the first place."

She squared her shoulders. "He cares for the tiniest of sparrows. And certainly for such a good, good—" Her voice choked, but her lips moved in a silent prayer.

He laid Taco on the seat and puffed two quick breaths into the dog. Aaron stopped, watching to see if Taco's chest rose.

Nothing.

"Come on, boy," he coaxed. "Where's my great, brave boy? Breathe, Taco. Breathe."

He followed with ten-fifteen-twenty breaths and waited.

"Jesus..." She breathed for them both.

His heart hammering, Aaron bent over Taco again.

Taco's chest heaved. His body shuddered as life returned. His tail thumped the seat.

He stroked the dog's head as his own heart returned to a normal beat. "Taco..."

"Resurrection power, I told you." She cast her eyes to the ceiling.

He scooped Taco into his arms as she bypassed Blue Corn Springs and headed toward Shiprock. He cuddled the dog inside the warmth of his sheepskin-lined jacket.

"Just a few more miles, Taco." She pointed at the highway sign with her lips. "Hang on, little guy."

If he hadn't been so scared for Taco, he would've laughed. *Shinali* would make a Diné out of her yet.

A redheaded Diné anyway.

"What's with the scorpions?" His brow furrowed. "I've never seen so many before."

She filled him in on how Taco had intervened. Her eyes glistened. "It's my fault. Better if they'd stung me. I could've handled the poison better than his small body could."

"Much as I love Taco, no way I'd exchange his pain for yours."

They passed into the city limits.

Had he just admitted he loved a dog? He'd learned the danger a long time ago of loving anyone or anything. He fought the moisture in his eyes.

Because Aaron Yazzie had also learned early—the hard way—not to cry.

Ever.

Tears reduced him to victim status. Made him weaker, made his stepfather despise Aaron more. Another weapon to use against Aaron and his mother.

Rivers of tears in no way mitigated the sting of the lashes. His stoicism, his control over—if nothing else—his emotions, became his only defense. His ultimate resistance, his defiance against the darkness. His unyielding, indomitable refusal to allow Michaels to win.

He whispered in the dog's ear. "We're almost to the doc. You're the best guard dog on the Rez, taking care of your human, keeping Kailyn safe."

She pulled into the clinic parking lot and rolled to a stop. "You think they've closed for the night?" She surveyed the darkened stucco building.

He released the catch and swung open the door. "Not yet. I think we're still in time." Taco in his arms and Kailyn on his heels, they raced into the clinic.

A white-coated Anglo doctor hurried from behind the counter at the sight of the listless dog. "What happened?" The vet removed a stethoscope from around her neck and checked Taco's vital signs.

"Scorpion stings. Multiple. Bark scorpion," Aaron rattled off.

The doctor reached for the dog. "How long ago?"

Kailyn glanced at the wall clock above the reception desk. "About forty minutes ago. Aaron?" She tugged at his arm. "You can let go now."

He blinked. "Oh..." He gulped and released his grip on Taco. "Sorry, I'm..." His voice wavered.

The vet placed Taco on a small metal gurney. "No problem. I'll take good care of your friend, I promise." She bent over Taco, examining the damage. Taco moaned.

She sighed and faced them. "Good thinking whoever removed the stingers and rigged the tourniquet. But I won't lie to you. This many stings coupled with the dog's small body weight..."

Kailyn's hand slipped into the crook of Aaron's arm. "He's in tremendous pain, isn't he?"

The doctor nodded.

Kailyn's lower lip trembled. "Should we—? Would it be more merciful to let him…?" A sob hiccuped from her throat before she could stop it. "…to put him down?"

"Absolutely not." Aaron swung around to face Kailyn. "Taco's worth trying to save. We don't give up on anyone we love. And Taco's a fighter, like us."

He cradled her face between his palms. "He's a survivor and deserves a fighting chance. Where's your faith?" He turned toward the doctor. "There's got to be something you can try."

"I'll give him methocarbamol to reduce the muscle tremors. If he goes into full-blown seizures…?" The vet's shoulders rose and fell. "Maybe diazepam."

She gestured toward the reception area. "Wait here and I'll see if I can get Taco stable. The main thing is to reduce his discomfort with pain relief, keeping him calm and quiet until the medication can begin to counteract the venom."

The doctor retrieved a clipboard from the counter. "Fill out these forms while you wait."

Aaron nodded and propelled Kailyn toward a cracked vinyl couch as the doctor wheeled Taco into the surgical area. She buried her face in her hands and wept as the double metal doors swung shut and Taco disappeared from sight.

"I promised I'd take care of him and now…"

Aaron drew her head upon his shoulder. Draping her arms around his neck, she buried her face into the fabric of his shirt. He savored the magnolia sweetness of her shampoo, wishing he'd had time to shower before the crisis erupted.

He dropped the clipboard on a side table. "I'm still dirty, Kailyn…"

In so many more ways, he reflected on the years of his undercover work, than she could ever imagine.

Things he'd seen. Things he'd done. Things done to him.

Kailyn's arms slid away as she released her stranglehold on him. "O-okay...S-sorry."

He immediately missed the warmth of her body. One look at her stricken face and he abandoned all attempts to keep his emotional distance. He pulled her close once more.

She nestled into him, the jerking from her sobs decreasing. His hand nuzzled the nape of her neck and he brushed his lips across the top of her head.

He'd reestablish his professional boundaries...Tomorrow, he promised himself. Or, maybe after Taco recovered.

No need to rush the healing process.

And he wondered if he was thinking of Taco or himself.

She straightened. "We need to call your dad. Warn him. What if *Shinali* returns home and—?"

Rising, he fished the cell out of his pocket. "Gid will clear the woodpile and make sure the varmints are long gone."

He speed-dialed Gid's number in Blue Corn Springs and apprised him of their situation.

"Never saw so many at one time," he repeated to Gid, trying to wrap his mind around it.

"This time of year," Gid responded, "packs of twenty to thirty bark scorpions are known to hibernate together till spring. I'll make sure my *shima*'s okay." Gid clicked off.

His innate caution couldn't dispel the notion that the scorpions weren't an accident of chance. Aaron shuddered at what could've happened to Kailyn without Taco's courageous defense. Had the Conquistadores or Flores found him? Was Aaron, as the resident woodcutter, their intended target? Suppose Grandmother had taken it into her head to restock her wood box?

But scorpions?

Not Flores's style. Too subtle for the likes of Villeda or the Conquistadores. Too much left to chance. Scorpion stings on an adult human were rarely fatal.

A warning? A threat?

The vet emerged.

Kailyn popped to her feet and swayed. She trembled underneath the safety of his arm.

"Taco...?" He struggled to control the quaver of his voice.

The doctor's tight mouth eased. "He's stable for now. We'll have to wait and see. If he survives the night, he's got a good chance of making it."

Kailyn closed her eyes and leaned into him.

He released a slow breath. "Thank you for all you've done, Doc."

The vet shook her head. "No need to thank me yet." She assessed them, her hands stuffed into the pockets of her lab coat. "You two go home."

Kailyn crossed her arms. "I'll stay with Taco."

The doctor raised her eyebrows. "Oh no you won't. Go home and get some sleep. If Taco makes it—"

Aaron and Kailyn stiffened.

"When Taco makes it," the vet amended. "He'll need lots of rest and special attention. He's sedated and won't know if you're here or not. I'm on call tonight. I'll monitor his condition and give you a call in the morning." She patted Kailyn's shoulder. "First thing."

The doctor reached into her coat pocket. "Oh, and I found this embedded under the skin on Taco's thigh." She held up a microchip. "It doesn't resemble any pet identification finder I've run across."

Aaron tensed and darted a look at Kailyn. The vet dropped the microchip into his palm.

He took out his wallet. Kailyn latched onto the hem of his coat. "I can give you a cash deposit now to cover any expenses incurred and we'll settle the rest when we check Taco out." He tucked the microchip into the fold and handed her a hundred-dollar bill.

Kailyn found his hand. "You'll give us a call first thing?"

The doctor nodded and escorted them out the door. Clicking his seatbelt in place, Aaron inserted the key into the ignition and surveyed Kailyn, huddled next to the passenger window. Misery reflected like twin blue lagoons in her eyes.

"You want to come over here?" He gestured at the space between them. "Keep me company on the way home?"

Lips trembling, she nodded before sliding over.

He chewed the inside of his cheek. "Did you know about the microchip, Kailyn?"

She jerked at the suspicion he couldn't quite remove from his voice. "No. Gaby must've..." She edged away from him, knotting her fingers in her lap.

"Gaby?" His voice rose. "You mean to tell me you got Taco from Gaby Flores? The woman whose husband murdered her in front of your eyes?"

She flinched.

"The dog of the man your testimony will put away for life?" He wrapped his hands around the wheel, tempted to throttle her instead. "And somehow this slipped your mind to tell me? You didn't think this might be relevant?"

He snorted. "No wonder Flores has Villeda and the Conquistadores out in full force looking for you."

She cringed. "Gaby gave me Taco before...Flores kept shouting at her. About something of his she'd taken." She moistened her bottom lip with her tongue. "Gaby volunteered at the animal shelter in Charlotte. I had no idea she'd inserted something into Taco."

Kailyn angled. "What do you think the microchip contains?"

He clamped his jaw. "Something Flores was willing to kill her for and you, too. Something that has put a target on everyone you come into contact with."

Kailyn wrapped her arms around herself, and he realized she'd gone outside with Taco and never bothered to grab a coat. "*Shinali* could have...Or you."

She averted her face toward the gathering darkness. "The marshals searched my stuff but never scanned for any device on Taco. I'm...sorry. I never thought..."

"This could be a game changer, Kailyn." He scowled. "I'll send the microchip to Rogers in North Carolina."

"I wouldn't lie to you, Aaron. I promise I didn't know." A sob caught in her throat. "And if Taco dies—" Her face twisted.

As did his heart.

He blew out a breath. This was Kailyn, he reminded himself. Not some double-dealing clique chica.

Aaron reached for her. "It'll be okay. Taco will be okay. You and I," he studied the play of rising moonlight on her profile. "We'll be okay."

Silence.

"Kailyn..." He sighed. "Would you please slide back over? When the sun drops out of the sky, it gets cold here on the Rez. Please . . ."

She swiped at the tears on her cheeks, but she complied, scrunching against his side. "Those scorpions won't be back, will they?"

He shrugged. "They hang out in wood or leaf piles, Gid said. Best thing to keep them out of the house—"

"They can get into the house?" she shrieked.

He chuckled. This was the Kailyn he knew.

"Those critters can get inside with only one-sixteenth-inch of an opening. If you shine a flashlight on them, they glow fluorescent green in the dark. *Shinali* used to have a cat. Maybe it's time to get another. Keep them from crawling up the sink or toilet."

She went rigid. "I'll never go outside again." She crossed her legs. "Or go to the bathroom without first turning on the lights and checking the toilet."

He laughed out loud. "Where's your sense of adventure, *dzani*? Don't go all deb on me now."

She huffed. "My sense of adventure bit the dust about the time I stepped off the elevator in Charlotte." She stuck both her hands into his jacket pocket.

He glanced in the rearview mirror, but they'd had the road to themselves since leaving Shiprock. "I'll pull over and give you my coat."

She snuggled closer, looked down and then up again at him through her eyelashes. "Don't bother. I'm fine. And this is way more fun."

His lips twitched, but he rounded his eyes at her. "You keep this up, distracting the driver, and we'll both end up in the ditch, *dzani*."

She laughed and the tension between them eased.

He pressed the accelerator to the floor as his pulse ratcheted up a notch. "Probably not a good idea to tell anyone about Taco's return from the dead."

She rubbed her cheek against the canvas of his coat. "God's still in the business of restoring life even if Taco was only gone for a few moments."

"It's time enough for most Diné, no matter how modern they claim to be, to avoid you and me both like the plague. The Diné have this aversion—an abhorrence for death. They fear it more than anything else. They believe the evil in a person remains behind, his *chindi*, and to say the dead one's name or touch his belongings, especially in the first four days after death, invites the *chindi* to take up residence with you."

"But God answered our prayers."

"God answered *your* prayers. The part in your gospel about your Savior dying, being buried, and then rising from the D-E-A-D? You lose 90 percent of The People every time."

"Is that where God loses you?"

"Your God lost me a long time before. Back when I watched my mother bleed out on an Albuquerque pavement."

He grimaced. "When I was at the wrong end of a belt buckle."

If Kailyn lived to be a hundred, she'd never forget the sight of Aaron's tender concern for the face-only-a-mother-could-love dog. How he cradled Taco in his arms. How he cradled her when she was sure all was lost.

The realization came to her in the middle of the dark, never-ending night when, unable to sleep, she waited for dawn to break and the doctor to call with news of Taco's condition. No need to try to fight it or deny it.

Because somewhere along the way from Charlotte to Shiprock, she'd fallen desperately, hopelessly, forever in love with Aaron Yazzie.

Or Rafael Chavez or whatever he called himself in the future.

Not that they had a future. Once the marshals relocated her, she'd be forbidden to ever see him again. And he had a whole other life, a career, of which she knew nothing.

This might be all she ever had with him. This pretend marriage. And this would have to be enough.

She'd never been in love before. Everything before him paled in comparison with the depth of her feelings now.

Kailyn liked the way he said her name—when he wasn't calling her "woman." Her insides lit and felt all floaty when he was around. The mere touch of his hand against her skin…

She flung off the quilt. Those kinds of thoughts weren't conducive to sleep. She dressed, glancing at the bedside clock. Sunrise wouldn't be far behind. She'd make coffee and have it ready whenever Aaron emerged from his room.

But when she padded on stocking feet into the kitchen, she found him seated at the table, nursing a mug of herbal tea.

"You look terrible."

He scrubbed a hand across his jaw. "Thanks. You really know how to flatter a guy."

"Did you get any sleep at all?"

He cocked an eye over the rim of the cup. "Probably about as much as you." He swallowed and made a face. He scooted his chair and emptied the contents of the cup into the sink. "Didn't want to risk missing the doc's call. I thought you'd never get up. Could use some of that brew you call coffee."

She smiled at him, patted his cheek. Her fingers lingered. "It's addictive, isn't it?"

He edged her against the counter. "Among other things." He played with a strand of her hair.

She held her breath as he leaned closer. Something glimmered in his eyes. The look liquefied her insides.

"Kailyn—"

The phone rang. They both jerked. He grabbed the phone from the table. He glanced at the caller ID and answered.

She kneaded his hand.

"You're sure he's going to be okay?" He met her gaze and grinned. "Great news. Kailyn will be so—we're both so relieved." He nodded as if the doctor could see him over the phone lines.

She sagged against him and released a deep gust of air.

"I'll pick him up before your office closes today. As soon as I—"

She pointed to herself and made a motion of driving.

"Kailyn will swing by after work…" He listened. "Thanks again, Doc. We'll follow your instructions to the letter, I promise." He clicked off.

She clasped her hands together. "He's okay?"

Laying the phone aside, he lifted her off the floor and swung her around. "Benadryl for any residual pain and inflammation. He'll need to wear a cone to prevent him from scratching the sores."

Kailyn laughed. "A survivor. Like us."

Something changed in his face and he lowered her to the floor. "Probably touting his battle cred to other canines in the clinic as we speak."

"But a cone?" She tilted her head. "A cone of shame. I'll buy booties for him instead and—"

"Don't you dare go unescorted into that shopping place."

Aaron ducked his head. "Not his usual sartorial splendor, but there's worse marks of shame, believe me."

"Shame?" Her eyes widened. "Aaron, what happened to you wasn't your fault. You've got nothing—"

He retreated, his hand upraised. "Yeah, yeah. So those counselors Steve and Nancy shoved down my throat informed me." He stuffed his hands in his pockets. "Are you going to get the coffee going or what?"

She narrowed her eyes, but turned on the tap water to fill the carafe. He always dodged the issue of his troubled childhood. It grieved her he didn't trust her enough to reveal the deepest hurts of his heart, but she'd learned over the last few months to give him space. To let him move forward at his own pace.

As she reached for the faucet to turn off the flow, his hand covered hers. She jumped. Sometimes she forgot about his stealth, courtesy of his heritage or military training or undercover work, take your pick.

"Maybe we could go get Taco together."

Kailyn shifted around as the emerging sun's golden rays angled across the planes of his stony face. Not unlike the rocks of his homeland. But no matter what he claimed, his heart wasn't the stone he allowed the world to believe.

She knew better. She'd seen him with Taco last night. And had glimpsed moments between him and her, giving Kailyn reason to hope he cared for her, too.

As more than Steve's witness.

He ran his thumb over the back of her hand.

This was his way of making up for his harsh words, for shutting her out. This much, over the last two months as his pretend wife, she'd learned.

She stepped around him and poured the water into the coffee-maker. "I'll text you when I leave the store." She removed the coffee from the freezer and sifted a few tablespoonsful into the filter.

"Can I text you my location?"

She glanced up and hit the On button.

"Gid's got a bee in his warbonnet about the crew doing community hours at the youth center. At-risk kids." He frowned. "Been there. Been them. I'm no good in those situations."

"Mr. FBI Agent? Mr. Ranger?" She let a smile tease her lips. "I can't imagine any situation where you're not good. And Taco would agree."

He folded his arms across his chest and leaned against the counter, his long, blue-jean-clad legs extended. "You're exceedingly good for my ego. But when're you going to learn appearances can be deceiving, *dzani*?"

"You'd rather I lived my life always expecting the worst?"

"At least then, you're never disappointed."

She sidled past him, grabbing the heavy iron skillet. "When're you going to learn life is full of cacti." He backed off a step when she brandished it. "And *you* make the choice to sit on it or not."

18

Aaron examined the sandwich. Fried Spam, lettuce, tomato, and mayo wrapped inside a burrito. According to *Shinali*, Kailyn informed him, The People's idea of a perfect lunch. In his opinion, Kailyn carried this going Native thing a little too far with the Spam.

He rewrapped the cellophane and sauntered over to Gid. "Want to trade?"

Gid's eyebrows rose and he lowered the peanut butter and jelly sandwich from his lips. "What is it?"

Aaron opened one flap of the sandwich.

Gid peered at the Spam. "You got something against Spam, boy? Not Anglo enough for you? And after your sweet wife got up at the crack of dawn to fix it for you."

He grabbed the Spam from Aaron's hand and switched with him. "Some people don't know how good they got it." Gid chomped on a hunk of fried whatever.

Aaron sprang up and slid next to Gid on the tailgate of the pickup. "Nothing wrong with peanut butter." He took a bite. "And there's nothing wrong with my appreciation of my wife, either."

Gid smiled around his Thermos. "She's going to love the manger you're making for—"

"Hey," Aaron's eyes darted. "She's got ears everywhere. Don't blow the surprise."

Gid's eyes probed him. "You've taken back your given name." He swallowed. "My name."

Aaron frowned. "Well, don't let it go to your head. Just came in handy. Easier in my current situation."

Gid's face fell. He heaved himself off the tailgate. His eyes dropped to the red dirt. "Guess we'd best head on over to the youth center." He shuffled over to the crew.

Aaron's conscience fretted him, watching his father's slumped shoulders as Gid moved away. He'd been surprised to find his former drunken excuse for a father highly regarded in the Blue Corn Springs community. Gid had proven to be an intelligent man, with his wits no longer dulled by alcohol.

A hard worker. An honest man. A father anyone would be proud to claim. If Aaron was in the market for a new dad.

Which he was not.

Another surprise as they'd worked together the last few weeks on the life-size crèche for the church—Gid's skill with wood and power tools. Lent proof to the argument of nature versus nurture in his own case, he supposed.

Gid, *Shinali*, Taco, and most especially, Kailyn. Their place in his life—in his heart—grew stronger every day.

Aaron spent a lot of sleepless nights worrying if January and the trial would ever arrive. And conversely—perversely—agonizing over what he'd do when they did.

He stilled his conscience—in regard to his father at least—by remembering the pain in his mother's eyes as she wrenched the cross from her neck, thrust it into his hands and told him to run. To get away while he had the chance. Before *he* returned.

Some protector Aaron had turned out to be. He should've…

He raked a hand across his head, dislodging and sending flying the construction helmet he'd forgotten.

"Saddle up," Gid called. "Let's head to the Center."

In the truck, Gid explained the situation. "For many of these kids, the Center, supported by area churches, is the only drug/alcohol/gang-free environment they can find. The guys and I stop by every few weeks to pal around and get a pickup game of basketball together with them."

Aaron grunted. Gid glanced at him before shifting his attention to the highway.

"These kids are ripe for gang recruitment. They're poor as any village child in Africa." Gid snorted. "Maybe worse off. Most of them come from broken homes. Parents most often never married. Themselves victims of violence and drug and alcohol addiction."

Aaron stared out the window. "I get it. You think me and them are gonna connect. Bond over our shared dysfunctional history."

"I think it'd do them good to realize theirs, unfortunately, isn't a unique situation."

Aaron's lip curled. "Do me good, don't you mean? Let you off the hook for your responsibility in the mess you made of my life and Mom's?"

Gid sighed. "I meant seeing how you'd overcome the obstacles, how you've risen above everything. They could identify with you and you could offer hope for their own futures."

Aaron held out his hands, palms up. "I made it. No thanks to you or this Rez. Any thanks for who or what I've become you can lay at the door of Steve Matthews, my real dad."

Gid winced.

"If I'd have stayed, I'd have probably ended up as sorry a drunk as you." Aaron shunted toward the window. "I got no hope to pass on, old man, other than to get out of here any way they can. And I'm not sticking around long, either. After Christmas, Kailyn and I both have…" He pursed his lips. "New opportunities to explore."

"Your grandmother—and I—hoped…"

Silence ticked between them.

Aaron bristled. "Your charity should've begun at home a long time ago."

His face inscrutable, Gid flicked on his signal and veered left in front of an aluminum-sided gym. A fleet of trucks followed and parked in the overflowing lot. The metal turquoise roof gleamed in the afternoon sun. Aaron smiled, thinking of how once Kailyn got a load of it, she'd probably insist on him reroofing the house.

But at the sight of multiple white SUVs sporting the Navajo Nation Tribal Police insignia, he swiveled around to Gid. "Don't tell me Runninghawk and his cohorts are involved in this charity project of yours."

Gid switched off the ignition and swung open his door to much dinging. "Stay in the truck. Or come inside. Your choice, Aaron."

Choice?

He glared as Jace Runninghawk strutted into the sunshine and embraced his father. Like anything had ever really been his choice. His mother had made her choice to go off-Rez and into the monster's lair with disastrous ramifications. Gid's choice to choose a bottle instead of them.

And then he remembered Kailyn's challenge to him yesterday. How he'd chosen to sit on the spiky spines of unforgiveness. Who was he hurting the most? Gid?

Or himself?

Runninghawk clapped an arm across Gid's back as they entered the gym. He flashed Aaron a look over his shoulder.

At his smirk, Aaron shoved open the door and strode forward to join them before he realized what he was doing. Gid looked pleased when he sauntered inside. Runninghawk gave him an aloof smile, looking down the long, arrogant nose Aaron itched to break.

Balling his hand into a fist, he plopped down on a set of bleachers. A boy edged a few inches away.

"Hey," he muttered. "Ever hear about personal space."

Aaron eyed the preteen. With strong Navajo features, the skin-and-bones boy huddled inside an overlarge parka. He fiddled with an electronic game. His hair hung long and unwashed down his back.

Gid disappeared into a room filled with weightlifting equipment. Jace and his pals drifted from bleacher to bleacher, encouraging the boys to put together a game. The guys ragged Runninghawk about his upcoming hot date this evening. Gid's crew dispersed, gathering balls and warming up with free throw shots.

Runninghawk swaggered over. "Mateo, my man."

He and the boy scowled.

"Join us. Show us your moves, dude."

The boy never took his eyes off the device.

He'd like to show Runninghawk some moves, bust his chops.

Runninghawk laid a hand on the boy's shoulder.

Mateo flinched.

Aaron narrowed his eyes.

"Take off your coat and stay a while, dude. Join us."

Mateo shrugged off Runninghawk's hand. "I'm busy. Don't want to play."

He didn't like to be touched without permission, either.

Runninghawk loomed over Mateo, his hands positioned on his sweatpants. "Where'd you get the toy? Your dad's out of work the last I heard."

Mateo's eyes shot up. "I didn't steal it."

Runninghawk wiped the smile off his face. "I think maybe you better explain where you did come by it."

The boy's face hung to his scuffed sneakers. "I didn't steal it. Mr. Gid"—he jerked his chin in the direction of the weight room—"he lets me borrow it. 'Cause he knows I'm no good at sports."

Mateo gulped. "I don't want to play ball. I'm just here till my mother gets off work. She doesn't want me at home without her."

He'd had about as much bullying from Runninghawk as he could stomach. Aaron remembered the awkwardness of thirteen even if Runninghawk didn't. The gangly, uncoordinated limbs until puberty caught up with potential.

But on second thought, Runninghawk bore the look of a lifelong athlete. His Anglo soccer mom's dream come true.

Aaron leaned back, resting his elbows on the bleacher behind him. "Leave him alone, Runninghawk. He's not causing any trouble. What's it to you?"

Runninghawk sneered. "What's it to you, Yazzie? You've got no stake in this community, no pony in this rodeo. Far as I can tell, you're just along for a handout from your dad."

His gaze traveled up one side of Runninghawk and down the other. The scathing, I'm-going-to-kick-your-butt-if-you-don't-get-out-of-my-face look had defused more than one potential conflict with the Conquistadores and Flores's bunch before it ever had a chance to blow up in his face.

Runninghawk stepped back, his eyes hardening, but he moved on to his next recruit. Leaving Aaron to consider that Runninghawk might be more intelligent than he appeared, wondering why Runninghawk worked so hard to push his buttons.

"I hate him," mumbled Mateo under his breath.

He glanced at the boy, once again engrossed in his game. "You and me both." He straightened, peering over the boy's shoulder at his score. "You're pretty good."

Mateo grunted, but the beginnings of a smile lurked at the corners of his lips. His fingers skimmed over the keypad, zapping an animated Titan-like figure.

"Take that, Runninghawk Dude," chuckled Aaron.

Mateo laughed, a rusty, underutilized sound. "You wanna have a go?"

Aaron raised his brows. "I don't want to mess with your score."

Mateo extended the device, his scrawny arm pushing out from the cuff of his coat. "No problem. Go ahead."

His eyes fixed on a burn mark on the boy's wrist. Following his gaze, Mateo coughed and wrapped his arms around his skinny chest, hiding the mark.

A choking feeling engulfed Aaron, along with a brief bitter memory of his own singed flesh.

"Mateo—"

A basketball shot across the court, missing Aaron's head by inches. He bolted to his feet.

Runninghawk raised both hands. "Sorry, dude. The ball got away from me." He didn't look one bit sorry.

Tossing his coat, Aaron grabbed the ball from Mateo and stalked out onto the court. "You want one-on-one with me, Runninghawk? Game on." He blasted the ball at Runninghawk, whose quick reflexes prevented the ball from making contact with his face.

"Sure, Yazzie." Runninghawk dribbled the ball. "*Hermano a hermano?* I'm game."

"You ain't no brother of mine, Runninghawk."

In a move he'd learned in Basic, Aaron sprinted forward, faked another direction and stole the ball right out from under the cop's nose. He dribbled to the basket for an easy layup.

Gid's crew clapped. Runninghawk's colleagues threatened payback. Runninghawk caught the rebound and dribbled wide of Aaron's perimeter. He hunched over, alert and ready for Runninghawk's next play. Runninghawk, sweat trickling down his pretty boy features, assessed him and future options to score.

With a suddenness that caught him off guard, Runninghawk made a move, weaving past Aaron's defenses, and headed toward the basket.

He planted his feet in Runninghawk's path and allowed him the shot. But feet in place, as Runninghawk surrendered to gravity's downward pull, Aaron twisted his torso, putting a shoulder in Runninghawk's descending stomach.

Runninghawk let out an oomph of air and came down hard. Aaron caught the rebound this time and moved away. Gid's crew whistled. The police officers jeered and urged Runninghawk to exact retribution. Runninghawk panted with the effort to regain his breath.

"Speed. Surprise. Violence of attack in dealing with an opponent." Aaron dribbled around him. "What the military taught me while you chased sorority girls around a college campus."

Runninghawk's mouth flatlined and he lunged. Aaron sidestepped and got off another shot.

He and Runninghawk circled each other, sometimes Runninghawk scoring, sometimes the basket going Aaron's way. One perfectly timed three-point shot from backcourt earned him an elbow in the neck when he returned to earth. The crew hissed Runninghawk. Letting the ball roll out of bounds, Aaron broadened his chest and Runninghawk lowered his head as if to charge.

Gid stormed out of the weight room. "What's going on out here?" He gestured at the cluster of schoolboys ringing the perimeter. "This is supposed to be about teaching them skills, giving them court time, fostering team building, and demonstrating sportsmanlike conduct."

He stepped between the two combatants. "All you two are demonstrating is testosterone." His eyes zeroed in on Runninghawk. "Jace, I expected better from you. You know better."

Implying, Aaron grimaced, he didn't? As if Gid expected nothing better from him?

Fine. Likewise.

But Runninghawk retreated and Aaron swiveled to the bleachers to find Mateo gone.

Runninghawk and Gid divided the remaining boys. The crew and policemen rounded out the teams. Runninghawk tossed Aaron the ball.

"Think you're up to playing by the rules, Yazzie?" He laughed. "Oh, right. My bad. You don't do rules, do you?"

Aaron held the ball against Kailyn's favorite purple—eggplant—T-shirt before propelling it in Runninghawk's direction. "Bring it."

Runninghawk caught the ball in one smooth motion. "Your team's shirtless." He gestured and Aaron apprehended too late he'd been set up. All eyes, including Gid's puzzled ones, rotated to him.

He flushed.

"Unless you got something to hide. Like tats we haven't yet seen."

He tensed. The heavy metal gym doors whooshed behind him.

"Whatcha waiting for, dude? Too shy? Whatcha hiding?"

The boys shuffled their feet on the court. The gym doors clattered shut.

His nostrils flared. "I haven't got anything to hide."

Runninghawk's lips bulged. "Prove it. Or you too ashamed to show some red skin to the brothers?"

Aaron's heart hammered. His hand drifted to the hem of his tee. He broke out in a cold sweat.

Soon everybody would see...Would know...

Aaron lifted his shirt to his belly button. Heels clip-clopped across the wooden floor. A wave of magnolia enveloped his senses. He turned, his fingers locked on the edges of his shirt, as Kailyn strode across the court.

"Husband," she greeted him. "Time for you to come home." The smile she gave him blinded Aaron, like a thousand flashbulbs popping at once.

She locked her fingers behind his neck. "I've been missing you too long today, baby."

Aaron froze. The noise in the background became a distant hum.

Her hand drifted down his back. She smoothed his shirt to his waist and her hand floated upward again. Coming to rest on the fabric covering his scar.

She drew his head toward her upturned face. He gazed into the deep blue sea of her eyes and drowned. His breath mixed with hers.

And she kissed him.

Kissed him failed to describe the sensation when her lips met his. She devoured him.

At first, he was too surprised to respond. But after a split-second hesitation, his arms went up and he pulled closer until the drumbeat of her heart thrummed through her shirt against his chest. His blood roared.

He returned her kiss for kiss, deepening his kiss. Reveling in the petal softness of her mouth. In turn, hungry for her. Ravenous. Starving, waiting his whole life for the touch of her lips on his, the sweetness.

The heat of his desire flamed inside him. His hands drifted down the length of her back, pressing into the contours of her spine. He stifled a groan at the sheer loveliness of her.

Her eyelids fluttered, smoldering blue fire. "Aaron...*mi querido*." Her husky, deep-throated words grazed his earlobe. His heart seized.

Aaron's world slid off it's carefully controlled axis. Rockets blared—actually he became dimly aware the crew stomped and cheered.

When Steve had asked him to protect his witness, Kailyn Eudailey cum Yazzie, he hadn't realized he'd also need to guard his heart.

And despite his reservations, Aaron Yazzie slash Rafael Chavez slash Aaron Matthews arrived at the jolting, sneaking suspicion that, despite his best efforts to safeguard his heart, he'd just kissed the love of his life.

19

Kᴀɪʟʏɴ ᴄᴏᴜʟᴅɴ'ᴛ ʙᴇʟɪᴇᴠᴇ sʜᴇ'ᴅ ᴋɪssᴇᴅ ʜɪᴍ ɪɴ ꜰʀᴏɴᴛ ᴏꜰ Gɪᴅ ᴀɴᴅ ᴡʜᴀᴛ looked like half the male population of the Navajo Nation. An impulse on her part when she perceived Jace taunting him, forcing Aaron to uncover and expose his shame. She'd die before she'd allow anyone to humiliate him.

Not on her watch. Not as long as she had breath in her body. Or a kiss on her lips.

God, how much she loved him.

She broke contact—much to her regret—from Aaron's mouth. She came down off her tiptoes. He refused to let her drift far, however, keeping her in the shelter of his arm.

"That's what I'm talking 'bout," shouted one of the crew.

"Get a room, why don't you?" yelled another, who proceeded to laugh. "Oh, yeah. You two got a whole house, I forgot."

Gid growled at his men. "Are you talking smack about my daughter-in-law?"

The men's eyes widened and they backed off with only a few more snickers. "No, Boss. Sorry, Boss. No disrespect meant, Boss."

Kailyn struggled to catch her breath, willed her heart to steady. From the pounding vein in Aaron's neck, he, too, was apparently having difficulty adjusting to the level of oxygen contained within the gym. Her gaze shifted over to Jace, his eyes narrowed and his face wary.

She stepped out of the circle of Aaron's arms. "Sorry to inter-rupt, guys." She flitted over to Gid and planted a kiss on his leathery cheek. "Would you mind if I stole Aaron away from the game? We need to check Taco out of the clinic."

Gid's face broke into a grin. "Why, of course, honey." He waved his hand. "You two take off. I'll finish this game for Aaron."

Aaron gaped at her.

She tugged him forward. "See you guys later."

He gulped. "Much later."

She trundled him out the door.

The last thing she heard before the gym doors clanged behind her was Gid—in a voice she didn't usually associate with her father-in-law—demanding to know why Jace rode his son so hard. Her eyes cut over to Aaron, already at the truck, and wished he could've heard, too.

She extended the keys. "You want me to drive or you?"

He raked a hand through his hair. "I think maybe you better." He moistened his lips. "Till I recover."

She laughed. "You said you wanted me to make it real."

If he only knew how real...

He stumbled around to the passenger side. Crawling in, he slammed the door shut behind him and studied the toes of his work boots.

"Thanks for..." He gestured at the gym as she pulled onto the highway. "...rescuing me from..." He sighed.

"You're welcome." She lifted her hand off the steering wheel to brush her fingers across the cleft in his chin. "I left some marks of my own behind. All over your face as a matter of fact." She held up her index finger, showing him the smudge of fuchsia-pink lipstick.

Aaron caught her hand and raised it to his lips. "Those marks," his breath whispered across her skin. He kissed her finger. "Feel free to leave anytime."

Her toes curled in her cowgirl boots. "Now who's distracting the driver?"

Aaron laughed. And she imagined something in his face more at ease, less defensive, than she'd ever seen him.

Ten minutes later, she veered into the clinic parking lot. He was out of the truck and around to her side before she had the chance to turn off the engine. He swept the door open with a flourish. She hopped down to find herself blocked by his body.

Her gaze flickered between his face and the clinic. "What're you doing?"

Aaron broadened his chest. "I believe in finishing what I started. Do you?"

She stroked the turquoise cross at her throat. "What do you mean?"

Aaron leaned closer. "Thought you might want to get the rest of your lipstick off my face." He gave her a lopsided smile. "The fun way."

"Here?" She eyed the people entering and exiting the building. "In front of Shiprock?"

"Didn't notice you had a particular problem with public displays of affection." Aaron placed his hands on either side of her waist.

"Affection...?" She applied a little extra drawl just for the fun of seeing his eyes go opaque.

He let out a gush of air. "For the love of sweet tea, Kailyn. Public places are about all I can handle with you. Safer."

Aaron's lips teased at her earlobe, explored the hollows of her throat above the cross. And he proceeded to kiss her thoroughly. And satisfactorily.

Five delicious minutes later, she came up for air. "Safer for whom? You or me?"

Indecision warred across his features. The light in his eyes struggled to break free of a sliver of panic.

Like Taco, one step forward, two steps back with this man.

Patience. Go slow, she reminded herself. She released him.

And was rewarded when he held on to her.

"Why else do you think I spend so much time away from home these days?"

He gave her a quick peck on the tip of her nose. And a grudging smile. "We'd best spring Taco, but..."

Another smile, this time the light winning over panic. "We need to talk tonight."

She nodded.

Once inside, he squeezed her hand. They listened as a tech went over further home treatment. Taco hobbled toward them, his tiny head bobbing. He licked their faces and scanned the crowded reception area with his head lifted—despite the cone—like a conquering hero.

Aaron carried Taco out to the truck. He settled the dog and strapped Taco in securely. She tossed Aaron the keys.

"You drive." She inched into the seat next to Taco. "I've got to give my brave, brave boy some much-deserved loving."

Aaron strutted around to the driver's side. Throwing open the door, he slid behind the wheel. He thumped his chest. "Only because this brave, brave boy has already got his."

He paused, made sure she observed his grin. "For today."

She made sure he saw her roll her eyes before she nuzzled her nose in Taco's pompadour. Taco made a sound somewhere between a cat's purr and a dying carburetor. She cut her eyes over to Aaron.

His lips twitched. He ruffled Taco's 'do. "I know 'xactly what you mean, little man. Me, too."

Cloud shadows drifted across the mesa, rippling over the wind-carved canyons. They pulled into the yard to find Willa's small compact sedan parked under the juniper. Kailyn bounced in the seat. "Oh, my friend from the shelter. She said she might stop by. The girls made us some Diné-inspired Christmas ornaments for the tree."

She unharnessed Taco. They exited the vehicle and approached the house.

At the sound of their arrival, *Shinali* emerged from the house onto the porch. Followed by Jace.

Behind Jace, Willa stepped out into the waning afternoon light. Taco in her arms, Kailyn strode forward, a smile of welcome on her lips.

When she beheld Aaron's face, Kailyn froze.

Shock, confusion, and something she couldn't decipher dawned across his high-planed features. He made a strangled sound in the back of his throat.

Willa's eyes enlarged. "Rafe...?" She ducked around Jace and hurried down the steps. "Is it you? Really you?"

Aaron covered the distance between them in two strides and swept her into his arms. "Willa?"

The look on his face...

Kailyn reeled. She'd never seen him come close to tears before. Not when Taco was hurt. Or when Steve died in his arms.

But as he clutched Willa to his chest, moisture like dew on a saguaro trembled on the edges of his eyes. Like joy rediscovered. Like someone who'd been lost and now found.

Like someone who'd reached home after a long, painful journey.

Willa's eyes filled with tears. "I recognized the cross, but I never dreamed Kailyn's husband and Rafe were the same." She buried her face into his strong arms and wept.

He stroked the top of Willa's shiny black hair, whispering into her ear.

And something shattered like exquisite crystal inside Kailyn, a sound discernible only to her. As her heart broke into a million, irreparable pieces.

Other sounds receded. She found it difficult to breathe, as if all the oxygen in the world had been sucked out by some giant tornado, starting with her lungs. She became aware someone, *Shinali*, tugged at her elbow.

The old woman's sharp eyes darkened with concern. Kailyn returned to reality to observe Aaron's arm twined around Willa—holding her up. The pair of them hobbled across the yard toward the truck. Aaron helped Willa into the passenger side.

Into Kailyn's seat.

Jace remained, one foot braced on the second step, the other on the bottom as if paralyzed momentarily in the act of setting foot on the ground. His face...like a storm cloud brewing above the mesa.

She realized, belatedly, that Grandmother spoke to her, had been speaking to her. In Kailyn's distraction, Grandmother had actually removed Taco from her arms. She dragged her attention from the truck, taking everything she'd been so stupid to hope for away toward the highway.

"Granddaughter…" *Shinali* repeated. She pressed Kailyn's elbow and urged her toward the porch. "I didn't realize my grandson knew her from that long-ago time."

Jace staggered as they passed him on the steps, as if he'd been mortally wounded, but didn't have enough sense to know he was dying, already as dead as she felt inside.

"They need to talk. To catch up." Grandmother threw Jace an anxious glance. "They will return." Her eyes cut to the cloud of dust hanging in their departure.

Jace's countenance was a mirror reflection of her emotions. It hurt her to look at him. The anger. The vulnerability. The deer-in-the-headlights shock.

"I left my vehicle at Willa's. I guess I should return her car and retrieve mine." His face hardened. "I'm not waiting around any longer."

"Don't jump to conclusions." Grandmother turned to her. "You, either. This is an area we don't yet understand. And gray areas must be pray areas first and foremost."

"Three years I've courted Willa Littlefeather. Half the time she wouldn't give me the time of day. These last months I'd hoped…" He swallowed. "I've cajoled. I've not been too proud to beg her to give us a chance. But something always held her back, something from her past."

He gave a short, bitter laugh. "Well, now I know why. Or should I say who?"

Grandmother reached for him. "Allow this adversity to grow your trust in the True God." She glanced at Kailyn. "At such a time, you both must walk in the comfort of His Presence, in the strength of His wisdom. Now is the time to wait for Him to act. Put your trust in Him."

Jace scowled. "I wait much longer, Kailyn and I both will be left in the cold." He stalked away.

"Granddaughter—"

"*Shinali*," she squeezed her eyelids tight. "I'd prefer to be alone now, if you don't mind."

Taco nudged her hand. Inside, she gave Taco his medicine, refilled his water bowl, and washed the dishes. As the kitchen clock ticked past nine, she swept the porch in the dark, spoiling for a fight with those glow-green monsters.

Her gaze roamed the living room from the handmade pottery *Shinali*'s friends had given them as newlyweds, to the worn leather ottoman in front of the armchair in which Aaron carved his animals, to the colorful small rugs hanging on the burnt-orange walls they'd painted together one Saturday.

When eleven o'clock came and went, she discovered the box of Christmas ornaments Willa left behind and decorated the tree with the beautifully crafted cloth and paper Navajo Grandmas, *Shimas*, and children. Many of the figures wore tiny strands of turquoise chips around their necks. And she took comfort in the girls' attempt to show their love.

At midnight, she grabbed the Navajo Cross quilt she'd made and tucked it around herself on the brown suede couch. At one a.m., headlights jounced along the rutted dirt road leading to the house. And suddenly, she dreaded him walking through the door. Dreaded what he'd say. Feared there'd be no going back after his revelations.

The porch steps creaked. The front door squeaked open. He bounded in, his step lighter than she'd ever seen. His shoulders broad and straight as if the burdens of a lifetime had been removed. He stopped, stock-still in the middle of the room, when he became aware of her presence.

He sighed, a long drawn-out trickle of air between those sensuous lips she knew would never kiss hers again. The tears, for the first time in this long, lonely evening, threatened to undo her. She dropped her eyes to the quilt, tracing the turquoise cross in the center of one of the blocks with her finger.

She mustn't, couldn't, wouldn't cry. Not now. She clamped her lips together.

"We need to talk."

But this time, so not the words she wanted to hear.

"I need to explain things to you."

"You don't have to explain yourself to me." She jabbed her fingernail into the palm of her hand, pleased with how even her tone came out.

He dropped onto the sofa, next to her. "I want you to understand."

Afraid she understood all too well, she drew up her legs, wrapping her arms around them, and rested her chin on her knees.

"When I was five, Gid and my mom divorced. She took a job, looking for a better life, off the Rez in Albuquerque. When I was six, she married my stepfather and instead found a nightmare." He stared out the picture window into the darkness. "For three years, she suffered indignities and cruelties of which I wouldn't begin to burden you."

His hands balled into fists. "My stepfather kept us isolated and friendless. I didn't go to school. He was a powerful man in the community. And there was no one we believed we could turn to for help. I've spent my life making sure I never feel as helpless again."

Aaron clenched and unclenched his hands. "He had a special hatred for Indians. Part of the beatings included rants on dirty, no-good Injun dung like ourselves. We lived on pins and needles, never sure in what mood he'd return from his job."

"He drank like Gid?" she whispered.

Aaron laughed, nothing funny in the sound. "Actually, no. Just chain-smoked. Been there, done that. My mom at first believed she'd found Gid's polar opposite." He snorted. "In more horrific ways than she could've ever imagined."

"Why didn't you go to the police?"

He blinked. "Oh, didn't I tell you? My stepfather was a cop."

And suddenly things she'd failed to understand before clicked into place. Like his refusal, once they discovered Whitten's betrayal, of going to the authorities for help. As a boy, he'd relied on his own resources. As a man, he'd reverted to form.

"When I was nine, he came home one day in a rage. Took off his belt..." His hands gripped his knees.

She scooted out of the quilt and caressed the scar on his back. His ragged breathing slowed.

He swallowed. "Afterward, he started in on my mom. When he'd run out of steam, he fell asleep." Aaron shook his head. "To this day, I don't know how she did it, but she managed to get us out of the house. I remember being in the yard when he awoke with a roar to find us missing. He chased us down the block, into the street."

"Where were you going?"

He cocked his head. "I'm not sure. There was another cop, not his buddy but from a division other than Vice, who lived at the end of our oh-so-respectable working-class neighborhood. I've always wondered if she was headed there. If she believed once he beheld her bruises...I was bleeding..." He gritted his teeth and Kailyn hugged his arm, willing him strength.

"Instead, we stepped out into the path of a delivery truck. Mom shoved me out of the way. She didn't make it. She bled out on the sidewalk while a neighbor called 911. With her last breath, she told me to run."

Kailyn wove her fingers into his.

"I've also wondered if..." His voice broke. "If she deliberately hesitated, wanted the truck to hit her and end the pain."

Kailyn took his face in her hands. "I don't believe that. She loved you, and she wouldn't have left you alone in your stepfather's clutches."

Aaron heaved a deep, shuddering sigh. "That's what Nancy used to say, too."

"What happened to your stepfather?"

"He hung back, tried to play the bereaved spouse, but the other cop had seen my back and the burns on my mother's—" Aaron clamped his lips together.

"Where did you go?"

A muscle jerked in his cheek. "As far away as I could go. Found myself a few hours later in the barrio section of town. Where Willa discovered me. She was thirteen."

Kailyn's heart thudded. "You were nine?"

"I endured physical and emotional abuse at the hands of my stepfather. But I've always been grateful it wasn't something more."

He swallowed. "Not the soul-shattering abuse Willa endured. That would've been…"

He sighed. "Do you know what happened to Willa when she was nine?"

Kailyn shook her head.

"When Willa was nine, her mother sold her to a man in Albuquerque to get cash for her next crack fix."

Kailyn lowered her eyes.

"When Willa was eleven, the man and his friends tired of her so they sold her to a pimp who specialized in preteen Navajo girls."

She bit her lip.

"When she was thirteen, by chance she met the local Conquistadores leader, Emilio Sanchez. He was only seventeen, but he kidnapped her from her pimp, brought her to live with him."

"So Willa exchanged one form of slavery for another."

"No, in his way, Emilio loved her. Took care of her."

"And when she found you?"

"She did her best to stop the bleeding. She convinced Emilio I was her long-lost cousin"—he caught her eye—"told me my name was now Rafael Chavez. Because Indians weren't any more highly regarded in the barrio than with my stepfather."

"So you became Rafe Chavez."

"Aaron Yazzie disappeared, although I later learned from Steve that my grandmother arrived in Albuquerque demanding they locate her lost grandson. Everyone assumed my stepfather had disposed of me one way or the other. Like Willa's mother or in a shallow grave somewhere in the vast desert stretches of the state. He went to prison."

"But you knew none of this and stayed with the gang."

He shrugged. "I was happy with them. They protected me, fed me, clothed me. This is why I fit in so well with them, even now undercover. I understand the draw so many kids feel for the gangs, whether they be Anglo, black, Latino, or Native. They're a family. A family most of us never had. Our identity."

"How long were you with them?" She took a breath. "With Willa?"

"I was their little mascot for two years." He displayed the Conquistadores tat on his hand. "Marked as one of them."

"But...?"

"But when I turned eleven, Emilio started making noises about proving my loyalty. He couldn't justify any longer to the other members why I was kept batted in sheep's wool away from the harsher realities of the enterprises keeping them in cash."

She closed her eyes. She'd read about the brutal gang initiations.

"Willa kept my nose clean—literally—from sampling the merchandise, saved me from becoming a crackhead like her mom. But she couldn't save me forever from the tests of loyalty. I'd witnessed initiations. I understood what was expected."

His shoulders slumped. "And ready to follow through with whatever my brothers expected from me. But Willa made an anonymous phone call to the Gang Task Force, of which Steve Matthews was a member. Ratted out the Conquistadores. Made sure narcotics would be found when they busted in."

"What happened?"

"In the shootout, Emilio died in the crossfire. The rest of us were rounded up. I was the only juvie without a record. Without any proof of existence in the system. Child Services, Nancy Matthews, waited at the station to take me into custody. She and Steve... You know the rest."

What she knew was there was a bond between Aaron Yazzie and Willa Littlefeather that could never be broken. A world of their own, set apart, none but they would ever understand.

Aaron—the one Willa mentioned being in love with so long ago.

"I never saw her again until this afternoon." He grimaced. "Tried not to imagine she might've been forced to practice her old trade again."

"But unbeknownst to us, Willa used to sneak away from the barrio and had befriended this elderly nun. Sister Mary Theresa." A smile lit his face and traveled to his eyes. "The Sister fostered Willa and established a halfway house for others like Willa. A second chance. A brand-new ministry, Willa described it, at the twilight of the good woman's life."

"Streams of life-giving water in the desert wasteland." Kailyn nodded. "A ministry Willa has made her life mission as well."

"It's more than I could've ever dreamed possible. Hoped for Willa."

Kailyn edged away from him. "God's grace."

Willa deserved all the happiness in the world.

As did Aaron.

His brow crinkled. "Grace...?" Aaron tilted his head. "I guess you might be right."

She hadn't been right about anything in a long time. Now this? But she knew, in her heart, Willa possessed the attributes she herself lacked. The skills, the personal and professional experience, to be all Aaron needed to fill the hole in his life.

For healing. To lead him to the truth of the Shepherd of his soul. To become everything the Creator intended for Aaron from the beginning.

Leaving him the quilt, Kailyn padded down the hall. And shut the door softly on Aaron Yazzie and her dreams.

20

THE NEXT MORNING, KAILYN AROSE TO FIND AARON EXAMINING THE ORNA-ments on the tree. He jolted at her footfalls on the wooden floor. He brushed a hand over the top of his head before jamming his hand in the pocket of his jeans.

She'd cried herself to sleep. One look in the mirror at her bruised eyes and she'd shoveled the makeup on in spades to cover the telltale signs of her distress.

Aaron, on the other hand, looked cheerier than she'd ever seen him. As if he'd shed years of secrets like water off a lizard's back.

"The coffee will be ready in just—"

"Don't bother."

She halted mid-stride into the kitchen.

He ran his tongue across his bottom teeth and shuffled his feet. "I called Gid to pick me up early today." His eyes dropped to the floor. "Lots of errands."

Tires spun gravel. He jerked toward the window. "He's here. Great—I mean, I'll see you…"

She swallowed past the lump in her throat. "You'll see me when you see me. Got it."

A flash of white, even teeth and he had bolted—yeah, that was the right word—out the door.

No sharing of coffee—or the sunrise—over the next few days either. He left early. He returned late. After dinner.

A fact not lost on her. Disconsolate one afternoon, she drifted toward the hogan where *Shinali* spent a great deal of time working on a custom rug.

"Come in," Delores barked at Kailyn's knock.

She waved Kailyn over to the stool next to the cast iron stove. "Wind's picking up. Probably get a cold spell before long. Warm up while I work on this rug for my favorite newlyweds."

The old woman lifted the treadle rod and thrust the batten through the warp to hold it open. "Two hundred hours of work for a small rug. My wedding present to you. It'll be ready by Valentine's."

Whereupon Kailyn burst into tears and buried her face in her hands. "He loves Willa, *Shinali*, not me."

"Not true." The old woman paused. "He's had a curveball thrown at him. But I've seen the way his eyes follow you everywhere."

Kailyn shook her head. "His eyes follow me because it's his job. Surveillance to keep his witness saf—" She clapped a hand over her mouth.

Delores cocked her head.

"I mean…"

Delores smiled. "I've known since the first day that you two weren't married. Figured it had something to do with an FBI case."

"How…?"

Delores flexed her fingers. "Confirmed when your first morning on the Rez you bought an extra pair of sheets from your favorite store. What newlywed couple needs sheets for the spare bedroom?"

Kailyn flushed.

The old woman returned to her weaving. The silence lengthened. Not an uncomfortable one. Delores giving her room to decide whether or not to trust her with the rest of the story.

She took a deep breath. "I never wanted to lie to you, *Shinali*. Aaron either. Being here has been the most wonderful…" She gulped past the boulder lodged in her throat. "You've been the grandmother I always…"

"Ayóó ánííníshní. I love you, Granddaughter. For yourself. That will not change no matter what you tell me."

Lips trembling, Kailyn detailed the events of her first encounter with Aaron, her friendship with Gabriela Flores, and Gaby's murder. When she spoke of Steve Matthews's death, Delores's shoulders slumped.

"A good, decent man. My grandson...He's lost so much already." The old woman, for the first time in Kailyn's acquaintance with her, manifested every one of her seventy years.

Kailyn, hardly pausing to draw breath, related the rest of the harrowing, on-the-run events of the last few months. "So you can see why Aaron was forced into creating this fake relationship with me."

It was important that Delores understand and not blame Aaron or in any way damage her relationship with her grandson. "I'm Steve's witness. He feels a tremendous obligation—"

"Poppycock."

"What did you—?"

Delores lifted her chin. "You think you Anglos are the only ones who watch PBS?"

Kailyn blinked at her.

"And I'm not buying marriage was the only option my grandson could come up with." She snorted. "Freudian slip, more like it."

"Freudian—?"

"I read." Delores rolled her eyes. "You're not the only one with a library card, either, wife of my grandson."

Kailyn's eyes fell to her shoes. "I'm not really his wife. It's just my fake ID."

"I'm not buying the fake relationship part." Delores crossed her arms. "I've seen you two together. My boy adores you."

Kailyn bit her lip. "You saw his face when he found Willa." She held back tears. "Jace knows..."

"Don't go mortgaging the sheep farm on anything he says on the matter. The both of you are too close to the situation, too invested to be objective."

Kailyn laced her hands together. "Doesn't take a rocket scientist to figure out from their reaction to each other and the amount of time they've spent together over the last few days where this is headed."

The old woman leaned over, placed a hand on the frame of the loom, and hoisted herself to her feet. "When my grandson was small, he was the sunniest, happiest child I ever knew. My husband, alive then, tried to fill the place my son was unable—"

Delores bit her lip. "My grandson followed his paternal grandfather everywhere. Learned to track, read the signs of the weather, gauge the changes in the wind."

She sighed. "Next time I see my grandson he'd been rescued by the Matthewses. Gone forever the sweet, gentle boy. In his place, this sullen, angry street kid I didn't know. I couldn't reach past his emotional barricades."

Delores shuffled toward Kailyn and draped an arm around her. "With you, I've glimpsed traces of the boy he was once. And I've been praying on this since you bought those sheets."

She placed her thumb and forefinger on Kailyn's chin. "You and my grandson give each other balance and harmony, *hozhq*."

Delores gazed deep into Kailyn's eyes. "You help each other to walk in beauty. You love him, do you not?"

Kailyn's eyes welled with tears. She nodded. "So much, *Shinali*. But unlike you, I'm not convinced, in the end, that Willa might not be better for him."

"I encourage you, my granddaughter, to go to the Source of your strength, to the Shepherd of your soul and seek His counsel. For His will to be done in both your lives."

Delores cupped her cheek. "Place your hope and faith in Him, not in anything or anyone else. Do not hide your pain from Him."

Shinali sighed. "Here's the life lesson I've learned from following the sheep. Despite what the sheep mean to our culture, sheep are essentially stupid creatures. Like me, easily spooked, weak, prone to wander. Prey. And they, like humans, were never meant to be load-bearing animals."

Delores patted Kailyn's cheek. "Oh, my granddaughter. This hard lesson I learned, a lesson we must each learn. A lesson I pray my grandson will someday learn. It's the Shepherd who carries the sheep, the lambs, in His arms in their difficulty. Not the other way around. In His arms, place your dreams. Let go of your plans and understanding. Because in the end, no man will ever satisfy if first your heart isn't right with your Creator."

Kailyn closed her eyes. "I'll try, *Shinali*. I will try."

But to Kailyn, her prayers bounced off the ceiling of the turquoise sky. Drifted and dissipated like the cloud shadows across the landscape of her heart.

After several days of silence under her belt, Kailyn had had enough. She'd move out of the house into a hotel room off the Rez.

It wasn't like she was his real wife, she scolded. For the hundredth time in an hour. Wasn't like he'd actually betrayed her.

After working herself into a fine yucca soap lather, she stewed through her shift at the fabric store and resolved to confront him about her relocation status. She'd visit the construction site, persuade Gid to grant them an early lunch, and have her say.

But Gid's truck wasn't among the vehicles clustered along the road next to the string of tribal houses the crew had erected. Hammers pounding, drills buzzing, she picked her way among the stacks of two-by-fours toward where Gid studied a blueprint.

"Where's Aaron, Gid?"

No response. He trained his focus on the blueprints.

She frowned. "If you'd direct me to where he's working today, I want to take him for an early lunch."

Gid rattled the paper in his hands. Didn't make eye contact. The background noise quieted.

She glanced around. "Where…?"

Heads down, eyes averted, the crew busied themselves studying the tools in their hands.

If you waited long enough…

She'd learned the trick from Aaron. Most people hated silence. Would say anything to fill the void. Less effective among the taciturn Diné, but she figured worth a shot.

Gid cleared his throat.

Kailyn raised her eyebrows.

"Sorry you missed him. He took my truck. Had errands." Gid coughed. "He said."

Kailyn folded her arms, shifting her weight. "I'm sorry to have bothered you."

Gid's dark eyes implored. "Kailyn..."

She marched toward the truck without a backward glance.

Two guesses where Aaron Yazzie roosted at this hour of the workday. And the first one didn't count.

Seized with an impulse, she pointed the truck toward Grace House. And discovered Gid's truck parked in its driveway.

Which served to further fire her Southern dander.

Long lost love—be that as it may—but highly inappropriate in front of the girls, she fumed shifting the truck into Park. Until she remembered that, at this hour, the girls were most likely in school.

And then her nerve deserted her. She wrested the gear into Drive and headed toward home instead. All the way there, she staved off the tears and counted on one hand her true friends.

CeCe—whom she'd never see again. Erin Silverhorn—whom she'd soon never lay eyes on again. She refused to drag Delores and Gid into what for them would be a conflict of interest. And Burke— her only friend in New Mexico.

Aaron returned home—albeit bedtime—to announce he planned to mail the microchip himself from Albuquerque. Taco pranced, delighted to see his best human bud any hour of the day or night.

More fool he.

He frowned when silence met his declaration. "What's wrong?"

She tightened her jaw. "Why, whatever makes you think something might be wrong?"

His eyes narrowed. "When you get that tone..."

She flounced toward the kitchen. "I do not have a tone."

"Yes, you do. Probably learned at your grandmother's knee. Snippy, imperious—"

She popped her head into the living room. "You keep my grandmother out of this." She jabbed a finger in the air. "And I'm nothing like my grandmother." She sniffed. "Just shows how little you know."

His face scrunched and he stared at her. Stared till she slammed the bedroom door behind her.

She awoke to an empty house the next morning. Aaron gone. The day went from bad to worse. She overcharged one customer, undercharged another. She almost dropped an open rotary cutter on her supervisor's stockinged, sandaled foot.

Hoping to console herself with a cup of coffee with her favorite volunteer, she ventured to the library. Burke, however, was in absentia. So she blew half her paycheck at her favorite discount store—just because she could—and stopped by Dairy Queen to indulge in a caloric brand of self-pity.

She returned home to find Gid and Delores huddled on the porch of her house—Aaron Yazzie's house—deep in conversation about her and him. She knew this because both their heads snapped up at the sound of the truck and their mouths clamped shut. She allowed the engine to idle, parking beside Gid's truck.

Gid's truck? She'd assumed Aaron... She set her mouth and got out.

She'd no sooner invited them inside when another vehicle approached.

"It's Jace," Gid called from the front room.

She and Delores joined him at the window, watching the SUV roll to a stop. Jace threw open the door, and stormed the steps.

"Look out," Delores murmured. "Here comes trouble."

"Where's that Conquistadores snake? That lowlife scum?" The door slammed in his wake.

Kailyn bristled. "Who do you think you are, busting in here, talking about my—?"

Gid reared. "He's in Albuquerque on business."

Jace's eyes boggled. "Albu—?" he sputtered. He slapped his hand on his khaki-clad thigh. "I don't believe this. When the weekend houseparents told me Willa had suddenly gone to Albuquerque today, I..."

She slumped against her sewing table.

Delores took hold of her arm. "Granddaughter."

She shook her off. "I think it'd be best if everyone left." She pointed at the door. "Now." She swallowed. "Please."

Gid and Delores exchanged glances. They moved toward the door. Jace looked stricken.

"I didn't realize, Kay. I'm sorry. They said she received an emergency call."

"What made you assume she'd be with him?"

"Because I checked the construction site first. One of the crew mentioned Aaron left in a red sedan. A sedan descriptive of Willa's."

"Whatever they do..." She tossed her hair. "They don't make a habit of coming here."

He crossed the distance separating them. "He's poison, Kay. God alone knows what he's up to." He clenched his fists. "Using you. Possibly dragging Willa into the underworld from which she barely escaped with her life years ago."

"It's not like that, Jace. He's not the man you think he is."

He peered into her face. "Are you sure? We've suspected Flores had Conquistadores connections for years. This Flores dude is into stuff, aided and abetted by our own criminal element, that'd peel your skin."

Jace snorted. "Actually peel your skin if you fell into his hands. And the men with whom he surrounds himself worse than him."

"You don't know what you're talking about. Believe me."

He grasped her forearms. "I believe you. It's him I don't believe. He's using you as a cover. For his own nefarious ends. I know men like him. I've hunted and jailed men like him."

She pulled, but Jace held her in a grip of steel.

"Despite your jaw-dropping kiss the other day, I know something isn't right with the two of you."

Her eyes darted away. She moistened her bottom lip with her tongue.

"Give me something to go on, Kailyn. You're in over your head with him. So's Willa," his voice faltered.

"You've got to come clean with me. Help me stop him before he hurts someone else. I'm your only friend here on the Rez. The best friend you've got. Trust me."

Trust?

She'd trusted Aaron and look where it landed her. Smack in the middle of a desert. She didn't speak the language. Miles from safety.

Her heart broken into pieces.

Was Jace correct in his estimation of Aaron? He'd told her himself of the difficulty of getting out of the gang lifestyle once in. Had Aaron been working both sides against the middle? Conspiring to land her right where Flores could most easily make her disappear?

Who was the real Aaron? Rafe Chavez, cartel thug? Aaron Matthews, grieving son?

Or Aaron Yazzie, her husband?

"Kailyn..."

She wrenched free.

Aaron was doing his best to protect her until the trial. He'd sworn an oath to the man to whom he owed everything. Aaron had no inkling he'd reunite with the love of his life when they'd begun this life-and-death game of hide and seek.

He couldn't be blamed for how he felt about Willa.

About how he didn't feel for Kailyn.

Despite her feelings of betrayal on a personal level, she'd never betray him. Who was to say, as Aaron insisted, Jace Runninghawk wasn't a Flores stooge?

"I've said everything I've got to say to you, Jace. I asked you to leave. Don't make me ask again."

Grinding his teeth, he stalked out the door. His engine revved. Kailyn slid down the wall to the floor.

And sobbed for all she'd lost. All that had never truly been hers. Never would be hers.

Burke telephoned the next morning before she left for work. Apologized for missing her at the library. Asked her if he could get a rain check at the coffee shop after her shift.

Like a lifeline, she accepted his offer and hurried through her morning. Thankfully, sans sharp potential weapons in regard to herself and her coworkers. Jace arrived during her shift. He waited for her to finish with a customer. She ignored him.

Went out of her way to dawdle over another customer's fabric indecision. She had nothing to say to him. And if he believed harassment worked on her, he failed to take into account her years under Carole Eudailey's emotional blitzkrieg. He finally left.

She held her breath later as she got off work, afraid Jace lay in wait. But he was nowhere to be seen. Relieved, she headed for her date with Burke.

Arriving at the always-crowded diner, she parked in the overflow lot behind the restaurant. Grateful she'd managed to snag the last available booth, she slid across the cracked vinyl cushion and waited another ten minutes for Burke.

He breezed in, his Stetson in his hand, apologizing for keeping her waiting. "Truck delivery went awry."

She fluttered her hand and gestured for him to sit across from her. "I took the liberty of ordering coffee for us." She stuffed the menu between the syrup bottle and mustard. She hadn't felt like eating all week.

He laid his hat beside him on the seat. He winked. "Won't be as good as the stuff you brew."

She sighed. "Mr. Burke, you do know how to tell a girl what she needs to hear."

He leaned forward, steepling his hands on the laminate tabletop. "Something got you in the dumps, gal?" He frowned. "Your husband's still treating you right, isn't he?" He growled. "'Cause I got horsewhips that'd soon put that 'un to rights."

She winced, but forced a smile. "What did you say about a truck delivery?"

The waitress returned, depositing their tea and coffee mugs in front of them.

Burke took a swallow. "It's how I made my money. In the trucking business till I retired and bought the ranch."

She reached for several packets of stevia. "I thought you'd always owned the ranch."

"Nope." He studied the menu. "But I kept a few trucks. Just to keep my hand in. Nothing like an open road before you and the wind in your face."

"What do you ship?"

He tapped his finger against the plastic-coated menu and signaled to the waitress. "A variety of products. Whatever I'm hired to transport."

The waitress approached, pad in hand.

He underscored the ham and egg platter. "Out too early for breakfast this morning. Glad you folks serve breakfast all day."

Kailyn declined to order. In between bites, Burke entertained her with stories of the latest escapades of the filly he was in the process of breaking. She managed to laugh in all the right places, surprised to discover he'd also coaxed her into eating one of his toast triangles. She leaned back, as relaxed as she'd been in days. A friend was, indeed, exactly what she'd been needing.

After he'd eaten his fill, Burke snagged the bill before she could grab it.

"Mr. Burke," she protested.

He wagged his finger. "Now who else has this old man got to spend his money on if not a beautiful woman?"

She patted his arm. "You're a dear."

"I mean it about the horsewhip, young lady." Burke's ice-blue eyes bored into hers. "If he's stepping out on you, I know how to deal with his kind. I'll not tolerate any man treating a good woman like trash."

His brow furrowed. "Like the pain my mama endured when my father abandoned her for a pueblo whore."

She forced a smile onto her face. "No worries, Mr. Burke. God's got everything under control."

Burke's nose wrinkled, but he shrugged and heaved himself upward to pay the bill with the cashier.

And she repeated her last statement over again. To convince herself and to shore up her own faltering faith.

Halfway between Shiprock and Blue Corn Springs, Kailyn detected a noise she couldn't identify. She tilted her head to listen.

There again. A rattling sound.

She glanced to the left and right, noting only steep canyon walls. "Great, the middle of nowhere and engine trouble."

Nobody on the road ahead. No one in back. Not a house or gas station or anything for miles.

She switched off the radio. At movement on the floorboards, instinctively, her foot retracted. Something slithered across her left boot. The hair rose on the nape of her neck.

Kailyn's heart skipped a beat.

Her right foot descended toward the brake, another automatic response. A hissing. More rattling.

Kailyn's eyes darted between the spokes of the steering wheel and she froze.

21

A COILED VIPER ARCHED ITS TRIANGULAR-SHAPED HEAD. ITS RED-FORKED tongue flicked out. Black and white diamond scales lined its skin. A series of raccoon rings encircled its rattling tail.

Kailyn's eyes widened, her foot poised mid-air. Gripping the wheel, she allowed the truck to decelerate. Her eyes darted from the empty stretch of road to the serpent at her feet.

Shivers of fear crawled up her arms. "Jesus..."

Her palms slick, she remembered the cell phone she'd plopped on the seat beside her. Oh so carefully, afraid to breathe, she removed one hand from the wheel. She groped for the phone. The snake wound its length around her boot.

She shrank against the seat, but her first order of business was to stop the vehicle.

Kailyn weighed her options. Should she allow the truck to drift off the highway to careen into the adjacent irrigation ditch and risk the rattlesnake striking when she applied the brake? One glance at the speedometer left her hesitant to try her first inclination. After crashing, she'd be rendered helpless and she visualized the reptile slithering and repeatedly striking her unconscious body.

She shuddered and froze when the snake, sensing her muscle movement, stirred. And thoughts of applying the brake flew out of her mind. Perspiration trickled down her neck.

Her hand shaking—*God, don't let me drop the phone*—she hit the redial button, trying to recall the last person she'd dialed or texted.

Aaron's number flashed on the screen as the call rolled over to voice mail. Her mouth quavered at the sound of his voice, but she whispered her predicament, gave her location, and ended the call with no hope of finding him this side of the state capital. She scrolled through her directory to Jace Runninghawk.

He picked up on the first ring. "Why are you slowing?"

"What?"

She glanced in the rearview mirror and observed his SUV rounding the canyon wall half a mile back. "You're following me?" But instead of chagrin, an enormous sense of relief flooded over her.

"What's going on, Kailyn? What's wrong?"

She hit the highlights of her dire situation.

"First thing you have to do is stay calm. Don't panic."

"Don't panic?" she shrieked and regretted it when the snake bumped against her foot.

"Take some deep breaths and describe the snake to me."

"Is this really necessary?" She cradled the phone between her ear and neck. "It's rattling. What further info do you need?"

"Turn on the AC."

"Why?"

She watched him gun his engine as his vehicle ate up the distance between them.

"Are you this much trouble to your husband?"

"Yeah, usually."

"Cold-blooded creatures, snakes, seek out warm places."

"Like my truck?"

"Probably got in somehow without you knowing, seeking the radiant heat of your engine. If you turn on the AC, the snake just might quiet down, go into hibernation mode."

"Just might?" she squeaked. "Does this actually work or are you making this up as you go along?"

"You've got to stop the truck before I can help you. Short of hypnotizing the thing into a trance, you're going to have to lull the snake before you hit the brakes. Trust me, Kailyn."

Trust? She almost snorted. Would've laughed out loud had she not been so terrified.

"Okay. Here goes nothing."

She dropped the phone on the seat to reach for the AC. She vented the air toward the floorboard. The rattling gradually subsided. Running parallel with her, Jace made a motion for her to retrieve her discarded phone. With bated breath, she complied, wedging the phone between her shoulder and ear.

Kailyn murmured a prayer between chattering teeth as the frigid air enveloped the truck. After detecting no further movement for a good five minutes—perhaps the longest of her life—she screwed up her courage and edged her foot millimeter by millimeter toward the brake.

Holding her breath, her boot descended and came to rest on the brake pedal. Gingerly, timidly, gently. She prayed no portion of the snake lay underneath the pedal to be vexed into an attack.

"Ease off the road," he coaxed in her ear.

She allowed the truck to coast on the shoulder and come to a complete stop. Out of his car and next to hers in seconds, he pressed the phone against his ear. She shifted to park.

"I'm going to open the passenger door."

Kailyn's eyes rounded. "But what about me over here?"

His gaze fastened onto hers. "I'm getting in on the other side, Kay, to pull you across the seat. I'm afraid if I open the driver-side door, the snake might…" He moved out of her view. The handle clicked.

"Jace…" She fought the hysterical note threading her voice.

"Hang on, Kay. When I say the word, lift both your legs as high and fast as you can. Let me do the rest."

Kailyn's hands white-knuckled the wheel.

"You're going to have to let go and trust me, Kay. Can you do that? Will you do that?"

Trembling, she pried one finger at a time off the wheel. She bit her lip.

"Okay," she whispered.

The upholstery creaked as he braced his weight against it. His shadow fell across her, blocking the early afternoon sun. "Now, Kay." He pounced.

She jerked and scrambled. His arms went tight around her waist and he dragged her across to the other side. Out of harm's way, into the sunlight.

The snake, open-fanged, darted upward.

Jace walloped the door shut with the heel of his boot. Her knees buckled and Kailyn collapsed into his arms. They hung on to each other, panting.

"You saved my life."

His eyes were big, black pools. His face paled.

"You weren't afraid, were you?"

He hugged her. "You were right." He sagged. "I was making it up as I went along."

She laughed.

Neither one of them heard the other vehicle drive up. Or the slam of a door.

"Get your hands off my wife, Runninghawk."

Swiveling, she found Aaron gripping a shovel, his face suffused with fury.

Gid exited the truck and sidled alongside Aaron. "Best give me the shovel, Son."

"Yeah, Yazzie," Jace taunted. "I've already taken care of the situation. And your wife."

Kailyn's arms dropped, but Jace didn't relinquish his hold until Aaron took a menacing step toward him.

She slipped out of Runninghawk's embrace. "Aaron—"

"I can't believe you called Runninghawk." He scowled.

She halted, halfway between the men. "I tried to call you, but-but I didn't know where you were."

Aaron grabbed her arm. "I told you where I was."

"Right, Yazzie. In Albuquerque. But you forgot to mention the part about your rendezvous with Willa."

Aaron positioned Kailyn behind him. "I don't like your insinuations."

Jace folded his arms. "What? You expect your little wife to keep the home fires burning while you pursue other 'interests' with your girlfriend at the state capital?"

Aaron lunged. She snatched at his sleeve. The fabric ripped in her hand.

"What's got you into such a tizzy is perhaps it's occurred to you that your wife might be already regretting a hasty marriage and not only considering other choices, but enjoying the comfort of someone else's arms."

Aaron drew back his arm and let his fist fly into the arrogant punk's face. Kailyn screamed. Jace staggered back, blood spurting from his nose.

Jace swiped the blood across his sleeve, stared at it, and then dove toward Aaron's middle. They both went down, arms and elbows entangled, legs thrashing.

"Gid, do something!" she yelled.

Aiming the wooden handle of the shovel, Gid prodded them until they rolled over the embankment and into the arroyo at the bottom of the ditch. Startled, both men released each other and tumbled apart.

"Gid, what's the matter with—?"

"Why did you—?"

Gid jabbed the shovel at the truck. "You, Aaron Yazzie, take your wife home. And you, Jace Runninghawk, are going to help me de-snake the vehicle."

Beating the dust off his once-immaculate trousers, Jace hoisted himself up the incline. "I ought to cuff you, Yazzie, for assaulting a police officer."

Aaron stalked up the embankment. "And charge me with what? Defending what's mine?"

"We'll see how cocky you are after your butt cools itself in the lockup." Jace reached for his handcuffs. "Is she yours, Yazzie? Are you sure? Or is that what's eating you?"

She inserted herself between them, touching Jace. "No, Jace. Please. Neither of you were without fault. Please don't arrest him." Her lip trembled. "Please, don't. For my sake."

His gut knotted at the sight of her familiar touch on Runninghawk's arm. "Don't go doing me any favors, Runninghawk."

"Shut up, Aaron," growled Gid. "Learn when to keep your trap shut."

"Please…Jace…"

It galled him to his soul to see her begging this Navajo wannabe.

Jace took a deep breath. "Don't go with him, Kay. He's not to be trusted. Who's to say Aaron wasn't the one who put the reptile in there in the first place?"

Aaron's eyes widened. "Me? I got into town an hour ago. I was catching a ride home with Gid."

Jace sneered. "So you say. Your only alibi your erstwhile girlfriend."

With a strangled cry, Kailyn clamped a hand over her mouth and hurtled toward Gid's truck.

Aaron balled his fists. "She's not—"

"Stop, Son." Holding him well away from Jace, Gid shook his head. "What possible reason would Aaron have to hurt his wife?"

Jace's mouth twisted. "Getting rid of Wife Number One to make room for Wife Number Two. Do you have any idea how often I've investigated those kinds of cases?" He stabbed his finger at Kailyn, perched in Gid's truck. "I'm not going to allow you to hurt her or Willa, Yazzie. I'm warning you."

Aaron stiffened. "I'll protect my wife. It's not me she needs protecting from." He broke free of Gid's grasp. "Stay away from my wife. From me and my family. I'm warning you."

Jace got in his face. "Or you'll what?"

He glared at Runninghawk, nose to nose with him before pivoting on his heel and stomping toward the truck.

Flinging open the door, he threw himself into the driver's side. Kailyn stared straight ahead, her posture rigid. He cranked the key in the ignition and yanked the gearshift into drive. Gravel spinning, he gunned the motor, jerking onto the highway. She scrabbled for the dashboard, lurching forward.

"I can't believe you called him."

She crossed her arms. "I had to call him. You were in Albuquerque," she spat. "With Willa."

He frowned at the unspoken accusation in her voice. "I told you where I was going."

"You told me you were going to mail the microchip. I assumed you borrowed Gid's truck until he showed up at the house."

"I went to Albuquerque because I didn't want the postmark to reveal our location on the Rez."

"You don't owe me an explanation."

He ground his teeth. That haughty tone of hers again.

"Willa happened to be heading there after receiving an emergency call from a street girl she's been urging to leave her pimp and return to the Rez."

Kailyn shifted in the seat so fast, he recoiled against the side of the truck. "And you knew this about Willa when even Jace did not, how?"

He fidgeted, averting his eyes. "We've kept in touch this week."

She snorted. "Yeah, I'll bet."

His head snapped around. "What's that supposed to—?" His mouth flattened. "What lies has Runninghawk been filling your head with?"

She frowned. "He's tried to be a friend. Apparently my only friend."

"After what we've been—?"

"Yeah," she narrowed her eyes. "After what we've been through, you ditched me for"—she threw her hands in the air—"Albuquerque."

"I told you . . ."

She held up her hand. "We've all gotta do what we gotta do."

He glowered at her. The silence thrummed between them. She broke eye contact first. Her lips aquiver, she turned toward the window.

Aaron tightened his grip around the wheel, wishing he could throttle his very uncooperative witness/wife. The most infuriating, oblique, read-my-mind-when-I'm-mad . . .

"Tell me about how the snake got in the truck," he asked when he trusted himself to speak. "What kind of snake?"

"Do I look like a snake wrangler to you?" She flounced in the seat. "How should I know what kind of snake it was?"

"Just tell me what it looked like, deb," he growled.

Were all women this way? The Southern species in particular? Or had he just lucked out?

Staccato-beat, as if she had to pay for each word, she gave him the lowdown.

A sick feeling settled in his chest. "That's a western diamond-back, deb." He blew out a breath. "One of the most venomous, deadly residents of the desert Southwest. Especially aggressive. This time of year it's usually in hibernation. How did it end up in the truck?"

Her eyebrows rose. She pointed to herself. "You're asking me? How should I know? Jace said it probably came out of hiding attracted by the warmth of the engine and slipped inside."

"Jace..." His lip curled. "First, scorpions. Now this? Runninghawk probably deposited the rattler in there himself."

"Why on earth would he do such a thing?" Her eyelids tensed. "And he said the same thing about you."

He stared at her. "You think I'd hurt you? You believe his lies about me?" His voice wobbled.

She sighed. "No, I don't believe you'd hurt me." She covered his hand on the wheel with her own.

His skin charged at the feel of her hand against his. He drank in the sight of her, having deprived himself of her presence for the better part of twenty-four hours for the greater good. He pulled into the yard, relishing the prospect of a long winter evening before them. A chance to talk.

Something had been off with her for days. Something bothering her. Something not right between them.

He'd hoped after he shared his painful past she'd understand how much faith he placed in her hands. How much of his heart. But instead, tension had sprung up.

235

The tension hadn't existed before his revelations. The thought worried at the back of his mind that she found his baggage too insurmountable to overcome the gulf separating his world from hers.

Was she as tired of living in limbo as he was? Living in the lies?

"Only a few more weeks, Kailyn. This'll all be over—"

She withdrew her hand and inched away.

His eyes cut to her. "The uncertainty will be over. After the trial, a slam dunk for Rogers with your testimony, you have a brand-new life to look forward to." He swallowed. "There's a lot of us who'd love to be in your shoes with a chance to start over."

She wrapped her arms around herself.

"Willa has contacts, and as soon as I told her about our situation—"

"You told Willa? About me?" She reared. "About us?"

His brow wrinkled. He clicked the gear into Park and switched off the ignition. He laid his arm across the back of the seat. "She can help me get you to Carolina."

Aaron's eyes flickered at a movement in the shadow of the porch. "You're the one who told me somewhere along the way I need to learn to trust someone."

"Someone...not Willa."

He bit the inside of his cheek. "You trusted CeCe. How's this any different from you spilling your guts to CeCe?"

She flung open the door. "It's completely different. And if you can't see that, then you are dumber than dirt."

He made a grab for her arm, but she wrenched free and ran inside the house. He slammed his fist on the wheel. So much for his happily-ever-after evening.

Shinali lumbered over. He rolled down the window.

"You two keep playing with fire long enough, you're going to get burned."

"What's that supposed to mean?"

She sniffed. "I think you know what I mean. Stop trying to pull the sheep's wool over this old woman's eyes. Granddaughter told me the truth."

"The truth?"

"About Flores. About the upcoming trial." She poked a bony finger through the open window. "About your pretend marriage."

His mouth hung open and closed with a snap. "She's got nerve, reaming me out over Willa, and then telling you."

Delores fluttered her hand. "Not news to me. I've known from the beginning."

He did a double-take. "But the bridal jar?"

The old woman gave him a slightly wicked grin, reminding Aaron of himself. "I've been messing with you. Wondering how long it'd take both of you to pony up the truth."

He raked a hand over his head. "I can't believe you. What was the point in that?"

A small, self-satisfied smile. "Kinda fun to stir the pot and see what rose to the surface. Help the natural course of events along."

His eyes narrowed. "What natural course of events are you talking about?"

"But I hadn't reckoned on my friend at Grace House." Her eyes bored into his. "Do you love the rescuer of doves, Grandson?"

"Of course I love Willa. After what we went through together…"

She shook her head. "I mean really love her. Passionately love her, the passion I see in your eyes every time your redheaded Southern girl comes within ten feet of you."

"I do not—"

"Don't lie to your *Shinali*." She squinted. "Or yourself. I know you."

He squeezed his hands around the wheel. "She's my witness. You and Gid have gotten attached to her—"

"Like we're the only ones?"

He set his jaw. "Kailyn will be out of our lives soon. Relocated after her testimony. And I'll—" He cleared his throat. "We'll never see her again. Best you remember it and guard your feelings."

Delores's eyebrows rose. "Like barring the corral gate after the sheep have wandered free, isn't it?"

He hunched his shoulders. "I have no idea what you mean."

Delores patted his arm and ambled in the direction of her hogan. "Sure you do," she called over her shoulder. "But what you need to ponder is, if that's an arrangement you can live with. Or not."

22

Aaron had no sooner walked into the house than his phone beeped. He glanced at the caller ID—Gid—and ignored the call. Kailyn, prickly as a cactus pear, scoured the sink. Taco rushed to greet him.

He refluffed Taco's Mohawk. "At least someone's glad to see me."

That statement resulted in the slamming of a cabinet door.

Aaron winced. He watched her wear out a Brillo pad on the porcelain sink. His phone vibrated. Taco meandered toward his bowl.

"Why did you tell *Shinali*?"

Kailyn went rigid. "I'm tired of keeping secrets. Living a lie."

A lie?

He traversed the short distance between them and seized her arm. "News flash, Sweetheart. Get used to it. The rest of your life's going to be one lie after another to keep yourself alive."

The phone buzzed again.

She jerked free. "Better answer that. Might be your girlfriend."

"I doubt it," he growled, but he extricated the phone out of his pocket. Gid, again.

Kailyn, her aquiline nose lifted high in the air, sidestepped him and disappeared into the front room.

He hit Talk. "Now's not a good time, Gid. What's so important—?"

"It's the kid you talked to at the gym."

"Mateo?"

"That's right, Mateo Benallie. He's been...hurt."

Aaron wheeled, propped one hand on the counter. "Hurt? What do you mean? Are you at the hospital?"

"Can't get him to go. Somebody's beat him."

Aaron flinched.

"I'm guessing his father. It's happened before."

Aaron pressed the phone to his ear. "Call the police."

"Believe me, I've tried that route with him."

Aaron scrubbed his forehead with his hand. "Call Child Protective Services."

"I threatened to the last time. He threatened to run away or join the gang. He doesn't want to be separated from his mother. I thought maybe you'd come to the gym and talk to him. Convince him he and his mother need help. After what you went through..."

Aaron tensed. "I told you I've got nothing to give these kids. Nothing to offer."

"You've got everything you need—yourself."

Expose his shame to the world? He didn't think so.

A silence ticked until Gid said, "Then I'll take him home myself. Have a talk with his father."

"Oh no you will not!" Aaron shouted into the phone. "Are you crazy?"

The notion of his lanky sapling of a father confronting a violent bully sent a wave of foreboding through his body.

He glanced at the wall clock. "I'll be there in thirty minutes. Keep the boy with you until I get there. I'll come and talk sense into both of you. Wait for me." He clicked off.

"Wait for you? How sweet. Missing each other already?" She sailed into the kitchen.

He spun on his heel. "I've got business to tend to."

"Go on, then. Don't let me keep you. Just so you don't expect your witness," she hissed, "to wait for you."

"I know better than to expect anything from you, Kailyn Eudailey. Nothing except pain and aggravation since you stepped off that elevator."

She crossed her arms. "Well, lucky for you I'll be out of your hair and in North Carolina in less than two weeks. Sooner, if you'd prefer."

Yeah, lucky for him.

He got in her face. "You can't begin to imagine what I'd prefer, deb."

Aaron wrested Taco's leash off the peg. "I don't know what's gotten into you lately, or, and I quote, 'who's stomped all over your tortilla.' End quote. But I've got something to take care of."

"Someone to take care of, you mean?" She made a grand gesture toward the door. "Don't let me stop you."

"You expecting company? Jace Runninghawk? Don't tell me you've spilled your guts to him, too."

"So what if I have? What's it to you?"

He whistled for Taco. "You're out of your league with that trickster. Runninghawk's nothing but trouble."

She snorted. "Despite what you believe, you are not the boss of me."

The truth was he'd been out of his league with Kailyn Eudailey since Atlanta. No need for her to know that, though.

He clipped the leash to Taco's collar. "You're *my* witness."

"So you keep reminding me."

"I'll be back—"

"Why are you taking my dog?"

He scowled. "Too much estrogen in this house for either of us."

She unclipped her hair, letting it cascade over her shoulders. "One day you might just come back and find me gone to a place where people don't share your aversion to my redheaded self."

Kailyn Eudailey made him madder than anyone he'd ever met in his life. And for the record, he'd developed a fondness for red hair.

Aaron yanked open the door. "Don't stick around on my account. You think you can do better out there in the darkness on your own, deb, then be my guest."

He'd scarcely made it across the threshold before the door slammed behind him.

Almost, but not quite, hitting him on the backside.

Kailyn kicked the door shut. She'd show him. She didn't need him. She didn't have to stick around and watch him romance Willa Littlefeather right under her nose. This farce of a marriage was over as far as she was concerned. She'd make her own way home.

Home? She gazed at the cozy home she'd spent the last months refurbishing. This was home.

The closest she'd come since her parents' deaths. She had people here. Friends, coworkers, Gid, and *Shinali*...family.

Her heart quivered. Not her family. Aaron's family. Soon to be Willa's family.

She'd seen Aaron Yazzie work his magic before. He'd convince Willa to surrender her reservations concerning marriage. A perfect granddaughter for *Shinali*. Provide her with those lovely children in her dream vision.

They'd all be so happy...

Except for her.

Kailyn chewed her lip. She refused to believe, like Aaron, that all law enforcement officers—LEOs he called them—were on Flores's payroll. And remembered the marshals had a field office in Albuquerque.

She peered into the gathering darkness as the headlights of the truck lurched away, a tiny pinpoint of light in the desert night. She contemplated calling Gid or Jace and rejected each. She'd not drag his father into this, and despite Aaron's declaration regarding her lack of good sense, she did possess enough to hesitate bringing an outsider into her situation.

A situation Jace would require her to explain before he made the three-hour drive to the city.

Had Jace planted the snake?

Was it designed to cast suspicion upon Aaron and thereby drive her into Jace's confidence? Plenty of time while she worked her shift to place the rattler in the truck. Easy accessfor someone like Jace.

Look at the mistakes in judgment she'd made in trusting Dex Pritchard. Or the mess she'd landed in by pretending to marry

Aaron Yazzie. Wasn't like she was the greatest judge of character as Aaron was so fond of pointing out to her over and over ad nauseum.

In the end, there was only one person you could trust—something she'd learned the hard way from Aaron—herself. And in the long run—she was so tired of running—only One upon whom she could completely rely—her God.

As she pondered that, the phone rang, startling her out of her daze. She snatched at the phone without pausing to examine the caller ID.

"Kailyn?"

And she had her answer.

The first sight to meet Aaron's eyes as he rolled into the deserted gym parking lot was Gid's truck and the two figures huddled near the side entrance. The taller figure—Gid—straightened from bending over the form on the ground as Aaron's headlights swept across them.

Aaron with Taco in tow swung his boots to the ground. He didn't know why he'd felt compelled to bring Taco along—besides annoying Kailyn—but he'd decided to act upon a growing hunch ever since he received Gid's call.

Gid threw up his hand. "Aaron's here, Mateo."

The boy kept his head tucked into the filthy jacket he wore—as far as Aaron discerned—night and day.

Aaron exchanged glances with his father. Gid gave a tiny, imperceptible shake of his head.

"Mateo, my man. Is everything all right with you?"

The boy turned his face to the wall, his eyes downcast.

"Did somebody hurt you, Mateo? Your father?"

Silence except for the muted din of engine noises along the busy highway.

He dropped the leash and allowed Taco to roam at will. Taco's nose pressed to the ground. With infinite caution, he sniffed his way forward, exploring new territory.

One sniff forward. Pause. Another sniff, two steps gained. Taco froze, poised for flight at the least sign of alarm.

Like him.

Pretty much—Aaron chewed the inside of his cheek—summarizing the extent of his life and his relationships thus far.

Regaining his confidence, Taco inched toward the battered boy. And became momentarily distracted by the garbage bag lying beside the boy.

At the sight of the garbage, Aaron darted his eyes over to Gid.

"Dumpster diving when I found him," Gid whispered. "He was hungry and his father's once again locked him out of the house."

A sudden memory of himself, younger than Mateo but equally hungry and cold during one particular Albuquerque winter, rose in his mind. A locked door. Lights out inside the house.

The darkness of the night. The strange sounds a Diné boy wasn't used to, scary city noises. The cold, concrete floor of the garage. His mother beaten unconscious.

Aaron raked his hand over his head. He clenched his fist to stop the trembling. He'd spent most of a lifetime trying to forget, refusing to revisit and reopen those old wounds.

Taco's wet nose nudged the boy's exposed cheek. The boy reared. For the first time, Mateo raised his eyes, to the dog and then toward the men.

In his eyes, a reflection of hurt, fear, and…shame.

And Aaron beheld himself. Alone. Without hope. The despair of the forsaken.

But it didn't have to be like this. Not this time. Not for Mateo.

Taco's tongue licked the boy's face.

Mateo blinked, his eyes traveling to Taco's bobbing head. "Your dog's ugly."

Aaron squatted beside them, brushed his hand over Taco's hairless back. "As a puppy, he was badly abused by someone who was supposed to love and take care of him."

Mateo pointed his dirt-encrusted finger at one of Taco's scars.

Aaron nodded. "He's forever marked by the wounds he suffered, but someone rescued Taco. And now, my wife"—how much he loved saying those words—"my wife, Kailyn, adopted him, and Taco knows he never has to be afraid again. Not all people are bad like the person who mistreated him. Taco knows he's safe and with people who love him."

Suspicion clouded Mateo's eyes, but he edged closer to Taco. "Can I pet him? Is it okay for me to touch him?" His mouth flattened. "I don't like to be touched."

"Taco's the one to give his permission. And I think it's okay, because he's already touched you. He knows you're a good person, a person he can trust."

Mateo's big, dark eyes probed Taco's unflinching, soft brown ones. Aaron held his breath. Moments passed. A lifetime of heartbeats drummed.

Then, the boy ever so gently reached for the dog. Slowly, with one finger, stroked the Mohawk fuzz on top of Taco's head. Taco stilled, never taking his gaze from Mateo.

"He said I was—I was lower than dog scum. Good for nothing but a whipping. My fault he hit me. If I weren't so stupid, so ugly, so clumsy, so..." Mateo looked away.

Mateo's words dropped like pebbles into the bottomless pool of Aaron's well-remembered pain.

"He—your father—is wrong."

Mateo shifted, wrapping an arm around Taco's neck. "Shows what you know." His eyes dropped to his sandals, inadequate for a December New Mexico night.

"I know, Mateo. Believe me, I know."

Mateo shook his head. Taco licked Mateo's chin. The boy cupped Taco's muzzle and allowed the canine to explore his face. "You don't know nothing."

No trace of tears. Aaron speculated that—like him—Mateo had gone way beyond that point years back. Only resignation and defeat shrouded his features.

"Where's your mother, Mateo?" Gid's soft voice spoke from behind. "Is she okay? Is she at work?"

The boy stiffened. "She didn't come home yesterday. He said she'd probably taken the money and cut and run on the both of us."

His voice wavered. "She only does that stuff 'cause he makes her. To get cash for his next hit."

"We need to get you somewhere safe and warm, Mateo." Aaron rocked on his heels. "Get food in your belly. Let the police find her. She may need help."

Mateo shook his head. Taco, with a soft whine, burrowed his snout in the boy's parka and tugged with his teeth. "She told me she'd never leave me. We just have to stay out of the house until he comes down from the high. Till he stops acting crazy. I'll be fine. Leave me alone."

"You don't have to be alone, Mateo."

Mateo turned away from him. "What do you know about anything?"

The temperature was dropping. Aaron scanned the distant peaks of the Chuska. It had snowed there last night. Forecasters predicted a Christmas snow in Shiprock, maybe tonight. Mateo's mother could be drugged out of her mind, too, or terribly injured by either his father or a john. Mateo, whether he admitted it or not, desperately needed their help.

His help.

Abruptly, Aaron yanked off his coat and tossed it to Gid. "I want to show you something. Something to prove I do know. That I am— was—you. Until, like Taco, I allowed someone to help me."

Seizing both sides of his shirt, he ripped the snaps apart, exposing his chest to the frigid night air.

Mateo's eyes widened. "What—?"

"I bear on my body the marks, the wounds, the scars, like you." And before he rationalized his way out of it, Aaron peeled off his shirt and eased onto the ground in front of Mateo.

Gid inhaled sharply.

Aaron twisted his torso, allowing the light cast from the street to reflect off his scar. "My mark. My shame. A broken vessel like Taco."

His back to Mateo, Aaron faced Gid, and was surprised to find tears running down the man's weather-roughened countenance. The pain in his father's face grabbed at Aaron's heart.

And a wall erected so long ago tottered in his soul. Aaron swiveled around to the boy.

"He said—my stepfather—said I was a dirty, no-good Injun. Worthless. Not worth the bullet it'd take to end my life. Excrement on the bottom of his shoe. Blight on the surface of the earth. Only good Injun was a dead Injun."

Funny, how after all these years the words still came so easily to his mind.

Mateo rose, his back pressed against the gym wall. Taco hugged his legs. "What…did that to you? When?" A mixture of pity, shared misery, and compassion flitted across Mateo's face.

Rising, Aaron tugged his shirt over his shoulders. His hands fumbled. His teeth chattered. "I-I was nine. A belt buckle." After misbuttoning, his hand dropped. "My mother was too afraid to reach out for help until it was too late. Until he'd killed her."

"Please, Mateo," Gid whispered. "Won't you let us help you? I should've been there for my son, but I wasn't. Let me—the both of us—help you." Gid draped Aaron's coat around Mateo's shoulders. He shrugged into its warmth.

Dawning hope flickered in Mateo's eyes. "You'll find my mother? You won't let them separate us?"

Gid nodded. "My friends at the Navajo police will find your mom. And another friend from my church runs an emergency shelter for battered women and children. You'll be safe there. Your mom will be safe there. And in time, the tribe's advocacy center will guide you to a new life. A new start for both of you."

The breath trickled out between Mateo's bloody, swollen lips. "Okay, I'll go with you to this place."

Mateo held both hands palm up. "But first?" He jerked his lips at the misbuttoned snaps. "Let me help you."

Aaron shot a grateful look over to Gid. "We'll help each other."

23

KAILYN PACKED THE ONLY PHOTO OF HER AND AARON—ON THE BEAUTIFUL autumn day outside the Loretto Chapel—and zipped the duffel bag closed. She swiped at the treacherous tears. With Delores at her weavers' meeting, she'd not have a chance to say a proper good-bye, to thank the old woman for all she'd done for Kailyn over the last few months.

Leaving the suitcase on her bed, she hastened into the kitchen. She'd leave Delores a note and place it in the hogan before Burke arrived.

Perhaps leaving this way was for the best. She wasn't sure she could've said good-bye to those she'd come to love.

She shied away from thoughts of Aaron. He'd be mad she'd taken matters into her own hands. But later, when his control-freak tendencies had a chance to cool off, she suspected he'd also be relieved. The burden of her protection taken off his shoulders and consigned once more where it belonged, with WITSEC. He'd be free of her then, free of his deathbed obligation to Steve, free to find healing and wholeness in the arms of his long-lost love.

And Taco? The pain in her heart doubled at leaving him, her most valiant champion. But her future after the trial was uncertain.

Taco loved it here. Taco had become more Aaron's dog than hers. Taco, if not Kailyn, had finally found a place to belong.

Headlights flashed across the front of the house. Burke? She'd only been off the phone with him ten minutes. How had he gotten here so soon?

She threw open the door. "Aren't you the quick one?" She ushered him inside. "I'm almost done packing."

Kailyn bit her lip, gazing one last time on the details of the life she'd so painstakingly—and foolishly—created over the last few months. The Christmas tree and the ornaments. The bridal jar... She blinked to clear her eyes.

Burke stomped his boots on the welcome mat. He blew on his gnarled fingers. "Cold out there tonight. Might see snow before morning."

She sighed. Morning for her would dawn far away from here. Far away from Aaron.

Burke shot her a long look. "You're not changing your mind about leaving, are you?"

Aaron's face at the sight of Willa Littlefeather superimposed itself upon her mind.

She shook her head. "No, it's for the best."

Burke nodded. "Good riddance to bad rubbish."

She drifted toward the kitchen to finish her note to Delores. "Aaron's not... It's not what you think." She couldn't bear for Burke or anyone to think badly about him. "It's me."

Burke snorted. He examined the Navajo Grandma ornaments the girls created for her. His lip curled. "Best to leave Yazzie to his own kind."

She straightened. "What're you talking about?"

His nose crinkled. "I seen your man 'fore I called you. He was at the diner with the Littlefeather woman."

Kailyn's heart sank. She'd been right. He'd left for an assignation with Willa.

"Only thing any Injun woman's good for is on her back."

She stiffened, anger flaring. "Willa's not... How do you know what Wil—wait." She blinked. "How do you know what my husband looks—" She sucked in a breath.

Her eyes darted toward the door, calculating the steps required and figuring she could outrun the older man and hide in the darkness of the night.

Burke stilled at her movement, the look in his eyes sharp and feral. He positioned himself between her and the exit.

Her mouth dry, she forced herself to take calm, even breaths. "Why're you here? Are you here for Flores?"

Burke folded his arms. "I got no beef with you." A momentary spasm of something almost human crossed his face. "You're a sweet gal. Remind me of my mother. Whose only mistake, like you, was to get mixed up with these featherhead huffers."

She fought to get control of her nerves. "I thought you said your father—"

"My father..." His face contorted. "After bedding the pueblo whore, he infected my mother, a good, decent white woman, with syphilis."

Kailyn put a hand to her throat. "Oh, Burke..."

"She died in disgrace, abandoned by our family, her church. In shame. Helpless, I watched her writhe in pain...in torment of body and soul..."

His chest heaved. "Ancient history. I've done my part to settle the score since. One piece of business to finish with Yazzie before I make my last delivery and retire permanently to the other side of the Rio Grande."

"What's Aaron got to do with you?"

Burke shrugged. "When I got out of prison, I knew eventually he'd return here. I waited. I established my operation on the edge of the Rez and after I spent five long years surrounded by these Fort Injuns, he finally came back." Burke smiled. "With you."

He withdrew a large syringe from his denim coat. "We can do this the hard way or the easy way. Your choice. I need you as bait to lure him into the trap I've been planning since he got away from me the first time."

She shrank against the armoire. "Why're you doing this? What did Aaron ever do to you?"

"Didn't Yazzie ever tell you?" He cocked his head. "I married his mother. I'm his long lost pappy."

She snatched the bridal jar and flung it at his head.

He ducked and then lunged. As he grabbed her around the neck, the last sensation she remembered was the pinprick of the hypodermic needle into her skin.

"You did good with him." The sheen of tears misted Gid's eyes. "I never knew about..."

Aaron folded his arms. "What's done is done, Gid. Like I told Mateo, we're both broken vessels."

Gid's eyes shot over to him. "Me, too. But a broken vessel mended whole by God."

"There is no wholeness for people like me."

At the station, he was pleased the police officer assigned to Mateo wasn't Runninghawk. Pleased until he wondered where the off-duty cop was spending his evening. Not as if he cared where Runninghawk was, as long as he wasn't hanging out with his Kailyn.

He sighed. His Kailyn...He wished.

"You certified long?"

He glanced at the child advocate conducting the initial forensic interview with Mateo. The fifty-something Diné woman inclined her head toward the other side of the room where Mateo kept Taco occupied—or was it the other way around?—with a ball.

"Certified at what?"

"Dog therapy for abused children."

His eyes widened. "Didn't know there was such a thing."

"Well, then you and the dog must be naturals. I began my career in Phoenix. An organization there often sends a trained dog and handler to help me interview the children. The dogs calm the children, lower their blood pressure, and ease anxiety for a battered child who's learned to fear authority figures."

He wished some dog had been there for him after the police raid, and he'd been sent scared and shaking into the interrogation room until Nancy Matthews rescued him.

The advocate smiled at him. "You should check into it. You and the dog."

Problem was—the dog, Kailyn's dog, would be long gone in a few short weeks.

A longing to get home, to get back as soon as possible to Kailyn, overcame him. To finish the talk he'd promised before the confusion of the past few days.

When Mateo caught sight of his mother as a policeman brought her to the station—Aaron looked away for fear he'd lose his own composure. The reunion between mother and son made sharing his secret worthwhile. Made his shame not feel as great.

If only Aaron and his mother... But life was full of if-onlys.

Nothing could be done to undo the past. But the future...? One tremendous if-only stared him in the face with Kailyn.

Aaron rushed to the station parking lot, eager to go home. Grateful for the safe place she'd somehow, when he wasn't looking, created for him, like Taco. Because no matter how ornery Kailyn Eudailey had been lately—maybe one of those female things—she'd given him hope, a balm to his soul.

Had he at last found a safe haven, a loving home, with a woman who'd love him, scars and all?

All of a sudden, all he wanted to do was to find out, talk to her, pour out his heart, tell her about Mateo and what had happened tonight—to him.

Getting out of the truck once home, the first thing he observed was the front door ajar. Setting Taco on the ground, he charged toward the house. No lights. He poked his head inside. Taco growled.

"Kailyn?"

No answer. Something stale tickled at his nose. A buried memory.

He flipped on the light switch. "Kailyn?"

Grandmother wasn't due home for another hour. Why had Kailyn left the door open?

Taco barked. The noise echoed the way sound does in an unoccupied dwelling. Something crunched under his boots.

The bridal jar lay smashed at his feet. Shards of pottery littered the living room floor. His heart constricted.

Aaron fell to his knees and fingered one of the shards. His arm shot out as Taco followed right on his heels. "No, Taco. Watch out."

He recalled the last thing she had said to him—the taunt she'd thrown in his face. A threat she'd obviously decided to make good on.

Amidst the shattered remains of the bridal jar, he closed his eyes. His shoulders sagged. Gid was wrong. So wrong.

Because some things once broken can never be mended.

Raw fury drove Aaron's fist into Runninghawk's face when he opened the door to Aaron's pounding. Only a quick sidestep by Jace landed the glancing blow to his cheek and backpedaled, groping for the gun on his hip.

"Where is she?"

It hadn't been hard to locate the jerk's address. Please . . . Compared to what he'd uncovered in the Flores operation, a piece of cake.

He swung his gaze and his fist around to find Jace's Glock .22 staring him in the face. "You tell me, Yazzie. Where's Willa?"

Aaron scowled. "Who's talking about Willa? I'm talking about Kailyn, my wife."

Jace reared, but positioned his index finger along the side of the barrel, Aaron aligned in the sights of the gun. "Why would I know where your wife is, Yazzie? I got a call from the houseparents. Willa received an anonymous tip a runaway was spotted underneath the bridge in Shiprock. It's been hours. Then, I got this garbled transmission—you know how spotty the cell coverage is here. She sounded scared. I was on my way when you barged in."

"Is she all right?"

Jace holstered his gun. "I don't know. But I aim to find out." He shrugged into his jacket. His face bore a look of resignation. "You wanna come help me find her?"

Aaron shook his head. "It's not that way with Willa and me. No matter what you think. Anyway, she called you." He grimaced. "Seems they all call you first."

Jace gave him a long look. "I've been pushing your buttons because I know something's going on. But I trust Gid and Delores and their instincts about you. And despite what you think, your jealousy about me and Kailyn's unfounded."

"The girl's besotted with you." Runninghawk raised an eyebrow and gave him the once-over. "Although why beats the tamale out of me."

Besotted? In Aaron's dreams. Dreams of turquoise skies, red canyon walls, and spring wildflowers.

A sudden, terrifying thought breached the white-hot anger consuming him since his discovery of the broken jar with its unspoken promises.

If Kailyn wasn't with Runninghawk, then where was she?

Runninghawk's brow knotted. "Is everything okay? Is Kailyn— are you—in trouble?"

Aaron strode past him. "It's nothing I can't handle."

The temperature had dropped another five degrees. He retraced his route home, searching his memory for any clue as to where Kailyn could've taken herself.

He frowned. Taken herself without transportation? Someone had to have taken her somewhere, not the other way around.

Aaron hurried inside the house to find Taco pawing at the door, whining and barking. Marching past Taco, he ventured down the hallway to her bedroom and found the duffel on top of the bed. But whatever she'd planned, something had interrupted Kailyn.

Or someone.

He stalked into the kitchen and found three envelopes on the table beside a blank pad of paper. Gid's name scrawled across one. *Shinali*'s on another. Aaron's, his heart plummeted, on the third.

She'd intended to leave. And leave him just a note good-bye?

He spotted her cell phone on the counter. He scrolled through her directory. Names of people he knew—people at church, coworkers, the Silverhorn woman in Arizona. And an unlisted number he couldn't identify.

But the last number dialed got his attention. He recognized the area code and fished out his own phone for comparison. He swallowed hard.

She'd placed a call to the marshal's office in Albuquerque. Had the marshal's office placed her into protective custody once more?

His boot ground slivers of pottery into the floor. He'd assumed that she'd broken the bridal jar as a sort of symbolic gesture aimed at him. But why, if she'd called the marshals?

As Aaron's eyes swept the room, he pushed down his tangled emotions, forced himself to draw upon his training not his feelings of abandonment. Had the marshal threatened her? The broken jar evidence of a crime scene?

Her peacoat hung upon its peg. No way with her thin Southern blood she'd have gone willingly into the night without her coat. He sniffed the air, noting the stale smell smokers carried on their clothes.

Something teased at the fringes of his mind. Something he preferred not to examine too closely. Something unpleasant.

"Kailyn..."

Taco pawed at the door.

"What have you done?" he whispered. "Where are you?"

The phone in his hand beeped. Kailyn's phone.

Jerking, he dropped the phone, sending it scuttling under the sofa. Scrambling on his hands and knees, he scavenged for the cell and clicked On just before it rolled over to voice mail.

"Aaron Yazzie..."

He tensed. Something about the voice.

The voice, the hate-filled voice, chuckled. "Why is it every woman in your misbegotten life eventually winds up on my doorstep?"

He hurtled through time and space to the memory of a man who'd died, according to Steve, in prison twenty years ago. Who used to laugh the same way. Just before he unbuckled his belt.

Aaron's heart hammered.

Monsters still roamed among the Diné.

Not Flores. Kailyn in Flores's hands a mercy compared to this. Neither she nor he could expect mercy from this creature.

"Michaels."

Burke Michaels whistled. "Very good, Yazzie. It seems I've managed to leave a lasting impression on you."

Aaron's lips twisted.

Michaels laughed. "I've never forgotten you. How I lost ten years of my life because of you and your blanket-squaw mother."

Had Steve known the truth? Why would he lie about the death of this man?

Aaron ground his teeth. "You are a criminal and deserved something far worse than prison."

"Only thing criminal I ever did was fail to teach you a lesson. A lesson you've still not learned. I should've done the world a favor and snuffed out your redskin vermin life the moment you stepped into my house. But I'm here to rectify my error in judgment."

"Where's Kailyn? What've you done with her?"

"A real treasure she is. A buried treasure you and your kind steal from your betters. I'll bet she'd take the lash better than you. Learn her lessons quicker than you."

Panic erupted. The thought of Burke inflicting such pain and cruelty—which Aaron remembered all too well—upon Kailyn dropped him to his knees. Taco whined, nuzzled at his hand.

The image of Burke hurting Kailyn, marking her as he'd done Aaron, or worse…

Aaron pictured what Willa and her girls had endured in the hands of such men, and blinding fear gripped his chest.

Bile rose in his throat. With effort, Aaron swallowed it down. "It's me you want, Michaels. Not her. Tell me where and when. I'll come. Exchange her life for mine."

"When will you get it through your nitpicker head you're not in control?" Anger laced Burke's voice. "Maybe I'll give you a call tomorrow. Maybe I won't. Going to be cold tonight. Might snow.

She probably won't last the night anyway. You'll never find her until it's too late."

"I'll come wherever you say. I'll do anything you say. Don't hurt her." His voice trembled. "Please...don't hurt her."

"Finally, you learn to beg, Yazzie. If not for yourself, then for her. But you still don't get it, do you?"

Aaron clutched the phone. "Get what?"

"You took my wife from me, Yazzie. Now I'm taking yours."

24

AARON STARED AT THE PHONE IN HIS HAND, THE DIAL TONE ECHOING IN THE empty room. He groaned, the sound welling from a place deep within. A place he'd tried not to revisit since he was a boy.

His knees scrubbing the floor, Aaron bent face forward. The shards of the bridal jar pierced his forehead.

"Grandson? What's wrong?"

He lifted his head at his grandmother's voice. Taco's tail whipped in a frenzy. The dog circled, pawing at the half-open door.

The old woman stepped around the broken pieces of pottery littering the floor. "What have you done to yourself?"

She brushed a stream of blood out of his eyes with a tissue from the pocket of her long traditional skirt. "Wh-where's my granddaughter?"

He fought against the tide of weakness flooding his senses. He'd prided himself on his ability to shove the unpleasant distractions to a corner of his mind so that he could concentrate on each mission before him. This skill made him successful in his army and Bureau career.

A trick he had learned at the hands of Burke Michaels. A coping device that enabled him to survive the horrors.

But his legendary detachment failed him now. All he could think of, all he could visualize, was Burke's hands on Kailyn... hurting her. The way Burke had hurt his—

Aaron's stomach heaved.

Delores snatched the trashcan beside the sofa, and he emptied the contents of his stomach. She sank onto the floor beside him.

He made a motion of protest. "You'll cut yoursel—"

"What's wrong, Grandson?"

"He took her." Aaron closed his eyes. "The monster. I can't believe he's still alive." He forcibly swallowed. "She'll be so scared, *Shinali*. I should've protected her...protected my mother. I thought he was dead. She'll be so afraid." He shook, recalling his own long-ago terror.

"Who?" Delores took his face between her hands. "Who's taken our girl? You're not making any sense."

"Steve told me my stepfather was dead. Said he died in prison. Why would he lie about it? He must've known the truth. He had to have known. Oh, God..."

Aaron's eyes widened. "The scorpions. The snake. Not Flores. Burke Michaels. It's me he's trying to hurt. And using anyone close to me to do it. You, Taco, or Kailyn. I've brought his evil upon you. *I* brought Kailyn here, *Shinali*."

He gripped the old woman's arm. "I brought her to the one place her enemies couldn't find her, but mine could. Into the clutches of the devil. He enjoys hurting people." His mouth contorted. "He'll do things..." Fear knifed his heart.

"We must call the police. Our tribal cop friend."

"No." Aaron shoved away from her. "Burke's playing a game. Calling the cops breaks the rules. His rules. Why do you think my mother never got any help?" He scowled. "She understood the punishment for breaking the rules."

Bolting to his feet, he paced the room. "It's me he wants. He'll keep Kailyn alive until he gets me."

He couldn't afford to panic. He had to remain calm. No matter what was happening to Kailyn right now, in the end what mattered was saving her life.

Shinali propped her arm on the sofa and heaved herself to her feet. "Exchanging your life for hers." She shook her head. "You don't have to do this alone. The People will get her back from this Anglo.

There's a justice in the land between the sacred mountains that supersedes Anglo law."

His lip curled. "If you're talking about God, once again where was this God of yours when that monster took my Kailyn? Where is He while the diablo is rap—?" He raked his hand over his head.

Delores caught his arm. "God is with her. She has committed her way unto Him and He will take care of His own."

"Some Shepherd, this Jesus of yours." Aaron jerked free. "Take her home to His heavenly bosom, you mean?" He clamped his jaw. "On behalf of Kailyn, no thanks."

He kicked at a ceramic sliver. "Her home's here. And I'll take care of her, my way, alone." He grimaced. "Like I always have."

"Alone is your choice. Not God's." *Shinali* folded her arms. "What did the man say exactly?"

Burke's words about the lash burned themselves into the forefront of his mind.

Aaron scrubbed his forehead. Think. He had to think past the horror. Ignore the buttons Burke had pushed.

"Buried treasure." His head snapped up. "Somewhere underground?"

"There're over six hundred abandoned mines on the Rez. And those are just the ones documented by the coal and uranium companies. We need more to go on if you hope to pinpoint her location."

We? But her solidarity with him strengthened his waning courage.

"Tell me how our girl fell into this man's hands."

Aaron strode over to the door and examined the lock. "The door stood wide open. The back door's still locked. Looks like she let him inside."

"You think she knew him? Should we start calling her friends?"

He sighed. "She knows more people here than I do. I warned her about being so trusting and accepting people at face value."

Unlike him, who never trusted anyone, until he'd trusted Kailyn with parts of himself he hadn't realized still existed.

"Most of the men my granddaughter knows are Diné, from church or your father's crew." Delores did a slow three-sixty. "The man she met at the library in Farmington was Anglo, I think."

She tapped her moccasin-clad foot, thinking out loud. "What was his name?"

Aaron recalled the Navajo penchant for long, thoughtful pauses. He possessed less patience tonight for it than ever. He rushed over to the window as saucer-like snowflakes drifted from a black velvet sky. Burke said something about her being cold.

He grabbed her coat off the wall and clutched it to his chest, burying his face in the traces of her scent. Kailyn was always cold here. Something cold lodged itself in his heart.

If the monster laid a hand on her, he'd make sure Burke suffered with excruciating slowness in the same way that Flores dealt with enemies who betrayed him. He'd make sure Burke understood hell on earth firsthand.

Delores tapped her finger against her chin, her head tilted. "His last name... On the tip of my tongue..."

He craned his neck, gazing at the disappearing stars as snow clouds filled the sky.

She joined him at the window. "He, the Creator, calls all the starry host by name and because of His great might, not one of them goes missing. My granddaughter is one of His, and He who stretched the heavens is in control of our present situation."

"It's cold out there, *Shinali*. The Rez is the size of West Virginia or," his voice quivered. "He could've taken her into three other states by now. I don't know where to start looking. I don't know how to get her back."

She squeezed his arm. "God is also our shepherd. He will lead you. A good shepherd guides, nurtures, and guards."

He clenched his teeth. "Some guard I turned out to be." He crumpled her coat. "Some tracker I've turned out to be."

"I am praying for our *dibeh-yazzie*."

He jerked. "Yazzie what?"

"Our little lamb. The Shepherd carries those who cannot walk. He will shelter her in His arms. Hold her close to the warmth of His heart tonight." Delores covered her mouth with her hand.

"What is it?"

"That's it, Grandson." Her brow creased. "That's what she called him. Shepherd. Burke Shepherd."

Aaron's eyes narrowed. "*Pastor* in Spanish."

He recalled Flores's reference to a "keeper of the flock" and the jokes about the *corderos*, lambs. With a sickening realization, too late he figured out Flores's new enterprise and Burke Michaels's involvement.

Aaron's face hardened. "It's meant as a mockery of the Diné culture and Christian faith. Michaels is back to his old tricks under an assumed name."

"His old tricks? What do you mean?"

The look he sent his grandmother was bleak. "Michaels was a vice squad cop who dabbled on the side running a prostitution ring. Sex trafficking."

Delores wilted before his eyes. She reached a hand toward the wall to steady herself. "He must've said something else to you on the phone. A clue to their whereabouts."

He put his arm around his grandmother's waist and settled her on the sofa. Her distress helped him get a handle on his own. His training clicked into place as the rational part of him gained the upper hand over his fear.

"Men like him are psychologically damaged. Bent in a perverse way. Strong narcissistic personalities. Proud of their cleverness. He was trying to goad me...Wait."

Aaron straightened. "Michaels said something about all my women eventually arriving on his doorstep. Suppose he meant it literally." He scooped Kailyn's phone off the floor. He scrolled until he found the name for which he searched.

Jace Runninghawk. He swallowed his pride and hit speed dial. All he cared about was getting Kailyn out of this alive.

He'd dance at Kailyn and the cop's wedding as long as he got her out of the monster's—"Runninghawk?"

"I thought this was—" Runninghawk grunted. "Yazzie, I'm asking you for the last time. Where's Willa? I found her car abandoned in a less-than-desirable side of Farmington. I'm there now."

Aaron set his jaw. "I told you I don't know anything about Willa. I'm calling about Kailyn. She's been taken."

"Taken? What do you mean she's been taken? By whom?"

He gritted his teeth and plunged ahead. "I'm with the Bureau, Runninghawk. I've been working an undercover sting in the Mexican Mafia. Kailyn and I are hiding from a drug lord she's testifying against in a few weeks. But I don't think that's what's—"

"Kailyn's a federal witness? Like WITSEC or something? She's not your wife? She's your witness?"

He clenched his hand around the cell. "Yeah, she's my witness. And I think someone from my past has taken her, a man she met in Farmington. A man who calls himself Burke Shepherd now, although when I knew him as a boy he called himself Burke Michaels. Flores calls him *Pastor*."

"Keeper of the flock." A long silence. "A connection between this guy and Willa's disappearance."

"Why would you—?"

"Before Willa disappeared she told me there'd been trouble recently. Some runaways were reaching out to her and then vanishing before she could rescue them from, and I quote, 'the keeper of the flock.'"

Runninghawk took a ragged breath. "She also told me her pimp back in the day had been a man everyone called *Pastor...*" His voice broke. "I assumed from the surname *Pastor* he was Latino. She said the guy went to prison for murder not long after Sanchez sprung her from the brothel."

Aaron's lips bulged. "The man I remember is arrogant. No hiding under the radar for him. If he's indeed living in Farmington and preying on the runaways in the Four Corners, he's also living in plain sight and living large. With your resources, could you find him?"

"The Bureau's got far more—"

"The Bureau and I aren't exactly on speaking terms these days, since I shanghaied Kailyn from a dirty marshal who sold her out to Flores."

"Okay. Give me thirty minutes to access our database and contact a source in the Farmington PD. Farmington's outside my jurisdiction. Off the Rez."

"Fine, but don't take too long. Michaels, Shepherd, *Pastor*, or whatever he's calling himself, is gunning for me and he's eager to torment me over Kailyn. Time's running out for her."

"Willa, too, if he has her." Runninghawk whistled. "You have a way of bringing death to everyone who cares about you. I knew you were trouble. Trouble you've brought on the heads of the innocent."

Aaron's mouth went dry. "Yeah, that's me. A regular dust storm of destruction." As if he needed reminding.

"Just find Michaels's address, Runninghawk. But watch your back. Michaels is a former Albuquerque cop and he knows his way around LE and the underworld better than you and I put together."

Aaron assembled a backpack of essential items while he waited for Runninghawk's call. Delores busied herself sweeping up the fragments of Aaron's fondest dream.

He deposited several bottles of water in the bag. In this arid climate, water was life. He stuffed Kailyn's coat into his pack along with a first-aid kit. And a flashlight.

Aaron checked and rechecked his Glock. And packed several clips of ammunition for tactical reload. He made sure the knife he wore around his ankle was easily accessible—just like his gang mentor, Sanchez, had shown him. He had to be ready for anything.

The phone rang. Delores jumped. He palmed the cell. "Yazzie here."

Runninghawk rattled off an address. "You were right. Hiding in plain sight. A big ranching operation on the west side of Farmington. Not far off the highway. Easier access to Albuquerque. Also backs up to the Rez. A barren stretch of desert according to the survey maps. Arroyos, mesas, and canyons. I've assembled a team, Navajo Nation and Feds. I've called in the Farmington PD and a SWAT team from the sheriff's office, too."

"You've what?"

Aaron banged his hand on the table. "You've signed Kailyn's death warrant. This is my operation, Runninghawk. What don't you understand about speed, surprise, and violence of attack?"

"I've got probable cause and as much at stake as you. He's bound to have Willa, too." Runninghawk's voice wobbled. "This keeper of the flock specializes in Native girls, Diné and from the pueblos. Turns out the Feds have been looking for *Pastor* for several years. A trucking firm's registered in Shepherd's name. The Feds think he's been running girls—here's the twist the Feds didn't catch till now— south across the border to ports unknown. Not north from Mexico like most human trafficking. They figure he and his Mexican connection, a silent partner—"

"Flores," Aaron supplied.

"Flores and Shepherd are likely responsible for a dozen disappearances, more if you take into account the runaways who live in the shadows with no one to report them missing. Probably sold to select clients in South America and Pacific Rim nations. Kailyn doesn't fit his MO."

"Kailyn's his twisted attempt at vengeance upon me," Aaron growled. "You go in with guns firing and you'll get her killed. She'll be his personal, last-ditch get-out-of-jail-free card hostage. I'm what he's after. Let me talk to him. Negotiate first."

"You're forty-five minutes out, Yazzie. Maybe more with the snow coming down. Leave it to professionals who've not lost their perspective. You're emotionally compromised."

"Like you're not?"

"We can't afford to wait on you. Willa's life depends on it. It'll be dawn soon and with the last slice of darkness as our cover, we're going in."

He slammed the phone on the table as Runninghawk disconnected.

Bending, Delores clipped the leash to Taco's collar. "Taco will find our girl."

"They've sidelined me, Grandmother." He rattled a chair underneath the table. "They'll botch it, I know they will. And Kailyn will be... If she's not already..."

He gripped the chair. "Although they couldn't possibly botch it more than I already have."

"I'll be praying they arrive in time. I'm praying you will, too. My granddaughter will want you when the dust settles. You and Taco."

Delores smiled and the wrinkles in her face rearranged themselves. "The first night you arrived I dreamed of happy children once again playing on this old farm. The Dream-Giver tells me to remind you. Trust Him, my grandson, with what you hold most dear."

"I'm going to leave the praying business to you, *Shinali*." He gave the old woman a peck on the cheek, as surprised by his gesture as she. But he perceived the pleased glint in her eyes.

She patted his cheek. "Go with God, Grandson. He is most strong in our weakness."

He shoved Kailyn's cell into his jeans pocket. "I'm taking her phone and leaving the line open in case Michaels contacts me again. I don't think he's finished playing his games."

Aaron pushed his cell across the table to her. "Keep mine and your double barrel close at hand, in case Michaels comes here. Call 911 right away if anything so much as the size of a rabbit spooks you."

Taco strained at the leash until Aaron pointed him in the direction of the door. Once inside the truck, he programmed the address into the GPS. The snow line stopped this side of Blue Corn Springs, just enough to cover the ground.

A string of red and green bulbs swayed in the wind as he bypassed the small town and headed for Farmington. The Christmas cheer of an isolated mobile home only served to remind him of how bleak the world—his world—would be without Kailyn in it. Barreling down 371, he passed darkened hogans and barns beginning to spring to light as farmers, in the age-old way, took care of the livestock first.

He white-knuckled the wheel. Taco perched soldier straight, his big brown eyes peering into the gathering light on the horizon. With every beat of Aaron's heart, Kailyn called to him.

The truck fishtailed and lurched on a patch of ice as he fought to maintain traction. If he ended up in the ditch in this weather, he'd never get to her in time.

"God, please…" he whispered as he grappled for control.

The truck righted itself and he sped on his way. No traffic this time of day, but Runninghawk had been correct. The drifts lay higher and deeper on this side of the Rez.

But the snow had stopped by the time he reached the outskirts of Farmington. Following the coordinates, he arrived at the remote crossbars of the Shepherd ranch with the milky sunshine still low on the horizon above the snow-covered mesa at the rear of the property. He bounced and jolted as fast as he could push his truck without breaking an axle.

He skidded to a stop halfway down the lane leading to the elaborate Southwestern style ranch house behind a bevy of LE cars, trucks, and EMS vans. Taco vaulted over his lap and onto the ground ahead of him.

At a run, he and Taco headed for the broad, terra-cotta-tiled porch only to be stopped by a burly, buzz-cut Anglo in a Farmington PD uniform who ordered him to halt.

Which he ignored.

The Anglo snapped off the safety latch of his side holster and in one smooth movement, which Aaron admired for its economy of motion, drew his 9mm and pointed the cold steel barrel. "I'm ordering you to stop or I'll—"

"He's okay. He's with the team." Runninghawk lifted a section of yellow crime scene tape. "He and I partnered in the intel on this."

The Anglo holstered his gun. His thin Anglo lip curled as he gaped at the dog between them. "The dog your partner, too, Runninghawk? Craziest K9 I ever saw. But I guess things are different on your side of the fence."

Runninghawk ducked out from under the tape and stood shoulder to shoulder with Aaron. "Yeah, they are. This dog's one of our best bloodhounds. And," he leaned into the Anglo's face, very unNavajo-like, never breaking eye contact. "Over there," Runninghawk sneered, "we train them to go ballistic at the sight of big, fat *bilagaanas*."

If his heart hadn't already been at a flatline since he heard Burke Michaels's voice, Aaron would've smiled as the Anglo retreated a step.

Runninghawk waved Aaron to follow him. A swarm of LE officers—county, state, and federal—filled the spacious foyer, gathering evidence.

He'd seen a lot of crime scenes in his career, death in Afghanistan, and the aftermath of what disloyalty to Flores wrought. But what he beheld once his eyes adjusted to the gloom of the interior took his breath. Bullets riddled the paneling. Pools of blood surrounded several bodies, contorted in strange angles of death.

A handful of girls huddled as female police officers questioned them and EMTs administered treatment for cuts and bruises. The girls were a range of ages and naked except for the blankets wrapped around their thin, frail torsos.

Jace bit his lip and crossed his arms over his uniform. "I-I know. It's bad."

Aaron cut his eyes at Jace. "Where's Kailyn? Is she…?" He searched among the dark heads for a red one.

"The goons were cartel-trained. They knew failure wasn't an option. They fought even after the flashbang. We couldn't burn them out for fear of harming the hostages. But Kailyn's not here. We didn't find her, just these…" Jace spat. "I won't dignify these monsters with the name of men. Guards who patrolled the perimeter while Shepherd stalked his prey on the streets of Albuquerque. Degenerates who drugged the girls he brought here into compliance. Animals who broke the ones who resisted until they could be shipped overseas."

The knife-wielding, lamp-smashing Kailyn he loved would never have gone down without a fight. Unless she'd been drugged or beaten senseless.

"She's got to be here." He surged forward, Taco on his heels. "Have you checked—?"

Jace caught his arm. "The hall's lined with…" His mouth worked. "Rooms. Holding pens."

Aaron released the leash. Taco trailed off, sniffing at the base-boards. "And Willa? Did you find Willa?"

"She's okay. When she got the call from the runaway, she arrived to find Shepherd hustling the girl. He took them both, but he hadn't time to harm her. Either of them. An officer is questioning them now."

Aaron swiveled to find Willa leaning against the wall, her arm around a teenage girl whose face already looked street-hardened. Willa gave him a small, gallant wave. Her eyes traveled to Jace and watered.

Holding his hand over the region of his heart, Jace nodded at Willa. She swallowed and turned to the police officer questioning the girl.

Jace dragged his attention to Aaron. "Will says there're graves out back. The ones who wouldn't be broken. Shepherd bragged about it." His mouth tightened. "Warned what he'd do to her, but he got busy. An opportunity to abduct Kailyn?"

"He must've had someone watching the house and when Kailyn was home alone..."

"That's what I'm thinking. Willa never saw Kailyn, but she did hear a commotion outside the padlocked room about midnight."

Aaron searched the corridor for signs of Taco. "If she's been here, Taco will find her scent."

Jace blocked his advance. "I've also put in a call for the county medical examiner. An awning was rigged to keep out the snow while a body was interred." His teeth worried his lip. "A grave, Aaron, recently dug."

25

SHOOED AWAY BY THE FORENSIC TEAM FROM THE FRESHLY DUG GRAVE, AARON and Taco returned to the house. Consulting the geological maps, Jace organized search teams with proper K9 dogs to scour the badlands around the ranch.

Taco's nose twitched and he dragged Aaron down a corridor to a far room. A federal agent Aaron recognized—they'd done their training at Quantico together—raised his eyes from the computer screen on Michaels's desk. Sometimes the world was very small.

"Heard you were mixed up in this, Matthews." The agent smirked. "You can kiss your career good-bye."

But sometimes, when it came to finding the person he most wanted to see alive, the world could be a very large place.

Aaron tightened his hold on Taco's leash. "It's Yazzie. And returning to the Bureau's way down on my bucket list for life goals."

The agent—Watkins—shrugged. "Also heard you managed to lose your witness. Correction, WITSEC's witness."

"You find any record of my wif—?" Aaron tried again. "Any evidence Kailyn was ever brought to this location?"

He couldn't bear to contemplate what lay in the grave outside. Couldn't—refused—to wrap his mind around the strong possibility the medical examiner would unearth a corpse with copper-red hair.

Something akin to sympathy glimmered in his colleague's eyes. "Here's a photo file you'll find interesting." He swiveled the screen as Aaron released Taco and sidled closer.

Five photographs. Taken from a location somewhere in the canyons behind the hogan. Kailyn getting into the truck with Taco. Another of Gid and *Shinali* underneath the cottonwood arbor. The presence of the loom in the picture timed the photo to sometime in early October, before he and Gid moved the loom indoors.

Another shot zoomed in on the woodpile. He clenched his jaw. A fourth depicted the Toyota-sized boulder—Kailyn's prayer rock—and her face lifted to a turquoise sky, her eyes closed. The long, wavy strands of her silken hair blowing in a desert breeze.

His fingers convulsed.

The final photo of him and Kailyn. A morning sunrise on the back porch, coffee mugs in their hands. He leaned against the porch railing, his head rotated toward her. She gazed at him with a smile curving her lips. Her eyes with the half-lidded, upswept Southern flirt she employed with such precision.

At him anyway.

He slumped.

Watkins touched the screen with his latex-gloved finger. "Pretty lady."

His lady.

Aaron gripped the side of the desk. "She walks in beauty."

Watkins scrolled through the photos again. "Looks like he monitored your place for several months."

"Biding his time."

Taco barked and growled.

He veered to find Taco burrowing his head underneath a red leather armchair. "What did you find, boy?" Aaron took hold of Taco's collar. "What have you got? Watkins—there's something wedged between the chair and the wall."

Watkins helped him shift the chair away from the wall and carefully, to avoid smudging any potential fingerprints, lifted the ivory candle from the tiled floor. "Used to sit on the side table." He pointed at the blob of wax beside a black iron candlestick.

Aaron's heart thudded. "There's blood on the end of the candlestick."

Watkins examined the crimson stain. "My guess is somebody seated in this chair grabbed the candlestick."

The agent squatted, peering from the table to the spot against the baseboard where the candle rested. "And the candle went flying, rolling under the chair. Somebody got whacked good."

Watkins rose, chagrin on his face. "Sorry, Yazzie. Not what you wanted to hear, I know."

A certainty defying logic seized hold of Aaron. "*She* smacked *him*, Watkins. Not the other way around. I'm sure of it." He yanked the seat cushion.

Taco jumped onto the couch. He held Taco back at the sight of a hypodermic needle buried between the cushions. "What do you make of that?"

Watkins plucked the hypo with the tips of his latex-gloved forefinger and thumb. He sniffed it. "We'll test it for sure, but probably the same stuff we've found elsewhere in the house to keep the girls subdued." He snagged a hair caught in the zipper of the cushion.

For the first time, Watkins smiled. He held the hair to the light of the chandelier.

A copper hair glinted in the refracted light.

"You might be on to something, Yazzie. We'll test the blood on the candlestick, too. But it appears your witness was seated here, because far as we can tell she's the only missing Anglo. Remember, Michaels specializes—"

Watkins made a face. "In Native girls. Maybe he believed her to be subdued, but even groggy, she managed to smash that iron bar on his head." He grimaced. "Dare I hope your lady took a big, honking piece out of the slime-ball?"

Aaron shook his head. "He doesn't like it when his vics fight back. If she did whack him, she'll pay for it in ways you could never dream." He averted his eyes. "Trust me, I know."

"But we know for sure, now, that she was here."

Footsteps pounded outside in the hallway. Jace poked his head around the doorframe. "Not Kailyn..." He panted. "Not her in the grave." He grasped the door casing. "A runaway, the M.E. thinks. From one of the Pueblo tribes."

His eyes locked onto Aaron's. "There's still a chance."

But where was she? And was she still alive?

Over the next few hours, with the police sifting through moun-tains of evidence, Aaron felt at loose ends. He needed to be doing something, anything, in the search for Kailyn. The crisp December day had warmed up enough to melt most of the snow in the arid environment around the ranch. The cell in his pocket vibrated. Her cell.

An unlisted number. He clicked On.

"I think you have caused me enough trouble, Yazzie. I'm done with you. You want Kailyn? You come and get her. Alone."

Clutching the phone, he twined Taco's leash around his arm, and darted to the edge of the porch. "You'll exchange her for me?"

A chuckle.

Memories prickled his spine. His knees buckled. He fought to overcome a remembered terror. A terror threefold for Kailyn.

"This is between you and me, Yazzie. Always been between you and me. Why do you think I dispatched the Conquistadores scout sent to locate you? Your worthless, sorry, dirty Injun hide belongs to me. Has always belonged to me. I'm in control, been in control, since you set foot on the Rez. I always win, boy. You ought to remember that if you don't remember nothing else."

Aaron swallowed, fear choking his throat.

"Maybe I'll transfer your lesson to this Anglo woman you've managed to make a whore of with her association with you."

"Don't call her—"

"You don't tell me what to do." An explosion of rage. "You stupid, good-for-nothing Injun. Too stupid to find her. What have I got to do? Leave a trail of breadcrumbs for you to follow?"

"I'll come..." Aaron tucked his head into his chest. "Wherever you say. Whatever you want to do to me. Just—"

"You weary me, boy." Michaels blew out a breath over the phone. "I'm standing here looking at your house. Waiting on you to do something intelligent. Clock's ticking. You got forty minutes, give or take, before time runs out on your redheaded woman." He punched Off.

Terror gripped Aaron's heart. He remembered Burke's words about buried treasure and he wondered if any mining operations had ever been conducted in the canyon lands in the vicinity of the Yazzie homestead.

In one bound, he leaped off the porch and headed for Jace's unmarked cruiser. He grabbed the survey maps and examined them. Wouldn't do Kailyn any good for him to go rushing off half-cocked. Probably what Burke counted on.

What Burke didn't know was that when Aaron was a teenager, *Shinali* had tried to make a Diné sheepherder out of him. Each summer they made the June trek into the foothills of the Chuska in these same canyons toward the higher elevations of pasture and water for *Shinali's* sheep.

His finger lighted upon a small red dot on the map in his hands. The Turquesa Mine. Turquoise in Spanish. Closed, the date in parentheses indicated, since the late 1930s. He scoured his memory—and the info he'd acquired through an underutilized engineering degree—for what he recalled about mining.

Turquoise lay close to the surface, often mixed in with the more valuable copper. In that period, unlike modern open-pit mining, shaft mining would've been the norm. Hammers, shovels and pick-axes used to extract the gemstone. *Shinali* and his grandfather had always given the spot a wide berth.

He closed his eyes and crumpled the map in his fist.

God, please let her be there.

Taco whined at his feet, his tail thumping the ground.

"We'll find her, boy."

But would they be in time?

He'd already wasted five of his precious minutes. Not wasted, though. Now he had a solid lead.

On a sudden hunch, he rifled through the glove compartment of Jace's vehicle, drawing out a road map.

"Unpaved, but there's a road, my man," he crowed. "Used by the trucks to haul away the copper, abandoned now like the mine. Straight through the desert aimed like an arrow in the quickest way to the highway."

The road would shave twenty minutes off his deadline. Reinvigorated, he scooped Taco up and edged his way around the police vehicles, praying—yeah, praying—that Jace or Watkins or the Anglo beefeater wouldn't question where he was going.

Because if Michaels got wind of LE, he'd execute her just for kicks.

Easing into the truck, he shifted into reverse, again thanking God no one hemmed him in. Out on the main highway seconds later, he spotted the turnoff—nothing more than a dusty track of muddy grooves and ruts thanks to the melting snow.

He pressed his foot onto the accelerator and surged forward. "Hang on, Taco, my man. We're going full throttle."

The engine strained as they picked up speed, jarring his head on the roof. The truck gradually inclined with the increasing elevation.

Three-quarters of the way there, the track came to an immediate and terrifying end. The ground dropped away. He slammed on the brakes.

"No!"

He thumped his hand on the wheel. A flash flood had eroded the ground into something resembling a pint-sized gorge.

Aaron scrubbed his hand across his mouth. "This the best You can do? Should've known You wouldn't be any real help."

Taco barked.

Aaron cut his eyes over the expanse of the impassable gulch and back to Taco. He could bridge the treacherous gap on foot. His little friend not so much.

He sighed. "I'll have to go the rest of the way without you."

Taco yelped as if he understood.

"I don't like it any better than you do. I know you want to see her almost as much as I do."

Taco laid his paw on his arm.

"Okay, maybe as much as I do. But you'll slow me down. Time's running out. I'll be back. Soon. With Kailyn. And you're going to have a mountain of tasty Pampered Pooch treats when she hears about your Superdog heroics."

He fondled Taco's bat-like ears. "I'm sorry, little man. You know I'd take you with me if I could. Michaels has hurt your human. Collaring this psycho belongs to you as much as me. But I gotta go the distance alone now."

Alone. Like he'd always been.

Taco stretched out on the seat, his head upon his front paws. Aaron left the windows rolled down and issued a warning. "Stay inside, little guy. No need to tempt the coyotes."

Aaron glanced at the cell phone. No coverage here. No surprise there. Service this close to the Rez was fifty-fifty at best. He unscrewed one of the two bottles of water in his backpack and poured the contents into a basin he had found in the truck bed.

"Stay safe, Taco. I'll return as soon as I can."

His boots sank into the snow-moistened soil and he skidded halfway down the embankment of the crevasse before he caught himself.

At the bottom of the ravine, he studied the other side. Digging his fingers into the steep wall, he gripped a rock and heaved himself upward, scrabbling for a foothold. He clawed his way to the top, soil and pebbles raining on his head.

Once out of the trench, he set off at a trot toward the range of mesas between him and the mineshaft. He sprinted past patches of yucca. Winded with a stitch in his side, he pushed himself past the pain, beyond the burning need to refill his lungs.

He skirted clusters of prickly pear. Rounding a curve in the rock buttress, he perceived the telltale signs of the mineshaft in the hidden canyon below.

Aaron froze, only his eyes moving. Roving, assessing potential threats and predators. Only the wind whistled through a distant stand of ponderosa pine. Observing no one hiding in the rocky cliffs, with a final jump, he jolted to the sandy canyon bottom. He raced toward the pile of rocks and debris obscuring the entrance.

"Kailyn!"

Slinging off his backpack, he fell to his knees and shoved aside the rotting timbers. His hands tore and bled as he thrust away the stones between him and Kailyn.

"Can you hear me, Kailyn? Are you down there? Honey..." His voice cracked and he saved his energy for uncovering the tomb Michaels had erected for her.

Using his shoulder to leverage an unwieldy boulder, the force of his momentum against its initial inertia almost sent him tumbling into the mineshaft. A cloud of dust and decay arose, sending him into a coughing fit.

"Kailyn. Answer me."

Directing the beam of the flashlight, he peered through the billowing particles into the darkness. When the dust settled, he eyed a rotting ladder hammered into the wall of the shaft. And scanned the form, perhaps twenty feet down, of a woman curled into the fetal position.

His woman. Wearing the jeans, high-heeled turquoise boots, and cream sweater in which he'd last seen her.

Would the ladder hold his weight? Flashlight clutched in one hand, he crawled over the side and tested it. Michaels had to have accessed the pit himself.

Unless he'd merely thrown her inside. And then left her to die.

Clenching his jaw, Aaron dropped the backpack into the hole, aiming for a spot in the tunnel behind Kailyn. He scrambled down and with a plop landed on the balls of his feet beside her. Another cloud of dust levitated, stinging his eyes, filling his nostrils with the stale, dank air in the cavern.

He tumbled to his knees and set the flashlight onto the ground, its light casting shadows on the cave wall behind him and Kailyn. She was so still. So unnaturally still.

"Kailyn, baby..."

Her skin so cold to his touch. Like a marble statue in a museum. Without warmth. Without life.

Like his world without her in it.

"No...Kailyn." He shook her. "Wake up. Kailyn, listen to me. Hear my voice. Open your eyes."

Aaron gathered her into his arms. "Please, Kailyn…Don't you dare die on me." His eyes shot to the crevice of light at the top of the shaft.

"Please…" he whispered. "Don't take her, too."

With her head lolling against his chest, he rubbed her arms. Freezing cold. He didn't know how long she'd been here. He didn't know how long it took a human body to die of exposure in temps like these. Aaron peeled off his own jacket and wrapped her in it.

"Deb, are you listening to me?" He took her face between his hands. "*Dzani*, woman, don't leave me." Aaron choked.

Tears rolled down his face. The tears he'd never found for either of his mothers or Steve. "Do you hear me?" he yelled.

And he placed his lips on hers, breathing his life into hers, willing her to respond.

He lifted his head, sucking in a lungful of oxygen. He ran his thumb over the contours of her cheek. "*Querida,* por favor." His mouth descended.

She quivered. A low moan escaped from her lips.

"Kailyn?"

He jerked and reached for the backpack. She needed water.

"Aa-aron…" She caught his arm. Her eyes flew open.

Those iris blues of hers dilated, but her lips curved into a semblance of a smile at the sight of him hovering over her. She raised her hand to his face. Her fingertips brushed the moisture off his cheek.

"Here, drink this." Unscrewing the cap, he propped her against his chest and helped her tilt the plastic bottle toward her mouth.

She guzzled the liquid, droplets dribbling down her chin.

"Take it easy. Not so much so fast. Don't want it to come right back up."

She surrendered her hold on the bottle and leaned back. "I knew you'd come. I prayed you'd find me."

He let out a shaky laugh, the air fizzing out between his lips. He'd almost been too late.

Maybe this God of hers had come through. He'd ponder it later. After he got her to safety.

She stirred. He jumped up and gave her the support she needed to get her feet under her. Weak as one of *Shinali's dibeh-yazzies*, little lambs, she swayed against him.

"Are you hurt, *querida*?"

He inspected her face in the feeble light, looking for signs of bruising, cuts. And burns. Hard to tell if underneath her clothes—

"Did he...?" He bit his lip, knotting his brow. "Did he hurt you?"

At his tone, her head lifted. "Not in the way you mean. But I saw..."

She gazed over his shoulder into the darkness. "I saw what he does...to others."

Kailyn wrapped her arms around his waist. "But no. He didn't touch me other than sticking me with needles."

He sagged against her in relief, thanking God—this was getting to be redundant—she'd been spared that. Maybe he and God were overdue for a long talk. Past overdue.

Sheltered by his arms, Kailyn huddled into the warmth of him. God had answered her prayers. Streaked with mud and incredibly dirty, they were both, however, alive.

And together.

He tightened his grip. "It's my fault you landed in his clutches. I should've never brought you here."

She cupped his jaw. "If it's anyone's fault, it's mine. It's because of me you came here in the first place."

"If he'd hurt you...?" He stiffened. "I would've tracked him down like the cockroach he is and killed him." A muscle twitched in his cheek. "I'm still going to kill him."

"Aaron, don't let his hate poison you."

He buttoned Kailyn's coat around her. "We need to get out of here before he returns. But I'll be back. For him. He won't find the weak, easily intimidated boy he remembers. I've learned a thing or two since then. From the Conquistadores and the Rangers. From Flores."

Aaron pulled her toward the steps fastened onto the cavern wall. "You go first. I'll be right behind, making sure you make it. I'll have your back."

She caressed his hand, turning it over and resting his palm alongside her face. "You've always had my back. You and God."

A flash of teeth as he gave her a lopsided grin. "And you've got mine. Like you told CeCe."

He shrugged. "Maybe this God of yours, too."

Something sweet seared her heart, and as her foot found the lowest rung on the ladder, she prayed God's grace would find him at last. For the Shepherd of his soul to gather this one lost lamb close to His heart.

One narrow rung at a time, they ascended. She expected any moment to hear the crack of wood sending them plummeting to the bottom. But as they rose, he filled her in on the events of the last twenty-four hours, including the call from Gid about Mateo.

Kailyn's mouth trembled. She'd wrongly assumed the call had been from…

She kept her face to the wall and lifted her eyes to the next handhold.

Aaron told her what the social worker had said about Taco. How Taco had proven himself a real hero. About what the police had found at Michaels's ranch. About Willa and the other girls.

She let out a breath of air. It always circled back to Willa.

At the top rung, she paused, her elbows clinging to the soil above the opening as exhaustion overtook her once more. Unable to summon the strength to haul herself out the rest of the way.

"Here." Slinging the backpack over his head, he groped for the surface beside her and swung himself up and over.

The wood underneath her boots splintered. She gasped, her eyes going large. Her feet dangled off into nothingness. Her fingernails fought for a handhold in the dirt, losing ground to gravity.

He grabbed her underneath her arms and with a tremendous heave propelled her skyward where their bodies rolled together in the red dust of the Rez, away from the gaping pit toward safety.

Or not.

"Get off the white woman, you Injun snake."

Burke Michaels hovered over them, the long steel barrel of a rifle aimed at Aaron's head.

Aaron tensed. She sensed rather than beheld his slight movement.

"No," she hissed, warning him.

His hand stilled upon his holster.

"Still hiding behind the skirts of your women, Yazzie?"

The taunt succeeded in driving Aaron to his feet. She caught hold of his arm, arresting his motion once more. He tried to shake her free.

Kailyn hung on. "He's just looking for an excuse to kill you."

"Smart lady. Smarter than you for sure." Burke pointed the gun at Aaron's chest. "She knows if you don't take out your gun nice and slow, I'm going to blow a hole in your redskin chest."

Burke nudged the gun in her direction. "Or maybe I'll take care of your girlfriend first. Hands up, little lady." He chuckled.

Swallowing hard, she raised her hands chest level. Aaron's focus never wavered from the gun in Burke's hands. But the cold hardness in his face—Rafe's face—took her breath, a resoluteness as intractable as one of the boulders rimming the canyon.

"Whatever you want, Michaels." His tone was soft, soothing.

He lifted his hands to show Burke his sincerity. With great deliberation, Aaron extracted the pistol from his belt. Holding the top of the gun, his fingers well away from the trigger, he raised the gun to shoulder level with his other hand.

"Now toss it, Yazzie." Burke gestured. "Over there."

Aaron complied. "It's me you wanted. Let her go."

Burke sneered. "Touching. You ransoming your life for hers. At the ranch she offered to do anything to save your skin." He spat at the ground. "Like your mother once upon a time. But 'fraid not, Son."

"I'm not your—" Aaron bit his lip. "She's—"

"Oh, I know all about who Kailyn Eudailey is."

Burke's bristly white eyebrows arched. "I've already put in a call to Flores. He's on his way. Personally." He jerked his head at a cloud of dust signaling the arrival of an incoming vehicle.

"Boy, you sure do know how to make enemies." Burke smiled.

The smile made her skin crawl.

"He's upped the contract on my friend Kailyn here to a cool mil if alive. Less if dead. For you he's offering two mil, only if delivered alive."

Burke swung the rifle toward her. "I'm afraid the time has come to end our recent and most pleasant acquaintance." He jabbed the rifle. "Move away from him."

Aaron reached for her. "No."

She clambered out of Aaron's reach, resisting his attempt to shield her with his body. Burke would kill him. If she created a diversion, perhaps she'd buy him enough time to seize an opening and turn the gun on Burke.

Even if it meant giving her life for his.

Kailyn lifted her chin, her eyes fastening on the azure-blue sky overhead. She knew the Shepherd of her soul. Aaron didn't.

Not yet…

Burke coughed.

Her eyes flicked to him.

Something passed across his face, something almost human. Regret shone out of his eyes.

"You were a real nice lady, Miss Eudailey. Reminded me of my mama. With your prayers on the rock every day."

Burke's mouth contorted. "Though, like her, little good they did you."

His eyes slid toward Aaron, who was inching forward. "You move another muscle and I'll blow her brains out this instant."

Aaron froze, his neck muscles straining.

Burke shifted his feet. "Because I like you, Kailyn, and because no decent white woman, should ever fall into the hands of Mexican scum like Flores, I'm going to accept the five hundred grand for your body."

She blanched.

"I'll wait for the two mil on your behalf, Yazzie. I'm an amateur at exacting revenge compared to a pro like Flores. You'll pay inch by inch for your betrayal of the cartel, but you'll do so knowing you failed her. Knowing she lost her life because of you. And the satisfaction I'll get from the look on your face when she drops to the ground will almost equal the financial compensation."

"Burke..." She trembled.

He swiveled the barrel between them, keeping them both arm's length from each other. "One shot—I'm a good aim, the Academy made sure of that—and it'll be over before you have time to register the sound. Quick. Painless as I can make it, Kailyn. I promise you that."

Kailyn's eyes traveled to the dried blood, a finger-length's rip, across Burke's forehead. She'd hefted the candlestick in her hand and landed a satisfying thwack across his head.

"Too bad"—she licked her lips and tossed her hair over her shoulder—"I wasn't strong enough to crack your skull."

She rolled her tongue over her teeth. "I hope it leaves a nasty scar. So you'll remember me."

Aaron shook his head. "*Dzani*..."

She twisted the ring on her finger. Her wedding ring. "Thank you for this."

Her gaze swept the immensity of the landscape. "For all this. I've been hap..." She swallowed. "But where I'm headed, I'll be okay, Aaron."

The desert light tinted his face copper. "Kailyn..."

She tilted her head, looking at him from underneath her eyelashes.

And something almost visceral passed between them.

Burke's face hardened. His finger tightened on the trigger.

Lightning forked from the rocks behind Kailyn, between her and Aaron. A shot cracked through the air.

With an instantaneous reflex, Aaron dove for her position and wrapped his arms around her waist. He tackled her to the ground, twisting his body to absorb maximum impact. She screamed as their bodies collided against the cold, packed earth.

In that split second, her eyes fastened on Burke's face, at the streak she'd left across his forehead. Which widened in front of her eyes, as it separated from the rest of his head. The top of his skull cleaved off. He crumpled, collapsing to the ground like a marionette whose strings have been severed.

She shut her eyes. The gunshot rang in her ears, reverberating against the high canyon walls. A silence settled once more over the ancient landscape, except for the whisper of a sibilant breeze.

"Aaron? Kailyn?"

"The Spirit, like the wind, whispers messages to those with ears to hear," she murmured to Aaron, his mouth inches below hers.

He sighed. "*Shinali*'s made you Diné, hasn't she?"

She gave a raspy laugh. "Almost."

He eased out from under her and hauled her to her feet. Gid rose from behind a sandstone boulder, a high-powered rifle with mounted scope cradled in his arms.

"Is she okay?" Gid emerged from behind the rock cairn. "Are you okay?"

"We're fine." Aaron nestled her closer. "Thanks to you…" Aaron's eyes brimmed. "Dad."

A transformational emotion flickered across Gid's weathered and life-beaten face. He straightened, broadened his chest, and crossed the remaining distance separating them. "Long overdue. For your mother."

Kailyn's heart stirred.

Gid's eyes sought Aaron's. "For you, Son."

She glanced at Aaron, at the vulnerability and love for his father sweeping across his sharp-angled face. Aaron's chest rose and fell as if he'd run a great distance.

Perhaps today, in so many ways, he had.

26

Emotion for his father welled in Aaron's heart.

He laced his fingers through Kailyn's hand. So much emotion for this woman he determined to never let out of his sight again.

Gid cocked his head. "*Shima* called. Said you needed help you'd never ask for. I followed you."

"But the road..."

"There's another way. A real shortcut only old-timers like me remember. I parked my truck on the other side and hiked over so I could get the drop on Michaels."

His father hoisted Aaron's backpack. "Michaels planned this well." Gid pursed his lips. "We're boxed in and the Enemy comes."

Aaron shunted around as two black SUVs churned to a stop in a billowing cloud of dust at the mouth of the canyon. Five black-suited men emerged with weapons drawn—the FN Five-seveN, unofficially known as the cop killer. Their polarized sunglasses glinted in the sun.

"We've got to get out of here." Retrieving his Glock, he swiveled, searching for another way. "Michaels funneled us into a kill zone."

"Only way out is the way I came." Gid's mouth tightened. "Over the mesa." He gripped his rifle. "I'll hold them off while you get Kailyn to safety."

Aaron shook his head. "No way I'm leaving you here to fight them by yourself. You won't stand a chance alone."

Gid's wide face broke into a grin. "I'm not alone." He squinted at the eye-searing blue sky. "I've got my Shepherd. And in case you've forgotten, shepherds, by nature of their occupation, are often called upon to be wolf-killers, too."

He smacked his palm upon the gunstock. "Time to go a-hunting."

"Dad…I don't think—"

Gid rolled his eyes. "You gonna protect our girl or what? Your problem…" he arched an eyebrow, "is you think too much. Now get going."

Aaron wrapped his hand around the sinewy muscles underneath Gid's flannel sleeve. "Don't you dare get yourself killed. You hear me, old man?"

Gid grunted and positioned himself behind a mushroom-shaped boulder, a hoo doo. "Go." He waved his hand. "Before you give away my location."

Aaron exchanged glances with Kailyn. She gave his father a fierce hug and then Aaron guided her along a serpentine track, more suited to mountain goats, not people. She stumbled with fatigue or the aftereffects of the drug. She'd have fallen on the uneven terrain except for his hand shooting out and catching her. He clambered over a jagged crag.

"I'm sorry." She gritted her teeth. "Not wearing appropriate foot-wear, I know. I'm slowing you down."

Gripping her hand, he leveraged his weight and pulled her through a cleft in the canyon rock. "Wasn't like you knew you'd be running for your life across a desert wasteland."

She smiled—as he'd intended—at his echo of her words in Atlanta.

"But Sweetheart," he rested his back against a rugged monolith. "You don't slow me down. Gives me a chance to catch my breath and admire the turquoise sky."

The toes of her boots clambered for a secure footing. "Don't tell me you're finally becoming a half-full guy."

"Ssh." He grinned. "Don't blow my cover. See what a positive influence you've had on this reprobate?"

He spotted Gid's truck in the distant valley below. "We're almost there, *dzani*. Hang on. A little further."

Shading her eyes against the glare of the midday sun, she nodded, matching his stride.

"And once we're settled at your new WITSEC location, you won't ever have to look over your shoulder again. I promise you."

She blinked at him. "We?"

He offered his hand to help her traverse a treacherous spot. "I'm not leaving you to face those jackals in court alone."

Aaron monitored the placement of her feet. "I'm good as my word. Curb-to-curb service."

She tottered.

He yanked her hard against his chest. "You're not the only one who might want a new start, a do-over. Never been to Wichita or Seattle or wherever they locate you after your testimony. I'm always up for an adventure."

Aaron tucked a strand of her hair behind her ear. "If you wouldn't mind me tagging along."

Kailyn cupped his face in her hands. "I need to tell you something. I…"

His mouth seized on hers and his arms wrapped around her shoulder blades. Her body swayed against him, her back arching. Aaron's lips welded to hers.

She stretched on the tips of her toes, her fingers combing through his hair. His mouth found the hollow of her throat above the turquoise cross. Kailyn lifted her face and closed her eyes.

And he breathed in her sweetness, the utterly beguiling magnolia fragrance of her being.

"Kailyn…"

The words he needed to say worked to get around his fear of exposing his heart. "*Ayóó—*"

A gunshot shattered the desert stillness. More blasts of gunfire followed.

Convulsing, he pulled back. "Got distracted. You distract me." He raked a hand across the top of his head. "Later. Definitely later."

He looked at her, hoping with his eyes to say what his lips could not. "You and I need to stop getting our signals crossed."

Rounding a curve, he halted in his tracks.

She plowed into his back. "What's—?"

He pointed at the natural stone bridge spanning the distance between the last two buttes between them and the valley. She dropped her gaze to the ravine.

"Is this Gid's idea of a joke?" she whispered. "One wrong step and next stop..."

"Coyote food." He glanced around. "We must've taken a wrong turn somewhere."

Gunfire peppered the trail behind them, the sounds drawing closer.

"We don't have time to backtrack. I'll go first. Test it to make sure it'll hold my weight. Then, you."

She caught his arm. "I don't think that's such a good idea."

"Like someone wise recently told me, 'You think too much.'"

Aaron shook her off and stepped onto the precipice, putting one foot in front of the other. "Can you never do what someone tells you without arguing?"

He wobbled and butterflied his arms to regain his balance.

She cried out.

"I'm okay," he called, not daring to turn and look at her. "A few more feet and I'm there."

He inched his way across. "Slow and steady wins the race. Make sure when it's your turn you don't look down. Just straight ahead to me on the other side. I'll be waiting for you."

Aaron froze, making sure his foot had traction before lifting the other forward. "See? No big deal. No problema. Just—"

"Stop talking and focus," she shouted. "Yak. Yak. Yak. Now you decide to become Mr. Merry Sunshine? Don't you dare fall off, Aaron Yazzie. Or I'll—"

"You'll what?"

He jumped the last few feet, hugging the solid sandstone cliff. "Are we talking knives, lamps, or those spiky-heeled boots?"

Aaron grinned and felt like planting his lips against the blessed solidity of the stone. Better yet—planting his lips against...

"Here's an idea —" Aaron pivoted.

The grin faded at the sight of Flores with his arm snaked around Kailyn's neck, pinning her against his chest. The steel of a knife gleamed at her throat.

"We meet again, mi amigo," Flores taunted. "Toss the gun over the ledge. Or I'll cut her."

Kailyn winced as the tip of the knife pricked her skin.

Aaron's features settled into the hard mask of Rafe Chavez. His posture subtly altered. No longer the man she loved more than life itself, but now the angry, violent gangbanger she'd first met at the hotel in Charlotte.

A lifetime ago.

He removed the gun from the waistband of his jeans and chucked it over the cliff.

"I gave your partner the slip." Flores shifted and she shifted with him to avoid being impaled on the blade of his knife. "Once my men dispose of him, your turn next."

Flores sneered. "And this chica who has cost me such time and money."

She turned her face from the overpowering aroma of his expensive cologne.

Aaron edged onto the narrow stone causeway. "Typical Esteban. Has to let his flunkies take care of the hard stuff." He spat over the edge of the precipice. "No wonder your padre distrusts you to handle operations stateside."

Flores's hold tightened. "I've tripled his profits. I've streamlined the production process on my brothers' end, too. If they'd listen to my ideas—"

"No one wants to listen to the illegitimate son of La Familia."

Her eyes never left Aaron's face as he moved forward one agonizing inch at a time.

Flores growled, clenching the knife. "You are wrong. Estúpido. I take care of my own messes. Like I took care of that—"

She flinched at the vitriol of rapid-fire Spanish Flores used in reference to Gaby.

"As I will take care of you, Chavez."

Flores angled her toward the drop-off. "I want what belongs to me. Where's the information Gaby copied, chica? What have you done with it?"

He shook her like a doll. Her arms flailed.

"Is that what this is about, Flores?" Derision colored Aaron's tone. "You losing control of your wife? Enraged, weren't you, when a mere woman threatened to bring the entire enterprise crashing to the ground? Gabriela was planning on taking it to the Feds, wasn't she? To make sure you rotted behind bars for the rest of your bitter born days."

Aaron wrinkled his nose. "You had to make sure your brothers didn't learn of it first. You were terrified Gabriela's revelations would permanently emasculate what amounts to the annoying ambitions of a bastardo half-brother."

Flores swung to face Aaron. "Where is it?"

"You mean the tiny microchip Gabriela inserted underneath the skin of a dog?"

Aaron folded his arms, swayed before regaining his footing. "*El perro* is smarter than you, *mi patrón*. A dog. The microchip's in the hands of the U.S. district attorney, courtesy of the good ole U.S. Postal Service."

Flores jabbed the knife at Aaron. "You lie. You lie to save your skin. The lies roll out of your mouth. But see how the lies flow after I flay the skin off this woman's face."

Because she'd spent the better part of three months learning to read his every nuance, every trace of emotion on his face, she interpreted the tightening of his jaw, the barest hint of his body shifting, the more telltale sign of the bulging muscle in his cheek.

"*Dzani*," he yelled. "Boot."

He leaped across the remaining distance of the bridge dividing them.

She brought the heel of her boot onto the top of Flores's foot and rammed her elbow into his stomach.

With a whoosh of air, Flores released her, clutching his midsection, and backed away, struggling to regain his breath. She twisted to the right and dived for a large outcropping.

Aaron landed on the balls of his feet in a crouch. In a motion so quick and smooth she almost missed it, he plucked a knife from underneath the leg of his jeans.

He threw the knife, steel tip over handle, handle over steel tip, whistling through the air, sinking into the soft underbelly of Flores.

Eyes wide with shock, Flores bent his head as if to study the strange protrusion sticking out from his body. Shook his head in disbelief at the slow, ever-widening red ripples that stained the front of his white shirt. His face convulsed.

Slumping to his knees, Flores fell face forward into the red dust of the canyon below. His body impacted the ground with a dull thud.

Aaron remained low to the ground, his eyes wild, his chest heaving.

She squatted at eye level. "Aaron . . . ?" She put out her hand, stopping shy of making contact so as not to startle him.

Aaron tore his eyes away from the gruesome spectacle beneath them and fastened onto hers. A light illuminated the blackness of his orbs, igniting from within as shock and Rafe receded and sanity returned.

"Kailyn." His voice a husky whisper, he pulled her close, kissing the top of her head. "We've got to get out of here. His goons will be right behind."

Aaron cocked his head to listen at the sudden silence. The color drained from his face. "Gid—"

Footfalls sounded on the trail and a shower of loose pebbles cascaded off the steep side of the track, raining upon the broken body of Flores. Aaron shoved her behind him.

"*Ya'at'eeh*, my son."

Gid's head sidled around the curvature of the rock. A grin slashing his face, he fist-pumped the rifle above his head. He let loose a series of sharp, guttural cries.

And if she hadn't known—and loved—Gideon Yazzie, the sound would've raised the hairs on her neck.

Cries that once ignited a primal fear within the hearts of the legendary Spanish invaders and the Diné's more recent adversaries, the U.S. Cavalry.

Give or take a hundred years.

Their hands locked behind their heads, three of Flores's men marched in single file over the rough track. Including Villeda. They were the worse for wear after their encounter with Aaron's dad. Their clothes ripped and torn, patches of red flesh marked Gid's accuracy where a bullet impacted their flesh.

Behind them, Jace's smiling face bobbed into view. He waved an arm. Then Adam Silverhorn also materialized. Followed by Gid's crew and a half-dozen men of assorted ages she recognized from church.

"Speed. Surprise. Violence of attack. Gid called me soon as you left Michaels's ranch, and I called a few of your friends." Jace nudged one of his prisoners forward with the butt of his pistol barrel. "Outflanked and outmaneuvered. Cavalry to the rescue, Diné style."

Kailyn glanced at Aaron. His friends. Here on the Rez.

She watched his face soften. And observed the conflicting, self-protective thoughts play across his broad features, as the emotional barriers of a lifetime tumbled. No longer an outsider, but at last one of The People.

"I sent Pastor Nez—" Jace laughed at the round-eyed look Aaron gave him. "Yeah, our pastor didn't want to miss any of the action, but he's not as good with a firearm nor does he possess a valid license, so I sent him to drive your truck and Taco the long way home. He'll meet us there."

Sirens blaring, vehicles from the county sheriff's department, Navajo Nation, and several unmarked cars jerked to a stop next to Gid's pickup.

Jace motioned down the rocky path. "Looks like our ride has arrived."

With Aaron's hand on the small of her back to support her, she picked her way across the boulder-strewn terrain.

"Tribal Council said to tell you, Yazzie," Jace called behind them. "Any time you want to join LE here on the Rez or employ your engineering degree Auntie told me about, you give them a call."

The police swarmed the prisoners, handcuffing them and stuffing them into various vehicles. Aaron was surrounded by his new Diné compatriots, and the not-so-touchy-feely Diné gave him their support with grunts of approval and muttered undertones of praise.

She found herself riding shotgun beside a New Mexico highway trooper. The officer remounted his handheld mike on the dashboard. "Marshals got a helo inbound to extract you, ma'am."

Her eyes fell to her boots. She nodded. The officer cranked the engine.

Aaron wheeled, his dark eyes darting, searching for her.

"I'll see you at the house," she called before touching a button to roll up the window.

But all the way home, she pondered how much the Rez meant to Aaron. How essential to who he was, a heritage he could no longer deny. Part of his DNA, deep in the marrow of his bones.

She reflected on how much this community could mean in making him whole again. She bit her lips to keep them from trembling as she recalled the first steps toward reconciliation between Aaron and Gid. His family needed him.

He needed them even more.

And then there was Willa...

She sighed at the passing desert landscape.

Despite the passion they shared on the mountaintop, Aaron was conflicted in his feelings for Kailyn. Caught up in the moment of the game they were playing, the roles they'd assumed. Doubt ate at her stomach.

He'd proven countless times he'd die for her out of his overinflated sense of duty to honor Steve. And now to accompany her into WITSEC? Even if it meant leaving behind the one true love of his life?

She'd never allow him to sacrifice his well-being for her. She loved him too much not to give him a chance at the happiness he deserved.

Kailyn sensed he was close to finding, at long last, the true Shepherd here among his People, with his family, and in Willa—a bridge from brokenness to healing. She'd never willingly take him from that path, his eternal destiny.

As he'd been willing to ransom his life for hers, she resolved to ransom her happiness. For his.

His sense of obligation ran so deep, she'd have to enrage him until the marshals whisked her away. Burn her bridges before she lost her courage.

Taco greeted Aaron from the front porch. Jace had informed him the marshals were on their way from Albuquerque.

"I'm going to check the condition of the corral." Gid slid out of the truck. "*Shima* said something about wanting to buy a few sheep and start the flock again."

Aaron clattered up the steps. He gave the exuberant dog an equally exuberant rubdown. "Kailyn! I need to pack— Oh, hey."

He smiled, the sight of her prompting pleasurable swirls in his insides. Her hair lay plastered in soft, curling ringlets around her face as if she'd just gotten out of the shower. "I didn't know where you were."

Aaron sniffed the air, inhaling her magnolia-scented skin. "Jace told me about the marshals. I'll pack a quick bag and update *Shinali* on our plans—"

She stuck out a hand, ramming it against his chest and stalling his forward momentum. "About those plans…"

He frowned at the hoity-toity tone of her voice. "What's wrong?"

She tightened her jaw. "What's wrong is I can't wait to get out of this backwater and return to civilization."

He stared at her.

Kailyn flicked an imaginary speck of something off her shoulder. "Dust. Constant dirt. Everywhere. Every crevice. Every corner. I couldn't pack fast enough."

He stepped back a pace, studying her. "Kailyn—"

"No need for you to pack. You've fulfilled your obligation to Steve."

With a supercilious smile, she patted his scar.

He flinched.

"More than fulfilled your obligation to this witness. Went way beyond..." She rolled her shoulders, unkinked the knots in her neck. "I'll finish the rest of my journey alone. Be good to get back to the land of shopping malls, sweet tea, and..."

He took hold of her arm.

She wrenched free. "...magnolias."

"What's happened? Talk to me. Did I do something to upset you?"

Kailyn twisted the ring off her finger. "Thanks for the memories." She held it out to him. "Actually, not so much. Here. Just until the trial, you said in Santa Fe. Mission accomplished. Finally, this charade and the lies we've told can end."

Aaron let the ring and her hand hang in the air. His heart pounded. He swallowed, disoriented, unsure exactly why the earth had tilted on its axis.

"Take it." She jabbed the ring in his direction. "I'm on to bigger and better things. Like you said. A new start. A do-over."

"*Querida*—"

Her face crumpled. "Stop calling me that."

She clamped both hands over her ears. "You were right the first time. Back in Charlotte. Debs and gangsters don't mix. Not in this life. Not in the life I intend to carve out for myself."

"Kaily—"

"Take it." She flung the ring at him and spun on her heel.

In a reflexive motion, he caught the ring in a one-handed swipe. He stood frozen, stricken, as she marched out of her bedroom with the fuchsia duffel bag and turquoise tote.

"Please, Kailyn...Why are you saying these things?"

She gave a heaving sigh. "Sometimes, Aaron, or Rafael or whatever you decide to call yourself, you sicken me."

Kailyn crinkled her lip, tilting her head. "Was all the pride beaten out of you, too, when you were a boy?"

He recoiled.

"I don't want you or this life. Let me speak a language I know you'll understand. Adíos, muchacho."

Kailyn kicked the door open and scooped Taco into the tote. A whirring sound, like a thousand roaring, devouring locusts, filled the air. The copter, rotors turning, settled with dust whirling amidst the fallow field. Several suited figures emerged. Their gold shields glimmered on their belts in the afternoon sun.

"My ride." She waved to the approaching marshals.

He broke free of the shock paralyzing him and in two strides gripped her arm. "Is this all we mean to each other? Are you really going to end things this way between us?"

Taco yelped inside the tote.

"Don't lie to me, Kailyn. Don't lie to yourself. And after the way your body responded to mine on the mountain—"

Her hand shot out.

The slap cracked like thunder across his skin. He quivered from the shock of her blow to his face.

Kailyn's eyes widened, her lips trembled, but her profile hardened. "You're more like Burke every day. Let. Go. Of. Me."

His eyes boring into her, he released his grip on her arm, raising one finger at a time.

She ripped the cross off her neck, snapping the leather band. "I believe this also belongs to you."

Kailyn grabbed his hand and closed his fist around it. "Unlike me."

Aaron's lips flatlined. "Some things, like some people, once broken can't be fixed."

His nostrils flared. "Don't let me keep you from your shiny new life, deb."

Stiffening, she cast her eyes behind him, scanning the walls, the room. Her face an unreadable mask, she dropped her eyes to her stiletto heels and swished away. Aaron stared after this strange person who'd taken over Kailyn's body.

His Kailyn, who had always worn every thought and feeling upon her face.

Aaron struggled to breathe.

Not his Kailyn. He'd never known her at all. A better actress than many undercover agents.

Better than him.

The marshal strode forward and gestured toward the waiting chopper. She nodded, started forward, and paused.

For one brief, gut-wrenching second, he believed she might turn and rush back to him, saying she'd changed her mind. Say the last few minutes had been a horrific mistake.

But she lifted her face and closed her eyes. As if saying good-bye. Then without so much as a backward glance, she and Taco vanished from his sight, climbing into the helicopter.

The blades of the chopper picked up speed. The craft hovered over the ground, kicking clouds of red dust onto the diminishing patches of snow. But beating the air into submission, the helo ascended, higher and farther until it disappeared into the brilliant sunshine of the turquoise sky.

Leaving his heart and his home empty.

In the helo, she cried all the way to the state capital.

Scalding, burning, disconsolate sobs.

The marshals let her alone. Taco licked the tears off her cheeks with his tongue, emitting whimpering noises.

She'd never forget the anguish glittering in Aaron's eyes when she found the right button to push. When she'd made the crack about his pride being beaten out of him.

And then, frantic to escape from the temptation to throw her arms around him, she'd done the unforgivable.

She'd slapped him, severing forever his obligation to her. She shuddered at the shock, the self-loathing, the pain of brokenness she'd glimpsed in his eyes. Like she'd taken a belt buckle to him herself.

Gouging this time at his heart.

"Forgive me, Aaron," she whispered into the tufts of Taco's hair. "Forgive me for hurting you for your own good."

She squeezed her eyes shut. "Be happy." Her voice broke.

"For the both of us."

27

Late January

How HAD IT COME TO THIS?

Aaron gripped the wheel as the truck lurched out to the highway. What had he done wrong? How could he have been so wrong about her?

He still listened for the sound of Taco's toenails upon the floor. He still expected to walk into the kitchen and find Kailyn, coffee cup extended, waiting to share a sunrise with him.

But his heart lay cold as a stone in his chest, and he knew there were no more sunrises for him. Not with her.

Would he always be alone?

He blew out a breath. He hadn't been truly alone, not physically, since she walked out of his life. Gid had practically moved in, and he'd given his room to his father.

Aaron couldn't bear to enter her room, much less sleep there. He'd taken to sleeping on the couch wrapped in the quilt she'd left. Slept when he managed to nod off from his angry, circling thoughts.

He wondered if Gid and *Shinali* were concerned if in his despair he'd harm himself. Or, take the slow route, like his father before him, with substance abuse. But they needn't have worried.

Not about that. Not his style. He'd learned early what couldn't be cured must be endured.

Or had it been Kailyn who taught him that?

Aaron grimaced.

He should've never trusted her. Never trusted anyone. Before her, he'd not comprehended what he'd missed. Now, the loss of things he'd just begun to believe possible gnawed at him.

Why didn't she love him the way he loved her?

He bit down on his lip so hard he tasted the metallic flavor of his own blood. Why was it so hard for anyone to love him? As the truck hummed along toward Blue Corn Springs, he recognized how his actions of late lacked any logic or rationale.

Aaron was utterly and completely lost. Like one of those stupid sheep Grandmother insisted they purchase. Only he'd taken a nose-dive, a death roll, off a canyon cliff.

He tendered his resignation with the Bureau and received his severance pay. With which he acquired a laptop. With which he hunkered down three days in a row accessing the library's WiFi and trolling through every society page reference to the Charlotte, North Carolina, Eudaileys going ten years back.

Aaron realized his behavior was pathetic at best. Obsessive-compulsive at worst. But he felt driven to know the details of Kailyn's life. To explain why she'd ripped his heart to shreds.

Scanning the Internet, he discovered a full-page spread in a Southern lifestyle magazine of the eight-thousand-square-foot mansion she called home for most of her life. He cringed at what she must've thought of his rustic, two-bedroom, eight-hundred-square-foot home.

But though he scoured the Web for news of the trial, he got nothing. Zip. Nada. Nothing.

Which worried at the fringes of his mind in the sleepless hours of the night.

He pulled up outside the construction site. With a farewell salute, Gid tucked his hardhat underneath his arm and strolled over to the truck.

Gid climbed inside. "Thanks for picking me up this afternoon, Son. Mechanic says my vehicle will be operational again by the end of the week." He frowned. "What happened to your lip?"

Aaron sucked at his bottom lip and winced. "Nothing."

His brow furrowed, Gid fastened his seat belt as Aaron put the truck in gear and moved onto the road. "How's Mateo and his mom?"

"Fine." Aaron glanced at the side mirror, turned on his blinker, and switched lanes.

"Silverhorn says it was a right good idea you had, Son, about taking the kids at the shelter to the pound every week. Teaching them to value themselves through valuing the unwanted animals there."

Aaron stared straight ahead as they left the city limits. "They learn they have worth, and they can make a positive difference in the world as they put the dogs through obedience training. When they finish the course, the dogs will be highly sought after, easily adoptable."

Gid deposited his hardhat on the seat between them.

"Adam says you have a way with the animals, Aaron. Even more so with the kids. There's a real chance, he thinks, your investment in their lives will keep these kids from repeating the cycle of violence they've experienced. Keep them from looking to the street gangs to fill the void, unlike the juvies he ministers to Arizona side who've already made one mistake too many."

One mistake too many? Like him.

At the house, Aaron shut off the ignition, but his hands drifted to the wheel. He peered at the darkened interior of the house.

Without Kailyn, no longer a home.

Being Diné, Gid said nothing, just sat beside him as the sun sat low on the horizon of the distant Chuskas.

Aaron laid his forehead upon the steering wheel.

"Why did she leave? Leave me? If I could just understand, wrap my mind around the fact that I'll never know, never see her again..." He choked.

And more broken since he was a boy, his shoulders shook.

"Did I ever tell you the story of the turquoise, Aaron?"

He lifted his head and squinted at his father. "No." Swallowing past the lump in his throat, he struggled to keep his chin from quivering.

Gid turned in the seat. "Do you have the cross your mother gave you? I can show you. Show you the lesson turquoise teaches The People."

Aaron fished the cross, bare of its leather string, out of his pocket. He'd meant to bury it at the Blue Corn Springs gravesite of his mother where she reposed between her parents. But somehow, he hadn't.

Couldn't get rid of the last thing his mother had ever touched. The last thing of his to touch Kailyn.

"May I?"

He extended it to Gid, who examined the turquoise-inlaid silver cross in the waning light.

"To the Diné, turquoise is life. Your maternal grandfather was a master silversmith. He was also a disciple of the Master, and he told me the story."

Gid sighed. "Told your mother and I both when we married. But neither of us at the time possessed the ears to hear."

"Mother, my *shima*, told me turquoise was for protection."

Gid nodded. "It's true. But there's more." He gestured at the bands of pink, purple, and indigo in the sky.

"The Creator paints a picture of Himself in each aspect of His creation. Each sunrise. Each petal. Each creature. The rocks of the *Dinétah* cry out the truth."

Despite the bitter fact that she didn't love him, Aaron recognized this truth in Kailyn as she'd drawn closer to her Shepherd. The unfolding of her soul like the opening of a magnolia blossom. One petal at a time.

In the Creator's time. Until Aaron could no longer deny the beauty at the center of Kailyn's being. A beauty she'd have been the first to tell him arose from the beauty of her Redeemer.

Gid, in true Diné fashion, let the silence speak first. "A lesson so those with discerning hearts might draw near to Him. Such it is with the turquoise, the sky stone, given by the True God to His Diné people."

"All my life," Aaron wetted his lips, "I've done what I must to survive. You adapt or you die. You learn to trust no one. I don't say this to hurt you. This was the only truth I knew."

Gid's face shadowed. "I've walked a similar path, my son. And I found when you live that way something vital withers inside. Like a desert flower too long without rain."

He fingered the cross. "Why did you enlist in the army, my son? Why did you become a White Eyes agent?"

"I don't know. Maybe I was trying to prove something to Michaels or Steve. To myself." Aaron shrugged. "Maybe I was searching for something to believe in, something meaningful to hang onto. Something to which to give my life."

Aaron studied the mountains. "To ransom my life—find atonement—because of the blood of my mother."

"You'll never find what you seek," Gid pursed his lips, "in the service of your country, no matter how great the cause. Nor find true purpose and fulfillment in any accomplishment."

Gid waited until the silence drew Aaron's gaze back to him. "Nor, my son, even in the love of a good woman."

Aaron's lips twisted. "Kailyn was right about me, Dad. I've done things…The wounds done to me…" He released a breath. "I'm marked. Scarred. What's broken in me can't be mended."

"Nothing is too broken for the True God. Let me finish the story of the turquoise." Gid held up the cross. "You see the line running through the blue? The crack in the rock?"

Aaron nodded, his eyes darting from the cross in his father's hand to Gid's face.

"This is what the turquoise tells the Diné. The line. The crack. The stone took it, my son."

Aaron tilted his head. "Took what, *Shizhé'é*, my father?"

Gid placed the cross in the open palm of Aaron's hand. "The sky stone took the blow you would've received. The one you and I deserved. The stone took it for you."

Aaron's eyes widened. "L-like Jesus…"

"Like Jesus did for you. For me. Those who come to the foot of the cross will be made whole. Like I was. The Shepherd carried your grief. He shouldered your sorrow. He Himself was pierced for my wickedness. Crushed for my sin."

Gid's eyes took on a faraway gaze. "For my transgression, he bore the stroke of my guilt. Pierced and scourged for my healing and yours, Son."

He grasped Aaron's hand. "You and I, we cannot go back, but with the True God's help we can go forward and turn what happened into a source of great strength."

"In our weakness, He shows Himself strong," Aaron whispered.

And for the first time in his life, he understood why Someone as great as the Son of God would've allowed mere men to kill him.

For love.

Love of Aaron and others like him.

For the first time he really understood how the Shepherd of his soul had pursued his heart. Never given this *dibeh-yazzie* up as lost. Called Aaron by name.

You are Mine and I will not let you go, the Spirit whispered on the wind, heard by one who at last had ears to hear.

And despite the wrongs done to him, he refused to use his suffering as a crutch to excuse choices he'd made later. Self-serving, consensually manipulative relationships that characterized his life until he met Kailyn.

He deserved judgment. He knew it. Instead, God offered him mercy, grace, and compassion. He'd never been alone.

A lamb bleated from the corral.

"Like a shepherd, He tends his flock," Gid murmured. "In His arms, He gathers His lambs..."

As He'd gathered this Diné outcast from the ends of the earth.

"His sheep hear the Shepherd's voice and follow."

"I want to return." Aaron took a ragged breath. "Return to Him. Live in obedience to my Shepherd. Walk in beauty."

He longed for the sweet fragrance of the Christ he'd seen in Kailyn and desired to make Him his own. "Will you show me how, *Shizhé'é?*"

And with Gid's arm around his shoulders covering the scar of his shame and with the cross held fast in his hand, Aaron Yazzie bowed his head and found the One who loved him best.

Early March

Aaron found himself—since sleep apparently wasn't an option these days—volunteering at the emergency shelter, helping the frightened moms and their equally frightened children. Embracing his true self, Yazzie, by becoming the defender of the little ones.

He experienced a tremendous, unexpected love for those kids, the first time he laid eyes on any of them. The runaways, too. Aaron looked beyond the filth and scars and saw the frightened child of God underneath.

Aaron reassured the easily spooked, the ready to bolt. In their eyes, he beheld a reflection of himself—at age nine. Read in their faces unspoken questions: Was this shelter for real? Was he for real? Could they trust him? Should they tell him the identity of their abuser? Would they be safe at the shelter?

He attempted to convince them, despite the terrible lies someone had hammered into their heads, that they weren't bad. They didn't deserve what had happened to them. Most of them were starving. Starving as he'd been before he found the Shepherd.

Starving for someone to offer them hope. To tell them they were worth something. Worth dying for.

And he'd take the turquoise cross from around his neck and share his story with them. Christ's story.

His life's purpose over the next few months derived from one of his grandmother's favorite Scripture passages in Isaiah—to comfort God's people. Aaron's people. The kids like him who needed to learn how to trust, how to accept kindness. How to respect and value themselves, because they were already so loved and valued by the Shepherd of their souls.

Broken vessels...Mended hearts.

Despite the purpose and joy in his life, a hole remained in his heart. An ache resided. A yearning for something yet undone.

He returned to the house one day to find *Shinali* folding—and refolding—the Navajo Cross quilt on the couch.

She jabbed her finger at him. "When are you going to find our girl?"

This, again.

He should've known only a direct approach would get Delores off his back. "She doesn't want me, Grandmother."

Delores rocked on her heels. "You read the quilt label lately? How she copied the Diné words *Ayóó áníínishní?*"

He shook his head and prayed for patience. "It was an act. She doesn't love me."

Delores crossed her arms over her ponderous chest. "You ever say those words to her?"

He flung himself into the armchair. "I tried once, but we were interrupted."

She snorted.

Aaron glared at her. "I'm afraid you got it wrong. The vision the Dream-Giver gave you."

Her eyes narrowed.

"At least the part about the children being mine and Kailyn's."

"I got nothing wrong." She lifted her chin. "The copper tints in their black hair glinted in the sun under the turquoise sky."

His eyelids drooped. "She wouldn't have pushed me away if she loved me."

"Because she loved you, she believed she was doing you a favor."

His lips parted. "A favor?"

"By not allowing you to be separated from your family and your heritage. From the rescuer of doves."

He leaned forward, his hands gripping his knees. "I'm not in love with Willa."

Delores, very unDiné-like, probed his face. "She thinks you are. The secret visits to Grace House. The trip to Albuquerque."

His eyebrows rose. "I explained about that. I'll always owe Willa a debt of gratitude for saving my life as a boy, but—but..."

Aaron scrounged in the willow basket beside the armchair for a dovetailed wooden box he'd fashioned—for Kailyn—and didn't have the heart to throw away.

He shook the box in Delores's direction. "I carved this nativity set for her. I didn't go to the house to see Willa. I went so the girls could help me decorate the figures and the stable with chips of turquoise. Their gift of love to her. My gift of love to her."

Aaron placed the box on the arm of the chair and eyed it as if it might sting. "I love Kailyn. Deeply. Passionately."

He grimaced. "Apparently, I'm permanently afflicted by her until the day I die."

Delores sank into the chair opposite him. "Again, I repeat, did you ever bother to tell her so?"

He blinked at his grandmother. "The gift was supposed to be a surprise. Gid knew. He covered for…" He closed his mouth with a snap. "Oh."

Delores rolled her eyes. "Yeah, a surprise all right."

She threw up her hands. "Idiots. Both of you. And I'm not talking about my girl."

"What should I do?"

"Bring home my granddaughter or, if that's not possible, stay with her, love each other, walk in beauty together with your Savior."

She glowered at him as he sat transfixed in place. "Well, get going, boy. Time's a-wasting."

First call he made was to U.S. Assistant District Attorney Rogers. Actually, it required three calls before he managed to speak to the attorney in person.

"Please," Aaron begged. "I know it's against protocol, but I'm desperate to talk with her. Just a few minutes. I'll fly to North Carolina. Meet you both at the courthouse during a lunch recess. You'll never have to compromise her location. Just—"

Rogers cleared his throat. "Only reason I'm even having this conversation with you, Yazzie, is because you mailed me the microchip. I owe you. Without that, we might never have nailed Flores's subordinates in the chain of command. The DEA got enough evidence off it to ensure that the entire La Familia enterprise is about to be dismantled, thanks to the intel we recovered from that chip and after Dex Pritchard turned state's evidence."

"Pritchard?"

Rogers laughed, or what passed for a laugh. "He was up to his eyeballs in the operation. He's been offered a fair deal at a secure WITSEC prison unit. A generous MOU, memor—"

"Memorandum of Understanding. Yeah, yeah. I'm still Steve Matthews's kid, too, Rogers."

"Right. And once we had his eyewitness testimony...And with Flores already dead..."

Aaron stiffened. This was what had niggled at the back of his mind. What worried him when he couldn't find info on the trial.

"She arrived about the time the techs decrypted the chip. We didn't need her testimony anymore. She only knew about Gabriela Flores's murder. And with Flores dead—"

"You sent her out there without protection?" He clenched the phone.

"No, Yazzie. You got it all wrong. Besides, La Familia doesn't care about her. In fact, you both did them a tremendous favor by getting rid of Esteban for them."

Aaron gritted his teeth. "You withdrew your offer to place her in the program."

"No, I'm telling you. She was relieved it was over on her part. She opted out of the program. We didn't kick her out."

"She's not...? Then, by God, you better tell me right now where she is."

The attorney sighed. "I-I don't know where she is, or I swear I'd tell you. I know what went down between you in New Mexico. She walked out of the courthouse with that dog into the rain without a single word. I haven't seen or heard from her since the New Year."

"You-you don't know where she is?" Aaron's chin dropped to his chest. "How will I find her? Where is she, Rogers?"

A silence. "I'm sorry, Yazzie. I really am."

Clicking Off, Aaron gaped at the phone in his hand with a growing sense of panic. What should he do now? Where to start looking?

He fumbled through the possibilities in his mind. She'd never return to the sterile existence of her grandmother's world. He'd stake his life on that. But CeCe—

"I don't know where she is, Aaron."

He set his jaw. "She's bound to have contacted you, Ce. You're her best friend."

CeCe sniffed into the receiver. "She called me. Early February. She told me what happened. How she left things with you."

The cell tucked between his ear and neck, he leaned his forehead against the bedpost in Kailyn's bedroom. "Please, Ce. I love her. I need to find her."

A silence punctuated by the rapid drumming of his heart.

"I know you love her. Or else I'd have already hung up on you. And I know she loves you."

He closed his eyes.

"But I don't know where she is, Aaron. I'd tell you if I did."

He slumped onto the mattress, scrubbing his forehead with his hand.

"But…" CeCe paused.

He lifted his head.

"I may have a clue as to where you can look."

"Anything, Ce. Anything you can give me to go on."

"You've got resources. Connections. You know her mama's name, Aaron?"

His mind flitted to Kailyn's name on their pseudo-marriage license. "Nolie is Kailyn's middle name."

"Kailyn was named after her mama. They called her mama Maggie."

She'd said she wanted to return to the land of sweet tea and… "Magnolia?"

"And one other thing to explore. Taco's a Pampered Pooch connoisseur. You put those two things together and track down a shipment of those fancy dog biscuits…"

He jumped to his feet. "Ce, you're an angel."

"Yeah, yeah. Be sure and invite me to the wedding this time, you hear?" She laughed.

Next stop, to beg a favor from his former case supervisor, Reilly.

"Please, Reilly. I'm desperate. You have access to the Bureau database."

The fifty-something agent growled into the phone. "You're asking me to hack into a company's records. On government time with government resources. And do you know how many towns in the South are named Magnolia?"

Aaron paced a groove in the rug in the hallway. "I know, I know. Like finding one particular needle on a cactus."

"If you hadn't saved my son's hide outside Kabul, Yazzie," he hissed.

But Aaron heard the click of keystrokes through the phone as Reilly scrolled through the database.

"Sure she wants to be found?"

Aaron swallowed. "I'm praying so. But I'm afraid she learned too well some of the tricks of the trade from me. How to blend in, how to hide."

Reilly grunted. "If even a small part of her wants to be found, I'll find her, I promise."

28

Mid-April

AARON LEANED BACK ON THE WOOD-SLATTED IRON BENCH ACROSS MAIN and monitored the front of the shop. His eyes darted to the sign above the entrance. MaeElla's Beauty Salon.

He scanned the light traffic idling by in Magnolia, North Carolina. In the end, Kailyn hadn't proved as difficult to find as he'd first feared.

She left him a trail of breadcrumbs. Make that a trail of fancy dog biscuits.

With Reilly's help, he established that no Kailyn Eudailey or Jones or Smith had ordered any dog treats anywhere in the continental United States. But an order had been placed by one Kailyn Yazzie and shipped to rural Magnolia.

He flushed with pleasure, thinking of how she'd kept his name. He only hoped Delores was right—it was because Kailyn wanted him to find her. And not because of convenience.

You are Mine and I will not let you go.

MaeElla and the other stylists had departed to begin their weekend early. He studied his watch. Because Kailyn was an apprentice hairdresser, her last customer should've been out of there by now. But knowing her, she was running her mouth.

Shooting the breeze. Little Miss Hospitality. Never met a stranger.

Observing movement through the plate glass window, he heaved himself to his feet and crossed to the opposite sidewalk. The customer sailed out the door, the bell overhead jangling.

He caught the door before it closed. And spotted a copper-colored head rearranging combs on the counter. He drank in the sight of her, a sight he'd feared he'd never behold again. And a profound sense of relief overtook him.

Just as long as she didn't boot him out the second she laid eyes on him. Closing his eyes, he took a deep breath and breathed a prayer. He yanked the door open wide and forged across the threshold.

With a sigh, Kailyn grabbed a broom to sweep the clippings left by MaeElla's last client. On the floor beside the turquoise tote, Taco didn't bother to get up.

Just lay there with his nose on top of his front paws. Staring at the glass-fronted door in the reception area. As if expecting any minute for Aaron to saunter through.

Pining.

Taco wasn't the only one. But though she ached for the sound of Aaron's voice, she'd destroyed their relationship back on the Rez.

Kailyn swept around Taco and pushed the hair into a scooper, which she deposited in the dustpan beside MaeElla's workstation. No need to hurry. Only delay the vast emptiness of her upcoming weekend.

She doused the combs into the Barbicide. She organized the brushes littering the workspace and hung the hair dryer onto the cart. When she finished her classes and training, she'd have her own station. She fiddled with the feather razor.

Taco barked once. Short. More like a woof.

"Kailyn..."

Her eyes widened at Aaron's mirrored reflection. She whirled.

Taco jumped to all four feet, tail wagging. He launched himself at Aaron's legs. But Aaron's eyes never left her face.

He stood there, a hesitant smile lurking at the corner of his lips. One hand stuffed into the pocket of his jeans, the other held a wooden box. And as befitted an already humid Southern spring, he wore a dark purple golf shirt. She swallowed.

Eggplant.

"I'd appreciate it, Kailyn, if you'd lower the blade in your hand."

She glanced down, surprised to see herself still clutching the razor. Schooling her features, she lobbed it onto the counter and put the salon chair between them.

Taco whined and pranced, his toenails clicking in a circle around Aaron. His hindquarters swished in a happy dance.

She squared her shoulders. "You better greet him; he'll never give up till you do."

Aaron gave her a look that scorched her cheeks. The hateful blush crept from her chest onto her neck.

Crouching, he nuzzled Taco. Taco licked his face. "You had it right from the beginning about me and Taco. We *are* a lot alike."

She raised her eyebrows.

His lopsided smile accelerated her pulse. "Neither of us give up."

Aaron fished a dog treat out of his pocket, tossed it to Taco who caught, ground, and chewed in one lunge.

"Looks like you could use another haircut." She gestured at the dark hair hanging over the collar of his shirt.

She lifted her chin. "You're a man who speaks three languages fluently and this is what you came for? An appointment?"

Rising, his mouth tightened. "I've come two thousand miles and that's all you can think to say to me, woman."

Aaron shuffled his feet and self-consciously tucked a strand of hair behind his ear. "My personal stylist and I parted company."

He swallowed. "Temporary arrangement, I hope."

She bit her lip. "I'm sorry for the things I said to you. Cruel things. None of them true."

"After I got over being mad and hurt, I realized that."

"I needed to go and you needed to stay. I never meant to hurt you." She gazed into his dark eyes. "To hit you was unforgivable."

"Not unforgivable." He fingered the turquoise cross around his neck. "A lot has changed in the four months you've been gone."

Her eyes flitted away from the cross, hanging by a sterling silver chain. He'd come to make sure she was okay. Classic Aaron in classic protector mode.

Kailyn whisked the cape from the chair and made an elaborate show of folding it into quarters.

Aaron frowned. "Gid, *Shinali*, and more people than I can give name to at this minute send their love." He paused as if waiting for her to say something.

God, please don't let him give me a blow by blow of his new life with Willa.

"Adam and Erin said to tell you baby John Adam loves his colorful Diné nursery."

She dropped the cape. "A boy? Oh—" She clapped her hands. "I'm so happy for them."

"Adam's friendship has meant the world to me." He took a deep breath. "Since I wandered back to the fold of my Shepherd. Returned to the Guardian of my soul."

She clutched the back of the chair. "You . . ." She pointed to the cross at his throat. "You found Him?"

Aaron smiled. "And with construction work slow during the winter months on the Rez, I've been sharing what I've learned with the kids at the shelter. A lot has happened since you left. A lot you've missed."

He cleared his throat. "A lot of people missing you."

Aaron gripped the wooden box. "You opted out of the program." A vein throbbed in his jaw.

"Why didn't you come home . . . ?" His voice wobbled. ". . . Back to where people love you?"

Her heart pounded against her ribs. "I'm making a new life for myself. A new career. Turns out Grandmother was right. I'm pretty good at bringing out the beauty in people. Like my mama."

"Like you brought out in me."

Tears, those treacherous tears, threatened to undo her resolve.

"I've prayed so hard for your happiness, Aaron."

He sighed. "I didn't say I was happy. I've found the joy of the True God. The Creator. But there's one last dream from the Dream-Giver yet unrealized."

Willa...

Better to pull the scab off this wound. Let it bleed and heal.

She took a deep breath. "So no wedding yet, huh?"

Aaron shrugged. "Willa and Jace wished you could've been at their wedding, but I'm sure you understand Jace's reluctance to wait in case Willa talked herself out of it again."

Her breath hitched and she came around from behind the chair. "Oh, Aaron. I'm so sorry."

She touched his arm. "After she told me about the love of her life...I know how much you love her."

His hand covered hers, warming her skin. "I think Willa meant Emilio Sanchez, the Conquistadores leader, not me."

Aaron ran his thumb over the back of her hand. Her insides fluttered.

"You're operating on bad intel. I'm not in love with her, Kailyn. I'm thrilled Willa found someone like Jace to love her. Heck, I'm delighted. I even stood up as Jace's best man at the ceremony."

"You don't love Willa?" She blinked rapidly. "But...you...she—"

"Here." He thrust the wooden box at her.

She tilted her head, examining the box from all angles. "What is it?"

He blew out a breath. "Look inside and find out, *dzani*."

Cutting her eyes at him, she raised the lid. Her mouth curved.

"Oh, Aaron. They're beautiful." She removed the tiny manger figure of the baby Jesus. "When did you—? How did you—?"

He folded his arms. "The day you came looking for me, the girls were out of school for Christmas break. I'd been stopping by Grace House after work. We were making this for your birthday."

Aaron stroked his chin. "Your birthday, which you neglected to mention, fell the day after Christmas."

He grimaced. "Some Christmas this turned out to be."

Kailyn's lips quivered. "Wasn't so great for Taco and me, either."

Aaron set the box on the counter. "See, you fold it back, and it becomes a stable."

He fingered the turquoise chips on the cornice of the miniature barn, outlining the points of a five-sided star. "Your birthstone. Turquoise."

Aaron propped his hand on his hip. "A special day not meant to get lost in the shuffle of Christmas. Not on my watch."

She arranged the tiny carved figures.

The holy family. The stable animals. Instead of an angel, a shepherd. And lots and lots of sheep.

"I love it."

"I love you, Kailyn Eudailey." He took both of her hands. "Or whatever you're calling yourself these days."

Aaron tugged her closer, cupping her face in his hands. "*Te quiero, querida.* I love you, *dzani*, in every language I know. *Ayóó ánííníshní.* Will you become my wife for real this time?"

Kailyn twined her arms around his waist. Beginning at the small of his back, she walked her hands over his spine, pausing at his scar, and draped her arms around his neck.

"I love you so much, Aaron. In my heart, since Santa Fe, I think I've always been Kailyn Yazzie."

His lips found hers and his kiss burned away the pain of the lonely weeks without him.

"We belong together, Kailyn. Belong to each other. The way we belong to God."

He curled a tendril of her hair around his finger. "We're better together, since a certain elevator door slid open."

She exhaled. "And you had no idea the trouble awaiting you."

"Or the joy ahead."

He leaned his forehead against hers. "Come home with me, Kailyn. Or we'll stay here if you prefer. Where doesn't matter, just as long as we're together."

A low moan escaped from his throat. "I've missed you so much."

Kailyn took a ragged breath. "I want to go home. Home to the Rez, where I belong with you."

She pulled back. "You didn't throw away my ring, did you?"

His brow crinkled. "I can get you another—"

"I want *that* ring."

She thumped his chest with the flat of her hand. "*My* ring, Aaron Yazzie."

"If you'd bothered to thoroughly examine your gift, you'd have noticed something hanging on the crook of the shepherd's staff."

She released him and searched for the figure in the crèche. She plucked the inlaid turquoise ring off the shepherd's crook.

Kailyn smiled at him over her shoulder. "You kept it."

He snorted and backed her against the linoleum counter. "I've still got the Christmas tree up, woman."

She wagged her finger at him. "It's dangerous, Aaron Yazzie, to keep a tree up so long. The needles must've fallen off ages ago."

"Yeah, a real fire hazard." He nibbled at her earlobe. "Waiting for you to come home and take it down."

His hand caught in the locks of her hair. "Did I ever tell you how much I love the scent of magnolia?" Aaron smacked his lips on her neck. "On you?"

She looked down and then up at him through her lashes. "You'll have to teach me the Diné word for 'husband'."

"I pray we'll have a lifetime to walk in beauty with each other."

Aaron tapped the end of her nose with his finger. "Grandmother said if you'd make an honest man out of me she'd have a new bridal jar waiting for us."

Her lips brushed across his jawline. "If we do not spill a drop, our lives together will be as sweet as the nectar."

Aaron unclasped the cross and placed it around her neck. "I have a story to tell you, *dzani*. A story about a cross and turquoise."

He traced the contours of her cheek with his fingertip. "You and I also have a front door to paint."

Kailyn touched the cross around her neck. "I promise my love forever, *querido*."

He gave her that slow, lethal smile of his.

Kailyn's toes curled as Aaron Yazzie made her go weak in the knees.

He leaned in, his hands palm down on the counter on either side of her. "Now you've had time to consider all the advantages, deb..." His lips quirked.

"Such passion, *mi corazón*." She caressed his face, recalling his words one night beside a certain elevator door.

Aaron's lips parted.

She closed the space remaining between them, stopping inches from his mouth. "Perhaps you and I, we could work out some arrangement..."

And she watched with glee as first his dark eyes widened and then went opaque.

Cocking his head, he drew her hand to his lips and kissed the tips of her fingers. "You know how I love it when you sweet-talk me, baby."

Kailyn smiled. "A sweet life together under a turquoise sky."

Group Discussion Guide

1. Who was your favorite character? Why?

2. Have you ever wished for a new life? Why? What would you do over?

3. If you were in WITSEC, which protocol would you have the most difficulty adjusting to?

4. Steve believed in God's love, the Constitution, and Aaron. What three things do you believe?

5. Although a demure debutante on the outside, inside Kailyn dwelled a knife-wielding, lamp-smashing protector of those she loved. What would people be surprised to learn about you?

6. What was your favorite moment between:
   - Aaron and Kailyn?
   - Grandmother, Aaron, and Kailyn?
   - Taco and anybody?

7. What was the biggest surprise to you?

8. When, where, and why do you think Aaron and Kailyn's initially wary relationship changed?

9. What was the significance of the names Aaron gives to Kailyn—*querida, dzani*? What was the true significance behind each of Aaron's aliases? Why, in the end, did the name Aaron Yazzie fit him best?

10. Have you ever known someone who has been abused—emotionally, physically, or sexually? Have you been a victim of abuse? How could you help them or yourself?

11. How were Aaron and Taco's situations similar?

12. Why were Aaron's and Kailyn's first impressions of each other deceiving? Have you ever been fooled by someone's appearance?

13. What was your favorite thing about:

- Kailyn?
- Aaron?
- Grandmother?
- Taco?

14. Kailyn struggled with a sense of inadequacy because of her grandmother. Believing himself dirty and unlovable, Aaron wore a brutal reminder of past abuse, etched forever on his skin. What hidden lies have been imprinted on your soul? About God?

15. In their romance-a-thon from Charlotte to Shiprock, when do you think Aaron fell in love with Kailyn? Why then? When did she open her heart to him?

16. Kailyn saw beyond Rafe to the real Aaron long before he did. What do you wish people would see in you?

17. What can you do to help survivors of abuse?

18. What do you think about the following statement, in terms of forgiveness: life is full of cactus and you choose whether to sit on its spikes or not.

19. Aaron told Kailyn to be herself. Why was it so hard for him to follow his own advice? How hard is it for you?

20. How did Kailyn, Aaron, Grandmother, and even Jace's feelings change regarding Taco?

21. Like the beautiful rugs Delores created out of tangled skeins of disorder, how has the Creator woven love and mercy into your life?

22. Do you walk in beauty with your Savior? Have you allowed the Shepherd of your soul to gather you in His arms and carry you through the arroyos and canyons of your life? If not, what holds you back?

23. What lesson does the sky stone reveal to you?

Want to learn more about Lisa Carter
and check out other great fiction from
Abingdon Press?

Check out our website at
www.AbingdonPress.com
to read interviews with your favorite authors,
find tips for starting a reading group,
and stay posted on what new titles are on the horizon.

Be sure to visit Lisa online!

www.lisacarterauthor.com